THE GATEKEEPER'S SON

A Novel

C. R. Fladmark

SHOKUNIN

The Gatekeeper's Son is a work of fiction. Names, characters, places and events portrayed in this book are the product of the author's imagination or used fictitiously. Any resemblance to actual persons, living or dead, events or locales is entirely coincidental and not intended by the author.

Fladmark, C.R.

The Gatekeeper's Son / by C. R. Fladmark.

p. cm.

Summary: With the help of a mysterious girl, a San Francisco teenager saves his grandfather's business empire from a ruthless businessman while discovering things about himself and his family that lead him back to ancient Japan and threaten to destroy the life he has always known.

ISBN: 978-0-9937776-1-5 (eBook)

ISBN: 978-0-9937776-0-8 (trade paperback)

ISBN: 978-0-9937776-2-2 (hard cover)

Edited by Shannon Roberts.

Book Design by Christopher Fisher; Cover Design by Pete Garceau

Visit their website: www.editorialdepartment.com

Printed in the U.S.A and internationally.

First Edition: September 2014

10 9 8 7 6 5 4 3 2

To Mika, who took me across.

THE GATEKEEPER'S SON

CHAPTER
1

I WAVED AT THE SECURITY CAMERAS as I crossed the cobblestones and headed toward the arched gateway of the old carriage house, and the wrought-iron gates began to swing inward. A little creepy, I always thought, but convenient. Behind me, the street sloped down a steep hill lined with manicured gardens. The Crescent was home to some of the finest mansions in San Francisco, including my grandpa's.

I was about to enter the driveway when I felt a weird sensation on the back of my neck, a tingling, like hot water hitting cold hands. I turned back to the street and looked around. The street was empty, nothing out of place—except the girl.

She was sitting on a park bench in the shade of a maple tree, legs swinging, her shoes barely scraping the ground. I saw long black hair and a school uniform.

She was looking at me.

When our eyes met, the space between us blurred and rippled as if the air were a giant tarp and someone had snapped the corner. I grabbed the carriage-house wall. I felt dizzy, ears ringing, chest tight.

The gates began to close. I wanted to slip through and escape into their sanctuary, but my body was frozen. A long moment later, the feeling vanished, but it left the air clearer, colors brighter. My body buzzed with energy.

The girl was still there, but she'd stood up. She gave me one last look before she turned and walked away, her short skirt swishing under a black backpack. I stared until she disappeared behind the bushes.

The ground began to tremble and flex, accompanied by a terrible roar. I flattened myself against the carriage-house wall and stared in horror as the cobblestones buckled and rose like a tsunami, higher and higher, racing toward me. I sucked in a lungful of air just before it smashed me against the wall, tossed me into the air, and dragged me under its boiling fury. I tumbled into the swirl of it, fighting the current, feeling the scream of my lungs as I slipped deeper.

Then the wave dumped me on the ground and was gone.

It took a minute for the pain to fade. When I could finally think straight, I sat up and looked around to see how bad the destruction was.

Everything looked the same. The carriage house still stood, and the cobblestones lay undisturbed. It was quiet except for the sound of someone running toward me.

A man, vaguely familiar, burst through the gate and skidded into me, slamming me back to the ground.

"Sprout's down, repeat, Sprout's down!" the man said as he shoved his knee into my back and pressed my head against the bricks.

Sprout? I gasped, my muscles aching and my head spinning. I tried to twist around to see who it was, but all I saw was a hand and the steel-blue semiautomatic it held, pointed toward the street.

⏤

When the bodyguard finally figured out I wasn't in danger, it still took a while to assure him that "Sprout" was fine. And why exactly did the protection detail have to give me that particular code name? Couldn't they have picked something cool?

When he pulled me up with one hand, I told him I'd fallen because of the earthquake.

He holstered his gun. "What earthquake?" He touched my forehead. "I'd better call an ambulance."

"No, no. I'm fine—I guess I just tripped." I forced a smile. "Did you see the girl on the bench?" I pointed toward the park—everything there looked normal.

He shot me a look, then walked into the middle of the street. "I don't see any girl."

"There was a girl there and … I got dizzy." I kicked my toe against the moss between the bricks.

He laughed. "She must've been one hell of a girl!"

I knew my face was getting red. I looked away and swore under my breath. When I looked back, he was smirking.

"Don't worry, Sprout, the Chairman's not home yet." He handed me my backpack. "You've got some seriously overactive hormones."

I heard him laughing into his two-way radio as he retreated into the yard. I stood just inside the gates, straightening my clothes and waiting for the heat to leave my face.

I glanced toward the bench one more time. Had I imagined the whole thing?

—

I climbed the wide stone staircase, but before I could knock, the front door swung open and there stood Grandpa's butler, wearing a gray apron over his dark blue suit.

"Good morning, Master James," he said in his English accent, looking down his thin nose at me.

I smiled up at him. "Morning, William. It's really good to see you."

"Thank you … but it's only been a week." He brushed the leaves off my coat and hung it in the hall closet, but he didn't say anything.

I handed over my backpack as if it were a newborn baby. "My new laptop's in there." It was three days old, custom-built, a birthday gift

3

to myself. He made a show of putting it away while I waited with my grubby running shoes planted on the thick rug in the foyer. Beside me stood an ornate round table weighted down by an enormous bouquet of flowers.

Grandpa's house was large, formal, and quiet, with something fragile waiting around every corner. But there was a familiar smell to the place that I liked—old wood, I guess, and maybe Grandpa, too. Today something smelled especially good.

William noticed my sniffing. A twinkle crept into his eyes, causing little lines to appear all over his face. "I'm baking croissants."

"Awesome." William baked one hell of a croissant. "Where's Grandpa?"

"Your grandfather apologizes for being late. He had a meeting this morning."

"On a Saturday?"

William shifted slightly. "Yes."

I frowned. "Everything OK?"

His face lost its stiffness. "I'm sure it's nothing." His hands toyed with the bow on the front of his apron. "It's just ... he's been looking a bit tired lately. I think perhaps he needs to slow down." He straightened. "In any event, the Chairman will be along shortly. You may wait in his study." He started toward the kitchen but stopped and turned. "Incidentally, I saw what happened outside."

I groaned. "Does Grandpa know?"

"Probably. You caused quite a hullabaloo out there." William smiled. "He's an eager fellow, that one. But that's why the Chairman hires them. Makes us all feel safer." With that, he turned and walked away, his heels clicking on the gleaming hardwood floor. As I climbed the staircase to the second floor, I was sure I heard him chuckling.

And what the hell was a hullabaloo?

CHAPTER
2

GRANDPA HAD ABOUT AS MANY BOOKS as a small public library. Tall bookshelves covered every wall—well, except for the walls with the large picture windows and the wide stone fireplace. But he had something the library didn't have: a rolling ladder that ran along the bookcases on a steel track. When I was a kid, maybe seven or eight, I'd run it along the track too fast and derailed it. I think William was angrier about it than Grandpa was.

I stood by the ladder and ran my hand over the smooth varnished wood. I still felt a buzzing, humming energy, proof that I hadn't just imagined the weird events outside. With a sigh, I sank into the soft brown leather of Grandpa's large chair, tilted back, and lifted my feet onto his desk.

For as long as I could remember, two Saturdays every month, I'd come here to visit. After William served tea and sandwiches, Grandpa would sit back in this chair and tell me the most outrageous stories while the fire crackled and the shadows grew longer. He told me about far-off places where beautiful women with long swords watched over the shrines of ancient gods, of shamans who lived in the desert, of spies and thieves stealing secrets and gold.

These days he told different stories in a not-too-subtle attempt to educate me about his business. I didn't mind. It was interesting to watch him buy a company or build an office tower and turn it into another piece of the Thompson empire.

A computer sat on his desk, yellowed with age. I slid the keyboard out and gave it few taps. No response—it was either turned off or dead. But when I shoved it back in, something fluttered to the floor—a yellow sticky note. On it, in Grandpa's curving writing, was a list of usernames and passwords. I rolled my eyes and put the note back under the keyboard.

"James!" a voice boomed from the doorway. "Get your feet off my desk!"

I jumped out of the chair.

Grandpa stood in the doorway, hands on hips.

"You do look good in that chair though," he said, his voice softer but still loud enough for William to hear in the kitchen. A smile started to lift the corners of his mouth, but it died. He looked tired.

"Sorry, Grandpa." I turned his chair around and wiped the desk where my shoes had been. He walked into the room and waved away my apology.

"I'm sorry for keeping you waiting. Business ..." His voice faltered.

I looked away, and that's when I noticed his assistant, Ms. Lin, standing in the hallway with a black leather notebook held to her chest. Ms. Lin was in her late twenties, maybe thirties—I didn't know, or care. She was gorgeous, the sexiest *real* woman I knew, and the subject of more than one late-night fantasy. Today she wore a short blue skirt with a matching blazer and dangerously high heels. My eyes started at her feet and traveled up. When I finally made it to her deep brown eyes, she was staring straight at me. She smiled like the stewardess she once was.

"Happy birthday, James." Her voice was silky smooth, with a slight Asian accent.

As usual, my brain stopped communicating with my mouth, and heat flooded my face.

"Uh ... thanks." I stumbled over to sit in my usual spot near the fireplace.

Grandpa scowled at me. "When are you going to get that hair cut?"

"Leave him alone, Chairman," Ms. Lin said, gliding like an angel across the rug to rescue me. "Let him be young and carefree while he can. Were you any different at that age?"

He hitched his thumbs in his vest pockets. "This isn't the sixties, and I was never carefree."

Ms. Lin looked skeptical.

He broke into a sly smile. "At least, not that either of you will ever know about." He turned toward the door. "There's a change of plans today, James. Let's go downstairs. William!" he bellowed as he strode down the hall, his back straight as a soldier's.

Ms. Lin turned to me. "You better not make him wait."

I ran after him. Halfway down the stairs, I stopped and gaped: there was a crowd of people in the foyer below.

"Happy sixteenth birthday!" they called out, not at all in unison—obviously they hadn't rehearsed. And I *was* surprised. Even my dad was there. My mother—my *okaasan*—clung to his arm, as if keeping him from running away.

Besides my parents, the only other people I knew well were William; two of the maids; the old Japanese gardener, Mr. Sugimoto; and John and Miles, two of Grandpa's regular bodyguards. That guy who'd flattened me earlier wasn't around—probably lurking near the gate, waiting to jump someone else.

The rest of the group was senior executives from Grandpa's company. A few I knew in passing, but most were faces I'd seen only on the boardroom walls. And, of course, there was Ms. Lin, standing so close behind me on the stairs that the scent of her—a hint of perfume and lipstick—made me blush again.

"How'd you all sneak in here?" I said.

"Maybe while you were napping in my chair," Grandpa said, chuckling at the bottom of the stairs. "Come on down, my boy. I promise this won't hurt a bit."

Okaasan met me at the bottom of the stairs. She wore a kimono, peach-colored with a trail of small flowers cascading from a wide silk belt. The color complemented Dad's tie.

Okaasan bowed to me, her smile changing to something more mischievous.

"You must pay attention, Junya," she said in Japanese. "What if we were ninja, coming to kill you?"

"You'd already be dead," I said, also in Japanese.

"You wish, little apprentice."

I heard Mr. Sugimoto chuckle.

I glanced at my dad and rubbed the fabric of his suit jacket, trying to get a read on him. "Looking pretty spiffy, Dad. I didn't know you owned a suit."

"I may need one for a funeral—yours, if you keep this up," he said, but he gave me a small smile.

I moved on to shake the hands of the people I hadn't met, knowing Grandpa would expect that, but I was still close enough to hear Grandpa address my dad.

"It's been a long time, Robert. Thank you for coming."

There was an awkward pause. I held my breath.

"Good to see you, too." Dad sounded tense. "The house looks good."

I released my breath and moved on.

Mark Smith, president of the Thompson Group, greeted me with a warm smile, a firm handshake, and a pat on the shoulder. Next to him was Mr. Barrymore, Grandpa's security chief and a former Marine sergeant. He was gray-haired and in his fifties—by far the most intimidating man in the room after Grandpa.

Near the back of the group, turned away from us and whispering into a phone, was Walter Roacks. He was Grandpa's chief financial officer and the longest-serving employee of his company. And since I knew Grandpa was probably watching, I went over to shake his hand.

He snapped the phone closed and extended his hand. It was cold and clammy.

I turned away from Walter and bumped right into Ms. Lin. I

reached out to catch her, afraid she'd fall off her high heels, but before I could touch her, she steadied herself. I paused, my hand in midair.

"Sorry, Ms. Lin." Not knowing what else to do, I thrust out my hand. To my surprise, she moved in close. Her delicate hands reached for my shoulders and she kissed me on the mouth.

"That's my present to you," she whispered, her lips beside my ear. "I wanted to be the first woman to kiss you now that you've become a man."

She pulled back, a bright smile on her face. I was pretty sure she'd done that to tease me because of the way I'd checked her out upstairs. I also knew I was glowing like a stoplight. I glanced around, wondering if anyone saw, but everyone else had drifted into the parlor.

The parlor was big and bright, with overstuffed leather furniture and glass doors opening onto the back gardens. Balloons and banners hung from the ceiling, and a string quartet sat near the doors. They broke into "Happy Birthday" when they saw me. I winced—this was getting ridiculous.

Ms. Lin pushed me past them and into the dining room, where caterers in crisp white uniforms were placing trays of hot food on the table. It was a birthday brunch. Grandpa had gone all out, something he'd never done before.

"Sit beside me, James," Grandpa said from the head of the table.

Okaasan sat next to me, with my dad beside her. All conversation ceased as we dug into brunch. Eggs Benedict, German sausage, Belgian waffles with strawberries and whipped cream and maple syrup from Quebec, even Japanese miso soup and broiled fish for Okaasan. And as promised, there were William's croissants, soft and buttery.

William was on hand to enjoy his creation, as were John and Miles, Mr. Sugimoto, and the maids. I was happy to have them there—I'd known them so long that they were almost like family. But why were there so many suits?

"Slow down, Edward," Okaasan said. "Didn't you have dinner last night?"

"Oh, Misako," Grandpa said with a laugh, a forkful of sausage on the way to his mouth. "That's what I like about you—and Lin. I wish the rest of my employees were so candid."

"She doesn't have to worry about getting fired."

The voice had come from down the table. When I looked up, John was whistling, looking outside. Everyone laughed, but Ms. Lin cut in.

"You do need to look after yourself better, Edward," she said, using his name for the first time that I could recall. "I've been saying that."

Grandpa grinned. "I know, but these sausages are so damn good."

"Yes, they are," Mr. Sugimoto said in accented English from across the table. "Would you pass them here, Junya?"

"Why'd you call him Junya?" Mark said.

Grandpa answered before anyone else had a chance.

"His *real* name is James Edward Thompson." He looked so proud. "His father named him after me."

I always suspected that Dad had slapped the name on me with about as much thought as a store clerk putting a price tag on a can of tuna. Just something to keep Grandpa happy, I suppose.

"*I* named him Junya." Okaasan's voice was low but strong. "It means 'the pure one.'" Then she looked up, perhaps becoming aware of the sudden silence. "And he'll stay that way if I can keep the young ladies away."

Someone chuckled, and then others joined in, a release of tension. I blushed again, my eyes still on the table. Okaasan had never called me James—like anything she disagreed with, she made her own way around it.

If anyone had bothered to ask me, I'd have said I preferred Junya. The older I got, the less comfortable I was with my borrowed name. It felt like a hand-me-down.

—

Grandpa started clinking a spoon against his coffee cup. I groaned as a man in a baker's hat carried in a huge cake, complete with the requisite sixteen candles.

"Make a wish, James," Grandpa said as he leaned back and loosened his tie. As if that were her cue, Ms. Lin walked around from her end of the table and placed a small wrapped package beside me.

I tried to smile. Maybe it was just this whole over-the-top party, but something about the gift felt … formal.

"James," Grandpa began as he watched Ms. Lin walk back to her seat. "When your father returned to San Francisco, bringing you and his beautiful wife, Misako, I promised I'd do things different with you."

I glanced at my dad. He was staring at the table.

"I've tried to teach you what I think is important about life, and about my business, and you've learned well." Grandpa addressed the room. "Are you all aware of his bookstore project?"

There were a few grunts.

"I'm not," my dad said.

"James found the classic undervalued property, an old building in a good neighborhood. Of course, I wanted to bulldoze the place, but he insisted on a heritage renovation. James led the project and it was a success." He chuckled. "I expected it to fail—which would've been a good lesson." Before I had a chance to process the insult, he continued. "Do you know how much profit you've earned?"

The question surprised me. I'd had fun working on the design and even hoped to impress him, but I never even considered the money it might make.

He hit the table so hard the cutlery rattled. "You've made one hundred and ten thousand dollars so far."

There was a whistle from the other end of the table.

Okaasan cleared her throat. "Edward—"

"Chairman." Walter Roacks glanced at me, then at Grandpa. "Given our situation, shouldn't this profit stay within the company?"

Grandpa glared at Walter. "This was a private project. I've taken my cut, the rest belongs to James." He paused for a moment and then turned toward Okaasan. "This money's not for video games or fast cars, Misako. This is for the future. Money is a seed—it must be planted to grow." Then Grandpa cleared his throat and stood up.

"I'm sure you've expected this, James, but I'm making it official."

I gave him a blank stare.

"Today, I'm officially naming you as my heir, the future chairman and sole shareholder of the Thompson Group of Companies."

I gaped up at him as murmurs rose. I stole a glance around the table—eight faces smiling, some of the smiles real, some forced. Only Walter Roacks looked surprised.

Suddenly I had trouble breathing.

"I ... I'm still in school," I said. "I need to help my dad ... I'm not ready, I don't—"

"You *are* ready, James," Grandpa said. "And don't look so worried. I'm not planning on dying anytime soon."

A thousand thoughts stampeded through my mind, most of them not good. Somehow, the words I managed to force out of my mouth surprised me.

"I'd be honored."

Grandpa laughed. "You know, some people would regard this as a curse."

My dad looked up. "You're right."

Grandpa's face fell. Slowly, he slumped into his chair. The room went silent, everyone's breath held.

"You understand, don't you, James?" He stared at me. "I don't want my work to die with me."

The awkward silence continued until Ms. Lin finally broke it. "Edward, perhaps James should open his present."

I grabbed the box, happy for the distraction. As I fought with the wrapping, I glanced at Ms. Lin. "Must own a tape company."

Someone laughed and the tension broke.

"Do I, Walter?" Grandpa asked.

"We own one in Minnesota." More laughter.

When I finally opened the box, a gold watch sat coiled like a snake in a cradle of blue velvet. It was beautiful, gleaming gold and crystal, with *James* and the Thompson Group logo engraved under the crown at twelve o'clock. I looked up at Grandpa.

"Put in on, boy. It won't bite you."

I reluctantly pushed my hand through the band. It fit as snugly as a handcuff.

"Do you like it?"

"Thank you, Grandpa. It's awesome." I forced a smile. "It's … is it gold?"

He nodded. "Very special gold."

I stared down at it. "This seems … maybe too much for me."

"Nonsense. That watch marks an important milestone in your life. You're stepping into manhood, and into my shoes."

—

Ms. Lin set the domestic staff and the bodyguards free, but when my dad pushed his chair back, Grandpa stopped him.

"Robert, I want you to hear this, too."

Dad sighed but sat back down.

"Something unexpected happened this morning," Grandpa said, "that puts us in a serious situation." He took a deep breath. "My biggest investors have backed out, which means the Bayview Complex project is in peril."

Loud conversation broke out around the table. The Bayview Complex was Grandpa's biggest project ever, his dream, ten years in the planning: three towers, one a Thompson Hotel with luxury condominiums on the top floors, and two office towers. He'd even talked about moving into one of the penthouses.

"The committee has never refused you," Walter said.

I frowned. "What's the committee?"

Grandpa glared at Walter. "A group of international partners," he said. "It's … an investment club of sorts."

I heard Dad cough.

"Are they crazy?" Mark said. "They're guaranteed a huge return on investment—not to mention they're breaching a contract. We'll kill them in court."

"We also lost most of our bank credit lines this week," Walter said, "the ones we use to operate our divisions."

Grandpa swore. "Then this is about more than just the Bayview."

"You're damn right!" Walter's face reddened. "And I can't be expected to factor personal attacks into my financial plans!"

"What does Mr. Roacks mean by *personal*, Chairman?" It was a woman I didn't know.

Grandpa hesitated. "He means, Barbara, that I've been blacklisted at the highest levels—the very highest. They mean to destroy me."

Something didn't add up.

"Wait a minute." I turned to Grandpa. "You're a billionaire. Why do you need to borrow money?"

Walter sighed. "We have billions in *assets*. We don't keep it in a vault in the basement like Scrooge McDuck."

I wanted to stick out my tongue at him.

Ms. Lin spoke up. "Chairman, isn't there something you can do?"

Grandpa gazed at his hands. "Of course, I could call Geneva—"

Someone swore—my dad. He looked mad, and he never got mad.

"You mean Bartholomew, don't you?" he said in a tone I didn't recognize.

When Grandpa didn't reply, Dad pushed his chair with a loud scratch and lunged to his feet.

"Goddammit! You promised me you were done with him!" His fists were clenched tight by his sides.

Okaasan touched his arm, but he shook it off and strode out of the room. She followed him, leaving me astonished and the room engulfed in another raging silence.

I took a deep breath. "Who's Bartholomew?"

Mark answered. "He's one of the top money men in the world."

I looked at Grandpa. "Why's he mad at you?"

He turned to me. "He lent me money years ago, helped me get my start," he said. "But why would one of the most powerful men in the world help out a young nobody like me?" He looked around the table. "Turns out I had something he wanted."

"What?"

"I had a small collection, ... antiques, just little trinkets, but he wanted them. I wasn't interested in selling, so I paid back the money I owed him and walked away. That was years ago." Grandpa let out a short laugh. "He's a sore loser."

"But why now?" I said. "Why'd he wait this long to do something about it?"

Grandpa's head drooped. "The bastard waited until I had the most to lose."

—

Everyone filtered out of the dining room, leaving me alone with Grandpa and Walter. I stared at my new watch. I still had an hour and a half before I was supposed to meet my friend Mack. For once I couldn't wait to do my homework—anything to get back to reality and out of the world of big business.

Walter paced. "Bankruptcy is a strong possibility," he said. "We may not last to the month's end."

Grandpa lunged to his feet, his face red. "We *just* lost the financing! So why did the Bayview project go under two months ago?"

"It's the economy. Everyone's suffering." Walter licked his lips. "Call Mr. Müller, Bartholomew's assistant. Maybe you can—"

"No!"

"You're risking the company—"

"It's *my* company to risk!" Grandpa strode from the room rubbing his temples. Not long after, Ms. Lin came in from the garden and followed him upstairs.

Through the open door, I felt the breeze and smelled the freshness it carried. Across the room, Walter now held a glass of scotch. He smiled, but it disappeared when he caught me staring at him.

"You've inherited a sinking ship," he said.

I was about to reply when something started nagging at me. I felt a pang of worry. Something was wrong—I just didn't know what.

Okaasan ran in from the garden and paused at the foot of the stairs.

A moment later, we heard Ms. Lin yell.

—

The red trucks of the San Francisco Fire Department were parked out front, paramedics waiting. Okaasan and I had run upstairs to find Grandpa slumped over his desk, his face gray, with Ms. Lin at his side. Seconds later, Mr. Barrymore and three men burst into the study carrying medical kits and a defibrillator. Everything after that was a blur.

Mr. Barrymore pleaded with Grandpa to go to the hospital, but he refused.

"I ate too much!" he yelled. "You're overreacting."

It was about then that Okaasan and Ms. Lin pushed the men aside. Within minutes, Grandpa was on his way down the stairs, strapped to a stretcher, grumbling the whole time but no longer resisting. The paramedics took him to the emergency department of UCSF Medical Center and my parents took me home.

CHAPTER
3

MACK WAS WAITING OUTSIDE our gate, kicking at the weeds poking through cracks in the sidewalk. Dressed in jeans and a gray hoodie, he looked older than sixteen. He was a big stocky boy with a curly mop of blond hair that had fascinated me since the first time I saw it in kindergarten.

I closed our gate. "Hey."

"Yo." He pointed to the book and pencil case I carried, and his face twisted in mock astonishment. "You're leaving home without your precious new computer?" He spun toward the street. "Call the media!"

I rolled my eyes. "I left it at my grandpa's house." Then I told him about my morning—most of it anyhow.

His face fell. "I hope he's OK."

"Me, too. Scared the hell out of me."

"I bet." He blew out his breath. "Well, happy birthday, I guess."

I frowned. "Where's my present?"

"My presence is your present." He grinned.

"Does it come with a gift receipt?"

He punched me on the shoulder.

We started up the Arbutus Street hill, under the shade of neatly trimmed trees, and it wasn't long before Mack was puffing. San

Francisco is a great place to live if you want a cardio workout every time you go out.

"So, what'd you do last night?"

He looked over at me. "I had a date with Isabella."

"No way!" Mack lived the life I dreamed about, at least as far as girls were concerned. "So how'd it go? ... Or should I even ask?"

"We met at the theater and had burgers before the movie. Her mom picked her up right after, so I didn't get any action other than making out during the movie."

I shook my head. "More than I get."

"That's 'cause you spend too much time with your computer."

I gave him a sly smile. "Guess who kissed me today."

"Your mom?"

"Grandpa's executive assistant—you know, Ms. Lin." I tapped my lips. "Right here!"

His mouth dropped open. "You gotta be kidding. She's a total babe!"

I beamed. "She said she wanted to be the first woman to kiss me now that I'm a man."

Mack looked dumbfounded. "Are you sure you didn't dream this?"

"Positive."

"Well, that sure beats my present." He paused to catch his breath. "What else you been up to, lover boy?"

"Helping my dad after school." I ran my hand along the iron bars of someone's fence, my lungs not feeling the hill yet. "He's almost finished that heritage renovation up in The Heights. I'm tired, but the money's nice."

"Yeah, I bet." He watched a white Mercedes climb the hill past us. "That's how you bought your new laptop, right?"

"Well, some of it was birthday money, but yeah." My dad paid me well, way more than I'd make flipping burgers. I'd been working with him since I was a kid, even helped him when we built our new house a few years ago.

We passed the old red fire box on the corner, turned onto

Sacramento Street, and walked past three-story apartments with shops on the bottom floor.

"So what happened with you and Tyler on Thursday?" Mack said. "He nailed you pretty good."

"Just the usual crap," I said as we passed a bus shelter with *The Thompson Media Group* spelled out below a perfume advertisement.

Mack sighed. "Use your stuff, man." He threw a few punches in the air. "Like you did in elementary school. No one messed with you then. Everybody thinks you're a wimp. It's embarrassing."

I shook my head. "My mom would kill me if I got into a fight again."

"Just don't break any bones this time," he said. "And who's going to tell your mom anyway?"

"She'd find out." When it came to me getting in trouble, I'd swear Okaasan was psychic—and she had a great imagination when it came to punishments. "Anyway, I don't need to kick his ass. I changed his Facebook page last night—he looks great in a bikini top."

Mack burst out laughing. "How'd you do that?"

"I found a picture on his hard drive of him posing by some lake in his sister's bathing suit."

"Oh man, I've gotta check that out." He was laughing so hard he had to stop walking. "Is it still up?"

"Yup, and *he* messaged all his contacts about it." I was feeling better now. "And he can't take it down—I changed his password."

"Man, remind me not to piss you off."

"You're doing it right now." I laughed. "Anyway, I'll change it back in a few days. That's more fun than hitting him, right?"

"Yeah, except no one knows *you* did it, so it doesn't count."

—

It was cool and dim inside the library when we burst through the doors, both of us laughing. The librarian hissed at us to be quiet as we dropped our stuff onto an empty table.

I hadn't even looked at our assignment, and when I did, I rolled my eyes. *Describe how settlement affected the American Revolution.* Mack was already scribbling in his notebook, but I didn't know where to start, especially without my laptop.

I glanced around, searching for inspiration.

A girl was sitting a few tables away with a thick book open in front of her. Two long braids fell over her shoulders. She was Asian, about our age, and wore a school uniform—a short gray plaid skirt and a blue blazer with a crest on the front that I couldn't make out. She had an odd-looking black leather backpack and tennis-racket case at her feet.

Our eyes met. She smiled.

The girl from the bench!

Mack noticed my reaction. "What?"

"See that girl?" I whispered as I tilted my head toward her. "I think I saw her earlier today, and she just smiled at me."

Mack turned to look while I hid behind my book.

"Don't be so obvious," I hissed, but the girl was busy reading and didn't even look up.

"I don't think she's from around here—I don't recognize the uniform." Then he gave me a skeptical look. "And cute girls don't smile at geeky guys like you." He went back to his work.

—

Mack left just after three-thirty. He'd finished his homework, but somehow, between doodling and stealing glances at that girl, I wasn't even close to being done. Not that it mattered. I had nothing planned for the rest of the day.

I must have drifted into a daydream, but a beeping noise snapped me out of it. I looked up and saw the girl standing by the door, the red security light flashing above her head. The librarian waved her away from the doors. Their voices rose, which didn't help, since the girl was speaking Japanese.

I glanced down at the table, then back up toward the girl. I sighed. Go on, Junya, be a hero for once in your mediocre life.

I walked over. "Excuse me," I said to the girl in Japanese. "You didn't check out those books."

She turned. Her eyes were cold—she looked at me as if I were blocking her view.

"What does that mean? Check out?"

I noticed she had very long eyelashes and the cutest little freckle below her right eye. It took a moment to gather my words.

"You can't *take* the books." I glanced at the librarian. She shook her head in frustration and went back to work.

The girl stared at me. I began to feel awkward as the silence stretched out. I noticed that the books in her arms were visitor guides to San Francisco.

"Are you on a school trip or something?"

She frowned for a moment. "I am visiting here." Then she tilted her head and looked at me from under those long lashes. "My name is Shoko ... Murakami."

"I'm Junya."

I ended up getting her a temporary library card, with me as the guarantor. I don't know what I was thinking. She could have run back to Japan with those books in her backpack and I'd be stuck with the bill.

Afterward, we stood outside on the library steps. Late-afternoon sun slanted through the tree branches above. I had my hands stuffed in my pockets, feeling like an idiot. A shiver ran up my spine. I was nervous, and that always made me feel cold.

"Do I know you from somewhere?" I said. "You seem familiar."

She shrugged. "Thank you for helping me. I get myself into trouble sometimes. My mother says I am not too bright."

What was I supposed to say to that?

"I am glad I met you," she said.

I knew she was waiting for me to say something, but I froze. The more I tried to think of something, the hotter my face got.

She looked away. "I guess I should go."

"Oh ... OK. Maybe I'll see you around." I tried to drink in every part of her—I seriously doubted I'd be seeing her again—and, of course, I stumbled on the steps. At least I managed to catch the handrail before I face-planted.

I walked away fast, cursing myself. What an idiot! Nothing was waiting at home except Okaasan and my old computer. If I had any balls at all, I would have turned around right then and gone back to her instead of walking home alone.

I decided I wouldn't mention this to Mack. He'd smack me in the head.

CHAPTER
4

THAT NIGHT I HAD THE weirdest dream. I'm halfway up a wooden staircase as wide as a country lane and taller than the trees around me. High above, supported by huge columns, sits a simple wood building topped with a massive X-shaped roof, like scissors pointed at the sky. It's a Japanese Shinto shrine, a place to worship the ancient gods. In the dream, it's both old and familiar, like something I've seen before.

I rest my hand on the thick railing and turn to look over the land. Beyond the forest lies the ocean, gray and foreboding. To the south and east, the distant hills are green with trees. A wide and fertile valley lies between, thick with crops and fruit trees. Tiny thatched huts dot the landscape, most of them clustered in what looks like a village. One house sits on the edge of a meadow, away from the others. I'm sure there's a girl standing in the doorway, looking at me.

I wave. She doesn't wave back.

People begin gathering outside their houses, pointing up at me. I hear a shout. At the bottom of the stairs, several old men in long black robes and tall pointed hats have gathered. Behind the men stand two women. On their waists they carry a katana, a long curved sword. I look closer. They're young, fierce, and beautiful.

One of the men waves his hand, motioning for me to keep going. I resume my ascent toward the shrine. My heart pounds and I
take a deep breath. As I reach the top, the shrine door bursts open
and a man walks out into the sunlight, standing straight and tall. He
doesn't smile. In his wrinkled face, etched deeply, I see only sorrow.
There's goodness in him, too, but it's faint, like a distant memory. It's
Grandpa.

"James. It is time for you to follow your destiny."

I feel a tingle of dread in my neck that turns into a shiver. Before
my eyes, Grandpa's shoulders sag and his face grows haggard. His
eyes lose their shine. Then he fades away.

In his place stands a much older man. His body begins to shudder
and it takes me a minute to realize he's laughing, his breath wheezing
through drooping lips.

A snake-like tongue flicks out of his mouth. I stumble back
against the railing, the tingle in my neck growing stronger. Suddenly
the old man's head leaps off his shoulders and tumbles down the
staircase, bouncing higher and higher with each step. There's a blur
of movement as it hits the ground below—one of the women stabs
her katana into the earth, piercing the head through the eye.

A hand touches my shoulder.

I spin around and bump into Ms. Lin. We're in Grandpa's foyer.
She grabs me, crushing her lips into mine, her tongue exploring my
mouth. When she finally breaks away, she puts her lips to my ear.
"God, I've waited so long for this!" she whispers as her hand slips
inside my shirt.

"I don't think so, old lady!" It's that Shoko girl from the library.

I turn and run.

—

When I opened my eyes, the clock on my nightstand read 6:42.
I heard a rhythmic banging coming from the kitchen—Okaasan
preparing breakfast—but it was Sunday. Didn't that woman ever
sleep in?

I pulled the pillow over my head and tried to shut out the noise while I replayed the dream in my head. I usually don't remember my dreams. The beginning made no sense, but the last part with Ms. Lin was worth remembering. Of course, seeing that Shoko girl just reminded me I'd let the perfect opportunity slide.

I tossed the pillow aside and glared at the ceiling. As usual, my eyes went to the nail hole in the third board from the left. My dad hadn't been able to see it when I pointed it out to him after I finished installing the ceiling by myself. He thought it was damn good work for a twelve-year-old. I didn't mind woodworking, but I liked architecture more, like the bookstore project, so helping with this house had been great. It wasn't your typical San Francisco dwelling—it was a modern structure of concrete, steel, and glass, with so many windows and skylights that even on cloudy days no corner was untouched by daylight, not even the laundry room.

The noise in the kitchen had stopped. I checked the clock again. It was 6:58, time for revenge of the ninja.

I tiptoed to my bedroom door. Okaasan had already opened the blinds, and light streamed in. I watched her walk along the gravel pathway in the Zen garden flapping her arms, apparently doing some kind of stretches, or perhaps she'd decided to start flying. I snickered. She turned and glanced toward my room and then continued to stretch.

I ducked back into my room. When I peeked again, she was gone.

I moved like a ghost past Tama, our chubby white tabby cat, who lay in the hall. She watched me with bored eyes as I sneaked past. I paused when a noise came from the kitchen. It was my dad, pulling on his work boots by the back door.

"Morning, James."

"Hi, Dad."

"What are you up to?"

I grinned. "I'm going to sneak up and scare Mom."

"Good luck with that. See you later."

As soon as he left, I moved toward the open glass door in the living room. Okaasan sat on a yoga mat near the koi pond, her back to me. Across the pond was the dojo my dad had built for our training room. It was a reproduction of a large traditional Japanese teahouse, complete with a steep straw roof. Dad's workshop was behind that, out of sight against the back fence.

My friends and I used to play samurai-versus-ninja here when we were young, running and yelling and tearing up the yard. Okaasan was a patient woman. She'd never said a word to us, not even when we tried to catch the koi fish with dad's fishing gear.

Speaking of ninja, I could climb above the doorway and drop behind her as she came in, but I'd tried that before—and was painfully unsuccessful. Instead, I started toward her, planting each foot carefully. I knew that the sand and the waterfall would mask any sounds. She was bent down now, her back to me, her head near her feet. I moved as silently as a soft breeze.

"Junya?"

I froze with one foot suspended in the air, still several feet away from her. "Yes, Okaasan."

"What are you doing?" She was still facing away from me.

"I'm conducting a test."

"And did you pass this test?"

I put my foot down with a thump. "No, but you did."

"Why don't you try to impress me with your skills in the dojo instead?"

I turned and tromped back into the house. I glanced back at her. She was in a downward-facing dog position now, her butt sticking up in the air.

—

Okaasan had practiced martial arts since she was a kid. I wished she'd picked another hobby, preferably something that didn't involve me. I'll admit, though, that for a woman fast approaching forty and smaller than me, she could sure kick my butt.

The dojo was a good-size building, with half the floor covered in hardwood, the other half laid with *tatami* mats, a type of woven grass that was softer to fall on. Along the back wall, rows of racks held her implements of death.

When I got to the dojo, Okaasan had opened the shoji panels, the sliding rice-paper doors, to let the sun in, and she'd already begun. She looked focused as she performed her *kata*, the repetitive routines used in martial arts.

We started with *iaijutsu*, a Japanese sword technique from something like the fourteenth century. Just like a cowboy's "fast draw," iaijutsu taught the samurai to draw his katana—while kneeling—and strike an opponent down in one fluid motion. Okaasan told me iaijutsu is moving meditation, a Zen art, but it looked pretty deadly if you asked me. Still, I rarely complained—it required concentration but never hurt.

Some days we did a little mother-son hand-to-hand combat, which did hurt, and was why I'd been able to snap a bully's elbow in third grade. Of course, once Okaasan heard about that, she forbade me to ever fight again.

Okaasan's favorite martial art was *kendo*. She called it "the way of the sword" and got misty-eyed when she talked about it, like she was passing me her dead grandmother's tea set. Kendo is fast and kind of funny to watch: two opponents run toward each other in body armor, hitting their opponent with bamboo *shinai*, all the while yelling at the top of their voices.

I couldn't stop any of her attacks today, which was nothing new.

"Junya," she said when she let me rest for a moment, "this is Zen, the goal is mindlessness. Stop thinking and let your body respond." She attacked again, striking me with her shinai while I fell back, barely able to stay on my feet.

She pulled off her mask.

"You're better than this." She looked frustrated. "Your mind is holding your body back." She pulled off her armor and planted her bare feet in a fighting stance. "Perhaps you can redeem yourself."

"Oh, come on." But she was already coming toward me.

I backed away from her, hands up, wary. As I circled away, she attacked, her hands and feet hitting fast and hard. I blocked and managed to force her back a few times.

"That's good," she said, "but you haven't hit me yet." She was fast and agile, and three times after that I hit the ground in pain, one of my limbs in a joint lock.

"Do something!" she yelled as she came at me again. I blocked her first strike, but she got through and took me down hard.

I lay on the tatami, not wanting to move, angry with her and with myself. I finally stood up and pulled my clothes and my pride back into place.

"You don't even try," she said, her hands on her hips.

"What's the point?" I glared. "I can't use any of this stuff! When guys hassle me at school, I try to keep away, but—"

She looked contemptuous. "So, because your mother says you can't fight, you run away like a scared mouse?"

"That's what you told me to do!"

"I never said that." Then a sly smile lifted the corners of her mouth. "Do you think you could beat Mack in a fight?"

I hesitated. Mack and I would push and body-check when we shot hoops, but in a real fight? "I don't know. He's huge."

She smirked. "What about his little sister then?"

I spun toward her as energy swelled inside me. "You don't—"

I blocked a shot to my head and took a punch to the stomach. She hit, I blocked, she hit, I blocked again. Finally, I found an opening and struck her neck. She faltered but didn't stop. A moment later, I hit the mats hard but surprised both of us when I jumped back up.

She fired a kick at my leg and her next punch landed harder than she'd expected. When she hesitated, I didn't. I hit her in the face, which shook her, and moved in close. The next thing I knew, she was falling toward the tatami. But she never got there. She cartwheeled on one hand—a move I'd never seen before—and attacked. My feet left the ground and I belly flopped onto the tatami. My breath burst from my lungs.

She stared down at me. "You're getting strong, Junya, … and fast." She bent down and helped me to my feet.

"But never fast enough." I started to ask about that cartwheel move, but I noticed her face. It was already changing from red to blue. I cringed.

"Don't worry. You'll still get your breakfast." She stared at me for a moment and then said, "You haven't talked about trouble at school in a while. I assumed that was over."

I rolled my eyes. "It's never over. Tyler calls me the bastard son of Edward Thompson."

She looked shocked. "He knows who your grandfather is?"

I shook my head. "Mack says everyone thinks I'm a wimp because I let him get away with it."

She stared out at the garden. "Weak dogs bark loudly."

I sighed. She'd never understand. Tyler didn't need psycho-analysis, he needed a kick in the head.

"But Mack's right," she said.

I raised an eyebrow.

"Appearing weak attracts trouble, but there's a big difference be-tween being weak and choosing not to fight." She headed to the door. "Make sure you clean everything up."

I glared at her back. "That's why this is a waste of time. Even if I'm good at this, I still have to let people beat on me."

She paused at the door and looked back. "Are you stupid?"

"I don't know, am I?"

Now she looked mad. "As your master, I will not give you permis-sion to fight. You don't realize your capabilities—you nearly broke my jaw today." She fell silent for a moment while she assessed me. "But you don't need permission to defend yourself. Use your brain, Junya. It's not a decoration."

She walked toward the house and I started to wipe the dojo floor, grumbling under my breath. I was sweaty and my shirt was heavy, so

I took it off and let the cool breeze wash over my bare chest. Maybe it would cool my anger as well.

I was on the way to the sword rack, going through a few routines and listening to Okaasan's katana whistle through the air, when I passed the full-length mirror. The lighting in here was different from in my bathroom, where I saw my reflection most often. Out here, the soft light created shadows that highlighted my chest and shoulder muscles.

I didn't look like a wimpy kid. I looked strong. I stared at my reflection for a long time. Okaasan was right—I was stupid.

CHAPTER
5

ON MY WAY TO THE KITCHEN I stopped to scratch Tama, who still lay in the hallway. She stretched herself out so I could reach her whole belly. Then I ran and slid on my socks and came to a stop in front of the kitchen door.

At least that was the idea. Actually, I overshot by a few feet and hit the concrete wall beside the doorway. I thought I heard a snicker.

Okaasan was busy cooking and wore an apron now, bright red with little cartoon cats all over it. Her long hair was tied into a loose bun.

She smiled at me. "Thank you for cleaning up."

I grunted and sat at the table, already set with cutlery. A glass of milk awaited me alongside the weekend newspaper. From the front page of the unopened business section, Edward Thompson stared back at me. The caption asked who would replace him if he died.

I shoved the business section away and grabbed the comics.

A cheery electronic tune sang out from the control panel on the kitchen wall, announcing that the washing machine was done with its cycle. Okaasan punched a few buttons and silenced the music.

She stared at the panel with her head tilted to one side and then nodded. "This is way better than doing laundry in the creek," she said.

That was a new one. I knew her life had changed a lot since she moved to San Francisco, but washing clothes in the creek?

She placed my plate and her cup of tea on the table and sat across from me.

"Have you heard anything about Grandpa?" I asked. "Real news, that is."

"He seems to be doing fine." She shrugged. "He'll have to stay there a few days for more tests, though."

"Good luck with that."

"I'll drag him back in if he tries to sneak out."

I laughed. "I'll go see him after school tomorrow if he's still there." Then I remembered. "I gotta go to his house today. I forgot my laptop yesterday."

Okaasan nodded and then pointed to my plate. "Eat. I didn't cook it for you to stare at."

The omelet was delicious, filled with chopped peppers and onions and chunks of ham and covered with melted mozzarella. Pieces of peeled apple and a thick slice of sourdough toast were on the side. I didn't look up again until every morsel was gone. Then I sat back with my glass of milk in hand and let out a small burp.

"*That* was delicious."

"You're welcome." She often complained that it took three times as long to cook food as it did for me to eat it, but I knew she was happy when I enjoyed her cooking.

"Remind me, if I ever meet her, to thank your mother for teaching you to cook." I arched my eyebrows and smirked. "Of course, I don't know where you found time to learn, what with washing clothes in the creek all day."

She made a face. "My real mother never taught me to cook. I learned that from my adopted Mom. And the creek was before I left my family."

Okaasan rarely talked about her life in Japan, but I knew she'd gone to live with another family when she was a teenager. I'd asked her about it once, a long time ago, but never got a straight answer.

"Why *did* you leave your family? Your real one, I mean."

She took a sip of tea. "My family lived an old-fashioned life, far from any cities. It was wonderful as a child—we could run barefoot in the grass and swim in the creek." She stared at the wall behind me. "But schooling was difficult, and I wanted a different life."

"Wait a minute." Something clicked into place. "Did you run away?!"

Her cheeks turned pink. "You can never tell your father I told you this."

I nodded, but I was never going to let her live this down.

She lowered her voice. "When I was fifteen, I spent a year in the city, as part of my studies. It was a rare opportunity, but I was a top student. It was so exciting, so much to see and do! When it was time for me to return home, I didn't want to. Of course, my family was furious, but I insisted and my mother finally relented." She smiled. "We had friends of the family in the city and my mother made arrangements. I became their adopted daughter and took their last name."

"Seriously?"

"That isn't so uncommon in Japan, even now."

She got up and started to pile the dishes into the sink. I stared at her back, wondering how I'd gotten to sixteen without questioning her odd life—which reminded me of what had happened in the garden that morning. I still didn't know how she'd heard me.

"You *were* very quiet," she said without turning, "but I sensed you from the time you got out of bed. Your thoughts were not pure."

I choked on my milk, splattering my shirt, the floor, the table.

She tossed me a towel.

As I cleaned the milk off the floor, I glanced up. She was staring down, but not at me. She looked a million miles away.

"Okaasan?"

She raised her eyes to meet mine. "For some reason, your energy is stronger today, easier to sense." She paused, looking uncertain. "No … it was harder to ignore."

"My *energy*? Give me a break." Then I remembered what I'd been thinking about in bed. My face went red. "Uh, can you hear *all* my unpure thoughts?"

"Who has time for that?" she said, facing the sink again. "I tune in to things that require my attention, that's all."

I stood up and tossed the wet towel onto the counter.

"But how do you know when to listen?" That she *could* listen, I never doubted. Okaasan had always had an eerie way of knowing exactly what I was thinking or what I'd done—especially if I'd done something wrong.

She shrugged. "Intuition is like …" She stopped, a wet hand going to her chin. "You just get this feeling, you know?"

"I *don't* know. That's why I'm asking."

"It's like becoming immersed in the stream of life," she said. "The stream is always flowing around us. If you listen, everything you need to know is available to you."

I stared at her. "The stream?"

She sighed and rolled her eyes. "How about a library? Can you imagine that?"

I nodded.

"Everything's already written and the book lies open. But you have to turn the pages and read the words." She smiled as if terribly proud of her definition.

"Is that what you did yesterday, at Grandpa's?" I frowned. "I'm sure you ran into the house *before* Lin starting yelling."

She thought a minute and then shrugged. "I guess so."

"But how did you *know*?"

"Why are you suddenly so interested in this?"

I hesitated. "Because I think I felt it, too. I just didn't know what it meant."

She frowned. "It's not common for men," she said after a while, "but anyone who chooses to listen can. And maybe it's easier for you. Nuts don't fall far from the tree."

I shook my head and left to get a new shirt. The only nut in this house was her.

—

She was still in the kitchen when I came back.

"I was wondering about something else."

She grinned at me. "I know."

I glared at her, trying to decide whether to continue.

"I'm kidding," she said, laughing. Then she sat at the table and looked up at me, expectant. "I'm sorry. Go ahead."

"Yesterday, some really strange things happened." I sat down across from her. "I don't know if it was this *stream* thing, but ... I felt something, this tingling feeling, like I needed to look behind me."

She gave me her full attention, her eyes wide. "And what did you see?"

"Well, I saw this girl and ... I thought there'd been an earthquake ... but it was more like an explosion. A strong wind hit me, like an energy wave."

Okaasan cleared her throat. "What kind of girl?"

"The female kind, what do you think?"

"Was she pretty?"

I paused. "Yeah."

Okaasan grinned. "Well, maybe you're smitten." She clasped her hands in front of her chest. "That happened to me when I first saw your father."

I stood up. "That isn't what happened." Well, maybe a little.

She shrugged. "I'm sure it's nothing to worry about."

"But I sensed something at Grandpa's, too—right before you ran into the house."

She stood and looked at me, her face serious now.

"Children can sense things that adults can't, but as we get older, we stop listening. I don't know why you'd start sensing things now, but I recommend you pay attention." She walked me to the door and put her hand on my arm. "By the way, ... you did well in the dojo today."

I forgot to say good-bye—I think I was in shock.

CHAPTER
6

WHEN I GOT TO THE BASKETBALL COURT, I found Mack sitting on a bench, gazing into the distance, his basketball under his arm. Without a word, we started a game of one-on-one. He had the height but I had the speed, so it wasn't as one-sided as you might think.

Half an hour later, we took a break and lay back on the grass, both of us sweating. A thick layer of clouds tumbled toward the east, but they didn't look threatening. Mack turned and grinned at me.

"I went out with Isabella again last night."

"How do you do that?"

He gave me a funny look. "Do *what*?"

"Not *that*." I rolled my eyes. "I mean how do you ask girls out?"

He emptied his metal water bottle. "If I like them, I just ask them."

"But what if they say no?"

He shrugged. "Sometimes they do, but so what? If you don't ask them, you'll never know." Then he gave me a suspicious look. "Why're you asking?"

"I just wondered." I tried to look innocent. "And you're such an expert."

He puffed up his chest. "It's so true," he said. Then he got serious. "You're scared of girls but they're as nervous as you. It's when they stop being nervous that they become a mystery. Or they become bitchy for some reason. That's when I dump them."

"Maybe you should try to understand them."

He just laughed.

I recalled my conversation with Okaasan that morning: if I couldn't understand my own mother, some strange girl was hopeless.

"Never mind," I muttered.

—

As I trudged up the steep sidewalk under a canopy of oak and maple trees, I noticed a shiny red sports car parked behind the iron gates of one of Grandpa's neighbors. I stopped to look. It was a Ferrari, a two-door convertible. Very nice.

I smiled and walked on. No matter what Okaasan and Grandpa said, I'd have a car soon. My bank account was already looking good, and I'd made a hundred and ten grand on a single project. If I inherited Grandpa's company, I'd have a car like that *and* his 145-foot motor yacht with the helicopter on the back.

A wave of guilt swept over me. What was I thinking? I didn't want a world without him. Besides, I had other plans for my life.

I was halfway across the boulevard when a chill ran up my spine. I spun in a slow circle, trying to find the source. When I found it, I faltered. That girl was back—same white socks and black braids, sitting on the park bench. She stared at Grandpa's house, just as she'd done yesterday, and didn't notice me until I was right in front of her.

It was Shoko Murakami.

She jumped. "Oh, it is you," she said in Japanese. "I am not used to getting sneaked up on." She still wore her school uniform. It looked neat and clean, but really, hadn't she brought anything else to wear?

"Hi again," I said. "What are you doing here … again?"

Sometimes I could just kick myself.

"I am sightseeing." She held up one of the books she'd checked out yesterday with my card. "It says The Crescent is a must-see." There was a picture of Grandpa's house. "That is your house?"

"No, it's my grandpa's house." It was the first time I'd admitted that to anyone.

"It is so beautiful. We have no such houses where I come from." She looked at me with wide eyes. "Do you have time to sit with me?" She patted the bench beside her.

"Sure ... I have lots of time." I sat next to her—well, not quite. I was nervous and kept a respectable distance between us. I knew I should ask her about yesterday, but my words evaporated when my eyes dropped to her legs. Her bare thighs were tanned and muscular—not the legs of a girl who sat around watching television all day.

"Do you run track or something?" I asked, my eyes still on them.

She turned her head fast, which sent her braids spinning. "What is *track*?"

"You know," I drew a circle on my jeans with my finger. "Run around the track at school or in races."

"Why would I run in circles?" She looked at me as if I were an idiot. "I run if I have someplace to go in a hurry."

"Right ... Never mind." Then I pointed at the black racket bag slung across her back. "But you play tennis."

She hesitated. "Yes."

I couldn't help it—my eyes dropped back to her legs. Her right hand rested there now.

"That's a cool ring."

"Cool?"

I couldn't strike out any worse, so I decided to plunge right in.

"Were you here yesterday?"

When she looked at me, her eyes had turned cold. "Why do you ask me that?"

"I just wondered," I said, hesitant. "I saw a girl sitting here. She kind of looked like you." I pointed toward the carriage house. "I was standing over there."

She shrugged and turned her head back toward Grandpa's house. "Is it ... amazing inside?"

"Is what amazing?"

"Your grandpa's house."

"Oh, uh ... yeah. There's lots of wood trim and stuff," I said, but I could do better than that. "It's a Victorian, built in 1910 by a wealthy banker."

"Victorian?"

"As in 'Queen Victoria.'"

She stared at me, her face blank. Couldn't she make anything easy for me?

"Victorian is a style of architecture named after the Queen of England at that time," I said, for the first time happy that I'd listened while Grandpa rambled on about this stuff. "The house is a Shingle style, built after the San Francisco earthquake in 1906."

"Ah, earthquakes," she said, nodding. "I know about those."

"I would think *so*."

"So your grandfather is rich?"

"He's the richest businessman in San Francisco, not counting those Internet guys," I said. "He owns hotels, banks, department stores, office towers—you name it. He even owns my favorite radio station."

"What about railways?"

I hesitated. "No, no railways."

She looked disappointed. "That is too bad. I like riding trains."

Why couldn't the man own a damn railway?

"So you are rich, too."

Again, I hesitated. "Well, no, not really ... but one day I'll inherit his company."

She looked concerned. "You are too young for such responsibility. It is best if Edward does not die soon." Then she stood and bowed. "Thank you. You have been too kind, wasting your time with a common girl like me."

"No, Shoko, I don't mind." I sprang to my feet. If I were Mack, I'd have been making out with her by now. She stopped and turned to face me, her eyebrows raised, smiling in a way that made her look older. "Maybe I could show you inside … sometime."

She smiled again. "Now would be good."

I hesitated. Well, I *had* offered.

—

William wasn't home and there weren't any security guys around, so I spoke to someone on the security intercom.

"This is my friend, visiting from Japan." I smiled at the camera. "She doesn't speak English."

Shoko smiled and waved.

"Welcome to the Thompson Manor, miss," the man said as the gate clicked and began to open. Shoko bowed low toward the camera. She looked impressed as we walked up the curved driveway and stopped several times to admire the flowers.

I gave her a tour of the main floor. She wanted to look at everything—the carpet, the furniture, the woodwork. Even doorknobs and light switches seemed to fascinate her. But it was when we walked into the huge kitchen with its rows of tall white cabinets and restaurant-grade stainless steel appliances that she looked like her eyes might pop out.

"What is this place?"

"It's the kitchen."

She held her breath for a moment. "My father could feed the whole village here." She ran her hands along the smooth countertops, shaking her head. "This is fit for a god."

"Yeah, it's pretty fancy," I said as I steered her out of the kitchen.

She stopped at the stairs. "What is up there?"

I shook my head. "Grandpa wouldn't—"

41

But she was already climbing. I hesitated and then followed.

She stopped in the center of Grandpa's study and turned in a slow circle, taking it all in. A breeze moved the air and I glanced down the hall, wondering if a window was open. Uneasiness settled over me.

Shoko was by his desk now, tracing the edge with her finger as she circled it. She looked so small next to it and even smaller when she hopped into his chair. Her feet didn't reach the ground.

"That's my grandpa's chair." My voice sounded hollow, like I was speaking inside a cave. "You probably shouldn't sit there."

She pulled the middle drawer open and looked in. She held up a stapler, turning it, peering inside. Then she put it back and pulled out a roll of tape. She examined it with the same curiosity.

"He has interesting things." Her eyes rose to meet mine and I took a step backward. Her eyes were hard, dark—the same look I'd seen at the library. Like I was in her way.

She pulled another drawer open and leaned forward to peer in. Swallowing a lump in my throat, I crossed the room and stopped in front of the desk.

"Please, I'm gonna get in trouble. There's nothing in there."

"Nothing?" The leather creaked as she leaned back in the chair. "What about a book where he records his thoughts?"

I blinked. "You mean like a journal?"

She shrugged, her eyes still on mine.

"I've never seen one." I glanced over my shoulder toward the stairs and lowered my voice. "And even if he did, my grandpa's stuff is private."

"I am interested in him," she said. "I am—how would you say it?—researching him."

I frowned. "Why?"

She put her shoe against the desk and slowly spun the chair. When it came full circle, she stopped and looked at me again, her dark eyes obscured behind strands of hair that cascaded across her face.

"Where is it, Junya?" There was nothing friendly in her voice now.

I stepped back. "I … if he has a journal, it's probably in his safe." I glanced toward the fireplace before I could stop myself. When I looked back at her, there was a smile on her lips.

"Please," I said. "We should go."

Her foot kicked out and she spun around in his chair again. She looked curious when she came back around. "What is a safe?"

My hands were flat on the desktop now, me on one side, her on the other.

"You don't know what a safe is?" I frowned. "Where in Japan are you from?"

She spun the chair again. "Who said I was from Japan?"

"You're visiting here, you speak Japanese, and you're wearing a Japanese school uniform!"

Her shoe hit the edge of the desk and the chair stopped dead.

"Then of course I am from Japan." She smiled, and a hint of red tinged her cheeks. "My family lives far from the city, so I seldom see modern things. That is why I do not know what a safe is."

"A safe is a strong steel box with a complicated lock—it's impossible to break into." I stood up straighter. "Now let's go."

She looked at me with big innocent eyes and then pulled the bottom desk drawer open with her shoe.

"I think it is in here." Her eyes held mine, daring me to stop her. When I didn't, she let out a deep sigh. "I did not imagine this would be so easy."

My stomach was in knots. What was I going to do, beat her up?

She reached into the drawer, to the very back, and withdrew a leather-bound book. It *was* a journal, the cover worn and darkened from years of use.

"How did you know?" I said.

"I could feel it speaking his words."

My mouth dropped open.

"I came a long way to get this, Junya. I *will* read it." Her expression softened. "But I will return it, I promise you."

My hands went to my temples. "So … you planned all this?"

Shoko nodded. "I want to see if Edward wrote about my mother."

"Why would he write about your mother!?"

She sighed. "My mother was in love with Edward."

If my jaw hadn't already been on the floor, it was now. I was dumbfounded but growing angry. "You're wrong."

She waved a hand, dismissing my comment. "I want to know what Edward thought. Did he know she loved him? Does he regret losing her, or did he throw her memory away as he has done with everything else he loves?"

"There's no way my grandpa knew your mother!" I felt something build inside me, a swelling in my chest. "Put the journal back—we're leaving!"

She clutched the book to her chest like a little girl. "Please, I will give it back. I promise."

I wasn't falling for it. "No way. You tricked me. Now put it back." I tried to sound strong, but the energy was already slipping away from me.

Shoko stood up and faced me and we stared at each other. Beads of sweat ran down my sides as my antiperspirant failed. Then I remembered the emergency button on his desk, within my reach, and a smug smile spread across my face. "One last chance," I said.

She took a step back to where she'd left her backpack beside the desk and leaned toward the drawer, but her eyes never left mine.

"Have you ever been in love, Junya?"

"I … well, no. I mean …" I glanced away.

The drawer slammed closed.

A wave of relief swept through me—she wasn't holding the journal. She must have put it back in the desk. She shouldered her backpack.

"He should have chosen love over gold," Shoko whispered.

I turned toward the fireplace, toward the painting with the steel safe behind it. There were gold bars inside that Grandpa had showed me when I was little. But how did she know?

When I looked back, Shoko was near the door.

"I am sorry about my behavior." She bowed low and her braids tumbled over her shoulders.

"You should be." I pointed toward the stairs. "Now let's go."

We went downstairs in a silence so dense that I could hear my heart beating. She kept her head down until she was through the gates. Then she turned to face me.

"Thank you for showing me the house. It is more beautiful than I could have imagined." Then she turned and walked out the gate, through the shadow of the archway. At the sidewalk, as the sun illuminated her again, she bent low into a formal bow. "I will see you again, as I promised."

What did that mean? I watched her walk across the cobblestone street. She never looked back.

There was a loud clunk behind me—the gates were closing.

"My backpack!" I darted through the shrinking gap and then slowed to a walk. I'd barely reached the front stairs when I heard the roar of the wave.

I spun in time to see it rush over the hedge, bending the trees as if they were blades of grass. It hit me and I flew backward. Then it was gone, leaving me breathless and flat on my butt in the garden.

Mr. Sugimoto came around the front of the house about then. His straw hat flew off as he ran toward me—he moved fast for an old guy in rubber boots.

"Junya, are you all right?" He reached out and pulled me onto the pathway without effort. He was in his late fifties, but bulging muscles showed through his damp work shirt.

"I'm not sure." I was trying to steady myself. "I hope I didn't hurt your plants." I always got nervous when I spoke Japanese with a man. I worried that I sounded like a girl because I listened to Okaasan so much.

He looked around, poised and alert. "What happened here?"

I hesitated. "There was this big gust of wind … It knocked me over."

"I felt something, too … but that wasn't the wind."

"Then what was it?"

He took in a deep breath. "It was like a door opened." He paused and an odd expression twisted his face. "And a breeze came through … a very pleasant breeze."

He touched one of the sharp, menacing-looking tools that hung from his belt and looked at me with interest. Then he walked away.

—

I got my backpack out of the hall closet and stood for a moment, trying to process what had just happened. I couldn't explain that wind, that wave of energy. At least I'd stopped Shoko from getting the journal, but I still didn't understand why she wanted it or how her mom could have known my grandpa.

I will see you again, as I promised.

A sinking feeling overtook me. I dropped my backpack and climbed the stairs.

When I sat down in the chair, the leather was still warm from her body, and there was a small shoe print on the dark wood of the desk. When I reached to wipe the print off, I noticed she'd left the bottom drawer open a crack. My heartbeat quickened as I stared into the thin dark space. Finally, I pulled the drawer open. Inside was a row of thin red file holders, each labeled in Grandpa's handwriting. But at the back of the drawer, so far back I had to open the drawer all the way to see them, were five blue folders. Inside each were thick manila envelopes. I leaned closer. There was one folder, the third from the back, that hung at an odd angle. Its contents had stretched it wide. I reached in to straighten it.

A lead weight dropped into my stomach. The file folder was empty.

She'd taken the journal.

CHAPTER
7

THEY MADE GRANDPA STAY in the hospital another night, which must have driven him nuts. Grandpa's driver offered to pick me up after school Monday and take me straight to the hospital, but no way was I getting into a Bentley in front of my classmates. I'd stick with the bus.

I sat near the front with my backpack on the seat beside me. I felt like crap. What was I going to tell Grandpa? *Hey, I let some strange girl into your house and she stole your journal. My bad.*

Grandpa's staff had taken over the waiting area. Two bodyguards stood at the end of the hall, and Walter Roacks was off in a corner with a phone pressed to his ear.

I headed to the bathroom to wash my hands. I'd barely finished when some guy in his early twenties barged in.

"What are you doing here?" he said. "This floor's off limits."

I blinked. "I'm visiting my grandpa."

"The old-farts ward is down two floors."

"My grandpa is Edward Thompson."

He frowned and then smiled. "I knew that," he said and slapped me on the shoulder. I stumbled. "I'm just kidding around."

He headed back out to the waiting area. I turned down the hall toward Grandpa's room. John stood outside the door.

"Hey." I jerked my thumb over my shoulder. "Do you know who that *jerk* is?"

John snorted. "That jerk is Anthony Roacks."

—

I found Ms. Lin sitting on the edge of the bed, holding Grandpa's hand. When she heard the door open, she let go and stood. Today she wore a short flowery dress and high heels. She looked less formal than usual, but to me that only made her more gorgeous.

She smiled. I blushed.

"Hi, James." She moved closer and lowered her voice. "He's saying some odd things, but don't worry, it's only the medication." I glanced past her. An intravenous line led from the suspended bag to his arm, but he looked OK otherwise.

"I'll leave you two alone."

I watched Ms. Lin leave before turning to Grandpa. His eyes were on the door, too. He let out a long sigh.

"That woman's got a beautiful body," he mumbled.

"Grandpa!"

"What?" His eyes were half-closed now. "It's true."

I agreed, but I wasn't about to say so.

"Did you know I met her on a plane?" He slurred his words. "She was a stewardess ... couldn't take my eyes off her." He laughed and pointed to his ice cup. I held it while he took a sip.

"So you hired her for her looks?"

"Listen, boy." He wagged an unsteady finger while he tried to talk around the ice chips. "Why can't I hire a beautiful woman? The airline did." He dropped his hand. "But no, it was her eyes ... Such confidence in them. Don't see that very often." He stopped again and stared at the wall, the only sound the rhythmic beeping of the monitors. "I've only seen that in a woman once before. Lin seemed so ...

familiar somehow. I couldn't let her go after that." His eyes drooped closed and his voice dropped to a whisper. "Couldn't let her go a second time."

I leaned closer. "Let *who* go?"

He cleared his throat. "This stuff's better than whiskey." He remained quiet, his eyes closed, and I began to wonder if he'd drifted off to sleep. I poked his shoulder and his eyes opened.

"Did you know someone else once, someone like Ms. Lin?"

He looked confused, but he nodded.

I put on my brightest smile. "I've never heard about this girl, Grandpa. Would you tell me the story, please?" Just like I used to ask for stories when I was a kid.

He made a clumsy attempt at scratching his face. "A long time ago ... I met a girl ... an amazing girl." His voice was clearer now. "I wasn't much older than you ... right out of college." He paused and his eyes slid closed, like a garage door coming down. I poked his shoulder harder this time.

"Where did you meet this amazing girl, Grandpa?"

His eyes opened a crack. "I went to the desert ... the Mojave—"

"You met an Asian girl in the Mojave Desert?"

His eyes opened and then he squinted. "I never said she was Asian." He glowered at me. "And ... I wasn't in the desert at the time. You wanna hear this ... or not?"

"OK, OK, I'm sorry. So you met this girl who happens to look like Ms. Lin ..."

He nodded. "I was looking for something ... treasure. My father told me about it before he died ... had a map." He looked past me. "Indians showed me the place, but ... they wouldn't go near ... said spirits lived there."

I nodded like it made perfect sense.

"Still couldn't find it ... but I found her. Well, she found me ... and I stayed with her for three days ... but they wouldn't let me stay, and I couldn't ask her to come. I had nothing ... I was broke." His eyes closed again and his words began to fade. "I should've found a way ..."

"Found a way to stay in the desert?"

"It wasn't the damn desert!" The machines started beeping faster. I kept quiet and after a while the beeping slowed down. He started to fumble around, and when he hit the intravenous needle, he mumbled an "ouch." Finally, he looked over at me. "Confusing for me, too," he said with a sniff.

I nodded. "You said you were looking for treasure?"

He blinked a few times before answering. "Remember that gold I showed you ... years ago?"

I glanced at my new watch.

"That's right," he said, nodding. "I used some ... in your watch." He paused and stared at me, his face perplexed as if waiting for something. "Well, don't you see?"

"See what?"

"The girl led me to the gold." His eyes returned to the ceiling. "Then she disappeared."

I looked up at the intravenous line and felt guilty. I knew I should stop and let him rest, but I couldn't.

"What was her name?"

He didn't answer. His breathing became regular and his eyes remained closed. I looked up at the ceiling, cursing inside. Then he grabbed my hand and scared the hell out of me.

"Tomi." His eyes opened a slice. "Her name was Tomi."

I held my breath.

"The perfect girl." A line of drool escaped his lips. "But money ... power ... they mean nothing now." He paused. "Sometimes I wish she'd never shown me that damn gold."

I looked out the window and tried to pull the pieces together. One thing seemed clear: Shoko hadn't been lying about my grandpa knowing her mother.

"You used the gold to start your business?"

He nodded.

"That Bartholomew guy helped you, too, right?"

Grandpa let out a growl. "Bartholomew ... helps himself." He let out a long, slow sigh. "Can't figure that bastard out ... He's been old since the day I met him." He chuckled, but it turned into a cough. When he recovered, he grinned at the ceiling. "Lin looks like Tomi ... but Lin has a better body."

A nurse came in to check his vital signs and shooed me away from the bed. When I moved back to give her room, I noticed Ms. Lin standing near the door.

How long she'd been there, I didn't know. She stared at me, her arms crossed, her face unreadable. "Why don't we go get some dinner, James?" There was no stewardess smile this time. "The Chairman needs his rest."

CHAPTER
8

WE WALKED OUT TO HER STEEL-BLUE BMW Roadster and headed downtown against the flow of rush-hour traffic. The BMW was a two-seater, small and powerful, with a retractable hardtop that Ms. Lin opened at the first light. She drove fast, swerved around slow cars, and shifted and cornered like a pro. As she peeled away from a traffic light, the car's engine roaring, she glanced at me.

"You like my car?" she yelled.

I nodded. "It's awesome!" I yelled back. *Grandpa must pay her a lot.*

A few minutes later, we lurched to a stop in front of a trendy Italian restaurant on the ground floor of a converted four-story brick warehouse. I could see massive wood posts and beams through the windows of the loft apartments above, as if the building were showing its bones.

The valet took one look at the car and hurried around to open her door. I let myself out and waited on the sidewalk, hands stuffed into my jean pockets. As Ms. Lin walked around the car, a breeze fluttered the hem of her dress. She eyed me as she approached and then shocked me by reaching out to adjust my shirt collar and fix my hair.

"That's better," she said as she stepped back. "You're a good-looking young man."

I felt my face flush.

"You take after Edward." She used his name with a familiarity that surprised me. "You should probably start dressing like his heir."

"Why?" I frowned. "I want him to get better."

"I didn't mean it like that, James." Her tone was softer now. "Let's go eat."

As we approached the glass restaurant doors, she nodded toward our reflection. I stood a little straighter, drawing myself up as far as I could, a hopeless effort against her high heels. Her long silky black hair brushed my shoulder as she tilted her head toward me.

"I look like a cougar." She frowned and then purred in my ear. We both burst out laughing—I'd imagined many things about this woman, but a goofy laugh wasn't one of them.

As we walked into the restaurant together, I wished Mack could see me. I looked at the beautiful woman beside me. "Ms. Lin, would you mind calling me Junya?"

"If that's what you'd prefer," she said. "And you can call me Lin. I feel like an old schoolmarm around you."

I smiled. "Deal."

"Table for Edward Thompson, for two," Lin told the man behind the reception desk while a surgically preserved middle-aged woman took our coats. The man said something to Lin.

"Put it on our personal account," she said.

I didn't have time to wonder what *our personal account* meant, because a short round man in a pinstripe suit pushed his way past the waiters and called to us in a thick Italian accent. He looked like a wise guy out of a gangster movie.

"Lin, what a surprise!" He kissed her on both cheeks. He looked at me, puzzled, and then his rosy face lighted up. "Ah, it is you, James!" He grabbed my shoulders. "You're growing up. Soon you'll be a big businessman like the Chairman, no?" He turned back to Lin. "I must apologize," he said, "but the cellar room is already taken." He forced a smile. "If I'd known you were coming ..."

"Please don't make a fuss, Antonio. Anywhere is fine."

He guided us to a secluded table for two, where a waiter appeared and spread napkins on our laps. Lin ordered a glass of red wine, and by the time I'd gotten my bearings it was already half-gone.

"Do all Grandpa's employees enjoy benefits like this?" I was also thinking about the BMW parked outside.

Lin gave me an "Are you kidding?" look, followed by a smile. "Only those Edward considers special."

I noticed a group of businessmen watching her and exchanging comments.

"Do you know everyone stares at you," I said, "even women?"

"I don't dress like this expecting to be ignored."

I flushed. "So ... you like the attention?"

"Dressing well is one of the joys of being a woman." She gave a small wave to the businessmen. Most of the men looked away, embarrassed. "But no, I don't need their attention."

One man in the group hadn't looked away, and she held his gaze for a moment.

"Confidence like that is rare," she said, turning back to me. "It's very attractive, more than good looks and money combined." Then she laughed. "Of course, if you're rich and handsome, you tend to be confident."

After the waiter took our orders, we sat in silence. Lin appeared to be content with that—after all, the only thing we had in common was *Edward*.

I checked out the other diners, who arrived in pairs or groups of four, all well-dressed and reeking of money. I noticed several people glance our way, probably because of Lin.

Our appetizers arrived after an agonizing wait. I grabbed the proper utensil from the cluster around my plate, happy to have something to do.

"Good, you know how to use cutlery," Lin said. "That's one less thing for you to work on."

I grabbed a lemon wedge and squeezed. Instead of squirting onto the raw oysters, a stream of juice shot straight into my eye. I yelped and attacked my eye, mopping up the tears with my napkin, sputtering and squirming. When I got things under control, Lin was staring at me with a blank expression.

"I see this will not be without its challenges." She burst out in that funny laugh of hers.

—

My filet mignon was delicious, but I was having trouble enjoying myself. I couldn't help noticing the people watching us. Lin was halfway through her meal and on her second glass of wine when she pointed her fork at me.

"You look so nervous," she said. "Relax."

I leaned toward her. "Everyone's checking me out," I whispered. "I feel like the newest panda at the zoo."

She nodded to the tables around us. "There are some very important people in this room. They know who I am and they're figuring out who you must be."

I crossed my arms. "Did you bring me here on purpose?"

She put her knife down and gave me a look I didn't like. "Yes." She lowered her voice. "Look, he'd never admit it, but I can tell your grandfather's scared. Something's eating away at the company like cancer. The losses are spreading from one department to the next, and with this credit problem …" Her face was dead serious now. "Your grandfather wants to show everyone that with or without him, the Thompson Group has a future."

I plunked down my fork. "So I'm the savior of the company?"

She raised an eyebrow. "Not quite, but you are the crown prince. And everyone knows it."

I let out a deep sigh. I'd probably never be able to go to school again.

"You can never forget you're *his* grandson." She signaled to the waiter for more wine. "I'd like to let loose in a nightclub once in a while, go dancing with the girls, but I won't. Everyone the Chairman does business with knows me, so any bad behavior reflects back on him." She paused as the waiter refilled her glass. "And you know how he'd take that."

I had to ask. "But what about dating and stuff? He can't control your personal life."

She paused, her wine glass suspended halfway toward her lips.

"It's hard to know where work ends and personal life begins." She took the sip. "Like now—is this business or pleasure? People are always watching, so I must adhere to higher standards. And you must, too."

I sat up a little straighter. "Do you like being his assistant?"

She got an odd expression on her face. "He's the best boss I've had—demanding but fair." She smiled, but it seemed sad. "He's given me one hell of an opportunity, no matter what his reasons for hiring me might be."

I winced. "You heard what he said?"

She toyed with her food. "I've never heard of Tomi, but he named his yacht after her, so she must be pretty special." She frowned at me. "Have you ever heard of her?"

I shook my head.

"Well, apparently I'm just like her." She kept her voice neutral. "I hope he's enjoying her memory."

A frozen silence followed and I stared down at my plate. I wiped my face with the napkin and looked up at her. "I'm sorry, Lin. Grandpa wasn't himself, all the medication and stuff ..."

Lin's eyes were shiny, but her jaw muscles were set tight. "Don't worry, Junya, I'm a big girl." She emptied her wine glass and the waiter reappeared to refill it, as if that were his only purpose. "And you and I both know I wouldn't still be here if my body was my only asset." She took another sip of wine and put the glass down with a thump. "I'm a businesswoman now, the right hand of Edward Thompson. The experience I've gained and the contacts I've made are a gift that'll last long after this asset"—she indicated her body—"is gone."

"You think he'd fire you if you ... lost your looks?"

Her eyebrows arched. "He'll move me somewhere else and get another, younger assistant. It's the way of things. You'll do the same."

"I won't."

Lin raised her eyebrows and, with a shake of her head, went back to her meal. I took a few more bites.

"May I ask you a personal question, Lin?" As if I hadn't been grilling her all night.

"Shoot," she said, but I sensed apprehension in her voice.

"When you were my age, what did you think you'd be doing now?"

She smiled. "I wanted to be a famous model, working in Paris and Milan, traveling to exotic places for photo shoots."

"So why didn't you?"

Her smile disappeared. "It didn't work out."

"But ..." *But you're gorgeous.*

"There are thousands of beautiful girls in the world." She stopped and stared across the restaurant. "But the truth is, I didn't even try. Everyone said to get my head out of the clouds, and my father expected me to go to law school and help my uncle with the family's law practice after I graduated."

"You have a law degree?"

She frowned. "A pretty girl can't have a brain, too?"

"That's not what I meant," I said. "I'm just thinking ... my grandpa said he met you when you were a stewardess."

She sighed and gave me a half-smile. "My father won the first battle, I won the second. It wasn't quite like being a model, but I got to see lots of different places, and that degree is coming in handy now, isn't it?"

"So, you're happy with the choices you made?"

Her eyes narrowed.

I plunged ahead. "What I mean is, do you like your life? Are you happy?"

She gave me a hard look. "Do you want to make me feel like crap?"

I flinched, caught somewhere between embarrassment and

frustration. "I'm sorry, Lin." I held my palms out in surrender. "It's just ..." Deep breath. "I don't want to be a businessman."

She tilted her head to one side. "Then what—"

"I want to be an architect, design houses and stuff." I sighed. "Grandpa decided this whole thing without asking me."

"But you know so much about his business." She looked confused. "You're the perfect choice."

All of a sudden I was mad. "I like being with him!" I said. "I don't care about the business. Besides that bookstore project, everything else is mind-numbing."

She looked worried. "It'll kill him to hear that."

"That's what worries me."

⁓

The rest of the meal passed in polite silence. After we finished dessert—warm chocolate cake with vanilla custard and ice cream—I excused myself to go to the restroom. On the way, I passed the cellar room and saw Walter Roacks and another man at Grandpa's usual table. Walter slouched at the table, but the other man sat tall and straight in a stiff blue suit.

"My employer is losing his patience," the man said. He had an accent—German, maybe?

"And *my* employer is getting suspicious," Walter said. "This credit freeze isn't necessary. The Bayview Project is already dead."

The man made a sound that might have been a laugh. "You can pick at the bones later—after you deliver."

Walter nodded. "Tell Bartholomew he'll get it and ..."

My ears started ringing, and then my stomach rebelled. I ran to the bathroom and burst through the door with my hand pressed against my mouth.

I stopped dead. It was cold and dank, and the air smelled of mold. Water leaked from the top of the urinal, dripping down and pooling on the cracked floor tiles.

I walked to the grimy sink, turned on the water and splashed my face with cold water. That made me feel a bit better, but the noises coming from the only toilet stall were threatening to change that.

I was washing my hands when a man came out of the stall. He was old, frail and stooped, dressed in a dark suit and a thin black tie. He sniffed the air and his eyes caught mine in the cracked mirror.

He looked like the old man in my dream.

"You are something special!"

I couldn't move. Darkness closed around me and blocked out everything else. I felt my heart speed up as I stared back at him.

"And you have the gold in your watch." He stared at me with hungry green eyes—I was sure they'd been brown a minute ago.

I pressed back against the counter.

"I ... I got it as a present." I reached to undo the strap. "Here, you can have it back."

"Keep it." Then he chuckled, although it sounded more like a cough. "But you're very perceptive—it is mine."

The watch suddenly felt tight and heavy. I couldn't get it off my wrist. I could barely breathe.

"What ... do you want?"

"To see you."

"Who are you?"

His lips parted and a long flat forked tongue flicked out at me.

I bolted past him, through the door, and into the hallway.

I collapsed against the opposite wall and stared at the door, shaking so hard I couldn't get a full breath. Sweat poured out of me and vomit rose in my throat again, but no way was I going back in there. I closed my eyes.

Then Antonio was beside me, his hand on my arm.

"James, are you sick?" He lifted me and steered me toward the bathroom. "Come inside and have a seat." I heard him snap his fingers. "Get some ice water!"

"I'm fine," I whispered, but he'd already pushed me through the door and lowered me onto something soft.

I opened my eyes. This room was clean and luxurious, with granite floors and shining fixtures. I looked up at Antonio.

"This is way better than the other bathroom."

He frowned as he handed me the water. "There is no other bathroom."

—

I waited for Lin outside the restaurant, breathing in the cool evening air while I tried to understand what had happened. Antonio had found me in the hall. Maybe I'd passed out for a second. The old man, the cold bathroom—it was probably just a weird dream. It had to be.

Lin came outside a few minutes later and looked at me with concern.

"Are you OK, Junya? You're as white as snow."

I gave her a half-smile. "I'm fine."

She glanced back at the restaurant. "I thought I saw Walter Roacks. I only saw his back, so I can't be sure, but—"

"Did you recognize who was he with?"

She hesitated. "He looked familiar ... very well-dressed." She snapped her fingers. "Yes, he's Mr. Müller, from Gen—"

"That's Bartholomew's assistant! We gotta tell Grandpa!"

Lin sat on the edge of a concrete planter while the valet stood beside her car, waiting with the car door open.

"Yes," she said, "but—"

"But what? Isn't having Mr. Müller in town enough? And I *know* it was Walter. I saw him, too."

She touched my arm. "I don't want Edward upset right now."

"He needs to know about this!"

Lin let out a deep sigh and turned toward the valet. "Can you call a cab? I drank too much and I think I'm seeing things."

CHAPTER
9

WE GOT BACK TO THE HOSPITAL just after seven and rode up the elevator in silence. When we entered Grandpa's room, we stopped dead. Walter Roacks stood over Grandpa's bed, a stack of papers in one hand, a pen in the other. When he saw us, something changed in his eyes.

Lin and I exchanged glances.

"Hey, you two," Grandpa said in his normal booming voice. "I hoped you'd come back." He looked and sounded much better. His intravenous lines were out and the monitors were unplugged and silent.

"Yes, finally." Walter scowled as he moved away from the bed. "Why weren't you at the office today?" he asked Lin in a low voice. "I need you there."

"The Chairman wanted me here." She said it loud enough that Grandpa heard her.

"Yes, I want her here, Walter," Grandpa said. "Are you complaining that I'm a control freak again?"

"Our situation's getting worse," Walter said. "Without one of you in the office, it's becoming overwhelming."

Grandpa eyed Walter with disappointment. "Look, you know how to fix this. Do what you have to."

"I'm trying."

Walter turned to go, but Lin blocked his path. "Where did you eat dinner tonight?"

"Downstairs in the cafeteria," he said. "Why?"

Lin's eyes dropped to the floor. "I just wondered…"

Walter stared at the top of her head for a long moment and smiled. "The food is terrible. You may need to get used to that again." Then he turned and walked out, leaving a cold silence in his wake. A moment later, Lin followed him.

I walked to the bed after the door closed. "When did he get here?"

Grandpa frowned at me. "Yes, James, I'm feeling great. Thank you for asking."

I moved closer. "I don't want to worry you … but something's going on."

His eyes narrowed. "What do you mean?"

"When did Mr. Roacks get here?"

"Not long before you did, no more than five minutes. Why?"

I glanced toward the door. "Lin and I had dinner at that fancy Italian place you like. We're both sure we saw Mr. Roacks having dinner with a man Ms. Lin thinks was Mr. Müller."

Grandpa's eyes went wide. "He went begging? I'll kill that bastard!" he yelled.

The door burst open a second later. It was John.

"No!" I grabbed Grandpa's arm.

He turned to look at me, surprised.

"What have you always taught me?" I whispered.

He stared at me a moment and then nodded. "Right." He looked up at John. "We're fine here, John."

John scanned the room one more time before backing out. Grandpa waited until the door shut again before letting out a sound like an unhappy grizzly bear would make.

"You need to get out of here and find out what's going on with *my* company." I grinned.

He nodded. "We'll look into it, real close and real quiet." A slow smile spread across his face, the first real smile I'd seen in a long time. "You see? That's why I chose you." He grabbed my hand. "We don't talk about this with anyone, got it?"

—

Lin came in a few minutes later and walked past me toward the bed.

"I need to get out of here," Grandpa told her.

"Why, do you miss me?" She giggled. Grandpa smiled up at her.

She leaned over the bed and whispered something into Grandpa's ear. He laughed and put his hand on her bare thigh, well above her knee. Then I watched, eyes wide in astonishment, as Lin kicked off her high heels, climbed onto the hospital bed, and sat on her knees, facing Grandpa, her dress slipping to the tops of her thighs.

Grandpa grinned at her. "Red or white?"

"A nice dark cabernet sauvignon, from Chile." She grinned at him, her hands on his. "But I think I had a bit too much."

I didn't know whether to look away or stare. I felt like a bone-headed, oblivious kid. They were *together*.

I sighed. The world kept getting more complicated.

I sat in the chair by the window and gazed outside. I couldn't help it—there was too much in my head and it spilled out.

"Grandpa," I said loud enough to interrupt them. "When you said the gold in my watch was special, what exactly does that mean?"

His hand, moving up Lin's back, froze. He looked past her at me. "What?"

I took a deep breath. "You said Tomi gave you the gold, in the desert ... or someplace."

He pushed Lin off his lap. "When did I tell you that?"

"You'd be surprised what comes out of your mouth when you're medicated," Lin said, her arms crossed in front of her. "I'm *so* happy I have a better body than *Tomi*."

Grandpa ran a hand down his face. "Oh, God."

I tapped my watch. "There's something strange about this gold."

He blinked a few times, avoiding Lin's gaze. Finally he turned toward me.

"Well," he said slowly, "I guess I'd better finish what I started." He gave Lin a quick look. "My dad had a map that he showed me a few times when I was a kid, usually when he was drunk. He said he got it from a buddy, a Navajo Indian that he'd fought beside in the South Pacific—my dad saved his life, I think. Anyway, Dad visited him on the reservation several times after the war. The last visit, it turns out the man was dying and he gave Dad a map, written on buckskin. Supposedly, it showed the way to an amazing treasure." Grandpa shifted himself up a little higher. "My dad took the map—didn't want to offend his friend—but he wasn't the type to believe in fairy tales."

"But you said—"

"Wait." He held up a hand. "My dad died of lung cancer my last year at college. The map was among his personal papers, so the summer after I graduated I borrowed a friend's truck and drove to the desert. I was broke—I'd worked my butt off getting through college, so I was inclined to *hope* for buried treasure." He hesitated for a moment. "I asked around. The local Indians set me on the right track, but they wouldn't go near the place. Said something about 'those who come from below' and if they felt the earth shake, they wouldn't leave their dwellings until the next day." Grandpa let out a snort. "Of course, I didn't believe any of that crap. I was a university graduate. I figured I'd be back in San Francisco in a few days, probably still penniless, enjoying the summer of love."

Lin was smiling again. "You *were* a hippie!" Then she poked Grandpa's arm. "So who's this Tomi girl with the big butt?"

Grandpa looked sheepish. "I'm sorry I said that, I truly am." He let out a long sigh. "I'm sure the whole thing was a delirious dream, a hallucination caused by sunstroke. There was no girl out there ... couldn't be, not in the middle of the Mojave Desert."

"It was a good enough dream to name your yacht after her." Lin sounded sarcastic.

"And what about the gold?" I said. "You didn't dream that."

"No, you're right." He glanced at me and then back at Lin. "I knew I was in trouble, I wasn't used to the desert ... At some point I passed out, and when I woke up ... there was a girl—a woman. She said her name was Tomi. I told her about the map and she led me to the gold."

I glanced at Lin. I got the feeling Grandpa was leaving a lot of things out.

"Anyway," he said, "I ended up back at my truck with a stack of these strange gold disks. But once I got home, I didn't have a clue how to sell them. I couldn't just walk into a pawnshop. At the time, I was working at an exclusive businessmen's club, so I started asking around, real casual, pretending I was an aspiring novelist, and I learned two things. First, Geneva was the place to go, especially if it was gold of a questionable source. And time and time again, one man was referred to, but no one would say his name."

"Bartholomew?"

He shot me a look. "Do you want to tell the story?"

"Sorry."

He cleared his throat. "There was a man who visited the club once or twice a year. The managers treated him better than they treated anyone else. He had a certain ... commanding presence. One night he got incredibly drunk and the manager assigned me to keep him hydrated and off the floor. When he mumbled that he was from Geneva, I started asking questions. He didn't have much to say at first, but when he sobered up he asked more about the gold. The next day he took me to Geneva to see Bartholomew, all expenses paid."

"Wow!" Lin said.

"He didn't want the gold, not at first, but he offered me a *lot* of financing. He became a mentor or sorts and encouraged me to start my Committee."

"Your investment club?"

"It's far more than that," Lin said. "True power comes from the production of intended effects."

I blinked. "What?"

"We *create* the market, James, and we control it." I'm sure I heard a hint of pride in Grandpa's voice. "Everyone else has to ride the currents we create."

"Isn't that … a little like cheating?" It sounded a little like *illegal*.

"Anyhow," he said with a dismissive wave, "Bartholomew never gave up asking about the gold. He became obsessed. I wouldn't sell it to him and he started putting financial pressure on me, so I paid him back, every cent with interest, and I cut off all ties—and that was the end of it."

"Until now," Lin said.

I looked from one to the other. "You had to know that Bartholomew was bad news from the beginning, right?"

Grandpa gazed at me in silence. When he finally spoke, his voice was low and cold.

"Your dad knows all this, but he still takes my money. I don't give a damn if you approve of my methods." Then he forced a smile. "It's just gold, James, bought and sold. Don't worry about it."

And so I sat staring out the window at the darkening sky as Lin snuggled beside Grandpa, trying to calm him. The more I learned, the less sense it made. The only thing I knew for sure was that the days of sandwiches and stories on Saturday afternoons were over.

CHAPTER
10

I SAT SLOUCHED IN THE BACK of Grandpa's Bentley, half-asleep, gliding toward my house. The driver had the stereo on, something classical and vaguely familiar.

Lin had persuaded me to let Grandpa's driver take me home, and I'd agreed once I realized how late it was. If I took the bus, I'd have to walk four blocks from the stop to my house. I hated being out alone at night.

Suddenly I sat up and looked out the side window. We'd stopped at a light, and across the intersection I saw three guys under the green awning of a coffee shop, just outside the reach of the street lamps. My face, reflected in the glass window, seemed more real than they did.

They were in their twenties, and the way they were pushing and staggering, I assumed they were drunk. My first reaction was to sink back into my seat. I was safe in the car and they weren't my problem. But something out there, maybe Okaasan's stream, demanded my attention.

The car lurched forward after the light turned green. As we passed through the intersection, I saw someone walking alone, almost at the end of the block.

"Stop!"

The driver slammed on the brakes. I flew forward and hit the back of his seat—my seat belt was already off.

"What is it?" he yelled over his shoulder as the car jerked to a stop in front of a narrow yellow building. He looked around, searching for the threat.

"I'm getting out here."

He spun in his seat. "Close the door! I'm taking you home!"

Our eyes met. My door was open wide now, and I had one foot on the sidewalk. I glanced outside. Across the wide sidewalk, a staircase rose into the yellow building, the steps disappearing into the darkness above. A shudder passed though me.

I heard the driver's seat belt click open.

"The Chairman's gonna kick my ass if I don't get you home," he said. "Now get back in!"

I shook my head, still staring into the darkness at the top of the stairs. Something awakened deep inside me, something urgent.

"Forget about me!" My voice was firm, clear, commanding. "*You* go home. Now!"

My other foot had barely hit the sidewalk when the car peeled away. I jumped back and tried to close the door but couldn't. The car door hit a tree and slammed shut. The driver kept going.

I stared down the street until the car disappeared into the distance. Then I turned and ran back the way we'd come.

Spruce Street was as bare and bright as a dry lakebed. There were no cars, no trees, nothing to hide me. But it didn't matter. The guys I'd seen were oblivious to me, staggering through the open parking lot behind the coffee shop, toward a back street.

I hesitated. Now that I was here, all alone on the street, I started to question my sanity. I glanced toward the apartments. I wondered if anyone was there, watching and willing to help, but the windows were dark and empty.

A light wind rustled my hair and blew past me, urging me forward. I moved with it, up the block and around the corner where the drunks had disappeared. The street was narrow, lined with cars on one side and a row of low apartments on the other. At first I didn't see them, but I *felt* something. That tingling in my neck, the whisper of the breeze—then I saw them.

They were hidden in the shadows under a tree, their gaze focused farther up the block, where a girl sauntered along the sidewalk, running her right hand along a hedge, unaware of the danger behind her. Even without the light of the street lamps, there was no mistaking those long white socks and short plaid skirt. It was Shoko.

I glanced around again, let out a sigh, and started up the street. I tried to stay behind the row of trees as I crept toward them. It didn't matter—they were too busy watching Shoko. As she turned the next corner, the men moved from their hiding spot and stepped out between the parked cars ahead of me. I bolted past them, running flat out.

"Shoko, run!" I yelled in Japanese.

As she spun around, the drunks saw me and started running. Shoko's eyes widened. I grabbed her hand as I went by, jerking her into motion. The tingling in my neck was overwhelming.

Something smashed into my back and I went down hard in someone's driveway. A shoe drove into my ribs, and then a hand grabbed my hair and hauled me up. I covered my head, trying to squirm away and escape the blows. Where was Shoko? What was the other guy doing to her?

As if in reply, I heard a girl's yell, followed by an ugly high-pitched sound.

I'd had enough.

The men fell back in surprise as I straightened up and started hitting them, hard and fast, dodging their flailing fists. I drove my knee into a stomach and turned. The other guy backed away, but I went in tight—elbow to chin. He fell, but now the first guy was back up, cursing, grabbing at me—or trying to. He aimed a fist at my face, but my elbow met it and I heard knuckles crack. I jumped and drove my head into his face. I spun away, fell to the ground and rolled, waiting for the other guy to get back up and attack me.

I looked around. Both my attackers were sprawled facedown on the sidewalk. Had I done that? My neck still tingled, but something felt different.

Shoko stood in a pool of light near the middle of the street, her face emotionless—a blank mask lined with loose hair and a streak of blood. Her blouse hung open, the buttons ripped to her waist. My chest tightened as I moved toward her.

"Shoko ..."

The third man pulled himself off the ground and cursed at Shoko. He didn't notice me, or his friends sprawled on the sidewalk.

"So you took a self-defense class." He pulled a knife. "Get over here, bitch!"

I picked up a board—maybe the one they'd hit me with—and glanced at Shoko again. She stood like a statue, her head lowered, so small compared with the man. I started to move, but when our eyes met through the strands of hair that fell across her face, I froze. She wiped a hand across her cheek and started slowly forward.

"Don't." Though my heart sank, I couldn't get my feet to move.

The man laughed, but his face changed as Shoko broke into a run. She closed the gap to about five feet before she exploded into action, her hands and feet a blur as she smashed into him. He staggered backward as her small feet and hands battered him, each impact like the crack of a home run. Then she jumped so high I couldn't believe it and smashed her foot into his head.

He fell sideways into a parked car. Shoko settled back to the ground, sure and steady as a cat as he slid down the car door.

She turned back to me, her dark eyes wild and dangerous. A smile curled the corners of her mouth. Light flashed off steel as a blade twirled in her hand, spinning from thumb to pinky and back again—she had his knife.

"I should take your head!" she screamed in Japanese.

The man's eyes went wide as she threw the knife so fast that I couldn't see it. I only heard the impact when it slammed into the center of his hand, pinning it to the car door. He was still swearing and screaming when Shoko kicked him in the head.

There was silence.

Shoko stood near the car, poised for more action, with one sock drooping, her blouse still open and her blazer askew. She glanced up and down the street, frowning.

"Are ... are you OK?"

She nodded. Lights came on in windows above us. Curtains opened and faceless silhouettes appeared.

"I called the police!" a lady yelled, fear in her voice, in her energy.

Shoko pulled her blazer closed. "What are 'police'?"

"*Keikan*—policemen. They'll take these guys to jail." Then I looked at the scene around us—three men down, unconscious, one with a knife wound. They weren't just hurt, they were a bloody mess. I looked at the guy I'd head-butted, his face a mask of blood. I remembered what Lin had said at dinner about making Grandpa look bad. How would we explain this?

"This is bad," I said. "The police will take us, too."

She glanced around. "I will not go with these police."

"You can't fight them."

She shook her head. "I will not go."

"Then we need to get out of here!"

We ran, staying in the shadows, until we reached California Street, back where I'd started. Once there, I stopped to catch my breath and check for pursuers. I caught my reflection in the pharmacy window and was shocked by what I saw. My face was bruised and bloody, already beginning to swell, and blood splattered the front of my shirt—not all of it mine.

There were sirens in the distance now. Shoko looked at me.

"Police cars."

She pushed past me and bolted toward the street. Without thinking, I lunged forward and grabbed her sleeve. She spun, rage in her eyes. I blocked her fist and yanked her back onto the sidewalk as a horn blared, so loud and close that I let out a yell. We both fell, her on top of me, as a trolley bus roared past, air brakes hissing.

Shoko rolled off me and onto her knees, but my clenched fist still held her sleeve. She tried to pull away but without much force, like a child tugging at an adult's pant leg. Then she sat back on the sidewalk as a low cry escaped her. She squeezed her eyes shut.

"This place is too much for me." She sounded more frustrated than scared.

The sirens were getting closer. I pulled her up and we ran across the street and dived into the shadows as two police cars roared up the street. They turned the corner where we'd just been, tires screeching, the reflection of their red and blue lights dancing on the buildings. A moment later the sirens fell silent.

I looked at Shoko crouched beside me. She looked small, vulnerable. I had a hard time picturing her throwing a knife into a man's hand even though I'd just watched her do exactly that.

I squeezed my eyes shut and focused on the moment. In the distance I heard another siren, probably an ambulance.

I stood up. "We have to get off the street."

As we jogged past the yellow building with its dark staircase, my body began to shake—leftover adrenaline—and it got worse as it reached my hands. I tried to hide it, but I was beyond scared. Maybe running away was a mistake. Maybe we should have waited. Instead, I turned toward my house.

Shoko looked to me. "I have caused you trouble?"

I let out a short laugh. "You could say that. A lot of people are gonna be pissed about this—my grandpa and my mom for starters—but that doesn't matter. They were going to—" I swallowed.

"When he ripped my blouse, I saw it in his eyes." She looked up at me, her eyes wide. "His grip was so strong and I froze." Another pause. "There is much wickedness here. More than I expected."

I nodded. I'd always thought so, too. "He didn't ... hurt you, did he?"

She shook her head. "He had no time. By then I was fighting."

She grinned. "I knocked that man down and kicked one of the men hitting you."

I sighed and felt a bit deflated. I'd beaten only one, after all. My gaze went toward the ground but stopped at her knees. I pointed at them.

"You're bleeding, a lot."

She bent to look, pulling her hair from her face. She looked embarrassed. "It is nothing. My mother says I am a clumsy girl."

"You're definitely not clumsy! My God, can you fight! But that knife throw was a little, um …"

She nodded. "Too weak, I agree. I should have put it through his eye, but"—she gave me a shy smile—"I do not know the rules here."

I stared at her. "What are you, an assassin or something?"

She looked confused. "Assassins kill a target with stealth, without warning. I only defended myself." Then she glanced around the empty street. Her apprehension reappeared. "They attacked me."

"What are you doing down here at night anyway?"

"I saw a movie," she said. "Then I went for a walk." She looked rather proud of herself.

"Tourists don't come to this neighborhood to see a movie. And not even a tourist would be stupid enough to walk alone at night."

"Stupid?" She crossed her arms, her eyes defiant. "I go where I want, when I want."

"And look where *that* got us."

She scowled at me. "If it is stupid to be here at night, then why were *you* here?"

"Because of you!" I felt that energy rising inside me again. "If I hadn't been there—"

She put fingers to her temples. "Did I ask you to come?"

I threw up my hands. "You didn't even know those guys were behind you!"

"So you came to *rescue* me?" Her words dripped sarcasm, but I sensed something else in her.

I hesitated. "I was getting a ride home."

Her hands went to her hips and she stopped walking. "How did you know I was there?"

I stopped, too. "I … I sensed something was wrong when I saw those men. Then I saw a girl—I didn't know it was you—but I knew I had to do something."

Shoko looked surprised. "Do you often have intuitive feelings and rescue girls?"

I felt myself flush. "Never before, but a lot of weird things have happened since I first saw you." I looked at the sidewalk. "Been getting these feelings, like premonitions."

"You felt my energy, or danger, from that far away?"

I nodded.

"Then you are very strong." She looked confused as she pushed a few strands of hair from her face. "There *is* something strange about you. And when you get angry … something is not right."

"What do you mean by that?"

"Inside your grandfather's house, your energy was … unpleasant."

"You lied to me and stole the journal!"

Her eyes narrowed. "I did not *steal* the journal!"

"Yes, you did!"

"I wanted to read it. I did what I had to do—I will not have any regrets in my life."

Pent-up frustration blasted out of me. "You can't just do whatever you want to other people!"

She stepped back, her face turned to the side, her hands on her head as if she had a bad headache. "I said I would return it."

Her little-girl act made my anger rise up like a wave. It was almost tangible, like I could ball it up and throw it right at her—

I saw her move, every detail in slow motion, felt the blows shake my torso and noticed my feet leave the earth. I became weightless as the world twirled around me. I saw the clouds against the dark sky, the street lamps, the trees, then the grainy surface of the sidewalk.

I crashed into the ground in a full belly flop and my lungs collapsed under the force. It took two or three seconds before oxygen could make it back into my body, and when it did, pain came with it. I lay there wheezing, curled in the fetal position. She stood back, wary, her expression blank as she assessed me.

"That was a stupid thing to do," she said. "Use your energy on me again and I will do worse."

I buried my face in my hands. "I don't understand."

She sat on the cold sidewalk beside me while I lay there battling my emotions—and pain. I don't know how long we stayed that way, but as I began to regain my composure, I noticed an unusual feeling growing inside me. At first, I couldn't grasp what it was, but slowly I realized it was peace and contentment. It washed over me, warm and gentle.

Her hand touched me and I felt a jolt.

"You are right," she said, her voice barely a whisper. "Even with your warning, that man had me before I could react."

I kept my eyes on the ground. "You didn't need me," I whispered.

"You are wrong. Had I been surprised by three men ..." She shook her head and looked frustrated again. "This place is difficult ... I cannot hear well."

She seemed to hear me just fine.

"I have offended you." She paused and then gave her head a little shake. "I said that I do not want any regrets, but I regret doing that to you."

In the pool of light from the street lamps, she looked very much like the girl I'd met at the library. But everything was different now.

"I don't know what's happening to me," I said.

"You are strange." She sighed. "And there are too many unexplained coincidences between us. I must ask—" She looked away.

I tried to sit up and was rewarded with a sharp pain in my ribs. She helped me to my feet and we continued toward my house in silence. As we climbed the hill in the dark, I noticed how peaceful it was. With the light from the street lamps scattered on the ground, diffused by the leaves of the trees above us, it was actually beautiful, and I realized that for the first time in my life, I wasn't nervous about being out at night.

I noticed that Shoko was crossing her arms, hugging herself to keep her blazer closed. I took off my jacket and placed it over her shoulders the way I'd seen my dad do with my mom.

Shoko looked surprised, but when she realized what I was doing, she pushed her arms into the sleeves and zipped it up to her neck. "Thank you, Junya."

I nodded and stuffed my hands into my pockets, determined not to show her how cold being valiant could be.

She flipped her braids over the jacket. "You fight well—very fast." Then the smile disappeared. "But that temper of yours, that energy, it must be controlled."

I frowned at her. "How can I control something if I don't know what it is?"

She didn't answer.

"I talked to my grandpa today. He told me a bunch of stuff ... weird stuff."

Her eyes lighted up. "About my mother?"

"What's your mom's name?"

"Tomi."

I wasn't surprised. "My grandpa said he went to the desert to find a treasure—he had a map."

She looked confused. "He had a map to ..."

"Yeah, apparently he passed out trying to find the place and your mom rescued him." I stopped and turned to her. "What was a Japanese woman doing in the Mojave Desert?"

Shoko gave me a sly smile. "The Japanese love to sightsee." Then her face grew serious. "My mother thought she did the right thing. But she regretted it when she saw how the gold changed Edward."

"What'd it do to him?"

"It made him greedy. I believe it changed his destiny, and my mother thinks she is responsible for that. I also know she regrets not going with him."

I couldn't wrap my mind around what I was hearing. "So did you read the journal?"

She wouldn't meet my gaze. "Most of it. Edward also felt much regret over losing my mother. If only she felt it, that would be sad, but that they both felt it is far sadder."

We walked on, lost in our own thoughts, until we reached the old fire box at the top of the hill. She stopped and rested a hand on top of it. "Can we start again?"

"What?" I was still lost in my own thoughts. "Start what again?"

"If you believe I stole the journal, then I did." She shook her head. "And yet you still came and helped me. I would not have done the same." A tear escaped her right eye and slid past that lone freckle. "Will you meet me tomorrow? We can talk more about all this." Her long eyelashes flashed at me. "I will bring the journal, and ..."

"And what?"

"Maybe we could ride the cable cars together and have hot chocolate." She gave me a sheepish smile. "I want to know you better."

I nodded, shocked. Did she just ask me out?

"I'm ... uh ... sure." I looked away for a second. "Let's see, tomorrow's .... ah, Tuesday. I could meet you somewhere after school, I guess."

She looked happy. Like a gentleman, I insisted she keep my jacket.

It wasn't until I was through my front gate and halfway to the door that I stopped. What was I thinking? I was letting her walk away alone at night—again!

I ran back to where we'd parted.

I felt the wave as I reached the middle of the intersection. It blew down the hill toward me, but somehow it didn't scare me this time. I didn't flinch and it blew past, nothing more than a warm breeze. Then I turned a slow circle, remnants of the wind still rustling my hair. Shoko had vanished.

CHAPTER
11

POWELL AND GEARY IS ALWAYS PACKED with tourists visiting Union Square, but I hadn't been able to think of anywhere else when Shoko and I made plans the night before.

I walked a block from the Muni bus. The day was warm, the sky cloudless, and I felt like a fish swimming upstream against the crowd that poured down Powell Street toward the cable-car turntable. But the closer I got to Union Square, the slower I walked. The excitement I'd felt earlier was gone, and I was growing more nervous with every step.

Shoko sat on the steps of Union Square, surrounded by palm trees. She still wore her school uniform and had my leather jacket folded beside her.

I waited on the corner and let the crowds sweep around me. I felt something nearby, nagging at me. Maybe it was coming from her, but I didn't think so.

Shoko waved, and I crossed the street to meet her. We didn't say much because the Powell-Hyde cable car was rumbling up the hill toward us, its bell ringing out. Shoko laughed as we hopped on and squeezed onto a bench near the driver. Everyone had cameras and San Francisco T-shirts still creased from the store. We climbed the hill, passed the cable-car barn and bumped toward Hyde Street.

The cable car was noisy—I'd forgotten that part—and made a terrible grinding noise as it reached the next intersection. Shoko craned her neck over the brass railing.

I tried to laugh along with her, but I was distracted. I glanced around the car, trying to figure out why, knowing I needed to listen to the stream.

When the cable car began its descent down Hyde Street, a few more passengers got on. They looked like locals. The feeling was stronger now, darker. I looked at Shoko, her eyes wide with excitement. Her energy felt warm and positive—it definitely wasn't her.

I leaned out and looked back to the street we'd turned off. There was a blue car sitting in the intersection even though there was no traffic coming. When we reached the end of the block, it finally turned the corner toward us. When I looked a few minutes later, the car was still behind us.

Someone was following the cable car.

When we crested Lombard Street, the view of the bay spread out before us. I pointed out Alcatraz and the commuter ferries and then glanced back around the cable car. Everyone was looking at the view except one guy, back near the brakeman. He was about thirty, but he was dressed like a college student. Our eyes met and he turned his head away.

"You are distracted," Shoko said. "You are bored? To me, this is spectacular."

"No, it's not that. There's something ..." I didn't know what else to say.

"I understand," she said with a nod. "You are troubled. I will leave you alone to listen." And she did, which surprised me.

When I stole another look at the man, it looked like he was talking to himself. I saw the wire that led up his sleeve from his hand. He was using a portable radio harness, the same type Grandpa's bodyguards used.

I touched Shoko's arm. She turned to me, her eyes alert. I leaned close to her. "I think I'm being followed."

Her face showed no apprehension. "Like those men last night?"

"No, something different."

She frowned. "Are you afraid?"

I shook my head. I had a sneaking suspicion that Mr. Barrymore had added me to his babysitting list and given me my own discreet protection team. I didn't recognize the guy, but he looked like the bodyguard type. I felt cocky for having spotted him, but I couldn't shake that dark feeling. I didn't like how he'd looked at me.

"Forget it," I said as I looked out at the view. "So, you like riding the cable cars?"

Her head bobbed up and down. "I have always wanted to ride them, ... but I was too afraid to try."

"*You* were afraid?"

Her cheeks turned pink. "This is my first time. And I like them, even better than trains."

I liked them, too. They were exciting, but I could see how they might be intimidating. They were kind of like a roller coaster.

The big guy driving, the gripman, rang a tune on the bell as we rolled down the hill. He made it sound Caribbean-style, as if he were playing a steel drum. As we crested the next hill, he threw all his weight against the brake lever, pulling it all the way back.

When we got to the turntable at Aquatic Park, I jumped down onto the cobblestone street while it was still moving. I'd always thought that was the coolest thing, but Okaasan never let me do it. Shoko reached her hand out to me and I took it. She let out a happy yelp as she hit the ground.

The red brick buildings of Ghirardelli Square weren't far away. Shoko was already half-dragging me in that direction while inform-ing me that Ghirardelli's was the best place to drink hot chocolate. I smiled—I'd been there a bunch of times with Okaasan. We'd come here on the cable cars, too, and she was like a kid when it came to sweets. The last time we'd gone was a few years ago.

I slowed. Had that been our last trip on the cable cars together? You never know when it's the last time—the last time your father carries you to bed, the last time your mother holds your hand crossing the street. It's only when you look back that you realize it's gone forever.

I decided I'd ask Okaasan to ride the cable cars with me again.

I grabbed Shoko's hand, an unconscious reaction, and pulled her in the opposite direction of Ghirardelli Square. She started to protest.

"Hang on," I whispered as I nodded toward the cable car.

That man was by the back door, blocking the other passengers from getting off. He looked right at us while he spoke into his jacket, not even trying to be careful. I didn't need to see any more.

"Let's go." I pulled Shoko's hand and we turned and ran the other way. The guy had to be one of Grandpa's new men, but that didn't mean I wanted him to follow me around on a date.

Shoko laughed as we ran through alleys and into stores only to exit out the back and run along another street, putting more distance between him and us. Shoko was in damn good shape, not out of breath at all. She got into the game and pulled me into a hotel through an open kitchen door. We ran past the astonished cooks and walked out through the restaurant, both of us laughing.

About twenty minutes later, we arrived at Ghirardelli Square. I stopped under the archway over the red brick courtyard to catch my breath while Shoko leaned against the iron gates and stared into the chocolate shop. I watched the sailboats on the bay sway on the blue water. I let my mind drift into a peaceful stillness, if only for a moment. There's no silence in a city, but the noise did fade, as if I'd put in earplugs.

At first my mind was empty, but eventually thoughts began to creep in. Was the man from the cable car still following me? And did I have to wait for that voice in the stream, or could I make it speak?

I closed my eyes and tried to reach into myself. At first I felt nothing, but then, little by little, a warm feeling began to well up inside me, rising from my stomach into my chest. It was peaceful at first, like I'd felt with Shoko last night, but it kept growing, swelling like a balloon. It got bigger and bigger and I started to panic. I tried to push it back down but it was too strong. I felt as if I were in the gym with Mack, trying to bench-press two hundred pounds. I clenched my teeth and then yelled.

The energy exploded out of me. The cobblestones leaped away from me like ripples away from a huge stone dropped in water. As I fell to the ground, I heard a gasp and the clatter of the gate hitting the brick wall. I spun to see Shoko fall back against the gate, her hands clutching her head. I lunged forward to catch her.

Her eyes snapped open. "I warned you not to do that again!" she yelled through clenched teeth.

"I ... what did I do?" I backed away in case she was planning to attack me again.

She let out a deep sigh and her hands dropped to her sides. Then she looked toward the sky. "Why me?" When no one answered, not that I could hear anyway, she looked back at me, her anger gone. "Well, after all that I hope you found him. With that much energy, you could knock the gods off their clouds."

"Find who?"

"That man from the cable car. Was that not what you were doing?"

To my shock, I realized I had an answer. "I ... he's still out there, but he's nowhere near us."

"Good." She pointed a finger at my chest. "I swear to the gods, I will rip your heart out if you do that to me again." Then she crinkled her nose and smiled up at me. "Now it is time for hot chocolate!" She turned and walked across the courtyard towards Ghirardelli's.

I watched her march into the chocolate shop. After a long moment, I got my feet to cooperate and I arrived in time to hear her order a hot chocolate and a hot fudge sundae—in perfect unaccented English. She turned to me with raised eyebrows. "Are you getting anything?" she asked, again in English. "My treat."

The chocolate factory had long since moved to another location, and the huge brick building had been converted into a trendy shopping complex. All that remained of Ghirardelli's was a busy chocolate shop with memorabilia covering the walls.

Shoko said it was too dark inside and she wanted to enjoy the sun. She walked out and sat on the bottom step of an old iron staircase. I followed and stopped in front of her. "Why did you pretend you couldn't speak English at the library?"

She looked up from her sundae and licked fudge off her spoon, her eyes expressionless. "I think it worked out better."

"So that's twice you've lied to me. What else aren't you telling me?"

She eyed me with curiosity. "Do you like hot chocolate?"

I stared at her, holding my cup. "What does that—"

She smirked. "You liar, you never told me that. And you certainly never told me you could do *that*." She pointed her spoon toward the gates.

I dropped onto the step next to her and put a hand to my head. "I've got a brain tumor, I know it."

"You have *something*." Then she held out her spoon and offered me a taste of her sundae. The ice cream sent a chill through me and I wrapped my hands around my cup of hot chocolate and tried to soak up its warmth.

"You are cold?" She put her hands over mine around the cup. "I will return the favor from last night." Her hands were warm and soft. I stared at them, studied the color, the curves, every line. Then I looked into her dark brown eyes. My heart fluttered along with my brain.

I gave myself a mental shake and pulled my hands away, spilling hot chocolate onto the step. I jerked my thumb toward the gates. "That's the same thing you did the first time I saw you!"

"You are right." It seemed to be the first time it had occurred to her. "You struck me with energy like nothing I have felt before."

I cringed. "Did I hurt you?"

She shook her head. "How can I explain this?" She paused,

eyebrows together. "To me, it was like a great noise, deep and vibrating. It overcame me."

I looked down at the step. "But why is this happening? These messages, this energy—I don't want any of it."

"Does a landslide ask our opinion before it sweeps us away?" Her eyes narrowed. "Do you regret hearing the message to help me last night?"

"No," I said without hesitation. "But I'd rather this stuff wasn't happening to me."

"Once awareness comes to you, it changes everything. Just as when we climb to a mountaintop and view the full majesty of a landscape, we can never be content to live in the valley again."

"But how did I become *aware*?"

She looked a bit guilty. "I think that when our eyes met that first day, you *awakened*. Now you must decide whether to treat it as fate or live it as your destiny."

I frowned. "What's the difference?"

"We make choices that change our lives every day." The edges of her mouth curled up. "You could have ignored me—twice—but you did not. Why?"

I probably should have. "I guess it was my fate?"

She shook a finger at me. "Fate is a passive response. Destiny is something in which we play an active role." She looked into my eyes as she continued. "To do otherwise is to view your life as a spectator and let fate carry you downstream like a twig."

I closed my eyes and tried to understand.

"You are not the same person you were that day," she said, "and you will never be again. You must accept that. It was the same with me."

I looked up in surprise. "You've been through this, too?"

She nodded and took another spoonful of ice cream. "I was eight. I woke up earlier than usual one morning and went outside. A thin fog hung over the grass and I felt the air ripple. Suddenly, all sorts of new sounds surrounded me—it was amazing. Every blade of grass whispered a message to me."

"Were you scared?"

She thought that over for a while. "I think knowing eliminates fear. It brings a new confidence. But it was frightening to realize something had changed *inside* me." She wiped her face with a napkin and smiled at me. "But it is not something to fear."

"So you hear messages, too?"

"Yes, but not here. The noise here overwhelms me, as if my head is under a waterfall. I have to block everything out, but that leaves me deaf, like last night. And I do not like that."

"But you can hear when you're in other places?"

She nodded.

"What causes that wave of energy?"

She frowned. "You ask answers for things I have never questioned." Then she held her hands toward the sky. "Can you feel that?"

I glanced around. I didn't feel a thing.

She giggled. "Actually, I cannot right now either, but it is the earth's energy. It is all around us, speaking to us, and if our energy is strong enough, we can disrupt the earth's energy field and make it shift, somewhat like a strong ocean wave." She paused and looked at me, eyebrows together. "And your energy is strong enough to do that."

She concentrated on her sundae until she'd cleaned the cup of every drop.

I sighed. "Do you ever get a tingly feeling in the back of your neck?"

"Sometimes when I eat ice cream then drink hot chocolate my head hurts," she said, still working her spoon into the edges.

I rolled my eyes. "I'm not talking about brain freeze." I hesitated, unsure how to explain myself. "I get this ... this tingling sensation before something bad happens—which is pretty much every time I'm with you."

She laughed. "Did you feel it last night?"

"Yeah, right before the guy hit me with the wood."

"Any time today?"

I nodded. "On the cable car."

She stood up and glanced toward the wastebasket. Then she threw her empty cups and they both went in, two perfect shots from eight feet away. She turned back to me. "There are many ways to sense things," she said, her eyes serious. "I suppose this tingle you feel may be a form of intuition. I have heard of such things, but intuition is a woman's gift. At least where I come from."

That's what Okaasan had told me. "And you come from Japan, right?"

She paused. "Yes."

"And you're not a crazy assassin or anything?"

She laughed as she shouldered her pack. "No."

I nodded and threw my cup toward the wastebasket. It missed by a mile.

—

We left Ghirardelli's and walked down to the beach, past artists under white umbrellas, their crafts on display. We stopped to look at a tall sailing ship docked at the pier, and Shoko pointed at the Golden Gate Bridge arching toward the low hills far across the bay. Cyclists, joggers, and couples holding hands passed by, everyone enjoying the warm weather. Three teenage girls wearing bikinis lay sunbathing on the thin strip of sand.

Shoko started laughing. "They are almost naked!"

I blushed.

After that, we walked along the shoreline in silence. The more I processed my thoughts, the more restless I became. The silence thickened and became uncomfortable.

"Shoko, what the hell is going on?"

She walked past me and stopped in the shade of a large concrete sculpture. It took a while for her to reply, and when she did, her uncertain tone surprised me. "I do not know how I can explain this." She kicked a dandelion head, sending its seeds off with the breeze.

"I'm ready to hear anything."

She gave me a tiny nod. "Junya, I was not supposed to come here, but I heard about Edward from my mother and became curious. I wanted to know more about him, so I watched his house for a while, wondering how I could get inside. Then I saw you."

I let out a deep sigh. "And you zapped me and woke me up—somehow."

She nodded. "Yes, but I did not know that until later. After I saw you, I followed you to the library and ..." She smiled. "I knew how to get you to help me."

Judging by the way she laughed, I must have turned eighteen shades of red.

"Boys are easy to manipulate."

"You think this is funny?" I felt like such an idiot. "I let you into my grandpa's house! I let you steal his journal! Do you know how much trouble I'm in?"

She stared at me through squinted eyes, her face blank now, perhaps confused.

"I told you, I did not steal it—"

"There you go again! One minute you're this ... this overbearing bitch, and the next you're all sweet and cute and ..." I rubbed my hands through my hair. "Everything you do is an act."

Her eyes narrowed, but she looked hurt.

"I bet you didn't even bring the journal!"

Now she looked sad. "I said I would," she whispered as she pulled the leather book from her backpack and handed it to me. "I told you at his house that I would return it." She dropped her pack to the grass and sat down beside it, landing with a thump. "I am sorry I tricked you. I am sorry I took the journal. I am sorry I did not tell you I could speak English. And I am sorry for whatever I have done or will do in the future that will make you angry."

"Give me a break," I said.

"I said last night I wanted to talk and get to know you better," she said without looking up. "I did not come here to argue."

I wanted to say more, but I was emotionally exhausted, my brain too overwhelmed to keep up. I looked away. I wanted to run—from her, from all of this.

The message was soft but clear, like a bell in the distance. The grass at my feet, the rustle of the trees, even the air whispered to me and told me to stay and listen to her. Surprised, I turned and when my eyes met Shoko's, I saw a girl who looked as confused and sad as I was.

I sat on the grass near her and stared out at the water. A tugboat chugged by the pier. It swayed from side to side, rocked by its own wake. I felt like that tugboat.

I turned to Shoko and stared into her eyes, but they were like pools, too deep to see the bottom. "I need to know which Shoko is the real Shoko."

"I am always me." She brushed a strand of hair from her face. "Perhaps I have more pride than I should—my mother says that— but I am the best at whatever I do, a leader of my classmates. I am not like people here, who act so proud but are nothing, like a golden temple with no foundation beneath it. They are too dependent, self-loving, and deluded, and yet they are oblivious to the evil all around us." She swept her arm to take in the whole city. "Emotions are a weakness."

I let out a grunt. "That explains a lot."

She scowled. "I thought you disliked lies. Is the truth too painful?"

"Brutal truth is my mother's specialty."

Instead of responding, Shoko gave a small shrug and looked at the water. I stared at the side of her face, the outline of her jaw. She was so strong-willed, so sure of herself. I wished I could be more like that.

"You've got that whole emotional weakness thing wrong," I said after a while. "We fight the hardest for the things we care about the most. What else is worth fighting for?"

She looked at me. "Duty and honor. There is nothing else."

"I think it's sort of the same thing."

She eyed me with suspicion. "Which one sent you into the dark streets last night?"

I hesitated. "I saw a girl in danger. I had to go."

She stared at me. "But you had no duty toward this girl, and certainly no emotional attachment." She shook her head. "I would not have done the same thing."

"Yeah, but aren't you glad I did?"

She rolled her eyes and leaned back.

"How come I can't feel you now?" I felt myself flush. "I mean, feel anything from you."

She didn't react. "I hide my presence here."

"How—?"

"I do not want my presence to be known here," she said, a small smile on her lips now. "But I do not mind if you feel me."

I swallowed hard. "You mean—"

"My energy," she said and I looked away, glad her eyes remained closed so she couldn't see me blush. After a while, she rolled onto her side and started picking at the clover. Sometimes she looked so young.

"How old are you?"

She thought for a moment, apparently having to concentrate. "It depends on how you calculate it, but … about fifteen."

I nodded, pleased and confused at the same time. I noticed the journal lying on the grass beside her leg. I reached over and picked it up. "Thank you."

"You are welcome," she said as she leaned up on one elbow and watched a floatplane rise off the water and soar over the bridge.

"That is so awesome!" she said in English. I laughed at her enthusiasm about such simple things. Then she turned her attention back to me. "It was interesting but also sad."

"Why?"

"Edward had one small moment to act that day in the desert, but my mother has no such excuse. She could have sought him out, but she was not brave enough. And I understand. Such a decision would take a will of iron."

I raised an eyebrow. "I thought emotions were a weakness."

Her eyes narrowed.

I held up my hand. "Never mind. What does the desert—and your mom and my Grandpa—have to do with you and me and this weird energy?"

She brushed a strand of hair from her eyes and swept it over her ear. "What do you think is happening?"

"I … I don't know. I keep searching for a reasonable explanation. I hate this and love it at the same time. There's so much …" I squeezed my eyes shut. "All of this is too much."

"Do you think you are an ordinary person, that all this is normal?"

I didn't look at her. "I'm an ordinary guy," I said. "And no, this ain't normal."

"Do you think I am ordinary?"

"You're definitely not normal."

"So, what do you think I am?"

I let out a soft laugh. "Well … I know you're no exchange student, but then again, I do play too many video games."

"I will not ask what a video game is."

"You see, that's just it. You don't know about stuff you should know about. And you've got some spiritual or magic power that can affect others… and you fight like crazy." I looked up at the sky and grinned. "I'd say you're a warrior monk from the Shaolin Temple."

She made a face.

"Or *maybe* you're a ninja," I said. "Your masters keep you hidden away, train you all day, and send you out at night to kill people." I smiled at her. "How was that?"

She smiled and shook her head and then reached out and touched my knee. Her energy flowed into me again.

My eyes met hers. "Your energy is so familiar," I said. "I feel peaceful when I'm with you."

"Even when I am a bitch?"

I looked down. "I shouldn't have said that. I'm sorry."

She nodded. "I also feel different when I am around you. Sitting next to you like this, my feelings get all tangled up. I feel happy and yet …" She shook her head. "Such feelings will make this assignment difficult."

My eyes narrowed. "Assignment?"

Her eyes met mine. "Will you trust me?"

I swallowed the lump in my throat. "I don't think I have any choice."

"All right." She let out a nervous laugh. "I do not think I am supposed to tell you any of this." She looked down. "But my … teachers have decided I must complete an assignment here."

"OK …"

She took a deep breath and put her hands together in front of her chest in a prayer position. "Please do not get angry at me," she whispered. "I did not mean for this to happen, and we have no idea how it *did* happen. You must understand that."

I leaned back, my hands against the cool grass, waiting, holding my breath.

She took a breath in. "*You* are my assignment."

I did my best to remain calm.

"Last night I told my … my teachers everything, what happened from the first time I saw you. I got in big trouble and they sent me back."

"You flew to Japan and back in one day?"

"They sent me back because of what happened—your awakening." Her face was tight with apprehension. "You must realize that what you are experiencing—these feelings, this energy—are not normal. My Elders are very interested. They want to know why you have these abilities and want you to use them wisely." She managed a weak smile. "I am here to help you, to teach you what I can, and to protect you."

I forced a laugh. "You know, that ninja-monk theory doesn't sound so crazy anymore." I took a deep breath. "Protect me from who?"

"Mostly from yourself," she said. "You do not want to be setting off tsunamis all the time, do you?"

"So tell me what's happening to me."

"Well," she said, sounding far less confident than I'd have liked. "That is what we are going to find out." She grinned at me. "This will be fun!"

I frowned at her. "You're not much of a teacher."

Her smile faded. "I cannot teach until I know what you need to know." She sat up and took a ceremonial poise. "We must make a pact. Then I will become your master."

"Whoa, hold on! I've had it with people telling me what to do." And technically, I think Okaasan already considered herself my master.

"Tradition must be followed!" she snapped.

"And why is that?"

"Because that is the way it is!"

"Well, I'm not doing it that way."

She glared at me. "Rules are rules."

I leaned toward her. "If it was a rule to kill yourself when you turn sixteen, would you?"

"Of course."

I blinked. "Well, that's stupid."

Now she blinked.

"Didn't you break a rule when you sneaked to San Francisco?"

She was silent. I stared at her, growing frustrated, and I guess I must have let some of my energy escape me. My body jerked as she hit me—not with her hands but with energy. I'm sure she would have been glowing if it had been dark enough. I fell backward, but I managed to listen, too. Amid her energy wave came a barrage of emotions, mainly anxiety and indecision.

My eyes widened. "I felt you." She'd told me something, whether she meant to or not. "You can't be my master if you don't have a clue what you're doing." I reached out and tapped her foot. "Think up a different way for us to work together, something on your own."

She stared at the water. After a few minutes, she sighed. "How about a vow of trust … between us?"

I smiled. "Agreed." I held out my hand to shake hers, but she ignored it.

"We need some sake." When she saw my expression, she said, "When two people form a bond, the sharing of sake is like a solemn oath."

I reached for my backpack. "I have a bottle of apple juice. No preservatives added."

She frowned, but a moment later a small grin appeared on her face. "Well, it *is* from the Mother Earth."

She moved so we were face-to-face, sitting cross-legged an arm's length apart. We both took a sip of the juice, first her then me, and for some reason the act felt momentous, almost intimate. I found myself blushing again, but for the first time in days, I felt good, like the world was full of new, exciting possibilities.

"So, where do we start?"

She stood up. "We should return the journal."

CHAPTER
12

IT WAS AFTER FOUR WHEN Shoko and I crossed the boulevard of the Crescent. Grandpa's house was quiet, no cars on the driveway. I punched the intercom button.

"Good afternoon, James." It sounded like the same guy from Sunday.

"Hello there," I said, "just me and my friend again."

There was a long pause.

"I'm sorry for the wait," the voice said. "You're not scheduled for a visit and the Chairman isn't home." Another pause. "I'll have to check with Mr. Barrymore."

I looked sideways at Shoko. "I don't need Barrymore's permission to be here."

"There's ... been a change to your status."

I glared at the camera. "Tell me."

"Yes, sir!" I could almost hear him sit taller in his chair. "You can't be at the house without a protection team." I looked at Shoko. She was staring at me with an odd expression.

"I want to go in."

"I'm afraid I can't—"

I tried to imitate Grandpa. "Open the gate now!"

"Yes, sir!" A moment later, the gate clicked and began to open. "But I'll still need to inform Mr. Barrymore."

"No you don't." I looked up at the cameras. "Are these recording?"

"Yes, 24/7," he said.

"Can the recording be deleted?"

"Yes, … but I'm not authorized to—"

"You are now. Do it, then forget you saw us here today."

"Yes, sir!"

I sneaked another glance at Shoko. I couldn't believe this was working—but now I was worried. Had Grandpa somehow figured out the journal was missing? Probably not, but why else wouldn't they let me in the house?

—

The house was dark and quiet. The flowers on the foyer table, the bouquet from my birthday, drooped toward the dusty tabletop.

"William?"

There was no reply, which was odd but also a relief.

I turned to Shoko. "Let's go." I climbed the stairs, two at a time, with her following close behind. I felt like a burglar, but the journal was back in the drawer within minutes.

Shoko pointed to a large portrait on the wall. "Who is the woman with Edward?"

"That's my grandmother. She died before I was born."

"She looks unhappy—they both do."

I didn't see what she saw, but their pose was stiff and formal, no fun about them at all. I glanced at the other painting—the one covering the safe.

"Shoko, … do you sense anything?"

"You know I cannot." Then her tone changed. "Why, do you?"

"Well …"

She followed my gaze. "Is it coming from that … *safe* thing?"

"The gold's in there." I started toward the fireplace but stopped and backed toward his desk. When I grabbed a roll of tape from the top drawer, I saw the yellow sticky note beside his keyboard again, unmoved from last time, the same digits and numbers staring up at me.

I rolled the ladder along the bookcase toward the fireplace and put a strip of tape over a small hole on the bookcase sidewall.

"There's a security camera in there. It watches the safe."

She moved back. "Something watches from the books?"

"It's a camera, for God's sake." I climbed down, my gaze back on the picture. "It's not alive."

"Are there other ... cameras watching us?" She sounded nervous.

"No ... Grandpa doesn't like them." I thought for a moment and then turned the brass candleholder on the right side of the mantle. The painting slid open just like in a scene from an old movie.

The LCD display on the front of the safe came alive when I touched it, but I nearly fell off the chair when a female voice asked for a password. I stared at the screen and concentrated. I felt energy rise inside me.

"You don't need to force it, just listen!"

"OK, OK, I'm sorry," I whispered. A moment later, I punched a code into the keypad. Then the voice asked for a thumbprint. "This is insane," I muttered. I took a deep breath and put my thumb against the screen.

"Good afternoon, James. Access granted."

The safe door clicked opened. I glanced back at Shoko. She leaned forward, her eyes wide in astonishment, and climbed onto the chair beside me as I pulled the door open. We peered in together.

"Oh ..." she whispered.

The gold bars lay there, rough and shaped like little surfboards with strange markings. They shone as if just polished—the same as when Grandpa showed them to me years ago. Beside the bars lay a rolled-up piece of leather—the map?

"So this is the treasure," Shoko said in a low voice.

The sight had me transfixed. They should have been in a museum somewhere, not locked away. Grandpa didn't need these anymore.

And I was starting to think he should never have taken them in the first place.

"I wonder how old these are." I reached out to take one, but Shoko slapped my hand away.

"Do not touch them! I told you it *changed* him—they are evil!"

I turned to look at her. "You don't know that for sure."

"And you know nothing!"

I shook my head and reached in again.

Shoko leaped off the chair, braids spinning out. Her hand flew back to her racket case. By the time she landed, a *wakizashi*, a short curved sword, was in her hand and pointed straight at me.

"Touch it and I will cut you down!" she screamed.

I jerked my hand away from the gold. She wasn't hiding her feelings now—her fear and sorrow hit me like a slap in the face. She took a step forward and placed the tip of the wakizashi just a few inches away from my heart. She looked upset, but her sword never wavered.

"Please, Junya, do not make me do this."

We stayed that way for a long moment, me on the chair, her below.

"OK, Shoko, I won't touch them."

She wiped a tear from her face with her left hand but held the sword steady.

I tried to smile. "Wouldn't killing me break our bond of trust?"

"Death is the only way to break the bond," she said. "And I will not hesitate if I must. I cannot let you become corrupted."

I wasn't about to remind her she was hesitating right now, luckily for me.

A car door slammed outside. I closed the safe, hopped off the chair, and ran to the window. Shoko crowded in close behind me.

"There are many men," she whispered.

I heaved a sigh. "I guess my protection team is here."

"Look ... it is Edward!" She sounded shaken.

"We've got to get out of here!" I punched the lock button and turned the candlestick back. The picture took forever to slide closed.

Shoko was staring at me, confused. "You will get in trouble?"

Panic rose in me. "I opened his safe!" I hissed. "He's gonna kill me!"

I heard the front door open as we moved into the hallway. There was the usual murmur of voices and then someone swore.

"Get the Chairman back in the car, now!"

Mr. Barrymore's voice came next, shouting from outside. "I need info, people! What're we dealing with?"

"Thermal detection upstairs."

"Get in there!" I heard Grandpa bellow.

"Not yet!" It was Mr. Barrymore again. "Weapons and vests—let's go, people! You three, cover the back and sides! Move, move, move!"

I imagined men pulling assault rifles out of the SUVs and struggling into thick Kevlar jackets. I'd seen them practice.

"Chief, control says no one came in the gate," a voice called out, calmer than the rest. "Perimeter alarms are negative."

I still had a chance to stop this. I could call out, feign innocence, although there would be hell to pay. But why had the guard lied about us not being here?

I suddenly thought of Grandpa's driver, how he'd driven off without a word when I told him to. Now the guard who let us in. Had I made them obey me somehow?

Shoko stared at me, waiting for some direction. The sound of ammo clips slamming into place made up my mind. I grabbed her hand and pulled her down the hall. I tried to be quiet, but with everything else dead silent, each step creaked.

They weren't rushing in. They were coming slowly, cautiously— and probably pointing their guns up the stairs. I pushed Shoko into Grandpa's bedroom. My heart pounded. There was enough room to hide under Grandpa's king-size bed, but...I stopped dead when I noticed that lingerie and a blue dress were draped over a lounge chair on the other side of the room. On the floor beside it was a pair of black high heels.

Shoko touched me. "Well?" she whispered.

I pushed her toward the bathroom, harder than I meant to, and she fell to the floor. The hilt of her wakizashi hit the floor, and the sound echoed off the marble walls. I swung the door closed and locked it. With my back against the door, I hit my fists against my forehead, as if I could somehow pound out a solution. But my brain had stopped working, frozen by the panic rising inside me. My whole body shook.

Shoko crawled over to me on her knees, her wakizashi pointed at the door. "I thought you had an escape plan!"

"I screwed up. We have to go out there—"

She grabbed my arm. "Edward cannot see me!"

"They're going to find us. We have nowhere to go." My neck was tingling. I felt their energy: fear, anger and something else.

One of them wanted to kill me.

The bedroom floor creaked. I tensed, waiting for bullets to rip through the door.

"Is this natural?" She pointed at the floor. "I cannot tell."

I could feel three men looking at the bathroom door.

"Yes, it's Italian marble," I whispered. It would be perfect for my tombstone.

"It better be," she said in a dead calm voice. Then she took my hand. "I am sorry, but I have no choice."

My mind collapsed as I watched her whispering to herself—probably a Buddhist death sutra. Then the door crashed inward and my head exploded in pain.

CHAPTER
13

I WOKE UP ON MY STOMACH, my head pounding. When I tried to open my eyes, the world spun around me in a blur, as if I were in the center of a wheel. I reached out to steady myself, but only one hand moved. Something warm and soft held the other.

"Lie still," Shoko said. "You are not dead ... yet."

I pried my eyes open. She was on her knees beside me. She let go of my hand and it dropped to the ground, which was soft and damp. I was lying in the dirt.

"It is always like this the first time," she said. "It will go away in a moment."

I let my head fall back and waited for my mind to clear. I had a worm's-eye view of the bushes around us. I saw trimmed branches, a park bench, the street, and, beyond that, Grandpa's house. I pushed myself up and was rewarded with sharp pain in my head.

Grandpa stood outside the carriage-house gates, near the rear door of an SUV, surrounded by men. John, the bodyguard closest to Grandpa, held a small MP5 submachine gun in one hand. I lay in the dirt, confused, as two more black SUVs skidded to a stop beside the others. Four men jumped out of each. When had Grandpa gotten so many bodyguards? And was this all because I'd opened the safe?

"They just kicked in the bathroom door," John told Grandpa. "Nothing there. They're still searching the top floor." John put his hand to his earpiece. "The house is clear, sir."

"Did they check the safe?" Grandpa yelled.

There was a pause. "It's secure," John said, "but someone put tape over the hidden security camera."

"What?!" Grandpa bellowed. "I'm going in there!"

"Sir, you should wait—"

Grandpa grabbed the MP5 from John's hand, cocked the weapon like an expert, and strode toward the house. "When we find out who did this, he's a dead man!" he said over his shoulder.

I looked at Shoko. "How did we get here?"

She didn't answer at first, her attention still on the house. "My mother told me he was a kind man with a pure heart," she said at last. "Do you see how he has changed?"

"Shoko, how did we get here? They're talking like it just happened."

"It did." She sat back in the dirt. "I cannot do many things here, but I can do that."

I sat up. "There's no way we got out of the bathroom and over here in less than a second."

She shrugged. "Use your eyes and decide for yourself."

I gave her a blank stare.

"We call it traveling," she said. "A way to move from one place to another." Then she stabbed her finger into my chest. "But this is a secret. You must tell no one!"

I gave my head a shake. "How ... how'd you do that?"

She shook her head. "It is not so simple ... and if you do not already know, explaining will not help."

"You have to tell me something! This whole mess is your fault."

She crossed her arms. "I did not ask you to open that ... that thing."

"We wouldn't even have been in there if you hadn't stolen—sorry, *borrowed* the journal!"

She let out a low growl as she slid the wakizashi back into the racket case.

"And why do you have a wakizashi?"

"How else am I to protect you?"

"Protect me?" I pointed a finger at her. "You were about to chop me in half!"

"I saved you." She frowned. "Did you not see your grandfather? I will not let that happen to you."

I sighed. "If it *is* evil … we need to get rid of it, take it back where it belongs."

Her eyes widened. "And you think *you* can do that?"

"Someone has to." I was staring at her, but my mind was a million miles away. "I think it has to be me."

She gave me an odd look. "Perhaps, but today is not the day we find out."

I leaned back against the thick trunk of the maple tree. I thought of all the things she'd told me that day. I should have had a million more questions, but my mind was blank. Information overload, I guessed. I laid my hand on a nearby tree trunk to steady myself.

My finger brushed rough bark and my body twitched as the tree's energy surged through the trunk and into me. It was vibrant, strong, pulsing like a heart. My mouth dropped open. "What the …" I started to stand, but Shoko pulled me back down.

"Be quiet." She nodded toward the house. "The men are starting to search away from the house."

"Oh, jeez."

"I will travel you home," she said. "If you are there, no one can accuse you of being here." She reached out for my hand, but I pulled it away.

"Wait! I … I still don't understand any of this!"

She heaved a deep sigh. "Use your eyes. It is what it is. And I will travel more slowly this time so it won't hurt as much."

I glanced back at the house. "OK, but make sure we end up behind my dad's workshop. My mom will freak out if we show up in the living room."

"When I travel here, I must go somewhere I know because I

cannot see my destination." She glanced at me, thoughtful. "Try using your energy and see where you want us to go. And try not to take my head off."

I tried to build my energy, tried to imagine what it looked like behind the shop. All I got was a bigger headache than I had a moment ago.

She looked disappointed. "Well, it is your house, so it should be safe. Hold my hand."

We sat cross-legged, facing each other, and I smiled as our palms touched. "They fit well together, don't they?"

She didn't reply. I blushed and wondered why I'd said that.

"Ready?"

"What should I do?" I asked, anxious, like I used to feel in a jet as it began its takeoff.

In answer, she slapped her right palm against the ground. A rush of air sucked the breath out of me and the world turned into a blur.

She'd lied—it still hurt like hell.

Before I opened my eyes, I did a mental survey. I was still sitting cross-legged and Shoko's hand still held mine. My head and body ached, but the pain was fading fast. If I opened my eyes and we really were in my backyard, I'd have to believe everything she'd said that day.

I opened one eye and swore. We were sitting in the narrow space between my dad's shop wall and the back fence, a neglected patch of weeds and discarded building materials—shady, quiet and private.

Shoko stood up and brushed the dirt from her legs. "That was not so bad, for you anyway." She sounded tired.

I didn't move. I felt drained. My mind and body were overwhelmed.

Shoko squatted in front of me. "Go and let your mother see you."

I looked up at her. "What will you do?"

"I must seek the advice of my Elders. And ... thank you for believing me."

I nodded. "Today was ... a lot to take in all at once."

She smiled. "I had fun."

"Really?"

"Well, not all of it was fun, but I enjoyed riding the cable cars and drinking hot chocolate with you."

"You'll come back, right? I mean, because of our training and stuff."

"For now, practice using your energy—carefully. I do not know when I will come back over again."

"*Over*? Where are you going?"

She smiled. "You have enough on your mind." Then her eyes narrowed. "Remember, you must tell no one about this. They may put you in a place where I cannot reach you. Now go."

I was halfway to the back door when the wind came, as I knew it would. It billowed through my clothes and my hair and then it was gone.

"Junya!" It was Okaasan at the kitchen door. "Is that you?"

"Yeah, I'll be there in a minute." I needed time to think before I saw her, both because of what had just happened and because I knew she was going to nail me about last night. I'd slipped out early this morning, before breakfast, just to avoid any questions.

The clock on the stove said four-thirty. Just thirty minutes ago I'd been walking up to Grandpa's gate with Shoko.

Okaasan barely glanced at me. "I thought I felt something ... odd. Did you notice anything?"

"Nope." I sat at the table and waited for what I knew was coming.

"Why were you so late last night?"

I swallowed. "I went to see Grandpa, and Ms. Lin took me out for dinner—she wants me to know what it'll be like being Grandpa's heir, apparently."

She turned to me and her mouth dropped open. "Oh my God, what happened to your face?"

"Ah ... basketball."

Her hands went to her hips. "And why was there a pile of dirty clothes on your bedroom floor this morning? Surely you didn't go to dinner like that?"

I hesitated. "I … they got dirty after—"

"What, playing basketball with Ms. Lin after dinner?" She glared at me and then turned to the counter and started hacking some celery.

"I fell down on the way home and—"

She spun around and pointed the knife at me. "Don't lie to me, Junya!"

"All right, I'm sorry." I held up my hands. "Grandpa's driver dropped me off on California Street last night."

She arched her eyebrows, waiting.

"You said it was OK to protect myself—or someone else."

"So you get into a fight the *very* day after I say that?" She shook her head. "And who was this *someone* else?"

I hesitated. "A girl. She got lost after a movie last night and … she got into trouble." I tried my damnedest to block my thoughts, not like I had a clue how.

Her eyes narrowed. "Do you know her?"

"Well …" I considered how much to say. "I met her at the library on Saturday. She's … she's an exchange student. Her name is Shoko."

"Shoko." She said the name as if sampling something new, unsure how it would taste. "That's an old name." Her eyes met mine. "This is the same girl who made you dizzy?"

I rolled my eyes. "I'm not in love!"

"But you got beat up helping her?"

"I didn't get beat up," I said a little too quickly. "Well, maybe a bit, but I did OK. She's OK, too."

"There was something on the news today about three men badly beaten, one of them stabbed, not far from here." She looked into my eyes.

I gave her my most sarcastic look. "Yeah, we beat up three men and stabbed them." I rolled my eyes again and sighed. "Give me a break."

She made a face, but it looked like she believed me.

"Can we talk about Grandpa now?" I said.

"This isn't over, Junya."

"Yeah, but this is way more important."

She didn't look convinced. I pointed to her chair and she sat down across from me.

"Grandpa was acting weird last night," I said.

"How was he different?"

I told her what he said about Lin and what I saw.

"I know about them," she said, although I sensed a bit of apprehension. "He shouldn't have to play the lonely widower so he can be the ideal grandfather."

"No, I agree."

"But I am surprised they acted that way in front of you."

"Yeah, it kind of shocked me when he put his hand halfway up Lin's thigh." I laughed, trying not to blush and failing.

"'Lin'?"

I cringed again. "She said I could call her that."

"Your world is changing rather quickly."

That was an understatement. "There's more." I told her about seeing Walter Roacks and Mr. Müller and about Grandpa's reaction.

She was silent.

"What's wrong?"

She forced a smile. "I worry about all this. After what happened with your dad on Saturday ..." Her words trailed off.

"Yeah, what's with that?"

"It's not my place to tell you."

I scowled. "There are a lot of secrets in this family."

"You should talk," she said, an edge in her voice now. "What's happening to you? Your energy is unusual—it wavers and disappears."

I stared back, trying hard to avoid thinking about today. "That stream you talked about is getting stronger. Way stronger. That's how I knew Shoko was in trouble—I sensed it somehow."

"Really?" She looked amazed.

I nodded. "And Shoko's a bit ... odd."

She scowled. "How so?"

"She's a lot like you."

I got a look. "Don't stereotype. Japanese society is completely different from American. She probably thinks you're weird, too."

"It's not that. She said she came from a small village, far from any city. Doesn't that sound familiar?"

She rolled her eyes. "Half the population of Japan lives outside the cities."

"And she can fight like you wouldn't believe."

She looked suspicious now. "Then why did you have to protect her?"

My eyes dropped to the tabletop. "I thought she needed help—I didn't know she could fight like that until after I got out of the car ... Maybe I didn't hear the stream right." I put my head in my hands. "It's really confusing."

When I looked back up, Okaasan was staring off into space. When our eyes met, there was something strange in them.

"You've had an overwhelming few days, with your grandpa getting sick and this new intuition—"

"Don't forget becoming the heir to a multibillion-dollar business that's going broke."

"Being emotionally drained is sometimes worse than being physically sick. You should take it easy the next few days. I'm worried about you."

Maybe she was right, but ... "I'm going to the Giants game tonight with Mack," I said. "I'll take it easy after that."

CHAPTER
14

I FOUND MACK AT OUR dining-room table, his thick forearms resting on either side of an empty but crumb-covered plate. He didn't notice me come in as he stared out the glass wall toward the teahouse.

"Hey, buddy." I plopped down beside him.

He sighed as Okaasan came in from the kitchen carrying a tray of drinks.

"I never get tired of that view," he said.

"The garden or the food?"

Okaasan saw Mack's empty plate and rushed back to the kitchen for more.

"Stop feeding him," I called after her. "He's like those bears in Yellowstone Park. They become habituated and you can't get rid of them."

"I'm always hungry and your mom never stops feeding me," Mack said. "It's the perfect relationship." He grinned. "In fact, I think she likes me more than you."

"Even if she hated you she'd still feed you. It's her culture."

"Perhaps." He winked at me as she came back into the room. "But in my case she really does."

She placed a large plate with melted cheese and crackers on the table.

"What are you two talking about?"

"Mack wants you to adopt him."

Mack dug something out of his pocket. "Ah, Mrs. Thompson, would you mind looking at this?" He handed her a piece of paper with a Chinese character drawn on it.

She made a face. "What's this?"

"I'm thinking of getting a tattoo," he said. "The guy in the tattoo shop said it means 'strong,' like the newest tough guy in town." He flexed his sizable biceps. "I thought it was appropriate."

Okaasan was smiling now.

Mack looked up at her in mid-flex. "What?"

Okaasan burst out laughing.

"What, what does it mean?"

When she regained her composure, she patted his arm. "I'm sorry Mack, but this means 'porcupine'!" She started laughing again.

"I'm gonna kill that guy!"

She waved a hand. "That's nothing. Last week I saw a guy who had *stupid foreigner* across the back of his neck!"

I looked at my watch and stood. "Come on, we're gonna be late." I was up and out the front door before he even got his shoes on.

"Why're you acting so stressed, man," Mack said as we walked up Arbutus Street to catch the bus downtown. "I'm the one who nearly got a rodent tattooed on his arm."

"What?" I had my hands shoved into my jacket pockets. "Oh, yeah, I'm stressed all right."

"Because of your grandpa?"

I looked up at him. "Do you think a person who's going crazy knows it, or would they be oblivious?"

He was quiet for a minute. "Ignoring the implications of that statement," he finally said, "I think if someone—you, for example—*were* going crazy, I don't think you'd know it. So, if you *think* you're going crazy, then I would have to assume—despite all evidence to the contrary—that you're not."

I stopped and stared at him. "Man, where did you get that?"

He shook his head sadly. "I," he said with a hand on his chest, "am far deeper than you'll ever know."

We started to walk again, but after a moment I gave him a mischievous grin.

He frowned, "Now what?"

"I went on a date today."

"You went on a *date*?" He grabbed my arm. "That's it, let's get you to the nuthouse!"

I pulled away, laughing.

"Let me ask you this," he said. "Did the girl involved know it was a date?" Then, before I could answer, he continued. "There was a *real* girl involved, right?"

"It was that girl from the library on Saturday, the one you said was cute?"

"A cute girl at the library," he said. "There were so many."

"The one in the school uniform," I said. "She smiled at me, remember?"

"Ah, the girl who *allegedly* smiled at you." He nodded. "She's not my type."

"Well, she's *my* type."

He glared down at me. "What are you saying? You landed a date with her?"

I grinned.

"Get out of here!" He gave me a slap on the back that knocked me off the sidewalk. Then he rubbed his chin. "So did you lose your innocence?"

"My innocence is none of your business." To my surprise, I didn't blush.

"That means no." He smirked. "But James's got himself a woman. Unbelievable." Then he frowned at me. "You're different from the last time I saw you." He looked puzzled for a minute. "You sure you didn't get laid?"

I laughed. "Pretty sure. It's just been … an amazing few days."

—

We got off the bus on Market Street not far from Grandpa's building. It was busy downtown, and for a while I almost forgot about my problems. I was busy just trying not to get run over or trampled by tourists.

"Gimme a minute," Mack said as he turned toward a deli on the corner. "I need a snack before the game."

"I think you've got a tapeworm, man." The deli looked packed, so I squatted against the building. "I'll wait out here."

I watched the restored streetcars rumble by. An orange Milan tram passed going north, followed by my favorite streetcar, number 1007, painted in the red and white motif of the Philadelphia Red Arrow Line. I fought the urge to run and climb on.

I glanced toward the deli. Mack was still far from the counter. I stuffed my hands into my pockets and began to pace in the shadow of the towers, at the bottom of a vast canyon. The crowds flowing past me made me feel like a stone in a stream. Energy seeped from every person. Excitement, indecision, fear, insecurity—so much negativity that it started to overwhelm me. I wished I could tune it all out.

I wandered over to the front doors of Grandpa's building and leaned against a newspaper box, thinking of Shoko. Okaasan and Mack were right: there *was* something different about me, and it had all started with Shoko. She was amazing—the things she could do, the things she understood. And she got me thinking about those stories Grandpa told me when I was young, about female warriors guarding the shrines of the gods. It had been only a few hours, but I already felt like I needed to see her again. I had so much more I wanted to ask her.

I glanced at the deli again. Mack was up next. I checked the time. There was only a half-hour until game time. It was when I started banging my toe against the newspaper box that I saw the headline: "THOMPSON GROUP ANNOUNCES LAYOFF OF 1600 EMPLOYEES AMID GROWING FINANCIAL CRISIS."

I skimmed the long story underneath. Walter Roacks spoke for the chairman, who was away due to "health issues," but I was positive this wasn't what Grandpa had in mind when he told Walter to fix things.

I'd blamed Shoko for starting this, but she was only a player, a small part of a much larger whole. Tomi and Grandpa had started something with that gold, but what? Seeing Grandpa with the machine gun had scared the hell out of me, but that didn't make the gold evil. Shoko said it had changed him, but how would she know? None of us knew what he'd been like before that trip to the desert.

I turned to face the crowd that flowed toward me. No one met my eyes or bumped me. Energy did though, a thousand voices blurring into one loud roar like the fans at a ballgame.

I clamped my hands over my ears and backed against the wall. The buildings around me started to feel like massive walls blocking out the sun—a trap slowly locking into place around me. I looked up and down the street, frantic.

I spotted the clock tower of the San Francisco Ferry Building. Behind it, the water and the bright open sky beckoned to me. I sucked in a long, slow breath.

"What are you doing?"

I spun, ready to fight, and then saw that it was Mack.

"Easy, man. What's up?"

"I had this weird ... Oh, boy."

"Are you OK? You're sweating."

"I'm ..." My head came up as a gust of wind blew past me and sent a newspaper page twirling down Market Street. It floated, aimless, carried by the wind of fate, and for some reason, ignoring Mack's protests, I followed it.

The wind carried the paper into the alley behind the Thompson Building. I turned the corner in time to see it flatten against the windshield of a white cube van backed up to the loading bay. Then, its message delivered, the newspaper carried on its journey down the alley.

Anthony Roacks leaned against the van, his back to me. Walter Roacks stood by the loading door, flanked by two tough-looking guys. The four of them watched two men in green uniforms load a huge stack of white legal boxes into the back of the van.

Mack came up beside me. "James—"

"Shhh."

Anthony turned, saw us, and tapped the shoulder of the big man in front of him. The guy started toward us.

Mack yanked my sleeve. "Let's get out of here!"

The man broke into a jog as we turned and ran. We spotted a bus and hopped on. As we pulled away toward the stadium, I used my cell phone to call the security office at Grandpa's building and told the duty officer—some guy named Johnny—what I'd seen.

"Mr. Roacks is down there, so there's nothing to worry about," he said, his voice all business. "As a matter of fact, he called a minute ago to say there were a couple of punks hanging around the alley. Was that you?"

"Yeah. Never mind," I said.

Mack was staring at me. "I take it back," he said. "Maybe you *are* going crazy."

CHAPTER
15

I WENT TO BED THINKING of Shoko, so it's not surprising I dreamed of her. It was the same as the last dream: the same long staircase leading up to the same shrine, the same house surrounded by a meadow, the same girl standing in the doorway—but this time she's wearing a uniform. I wave to her and she waves back.

Grandpa shows up and gives me the same speech: "It's time for you to follow your destiny."

And again, his shoulders slouch and his face grows haggard. His eyes lose their shine. Then he begins to fade away until he's gone. In his place, the elderly man appears—it's definitely the old man from the restaurant bathroom. His forked tongue flicks out at me. I tense up.

Ms. Lin's up next.

But when I turn around, there's no Ms. Lin waiting for me. It's Okaasan with her katana, its handle revealing accents of gold beneath the well-worn black cord. Her energy overwhelms me. I drop to my knees and touch my forehead to the wooden boards at her feet. She speaks softly but sternly to me in Japanese, in a voice that sounds far away.

"Junya, you must get up." She glares down at me. Then, with a look of disgust, she raises her katana. Sunlight glints off polished steel as it swings up over her head. She steps forward and I squeeze my eyes shut as the blade begins its descent.

—

I struggled to free my mind but couldn't. I felt the air move beside me, heard the rustle of fabric, and the darkness began to recede. When a hand touched my shoulder, my eyes opened.

Okaasan was leaning over me!

"Yaaa!" I yelled and rolled away from her, knowing I'd die if I landed at the bottom of the shrine, but I hit the ground a second later.

I looked around. There was no wooden shrine towering above me, just the familiar wood ceiling of my bedroom.

Okaasan rushed around the bed and dropped to the floor beside me. I was on my back, one foot still up on the bed, my pajama pants falling down, cartoon boxers exposed. I looked up at her, eyes wide. I panted for air, my heart about to explode out of my chest.

"You had a nightmare." She laughed as she patted my arm. "Relax, Junya, breathe. You're safe."

I nodded but still couldn't speak. Her words and the swish of her katana stayed with me.

"I'm sorry I startled you," she said. "I came to tell you it's time to get up."

Still I lay there and stared. It was just a dream, but my intuition was screaming at me, insisting it was real.

Her smile faded and a worried furrow appeared between her brown eyes. "What is it, Junya?" She reached out to touch my face, but I swatted her hand away. She pulled back, surprised. "What's gotten into you?"

I lay there panting, "You tried to ... tried to ..."

"To do what?"

"You wanted to kill me!" I pushed myself up and glared at her. "I saw it in your eyes!"

Her hand moved to cover her mouth. "You were dreaming, Junya."

"Why do we have to live like this?" I was yelling now. "The stream, the training—I'm so tired of all this crap!" I punctuated my rant with a fist slammed against the floor.

Her expression changed, first to shock, then to anger. She pulled herself up straighter.

I knew I'd gone too far. "I'm sorry, Okaasan," I said. "I dreamed you were raising your katana to cut me down. Then *you* came in here and woke me up." I spoke to her in Japanese, hoping to make up for my outburst. But it was halfhearted and we both knew it.

"Once spoken, words can't be taken back," she said. "I'm sorry I scared you, but I didn't create your dream." She stared down at me as she had on the staircase. "And if you don't like your life here, then leave!"

We stared at each other, both of us angry.

After a while her face broke into a crooked little smile. "I don't live like this to punish you. This is how my mother raised me and her mother raised her. I didn't know how to live here or what to do with a son. Both were beyond my experience. And I had no one to help me."

I closed my eyes. "I'm sorry Okaasan." I meant it that time.

She rolled off her knees and stood up again. "Get ready for school," she said as she brushed her hair back. "You don't want to be late."

—

I threw on a T–shirt and pulled a worn sweater over it, one of my favorites. It was my dad's, but he'd never asked for it back, so it had become a regular part of my wardrobe.

I heard pots and dishes banging in the kitchen when I left my room, which was a good sign. If Okaasan were mad at me, the only breakfast I'd get was whatever I made myself. Okaasan was easy to understand that way: either she was mad or she wasn't.

Tama lay in the hallway in her favorite place, near the windows. I stopped to rub her soft coat. She closed her eyes and purred and then raised her chin to let me scratch there.

"What do you think of all this?" I asked her.

She opened her eyes and let out a loud meow.

Okaasan was wearing an apron now, royal blue with white splotches—a traditional wrinkly tie-dye style. On the stove, an egg bubbled in the fry pan, sunny side up, and a bowl of steaming rice sat nearby. It looked like I was having a Japanese breakfast, although she wouldn't call it that. When I was younger, I thought everyone ate rice three times a day.

It wasn't until I'd started junior high school that I got the nerve to ask Okaasan to stop packing anything weird in my lunch: no rice balls wrapped in seaweed, no sandwiches with ketchup smiley faces. There's nothing more humiliating than opening your *An-pan-man* cartoon lunch container to find a carrot-stick man with a boiled egg for a head and a mayonnaise happy face looking up at you. Even your best friends laugh you out of the room. For some reason, remembering that made me sad now.

I sat at the table and watched her work. Her hands moved fast, her knife slicing through the skin of an orange. Dad kept them razor sharp, which was the only job he had in the kitchen. Okaasan stood on her toes to grab a cup from the lowest cupboard. Her shiny hair hung down her back in a single loose ponytail. I hadn't noticed earlier, but she was wearing dress pants and a nice blouse, which meant lunch and shopping downtown were in her plans for the day.

I was still feeling shaky. As I looked at her, I realized some of that anger, however irrational, still remained.

She set my breakfast and her cup of tea on the table and sat across from me. I took a bite with my chopsticks, chewed slowly, and enjoyed the taste of the soy sauce mixed with the runny yolk.

"Delicious," I told her. We both knew I was sucking up.

"You're welcome," she said as she filled her cup from a small pot. She watched me eat for a while before she set her cup down. "How was the game last night?"

"The Giants won and the food in Grandpa's private suite was amazing. Mack gorged like a pig."

She smiled, but it didn't last. "Tell me about your dream."

I continued to chew, stalling. I didn't know where to begin or how much to say.

"I'm sorry about that," I said after I swallowed. "I was a total jerk."

She nodded and a faint smile appeared on her lips.

"You know the Izumo-taisha Shrine, in Japan?" I said.

"Of course. I often went there as a young girl."

"That's what I was dreaming about." I described it, but when I mentioned the massive red posts, she got an odd look on her face.

"You saw three trees tied together and painted red?"

"Yeah," I said. "Everything seemed so real. I guess that's why I freaked out when you woke me up. Sorry."

She placed her cup back on the table with a loud thud. "The grand shrine at Izumo doesn't have a long staircase, and it's certainly not high off the ground. I took you there enough times, you should re-member that."

"Wasn't I, like, five or something?"

She considered that and shook her head. "This is impossible."

"It was just a dream, Mom."

She studied my face for a moment and then stared down at her teacup. I could tell she was upset because her hands shook as she rubbed the ring on her right hand.

Something clicked.

"Where did you get that ring?"

She glanced down at her finger and moved her left hand to cover it. As she did, she frowned, revealing small lines around her mouth that I hadn't noticed before. "I've worn this for years."

"Yeah, but where did you get it?"

"My mother gave me this when I graduated. The silver is from the Iwami-Ginzan mines, near Mount Sennoyama."

"Which mother?"

"My birth mother." She looked at the ring, and then our eyes met.

"Only the women in my family clan wear this. It meant something to me once—an honor of the highest order. Now it's just a reminder of another life."

"Shoko has a ring like that."

Okaasan sucked in a quick breath. "That's impossible."

I studied her face. "I told you before—you and Shoko are a lot alike."

"So we Japanese girls are all the same?" She stood and took her cup to the sink, as if she were running from me. She began to wash the dishes, banging the pots in the sink.

"Remember I told you I was sensing things?" She didn't answer. "Well, it's more than that now. I can feel energy, even feel people's emotions, I can *project* energy, and I get a tingling in the back of my neck when there's some kind of threat nearby."

Her hands gripped the edge of the sink.

"Are you OK?"

"No, I'm not." She turned to look at me. "Even if you take after me … this isn't possible. You're a boy."

"Shoko said that, too!" I stood up and faced her. "That exact same thing."

She hesitated. "I think you should stay away from that girl."

"Why?"

"Because she's changing you."

CHAPTER
16

As I trudged up the Arbutus Hill, I played the morning's events over in my head. The more I thought about it, the more I realized Okaasan was hiding something from me. She and Shoko definitely had the same ring, and the similarities between them were too obvious to ignore.

I stopped and looked back toward my house. I knew Shoko was trouble, but she was also part of some larger mystery involving my family. I needed to see her again, but I didn't even know how to contact her.

I started to jog up the hill.

Mack was standing by our lockers, looking into his with disinterest, when I ran up and slammed into him. It was like hitting a wall. I bounced off and hit the lockers with a bang.

"Morning," he said. "How come you're late?"

"My mom's fault."

We both ignored the second bell as I told him about the dream and Okaasan's reaction to it.

Mack leaned back against his locker. "Dreams are movies in your head, man—garbage in, garbage out. You do all that martial-arts crap, so no wonder you're having crazy dreams. But that doesn't make it real, right?" He got a dreamy look on his face. "I had this dream a couple of weeks ago. A brontosaurus was chasing this hot cave babe and me through the jungle. Her tiny fur top kept slipping off as we ran. Nice."

"A *hot cave babe*?"

He nodded. "What I'm saying is, it ain't too likely I'm gonna see a dinosaur or a topless babe running through the jungle, is it?" He paused. "Well, I won't see a dinosaur anyhow."

"Where do you get these ideas?"

"A new poster I've got in my closet. You should see it."

"In your closet?"

He grunted. "Gotta hide it. You remember what happened when my dad put that bikini calendar in the garage?" His mom had poured gasoline on it and burned it in the street in front of their house. The fire department even came. "You see why I want your mom to adopt me?" He looked away. "Anyway, I've gotta go, man." He shouldered his backpack and walked away. "See you at basketball practice."

—

I got home after seven and found Okaasan in the kitchen preparing for a late dinner. Dad wasn't home yet. I felt nothing from her, good or bad. She was peeling a yam with smooth strokes, but as soon as I tried to sense her energy, she jerked and dropped it. Her hand went to her temple and she looked at me.

"If you're going to stand there, you can cut these carrots."

I reached for a knife.

"Wash your hands first." She began to peel again, her face a mask of concentration while I started on the first carrot. She glanced over. "Smaller please."

"Yeah, yeah."

After a few minutes of silent work, she said, "Your grandpa called. Someone broke into his house yesterday."

My hands froze in mid-cut. "Really?" I tried to keep my voice neutral and get my hands moving again before she noticed.

"They opened his safe, and apparently there are only a few people who even know it's there. Do you?"

I swallowed hard. "He showed me inside it years ago."

"The burglar used your code—your fingerprint—to open the safe, but the security cameras weren't recording, and the guard on duty doesn't remember anyone going into the house."

I closed off every thought in my head and concentrated on the carrot in my hand.

She stopped working and stepped back from the counter. "You're thinking about carrots? What do you know about this?!"

I glared at her. "Stop doing that!"

"Tell me what you know, Junya!"

I hesitated, but guilt churned my stomach like bad food. I hated lying. "Shoko and I were hanging out yesterday afternoon, and there was a book I needed to return to Grandpa's."

Her eyes widened. "You were there, with Shoko?"

I started cutting again. "We went inside and put it back."

"How did you get in and out without anyone seeing you?" Her voice had an edge now, anxiety turning into fear.

The carrot pieces were the size of peas and getting smaller.

"I talked to the guard and told him to erase the camera footage." I turned to look at her. "And I opened the safe."

Her face went from surprised to furious in under a second. "You idiot!"

I spun to face her. "And you're a liar!"

Okaasan slapped my face.

The sharp crack froze us both for a moment. Then she backed away and something flickered in her eyes, just for a moment.

I stared. "You're afraid of me?"

She pointed to my hand. I held the knife in a throwing position, my arm cocked and ready—I didn't remember doing that. The knife slipped from my fingers and hit the floor, its point embedding in the wood.

Okaasan stared at the knife, still wobbling in the floor, and then her eyes rose to mine. "I'm afraid for you."

"Mom ... You know something. You have to help me out here."

She dropped into a chair. "Tell me everything that's happened in the last few days."

I told her enough to explain some of what had happened.

"So that's where he keeps the gold?"

"Yeah. It's a shame to keep a collection like that hidden away."

"Did you see the map?"

"The treasure map?" I had to think for a moment. "There was a rolled piece of leather. I didn't look at it."

She thought for a moment. "So you didn't touch anything?"

I shook my head. "I'm still alive, aren't I?"

She looked confused. "What does that mean?"

"Shoko pulled a wakizashi on me. She said if I touched the gold she'd kill me. She thinks it's cursed."

Okaasan closed her eyes and nodded. "I see."

"So that sounds normal to you? I thought she was a ninja assassin or something."

Okaasan's eyes remained closed. She was thinking hard. The effort showed on her face. "Did Shoko say why she wanted to see his journal?"

I nodded. "She wanted to see if Grandpa wrote anything about her mom. They were in love once, apparently."

Okaasan's mouth dropped open. "Oh my God!" she exclaimed. "Shoko's mother is Tomi?"

"How do you know that?"

A short silence ensued. "He named his yacht Tomi," she said. "It's obvious that woman was once very special to him—"

"Would it be so frickin' hard to tell me the truth here? Just once."

Her mouth twisted, as if she was struggling with something she'd never prepared for. "I knew Tomi a long time ago."

"In Japan?"

She nodded. "We went to the same ... school."

"But isn't Tomi way older than you? She knew Grandpa when he was young."

"We weren't in the same grade." She looked at me. "Why did Shoko become interested in you?"

"At first she was just using me to get to the journal, but I guess I became her new assignment or something."

"How do you know that?" She looked incredulous.

"She told me. They made her come back because she *awakened* me."

"That explains everything!" She grabbed her face. "You should've told me this sooner! You said she tried to kill you?"

"Only because I tried to touch the gold."

A few of the puzzle pieces fell into place. If Shoko was an assassin, that explained a lot, including the traveling. It was a trick, an illusion. Ninja were famous for that.

Okaasan heaved a deep sigh. "No, no, this is OK." She sounded like she was talking to herself. "If she was supposed to kill you, she would've done it on your birthday."

"How do you know all this?"

She stared at me, her face blank.

Then it hit me. "Oh, God."

"Junya, I—"

I grabbed her hand. "It *is* the same! You and Shoko ... you're the same!"

She slapped my hand away. "I wear the same ring, but I am not like her."

"It's not just intuition you ... we ... have. It's some kind of magic, right?" I tried to piece it all together. "Can you travel?"

"What do you know about *that*?"

"Shoko moved us out of Grandpa's house somehow and she brought me here. She called it traveling."

She raised her hands to cover her face. "What else do you know?"

"I know nothing, except that you've been lying to me since the day I was born!" I stood up, confused but furious. "You knew about

Tomi. You knew Grandpa took the gold. Did you *expect* someone to come for it—for me?" Tears blurred my vision as I backed away from her. "Is that why you've been training me? You knew somebody would try to kill me and you never warned me?"

She stood up, her hands on her temples, but I turned away. My head felt like it would explode.

"Junya, calm down," she whispered. "It's not like that."

I was at the door now, jamming my feet into my running shoes.

"You need to stay with me." She reached out for me, but I pushed her away.

"Get away from me!" I turned and ran out the door.

CHAPTER
17

BY THE TIME I GOT TO Sacramento Street, my lungs were screaming for air and my sides ached. I stood with clenched fists, bent over, panting, and considered my options: I could head east toward Grandpa's, south into the unknown, or west toward Mack's house.

I chose west.

Mack's mom peered through the curtain when I knocked, but she didn't open the door. I was about to leave when I heard yelling, so I sat on the steps and waited.

Mack came out a minute later, shrugged into a jacket, and slammed the door behind him.

"What're you doing here?"

I waved for him to come along and I started walking. He trotted up beside me and grabbed my arm.

"Slow down."

I spun toward him and he jumped back.

"Why're you pissed at me?" he asked.

"I'm not …" I choked. I couldn't say any more.

Mack was silent for a bit. "Did something happen to your grandpa?"

I shook my head and kept walking.

"Come on. Give me something here."

"Please," I whispered. "I just … need to clear my head. Then I'll talk."

He stayed quiet, but after a while I sensed his growing apprehension. I stopped and looked up at him.

"What's wrong?"

"We've been walking for twenty minutes. Look around, man."

I did and realized I had no idea where we were. Except for a bar across the street with a group of guys outside smoking and laughing, the street looked dark and the buildings deserted.

"I don't care." I started to walk again.

"Well, I do. Start talking or you can walk home alone."

"Whatever."

He stopped. "Screw you, man. I'm going home."

"Why? You've got nothing at home and neither do I."

His face changed. "Just tell me what happened."

I started to ramble, probably incoherently, about old shrines, trained killers, and weird dreams.

Mack stopped me. "Take a couple deep breaths, bro. You're not making any sense."

The world grew dim and my body began to shake—I think it was that tingle—but before I could react, Mack let out a yell that was drowned out by the screech of tires. Something slammed into me from behind. I flew forward and hit my head on the sidewalk.

I rolled to my knees, clutching my head. Someone grabbed my arm and yanked me up. Two shapes loomed in front of me. One hand jerked my arm down and another grasped my throat.

"Get him in the car!" someone said. "That other kid saw us last night. Deal with him and let's go!"

My eyes opened. Mack managed two good punches before he took a fist to the face that rattled him. Two large men punched him until he hit the ground.

I caught my breath. These guys were Grandpa's new security team.

"What're you doing?!" I yelled. "Leave him alone!"

"Shut up!" A man shoved me toward the open rear door of a black SUV. I glanced back. Mack was on the ground, black boots driving into his body, trails of blood running from his nose and mouth. He'd rolled into the fetal position—he wasn't fighting back anymore.

"No!"

A hand grabbed my collar and tried to shove me into the truck, but I kicked against the door frame and drove my head back. It connected and the hand let go. I spun, slammed my forearm into his neck, and kneed him in the balls. Someone else grabbed me from behind. I dropped, rolled under the door, and kicked it shut on him.

When I came up behind the man who was kicking Mack, my fury was uncontrollable. I attacked him—elbows, knees, a wristlock and a twist, a palm to his elbow. His body jerked, bones snapped. I drove a knee into his head and he dropped to the ground.

Two more men came at me. The first one collapsed unconscious, his right arm dangling like a piece of rubber. The other one grabbed me from behind in a bear hug that tightened as he lifted me off my feet. He swore at me and then yelled to the others. I let out a growl and bit into his hand. The man cried out and dropped me. There was more cursing and yelling, a rush of feet behind me. I rolled out of the way as the guys who'd been standing outside the bar attacked the men who'd jumped us.

I rushed to Mack and tried to pull him up. His eyes fluttered open and he struggled to his feet, his face bloody. I half-carried him away from the brawl, and then we ran past parked cars and dark storefronts, staying in the shadows.

Mack finally stumbled to a stop in an orange puddle of light, his back against a brick wall, panting, clutching his stomach.

"I can't," he gasped. "I'm done."

I glanced down the block. Most of the men were down, sprawled on the ground. The only one still upright had a two-way radio in his hand.

"We've got to get out of here!"

Mack struggled upright and we managed to get back into the shadows.

"Who the hell are those guys?" His teeth were clenched. "I thought I was gonna die."

I sank to the ground beside him, suspended in a fog of disbelief. "They're my grandpa's bodyguards."

"Did you hear them say ... they saw me last night?" Mack struggled to keep his voice level. "That truck ... in the alley ... What the hell, man?"

I couldn't answer. Why would they want to hurt us?

We heard tires screech and another black SUV roared up the street behind us. We were crouched behind a parked car, but it wasn't good enough.

"We've got to get further away."

"I can't."

I reached down and pulled him up. We disappeared into a narrow space between buildings as the SUV roared past. I didn't stop moving until we were behind one of the buildings.

Mack looked up at me from where I'd dropped him.

"You ... you carried me?"

"Listen," I said between breaths, "you need to stay here, OK?"

He looked awful. "What're you gonna do?"

I heard engines roaring all around us. They'd started circling the block. It wouldn't be long before they started looking for us on foot.

"I'll run and let them chase me, draw them away from here." I tried to hide the panic that was starting to overtake me. "Stay here until they're gone. Then call the cops."

"But ..." He looked groggy.

I grabbed his collar and focused my energy at him. "You're OK, all right? Now do what I said."

His eyes opened wide. "I will. Good luck."

—

The stream was screaming at me, warning me. What was going on? If Grandpa thought I was the one who opened the safe … No way. I wouldn't—couldn't—believe he'd send these guys after me, not like this, no matter how much the gold might have changed him.

But the man said they'd seen us last night. The stream was still whispering to me, insisting that all these things were somehow connected—if I could just figure out how.

Right now I didn't have time. I had to lure those men away from Mack.

When I stepped onto the sidewalk, there was a black SUV parked up the block with its lights on, facing away from me. A man stood at the passenger door, talking to the driver and looking toward the building Mack lay behind.

I started to jog up the street, away from them, letting my shoes slap the pavement.

They heard me. Over my shoulder, I saw two men running after me. The SUV swung around and barreled up the narrow street behind them. My adrenaline spiked and I started to sprint between the parked cars. I turned the next corner. The street was empty—no trees or parked cars to use as cover. Behind me the men were still coming, but they sounded farther away.

My neck started tingling as headlights flashed on up the block. I darted into another narrow space between buildings, barely two feet wide. I ran down that and then turned up another narrow lane, with nothing to hide me while the sounds of pursuit closed in around me. Headlights appeared behind me and a dark sedan skidded to a stop in the intersection ahead.

I turned in a slow circle, looking for an escape as doors opened on both vehicles. I waited until the men had climbed out and moved away from their cars and then I vaulted the fence beside me and crashed into a row of garbage cans. I startled a cat as I raced into the next street and then through a yard. I still heard the squeal of tires and the occasional shout, but they began to fade.

On a dark residential street, I slowed my pace. I'd led them far enough away from Mack, but I had no idea where I was. While I caught my breath, I studied the houses and looked for clues. They were all Victorians, but that was no help. There were thousands of Victorian houses in San Francisco, from mansions to dumps, and they all looked the same at night.

I stopped in front of a house and tried to make out the street number. The gate hung by one hinge and the building behind it looked to be in similar disrepair. From inside came voices, a couple yelling at each other, punctuated by a smashing sound like a plate crashing into cupboards.

Dark clouds swirled above me. I began to shiver as the breeze touched my sweat-covered skin. My shirt was soaked. I sat down on the curb, head in hands. I felt raw inside. Was there anyone I could trust? I had no idea anymore, but I decided I'd run far enough.

I reached out with as much energy as I could muster. I sensed them, still searching—these guys didn't give up easily. A few minutes later, I felt them approaching.

I stood up.

An SUV rolled slowly down the hill, windows open, its occupants searching both sides of the street. My sides ached and my legs felt like rubber. I leaned against a tree trunk for support and waited. I needed to find out why they were doing this.

They were right beside me when they finally saw me. The truck jerked to a stop.

"Did my grandfather send you?" I asked.

The driver looked surprised, and then his energy changed. I was already moving behind the tree when the Taser gun pointed out the window. The projectile slammed into the tree beside me, sending sparks into the night.

And I swear to God I heard the tree cry out in pain.

I stepped out from behind the tree as the man got out of the SUV. He was only five feet away when I lunged at him. He didn't have time to fire a second shot before my knee connected with his solar plexus. There was an ugly crunch. As he dropped to the ground, eyes bulging, gasping for breath, I twisted the Taser from his grip and fired through the open door of the SUV. The projectile hit the passenger. He screamed as his body convulsed so violently that the truck shook.

I turned and walked away. I was really scared now—not of them but of what I'd just done.

CHAPTER
18

I CROSSED A SHADOWY PARK, pushed through a hedge, and stopped in a narrow, cluttered alley that reeked of garbage. About thirty yards ahead, a gate crashed off its hinges and clattered to the ground, and a man burst into the alley. When he saw me, he yelled into his portable radio.

I started running again. The streetlights became a blur. I felt them coming faster, closing in. The wall beside me spit sharp bits of brick at my face.

Were they *shooting* at me?

"Shoko!" I yelled as I exploded into a sprint with a burst of adrenaline. I took the first left I saw, swerved around a dumpster, and leaped over the legs of a sleeping homeless man. I didn't know how much longer my legs and lungs could handle this.

I turned another corner. Up ahead, in a pool of light cast from a single overhead lamp, someone stood. Panic rose—had they managed to cut me off?

It was a girl in a school uniform.

"Shoko!"

She spun toward me. Her eyes widened as she looked past me. I glanced over my shoulder as seven men careened around the corner after me. Her wakizashi slid out, and then they were on us.

Shoko became a blur of movement, spinning and twisting, her sword catching the light as it sliced through the air. The first man hit the pavement, a red line expanding across his chest. Another went down, blood pouring from a dangling, half-severed arm. The men scattered amid yells, spinning, bumping into each other, trying to readjust to this new threat. Gunshots rang out, wild shots that disappeared into the ground or ricocheted off the walls. I'd fallen into a stack of garbage and lay there, astonished, as Shoko danced among the men, her face expressionless, her wakizashi whirling.

A man with an MP5 leveled it, trying to get a clear shot. Cold fury washed over me as I pushed myself upright. A second later, the man hit the ground with me on top of him. I kept punching until he went limp. I rolled off and kicked the gun under the dumpster. Two more men fell, one with his hand sliced off, the other with a growing circle of blood from a stab wound to his chest.

The last man stood with his back to the brick wall, gun raised, eyes filled with panic. At first he aimed at Shoko, and then he shifted the gun toward me.

Flame burst from the muzzle as I charged toward him. My hands and elbows smashed into his throat and face. I drove his head into the wall until he collapsed unconscious, and then I wrestled the gun out of his grip.

I spun around, panting. Shoko stood among the fallen men, in the middle of an expanding pool of blood, her wakizashi pointed at the ground. Bathed in the light from above, she looked calm but fierce.

"Are others coming?" she asked.

I paused to listen, but my heartbeat was all I could hear. "Give me a minute."

She bowed her head and squeezed her eyes shut, enduring the pain I was causing her in silence.

"There are more out there … but none close by."

She nodded. "You are like a blur, so fast." She swung her wakizashi, flicked the blood onto the ground, and slid the blade back into her racket case.

I studied the men—the one with the severed arm was the worst off.

"That last man was trying to fulfill his mission," she said. "I was the immediate threat, yet he chose you. You are marked for death."

I didn't want to believe that, but what other explanation was there? I glanced around, unable to get my feet to move.

"How'd you know to come?"

She'd moved into the shadows, eyeing the men, still wary. "You called me."

I nodded as if that made perfect sense. "You'll need to explain that sometime … soon."

I still had the gun. It was heavy and I considered dropping it. Instead, I flipped the safety switch on, a skill I learned by watching cop shows, and shoved it into the back of my belt. Then I reached down and pulled a two-way radio from one of the men's belts. As I put the earpiece in my ear, the radio chatter confirmed what the stream was telling me. More men were gathering to the west, trying to make contact with these guys.

Shoko whispered to me, "Who are these men?"

I didn't want to say it aloud, but there was no denying it. "They work for my grandpa."

Even in the dark, I could see her eyes widen.

"But … why?"

That was a good question. "Let's go this way."

—

We were a few blocks away when we heard the first sirens. I could tell they were police sirens—no ambulances yet—and I felt the weight of the gun in my belt. Now I regretted taking it. I was armed and the police would soon know that.

I glanced at Shoko. "Where've you been?" We were walking fast, keeping to the shadows and off the main roads.

"I went home," she said.

"I really wanted to see you."

"You wanted to see me?" She smiled "You only need to call me, as you did a moment ago."

"And you'll just appear like—"

Voices in the earpiece interrupted me. The police were at the scene and a serious search for me had begun—but not by them. Grandpa's men were hunting me again, and it was clear they didn't want the cops to get in the way.

—

We walked down a residential street far from my neighborhood and far from where the men were searching. It was after eleven and the streets were empty and quiet. Only a few lights and the blue flicker of TV screens shone from the houses we passed.

I turned to her. "How did you *hear* me?"

"I told you, your energy is strong."

"But I thought you couldn't hear anything here."

She gazed at me, expressionless. "I was not *here*."

I licked my lips. "So, in some other place you can hear me?"

"Yes, and I can travel to where you are, knowing what I am getting into. It is once I am here that I become deaf."

"Is … is traveling some kind of illusion?"

"It is how we move from place to place or across from my world to this one."

"What the hell does that mean!?" I stepped back from her. "Look, my mom said you were like a ninja or something, and I think she is too—"

"The ninja are nothing compared to us!" Her face twisted as if she'd bitten a lemon.

My brain felt like it might explode. "What are you then?" I glared at her. "My mom knows your mother, so what is she?!" I paused to catch my breath. "What are you all … and what does it make me?"

Shoko lifted her right hand as if that were an answer.

"Yeah, what's with that ring anyway?"

"What did your mother tell you?"

"That it was a graduation present from her mother. A great honor that only women in her family clan wear."

Shoko nodded. "That is correct. The completion of years of training and the beginning of a life of service."

"So, you're some kind of Japanese … assassins?"

"I am not Japanese."

"Oh, for God's sake, you *are* Japanese!" I threw up my hands in frustration.

Shoko crossed her arms and spoke a sentence in a language that sounded like German and another in Spanish.

"What was that?"

"We are nothing—and everything."

I put my hands to my face, more confused than before. "Okaasan … we had a big fight tonight." I gave her a brief rundown. "She and you … She's been lying to me my whole life!" I spit the words out.

We'd stopped on the sidewalk in the shadow of a large tree and the street lamps lighted her face.

She smiled. "You are very cute when you become annoyed."

My heart jumped inside my chest and I faltered, my anger dropping like a windless sail.

"You cannot expect her to explain the unexplainable," she said, "but I will try to tell you what I can." She glared. "*If* you stop yelling at me."

We began to walk again, side by side, and it occurred to me that her energy was flowing toward me, a warm peaceful sensation that eased the anger and terror that had held me most of the evening.

"My people were once inhabitants of the lands of the god Ōkuninushi, the savior and guardian of ancient Japan. He controlled the islands from Izumo, the realm of gods and the land of myths."

"Izumo?" I could barely breathe.

She nodded. "As time passed, men began to encroach upon the shrine at Izumo, and Ōkuninushi decided he could no longer remain in this world. He moved to another world and re-created the Izumo shrine there." She smiled at me. "Ōkuninushi brought a few mortals—my ancestors—to accompany him."

"OK …"

"That place is much like this." She spread her hands wide. "The mountains, the water, the sky, the stars—all are the same."

"You're saying you—and Okaasan—are from … some kind of parallel dimension?"

She nodded. "My world is the home of the gods." Her voice took on a proud and passionate tone. "It is where they live when they are not in this world."

"You mean like … heaven?" I grinned. "Don't tell me you're an angel."

"You just called me an assassin," she said with a laugh. "No, we are not angels and my world is not heaven." Her smile faded. "I know nothing of heaven and hell. If they exist, then they exist in each person's heart. This is all the reward anyone will ever get."

I nodded, trying to comprehend what she was telling me, but something distracted me—some message in my head.

"This is too much for you?"

"No … Well, it is a lot, but that's not it." I touched the earpiece. "They aren't talking anymore." I realized I'd been ignoring it for a while. "And someone's close by."

I pointed to a thick hedge at the front of someone's house and jumped over it. I waited a moment and then stood up and peered over the top. Shoko stood on the sidewalk staring at me.

"Why do you always run and hide?" She looked annoyed. "It is not the way of the warrior."

"It's the *way* of staying out of trouble," I whispered. "Come on!"

She sighed and walked toward me, taking her time. She'd barely squeezed between the bushes when I heard the click of a car door closing—someone was trying to be quiet. A minute later, farther away, a car door slammed. I glanced at Shoko. She was lying on her back staring at the clouds.

I elbowed her. "Come on! This is serious," I whispered.

"I think they're close, Johnny," a man said in a low voice from the other side of the hedge.

I stopped breathing. Shoko grasped the hilt of her wakizashi.

"Good," said an older voice, presumably Johnny's. He wasn't trying to be quiet. "Let's see what that thingamajig says."

There was a pause, and then the first man said, "The signal's really screwed," still keeping his voice low. "It's jumping all over the place."

"Damn technology," Johnny said.

"They're not doing any better from the control center."

"Those pencil-pushing office pukes couldn't find that radio if it was halfway up their ass."

I looked at Shoko. She looked like a coiled snake. I tapped the radio.

"They're tracking us because of this," I mouthed.

"The old man must be one cold son of a bitch," the younger guy said. "How could he do this to a kid?"

"I've worked for him for years," Johnny said. "I gotta say, this surprises me."

"Oh, well. The money's good, right? We'll need more guys here— I think he's close."

"No," Johnny said. "If we get the kid, we can split the reward. Why share with the rest?"

My mouth was dry. Old man—my grandpa?

"Yeah, why share?"

Johnny laughed. "Let's see that thing again," he said and I heard a beep. "Look, the radio should be right behind there."

"You go look," the younger man said, followed by a sound I'd heard a thousand times in the movies: the cocking of a gun. The young guy laughed. "Go on, I'll cover you."

"All right."

The bushes started to rustle and I turned to look at Shoko.

She was gone.

—

I lay just a few feet away, frozen with fear. My neck was tingling like crazy, but I couldn't make my body react. Where the hell did Shoko go?

"Did you hear that?" Johnny said. The bushes stopped rustling. "Control said the signal's confirmed, coming from two blocks away." There was a pause. "Put your gun away, rookie. I'll go check it out." He sounded relieved.

Footsteps retreated down the sidewalk. Johnny was leaving, but the other man didn't budge. I felt his presence, heard his breathing.

The hedge began to wiggle. This time I did react—I pulled the gun from my belt and raised it.

When he emerged from between the branches, not a dozen feet away, I had the gun pointed right at him.

He carried a gun in his right hand but was pointing it at the ground. He didn't try to raise it. Maybe he didn't like the odds, but I doubted that.

He smirked. "Aren't you going to say something corny, like 'Drop it'?"

I gripped the gun tighter. "Who's the Old Man and why does he want me dead?"

"Easy, kiddo."

I struggled to my knees, trying to keep the gun aimed at him as my fear turned to panic.

"Is it my grandfather?" I tried to keep my voice strong, but I failed and choked on the last part.

In the distance, a dog barked and someone started yelling. The man put a finger to his earpiece and then let out a chuckle.

"You stuck the radio on a Doberman's collar? Now, how'd you do that?" He tilted his head. "I *know* it was here a minute ago."

I didn't reply. I still held the gun, but it was heavy and starting to droop toward the ground.

He started toward me with a smug grin on his face. "I don't plan to share the reward."

I struggled to my knees and raised the gun. "Stay away from me!" When he didn't, I pulled the trigger.

Nothing happened.

"You forget the safety," he said as he raised his gun, his thumb clicking off his own safety. I focused on the tip of the barrel, wondering if I'd see the bullet.

Suddenly, he jerked sideways. His gun spun away. I lunged to my feet, but he was already falling, his arm spurting blood.

Shoko stepped out from behind him and drove her wakizashi through his heart. There wasn't much blood—until she yanked the sword out.

She spun her blade, flinging the blood from it, and slid it back into the racket case.

"Did you ... Is he dead?"

She stared down at me. "Do you have a problem with that?"

"Shoko, please get us out of here."

—

Shoko was sitting beside me, legs crossed, looking out over the city toward the water when I managed to open one eye. We were in the park near Grandpa's, behind the bench, the same place as the other day.

"Why'd you come here?"

She shrugged. "I told you, on this side I only go where I have been before, somewhere that should be safe, but even then there are no guarantees."

I moved up beside her. "Why'd you take off and leave me alone?"

"You told me that radio thing was a problem, so I got rid of it." She turned to look at me. "And you *should* be able to handle two men yourself." She lay back on the grass and her eyes drooped closed. Bathed in moonlight, she looked exhausted—like I felt.

"Killing that guy ... doesn't that make you feel ... bad?"

"I would feel bad if *you* were dead," she said, her eyes still closed.

I sat back on the wet grass. "Did you hear what they said? My grandpa wants me dead!" I grabbed my head. "Did he find out about the journal? It can't just be because I opened the safe!"

Her eyes snapped open. "I warned you. That gold has cursed him and it will curse you, too."

I pointed a finger at her. "Everything was fine until you got here!" I backed away from her and struggled to get a breath in. "Why are you really here?"

She sat up. "I am here to help you!" She yelled so loud I worried the neighbors would hear her. "Did I not kill to protect you? Be strong! Take control of your emotions and fight against this evil or you *will* be dead!" She spit the last word out, her anger now as strong as mine.

I grunted. "But I have you to protect me, don't I?" I meant it to sound sarcastic.

"But who will protect you from me?" Her eyes took on that hard expression I didn't like. "If you let evil overtake you, I will kill you."

I looked down at the grass, at the gun lying there—blue steel shining amid a field of glowing dewdrops. I picked it up. "Can you die? Could this gun kill you?"

She looked at it. "I am flesh and blood, the same as you. Cut me and I will bleed—but I assure you, I will not die alone."

I bowed my head. I wanted to fall over and cry. Let them come and find me—the police, Grandpa's men, I didn't care who.

"The bloodshed and this talk have made me sad," Shoko said as if speaking to herself. "I want to go home for a while. I need some peace."

"Go," I whispered. "Just leave me here."

Silence descended as I slipped further away, my heart dropping further and further.

"Would you like to come with me?" she said.

CHAPTER
19

I STARED AT HER, SPEECHLESS, as thoughts and emotions stampeded though my head. She watched me struggle with something like sad amusement on her face.

"You mean travel ... across?"

Her dark eyes reflected the city lights. "It is against the rules, but this whole assignment is bewildering." She knelt on the grass and looked at me. "Do you want to come?"

"But how—"

"It is either yes or no."

I took a deep breath. "Yes," I whispered, "but would you really kill me?"

"That is up to you." Then she broke into laughter. "But I am an excellent teacher, so I *probably* will not need to."

I frowned. "I don't think that's funny."

"I am sorry," she said. Giggling, she added, "Do not fear me."

"I'm not scared."

She was still smiling as she reached out and took my hand. Immediately, the warmth of her hand radiated a peaceful energy into me. I took a deep breath and felt my anxiety lessen.

"We will go straight across, to the exact same place on the Other Side. This is the way I started." She made a face. "But that got me into some awkward situations, let me tell you." She let go of my hand and knelt. "I should do this the proper way." She bowed low and touched her head to the earth, the same way Okaasan and I bowed in the dojo. She was silent for a moment before sitting upright. "One must thank the gods and the Mother Earth. Without them, this is not possible."

"But if you can't see where you're going, how do you know it's safe there?"

"Anywhere there is safe." She took my hand and slapped her right hand on the grass.

The dizziness came, along with swirling lights. I closed my eyes and we tumbled through the darkness, for far longer than we had before, but Shoko's hand clasped tight with mine eased my fear.

—

I felt a cool breeze against my face and sensed movement around me. Scurrying sounds, leaves rustling, the creak of tree branches—night-time sounds. And my head didn't hurt.

I opened my eyes.

We knelt on soft ground covered in needles, still holding hands, bathed in the light of the moon. Huge green ferns and cones as big as footballs lay scattered on the ground. Trees towered above us, hundreds of feet tall, some at least twenty feet across, larger than any redwood I'd ever seen.

Shoko inhaled deeply. "This is what air should be like."

I took a deep breath too, filling my lungs. My head cleared and my exhaustion lifted.

It was a while before I realized we were still on top of the hill where the Crescent was. Man had changed the landscape somewhat, but it was obvious that this was the same place. Through the trees, moonlight shimmered on water. The outline of the distant hills, Alcatraz Island, Angel Island, even the shape of the bay were the same, but the familiar bridges and buildings were gone. This was San

Francisco Bay, the way the Spanish explorers must have seen it when they arrived in 1769.

"Did we go back in time?"

She shook her head. "This is a parallel world that follows a different destiny, free from man's relentless conquest and suffering. Our population hasn't changed in a thousand years. Each generation leaves the world *as is* for the next. No tree is cut without asking the Mother for permission, no animal taken without need."

Shoko smiled at me. In that moment, I knew I was looking at an angel.

"I told you Junya, I am no angel."

"Hey! I thought you couldn't hear my thoughts!"

She grinned. "In your world, I cannot. Also, from here I can see where I want to travel in your world—and I can hear you call me."

I looked at her. Angel or not, she was something special, and despite her warning, I couldn't help thinking how much I'd like to kiss her.

She gave me a sad smile. "I have that desire, too, at times. But nothing must distract me from my duties."

I nodded, both happy and disappointed simultaneously.

She pointed to the gun, still dangling in my right hand. "I do not like that thing. Dig a hole and bury it deep."

I grabbed a broken branch and dug into the soft earth. At two feet, I dropped it into the hole. After replacing the soil, I scattered a layer of needles over it.

She nodded in approval. "I am hungry," she said as she started down the hill.

—

A man was waiting when we came out of the trees. He wore a knee-length skirt and an elaborate headpiece, both made of supple bark. His chest was bare, revealing a powerful body. He bowed in greeting. Then he looked at me.

"He is one of us?" the man asked.

"A guest," Shoko said. Even in her school uniform, she looked confident and strong, easily this man's equal. I doubted I looked the same.

The man squatted. "You are from Izumo?"

Shoko nodded.

"We see warriors only in times of trouble, which is rare." He assessed her. "Others will come because of him."

"No one will come." Shoko's tone had a note of finality.

He nodded, but not in agreement. "I sensed your arrival, and your needs." He indicated a basket. "There is food and a blanket."

"Thank you for your kindness." Shoko bowed. "I would prefer this event to remain between us."

"They will come."

I glanced over my shoulder, suddenly nervous. "Who will come?" I started to reach out with my energy.

The shaman looked surprised. Shoko looked angry. "Close off your mind, now!" She grabbed the basket with one hand and my arm with the other. "Let's go," she whispered.

The man was barely out of view when I jerked to a stop. "Something's coming." I couldn't define the energy as good or bad.

Her head snapped up and she listened, and then her eyes widened. She dropped to the ground and put her hands in a prayer position. Energy began to radiate from her so intensely that I had to grab my head. Then, slowly, as if she'd pulled a curtain around us, all sounds vanished—the waves, the night sounds, even the wind. I didn't move. I tried not to even think. Finally, after several minutes, Shoko turned to me. "You sensed them before I did."

"What was coming?"

She was quiet for a moment. "Before I tell you, I need to explain some things. But before that, let's eat!"

There were several bowls filled with nuts and berries, mussel shells and smoked fish. As we ate, the evening became cooler and Shoko moved closer to me. When I pulled the blanket around us, she smiled.

"This is nice."

I nodded, although I imagined she thought it was nice only because it was warmer. For me, the blanket made my body as warm as my heart had become.

"This really feels like God's world," I mused. "I feel so relaxed, like nothing bad happened tonight."

"It is difficult to feel negative here," Shoko said. "And it is not God. There are thousands of gods here, both small and powerful, gods of the shrines of Japan and gods from around the world, gods of the desert, of the mountains, streams, and lakes. Worship is what gives them strength, but as the years pass, there are fewer believers. New religions or disbelief have replaced the ancient ways, and the gods grow lonesome."

I turned to look at her. "Why do these gods need someone like … you?" I couldn't find a delicate way to say it. "You're a killing machine."

Shoko snorted contemptuously. "Show me one great civilization that survived because of their kindness. Ōkuninushi commanded my people to be the guardians of this world, to keep out the evil that had infested your world."

"But why women?"

"You think us incapable?"

"Of course not."

"Ōkuninushi considered women to be the daughters of the Sun Goddess. He knew the strength of a woman's heart and decided we—the life-givers—would also be responsible for taking life."

"So that makes you …"

"We are the Gatekeepers. Ōkuninushi created gateways between our worlds so the gods could pass back and forth. Most are locked, and some allow passage only temporarily—only Gatekeepers can travel at will as I do. The ancient peoples of your world had their shamans, their witch doctors, medicine men and druids, who knew the location of gateways and had permission to cross. But there are few left since your people began spreading around the world, crushing the old religions and cultures. And there are intruders, those with stolen knowledge, who cross over without permission and with evil intent."

I thought for a few minutes. "You haven't told me what was coming. Was it those Gatekeepers?"

"Yes." She took a deep breath. "There is a break in the energy field of the Mother Earth each time someone crosses."

"That wave that knocked me over?"

She nodded. "When that break is detected, whoever has crossed over is intercepted. Depending on their intentions, they are accepted, returned ... or killed."

I chill ran up my spine. "But my grandpa wasn't killed."

"When Tomi and the other Gatekeepers arrived, Edward was on the floor of a hut, the home of an old Indian—a shaman from your side. The old Indian spoke of destiny and showed Tomi Edward's map. And thus," she said, opening her arms, "the continuation of that fateful moment."

A lump came to my throat as I stared at the ring on her finger. "Is my mother a Gatekeeper, too?"

Shoko was looking toward the water and didn't reply. She had a screen around herself, guarding her thoughts.

"Come on, Shoko, tell me. You can't go this far and then clam up."

I felt sadness seep out of her, but she managed a smile.

"*Clam up*, I like that." She let a few more seconds tick by. "She *was* one of us. And that, in part, could explain some of what you can do." She shrugged. "But I, too, am in the dark about many things."

152

CHAPTER
20

SHOKO BROUGHT US BACK TO the beach near Ghirardelli's where we'd made our vow just days before. I was surprised to see it was already dawn—

I grabbed my head and fell to my knees in the grass. Through squinted eyes, I locked my gaze on the Golden Gate Bridge as darkness overtook me. I tried to block it out, but it pressed against me and shoved me down like a stone into mud.

"Junya!" Shoko grabbed my hand. I felt her energy begin to push the darkness back. When I opened my eyes, she looked at me with curiosity.

"Thank you," I whispered. "There's so much negative energy here. I never felt it before."

"You repelled it, not me." She let go of my hand. "Your energy is powerful. I felt it growing inside you, trying to seep into me." She shook her head. "I do not understand any of this."

"Welcome to the club," I said as another chill shook my body.

She sat back, cross-legged, and put her chin in her hands—a most unladylike position, as Okaasan would say.

"Your power thrives in both worlds. Everything I have ever believed is shaken." She stared out at the water. "How can this be?"

I stood up. "I want to walk home. Will you come with me?"

"As you wish."

I didn't know what to expect when I got home, and the closer I got, the more overwhelmed I felt. I slowed down, wanting to stall for as long as I could. By the time we climbed the last hill, with only a few blocks to go, the sun had cleared the horizon—a new day dawning.

I stopped when I saw Grandpa's Bentley in front of my house, flanked by two black SUVs. If he was here, it was the first time he'd ever set foot in our house that I knew of.

Shoko gave me a small push. "Be strong, Junya."

I couldn't bring myself to go in the front door, so Shoko and I climbed over the back fence and sneaked into the dojo. I slid the shoji open and we sat down to watch the first rays of light peek into the Zen garden.

I heard the murmur of male voices coming from the house, including Grandpa's unmistakable booming voice. I couldn't make out the words, but I could tell he was angry—which, in turn, made my own anger rise.

"Junya, stop … please," Shoko whispered.

I reached for her hand, but it was limp. She was staring toward the pond and I followed her gaze.

Okaasan stood on the small bridge over the pond.

Like an exhaled breath, the energy drained out of my body. I felt like a wrung-out dishrag. I wanted to cry, from anger, exhaustion, relief.

Okaasan didn't move. She stared at us, an odd expression on her face and a look in her eyes I'd never seen before. I don't know how long we stayed that way, frozen in time, but eventually my eyes dropped and I felt my chin quiver.

Shoko let go of my hand. Okaasan was walking toward us. Shoko dropped to the ground and stood in front of me. Her hand moved toward the hilt of her wakizashi.

Okaasan looked Shoko up and down. "You won't be using that here, young one." Her voice was like ice.

"Misako-san." Shoko didn't bow. "This is an honor."

My eyes moved from one to the other, and then I glanced up at the house. Grandpa and my dad stood side by side, staring at us from the back door. They both looked tired and angry. Mr. Barrymore was behind them, his face expressionless.

"You've scared the hell out of us!" Grandpa bellowed as he strode through the garden toward me. "You think you can hide from me?"

My chin rose. "Did you do this because I opened your safe?"

"So it *was* you!" His face was already red with anger.

I jumped down to face him. "I'm not that easy to kill."

"Junya?" It was Okaasan.

I kept my eyes locked on Grandpa's. "His men have been chasing me most of the night." I pointed a finger at him. "I heard them say they had orders to kill me and they damn near did!"

"What?!"

My voice choked with emotion as I whispered, "Tell me you didn't do this."

Grandpa looked like I'd punched him square in the chest. It was like watching a mountain crumble. The man I respected shrank before my eyes, just as he had in my dream.

"What ... what are you talking about?" He turned to Mr. Barrymore. "What's he talking about?"

Mr. Barrymore stepped into the garden, not standing as straight as usual. "I have no idea sir, but"—he took a deep breath—"almost a dozen of my guys were injured tonight—seriously wounded—with edged weapons." He turned to look at me. "One had his arm severed and nearly bled to death. Another is still missing."

Okaasan looked like she was going to faint.

Grandpa looked back at me. "Did you do that?"

"It was self-defense."

"Defense against what?" Mr. Barrymore yelled.

I took an involuntary step back. "They tried to kidnap me!" I yelled. "They beat up Mack, they fired a Taser at me, then they shot at me!" I took another step backward as I glared at Grandpa. "Why would you do that?!"

His mouth dropped open. "You think I ordered you killed because you opened my safe?" Grandpa turned to Mr. Barrymore. "What do you know about this?"

"Nothing!" Mr. Barrymore yelled. "You've hired so many new employees I can't keep track of them all!"

"That's unacceptable," Grandpa said through clenched teeth.

Barrymore glared back. "I was hired to lead a professional protection team, not field an army of mercenaries."

I thought Grandpa might explode, but he didn't. He'd finally noticed Shoko.

"Who ... who are you?" he stammered.

"I am Shoko, sir," she said with a low bow. "I am visiting. Your grandson has been most kind to me."

"Visiting?" His face drained of its color. "Did you ... did you help James tonight?"

She nodded. "Those men meant to kill him. It was I who cut them down."

Mr. Barrymore's mouth dropped open. "You?"

I looked back and forth between Okaasan and Shoko. I needed to get to the bottom of all this, but suddenly my exhaustion caught up with me.

I turned to Grandpa. "I want you to go." My words came out in a hoarse whisper, but with force.

And to my surprise, he left.

I trailed after them to the front door. When it closed behind them, I heard voices in the garden and I walked back outside.

"So ... Shoko," Okaasan said in Japanese, her arms folded on her chest. "You are far from home. Why?"

Shoko faced Okaasan, her chin lifted. "I have my duty, Misako-san. Please excuse me, but this is not your affair."

"Please excuse *me*, but it's a mother's place to worry. Junya hasn't been himself since he met you."

"I will take the blame for awakening him. That he does not understand his heritage is your responsibility."

Okaasan's eyes widened. "There was no need ... He's a boy."

"It is true that no one could have predicted this." Shoko looked at the ground. I felt anger rising in her. When she finally looked at Okaasan, her eyes were filled with fury. "The Elders do not know what to make of him and the gods have not made their will known. The outcome of this situation is ... unpredictable."

Okaasan looked confused. "Then why did the Elders choose *you* to handle this?"

"Because I am not like you," Shoko said. "I will not forsake my duty."

"You know nothing," Okaasan whispered.

"I know what is before my eyes."

I stepped between them and faced Shoko. "Stop it ... please." I turned to Okaasan. "If it weren't for her, I'd be dead."

"I will see this through, Misako-san," Shoko said. "You no longer have the blessing of the gods. Do not get in my way," she said as she sank to her knees.

"Shoko, wait!" I ran toward her as her palm hit the ground.

—

My clock read 7:35 when I opened my eyes. I had no idea whether it was morning or evening. As soon as Shoko had left, I went straight to my room, collapsed onto the bed, and fell into a dreamless sleep. Now I was having trouble waking up, as if I'd taken too much cough medicine.

The house was quiet, although I could hear Tama purring at the foot of my bed. I didn't move at first, but slowly the events of the past few days rolled through my head like a banner unfurled.

I reached up to touch my head, where I found a bump on my forehead, a big one. My arms and shoulders ached, and my knuckles were bright red and swollen.

I might have stayed in bed all day if my bladder hadn't been about to burst. When I came back from the bathroom, Tama was lying outside the door, her back against the sunlit glass. I bent to pat her, but I saw something that made me stop dead. Two suitcases stood by the front door—Okaasan's.

Panic began to rise. "Okaasan!"

I looked for her in the kitchen, her bedroom and the living room. I finally spotted her in the dojo, going through her sword kata with more intensity than usual. I made my way across the yard. She watched me come, her katana pointed at the tatami.

I glared at her. "I saw your suitcases." I was struggling with so many conflicting emotions. "Are you leaving?"

"*We're* leaving," she said. "Mr. Barrymore called this morning. You're right. Those were your grandpa's men, but they weren't acting on his orders. Both he and Mr. Barrymore have no idea what happened out there."

"You really believe that?"

She nodded. "And until they find out, you're not safe here."

"So we're just going to run away?"

"You want answers and I need some, too. We're going to Izumo."

CHAPTER
21

WE FLEW TO VANCOUVER and then transferred to a Japan
Airlines Boeing 747 for the long flight to Narita Airport, outside
Tokyo. As the jet circled over snowcapped mountains north of the
city and began to climb out over the Pacific, I couldn't help but feel I
was leaving all that I knew behind.

We sat next to each other in first class. Our seats were like co-
coons, offering immense privacy and luxury but little opportunity
for conversation. That was fine by me, since I didn't feel like talking, and Okaasan had transformed her seat into a bed as soon as we
reached cruising altitude. She slept through most of the flight while
I zoned out with one movie after another.

The immigration hall at Narita Airport was huge but squat, the
ceiling oddly low for its width. It felt as confining as a concrete bunker and was about as attractive. The single line marked for foreigners
was long, winding back and forth between black ropes, but Okaasan
headed straight for the booths reserved for Japanese citizens—their
lines were short and clearing quickly. When she presented Japanese
passports for both of us, I looked at her in surprise. I had no idea I
even had one.

The immigration agent in the booth looked tired, lost in the boredom of his mundane routine. But as he looked at our passports, his energy changed. He looked up at us.

"Is there a problem?" Okaasan asked.

"There is an irregularity with your passport."

"I'm sure everything's fine," Okaasan said. Her tone was polite but I sensed a trace of alarm.

The agent passed our passports to an older man who'd walked over, a textbook bureaucrat if I ever saw one. Dressed in an ill-fitting dark blue suit, white socks showing beneath his pants, his face was red and swollen, his head shiny and balding. He reeked of cigarettes and coffee—a walking cardiac event waiting to happen.

He held up one passport—mine, I assumed—and stared at it and then at me, his dark eyes flicking back and forth several times. When he was satisfied, he studied Okaasan's passport, but when his eyes rose, his face turned an even deeper shade of red.

I turned to look at her and felt my jaw go slack. The way she stared into the man's eyes made me feel like blushing, too.

"There's no problem," she said, her voice silky smooth. "I'm sure it's a computer glitch."

The supervisor didn't budge, but the agent cleared his throat.

"Sir, the computer indicates an irregularity with her identity."

The supervisor snapped out of his trance and glared at the agent. "Then do something about it," he yelled. "You're no better than a photocopier, spewing useless information. Do whatever is necessary to correct this problem." He turned back to Okaasan. "These people are Japanese citizens."

"Of course." Okaasan continued to stare at the man. "I want to leave now."

The supervisor handed us our passports.

"Thank you, sir." Okaasan bowed low to the supervisor. "You are a fine leader," she cooed. "I will be sending compliments to your superiors."

The supervisor blushed deeper as he returned the bow. "Please accept my apologies," he said, still bowing. "Welcome back to Japan."

Okaasan turned to me and tugged my arm. "Let's go."

We cleared customs without further incident and strode through the terminal past rows of identical-looking young women who smiled and bowed and waved their white-gloved hands at us. It wasn't until we were on the bus, speeding along an expressway on the edge of Tokyo toward Haneda Airport, that she finally spoke.

"I don't know what that was about," she whispered in English. The bus was half-full, and most passengers had dozed off the minute we left the airport. "I guess I need to be more careful about these things."

"What'd you do back there? You looked ... different."

She smiled at me. "Sometimes, if you believe something strongly enough, you can convince others of your point of view. Of course, being a woman is advantageous."

"You're freaking me out."

"I merely made a suggestion. Bureaucrats are easier than most people are. Their minds are weak from the monotony and mediocrity of their lives."

"That's mean."

A mischievous smile crossed her face. "It depends what your intentions are."

I shook my head. "Unbelievable."

She smiled again and turned back around in her seat.

I looked out the window and considered what she'd said. Was it that easy to change people's minds? But, hadn't I done the same thing to Grandpa's driver and to the guard on the intercom?

As we sped through Tokyo, Okaasan slept with her head against the window, but sleep wouldn't come to me, exhausted as I was. Train tracks, overpasses, tunnels and bridges intertwined with the expressway, coming and going, as random as spaghetti on a plate. Tokyo went on forever, as far as I could see, an endless sea of grey concrete mirrored by a layer of gray haze in the sky that spread all the way to the hazy mountains far in the distance.

~

When we reached Haneda Airport, I was in an exhausted daze, but Okaasan was bright and perky. While we stood in line at the All Nippon Airways check-in counter for the next leg of our trip, Okaasan gave me our tickets and passports.

"You do it this time, in case there's still a problem," she whispered in English. "You've proven you can manipulate people. Make sure we get through here."

I sighed, too tired to argue. I studied the clerks, wondering which one would be the easiest to manipulate, but they all looked the same. All were young women, about the same age, with the same hairstyle, the same makeup and the same uniform, like pretty robots in a row. Even their smiles were identical—rehearsed, mechanical and insincere. One of them motioned to me.

"Here you go." I gave the girl my best smile as I handed over our tickets and passports. I studied her face as she stared at her computer screen.

"I like your scarf," I said. "It's very nice on you." I wasn't lying—it did look good.

She looked up at me, surprised. A smile came to her lips, along with a touch of pink to her cheeks. "They make us wear these," she whispered. "But thank you."

I smiled back and felt my cheeks redden as well. But when her eyebrows came together and her fingers paused over the keyboard, Okaasan elbowed me from behind. And when the clerk glanced over her shoulder toward the office, Okaasan tried to push past me.

"Window seats would be awesome," I said to the clerk.

She turned back to me and cocked her head and smiled.

"Actually, I'm upgrading you both to business class." Then her voice dropped to a whisper. "I was just checking to see if my boss was looking."

When she passed me the boarding passes, our hands touched and we both froze—our eyes locked for what felt like an eternity. When I finally took the passes from her, she looked shaken. I felt pretty shaken myself.

"Don't give up, Kiyoko," I said. "You deserve better than him, and this. You can do it."

Her mouth dropped open, and as I pulled Okaasan away, I felt her gaping after me until her boss tapped her shoulder and called the next passenger.

—

We'd barely buckled into our business-class seats for the one-hour flight across Japan before Okaasan started grilling me.

"Why did you say that?"

I patted the arm of the chair. "Nice seats, eh?"

She began to form a reply but instead grabbed the armrests as the pilot released the brakes and the jet's engines roared to full power. We banked over Tokyo and circled to the west.

"You're not taking this seriously," she said when we leveled out of the steep climb.

I glanced at her. "I think I'm taking all of this rather well, actually."

Okaasan accepted two cups of tea from the stewardess and handed one to me. I took a sip and let out a yelp. It was like molten lava and I sucked in a dozen fast breaths to cool my tongue.

"Did you do something to her?"

"Not like you did to that supervisor," I said. "I'm sure he's still fantasizing about you, by the way."

"I just asked you to—"

I banged the teacup down and fought the sudden anger that surged inside me. "Did you feeling anything from that clerk, anything at all?"

Her face stiffened. "Don't you look at me like that," she said. "I was distracted—"

"There was nothing on her computer. She gave us these seats on her own."

"But still—"

"She had toast for breakfast with strawberry jam. She thinks her boyfriend isn't interested in her anymore and her parents wished they had a son instead of a useless girl who couldn't even finish business school. And two days ago, she stood at a train station and imagined herself jumping in front of the express." I paused for a moment to catch my breath and lower my voice. "That was the day she was offered a front-desk job at a resort hotel in the Maldives, but she's not brave enough to go."

Okaasan's hand went to her mouth.

I turned toward the window, overcome with emotion.

CHAPTER
22

MIHO-YONAGO AIRPORT, which is not far from Matsue City, was the exact opposite of Tokyo. Our flight was the only commercial jet at the airport, and the terminal was no larger than your average elementary school. But there was a long row of military aircraft parked along the runway, marked with the red circle of the Japanese Self-Defense Force. I asked the stewardess about it.

"Right over there is North Korea," she said, pointing past the mountains. "We won't start any wars, but we're well-equipped to defend ourselves."

We drove to Matsue City in a small taxi, a boxy black sedan with white fabric seat covers that matched the driver's white gloves. I sat in the back with Okaasan and watched the scenery go by. I hadn't known they drove on the left here. The buildings, the cars, the people—nothing was like I'd imagined.

After a quick meal in Matsue, we dragged our luggage along the narrow streets for three blocks to Matsue Onsen Station, which I thought was a weird name because onsen means "hot springs." Our destination was Izumo-taisha, a small town on the Japan Sea, and Okaasan decided to take the Ichibata Line. It was a small local line, owned by the Ichibata Department Store Company, and it had only one route: Matsue to Izumo.

Okaasan bought our tickets at the machine, but we still had twenty minutes until the next train left. I hunted around for empty seats in the small, crowded terminal. I found two, but when I turned around she was on her way back outside, looking pleased. By the time I got outside, I couldn't see her anywhere and I started to panic.

I found her a few minutes later inside a small traditional building just outside the station. She sat on the edge of the shallow pool, soaking her feet and calves in the steaming water. Several tired-looking commuters—businessmen, students and a few elderly people—were doing the same. I took in the surreal sight and then took off my shoes, rolled up my jeans, and sat beside her.

She smiled at me. "Why do you think it's called Onsen Station?"

—

The train, if you can call two cars with a driver a train, left on time. We sped west beside Lake Shinji-ko, following the shoreline, with a tree-covered ridge on one side and a narrow winding road on the other. Small houses dotted the shore, but unlike the lake cottages you'd find in America, these were the homes of fisherman, with nets and narrow boats tied up outside.

Past the lake, the single track sliced across fields, occasionally speeding between little clusters of old houses and barns that stood dangerously close to the tracks. Okaasan, as usual, was sound asleep, her head resting against my shoulder.

We stopped at a few lonely concrete platforms to pick up schoolkids or drop off weary salarymen in identical blue suits. The more kids I saw here, the more I understood why Shoko always wore her uniform. Every teenager wore one here. The styles varied, but I didn't see one kid in street clothes.

The station at the end of the line was smaller and older, with one elderly ticket checker standing to greet us as we struggled through the turnstiles with our luggage. We found a taxi and were soon on our way. I didn't pay attention to the address, but within a few minutes it was obvious the driver was having trouble finding the place.

"What's the problem?" I asked Okaasan. "This isn't a very big town."

"Addresses are different in Japan," she said in English. "Most streets are nameless, just spaces that separate blocks. The address is actually the name of the block of houses."

"OK, but I still don't see why it's so hard to find one."

"They number the houses in the order they were built," she said, "so house number twelve might be in between numbers seven and two."

The street he finally dropped us off at was barely wide enough for the taxi.

"I also gave him a fake address," Okaasan said, chuckling. "The poor guy will probably be up all night trying to figure it out." She waited until the taillights disappeared around the corner and then set out at a fast pace up another narrow lane. We towed our suitcases over the cobblestones and open drains through a maze of passageways, getting farther and farther from the main road. I could have sworn we were going in circles. Few houses had lights on and the rumble of our suitcase wheels was the loudest sound, but whenever we stopped, I heard the sound of waves washing over the beach.

"The ocean is two blocks that way." Okaasan pointed as we turned up a different alley, which took us past more dark houses. "Do you feel anything? You're better at this than me."

I shook my head. I couldn't even feel my feet.

"I hope that's a good thing." She took a deep breath and stretched. Then she was off again.

About a block later, she stopped and nodded at a rundown little house with rusty, dented corrugated steel walls. It looked bad even in the dark.

There were no lights on, but the sliding door, which opened right off the narrow alley, was unlocked.

"It's my grandmother's house, on my adopted mother's side. She lived here most of her life." She looked around with a sigh. "No one lives in most of these houses anymore."

"Why?"

She rested her hand on the door frame.

"Things changed after the war. Farmers and fishermen didn't want their children to work as hard as they had. They wanted them to become doctors and lawyers and businessmen. But to do that, the children had to go far away to university. And professional jobs were in the big cities, not here. So they stayed in the city, got married, had families, and most never came back." She paused. "I suppose I'm one of them."

"But this is prime waterfront property. It must be worth a fortune. That should bring them back eventually."

She let out a small laugh. "This is not America. The Japanese are too busy working to relax at the beach. This land is worthless to them. This place is dying, like a fire burned down to the embers. Even the great shrine is growing cold."

The town might have been dying, but someone was paying attention. We'd been inside maybe five minutes, with a few lights on, when the front door slid open.

"Who's there?" someone called out.

"Please excuse us!" Okaasan rushed across the tatami to the inner doorway and then knelt and slid it open. There stood a gray-haired, tired-looking man, his skin wrinkled and tanned, probably from years spent on the ocean. He stared at her, and then his eyes opened wide in recognition.

"Misako? Is that you?" He bowed. "I apologize for bothering you in your grandmother's home. I thought you were an intruder," he said as he bobbed up and down in a series of low bows.

"Please excuse us, Mr. Ito. Thank you for taking care of Grandmother's property." She returned his bows while I stood behind her and wondered if they would go on bowing and apologizing all night.

"Let me turn on the gas on for you. Do you need groceries? I will get my car—"

"No, no, Mr. Ito, please don't worry. We're tired and need our sleep. We'll go for groceries in the morning." She turned to me. "This is my son, Junya. This is Mr. Ito, my grandmother's neighbor."

I bowed to him and he returned it. "He is growing tall in America. The last time I saw him, he was this big." He held his palm near his knee. Then, after more bowing, he left.

"Nosy neighbor," I said after the door had closed.

"That's the way it is here. Everyone knows everything." She smirked. "Well, at least they think they do."

The house smelled musty, and everything was covered in dust. Okaasan found a broom and began sweeping the floor while I pulled the futon mattresses out of the cupboard and laid them on the tattered tatami mats. Then I sat and looked around as exhaustion settled over me, leaving my body heavy.

The house was a traditional post-and-beam style, with yellowed and water-stained shoji panels that divided the small rooms. Electricity had obviously been an afterthought, with wires running across the low ceiling beams to the outlets and switches. The small kitchen didn't have a refrigerator, and there was no hot water. The best this place could hope for was to make it into a renovation magazine as a "before" picture.

It was cold, too. The windows rattled in their frames whenever the wind gusted, and there was a constant draft. Okaasan laughed when I asked her to turn on the furnace. She pointed to a small portable heater at the end of a frayed orange cord, but I decided against it. I'd be warm, all right—that thing would probably send the whole house up in smoke.

"Your grandmother lived here all her life?"

"Until she was ninety-three," Okaasan said. "The simple life is the best life."

I gave her a look. When we'd visited Grandpa's yacht last year, she'd flopped onto the king-size bed in the master cabin and asked Dad if they could go on a cruise—forever. Simple life, my ass.

"This'll be our home for a few days," she told me as we slid under the covers of our small beds. It was about nine o'clock local time, but for us it was almost five in the morning. "Tomorrow you can visit Izumo."

For some reason, the thought sent a shiver up my spine.

—

The next morning, we were awake before five o'clock local time, our jet-lagged bodies confused. It was too early to buy groceries, so after wasting as much time on our futons as we could, we dressed and walked to the beach as the sun came up. The little bay reminded me of the beaches in Carmel. I headed toward the water.

Any beach was reason enough for Okaasan to kick off her shoes and I was never far behind, but not here. There was garbage everywhere—plastic containers, bottles, Styrofoam—anything that could float had washed up. I kicked a cup and asked her what we were doing today.

"I have people I need to see," she said, looking out at the water. "But you cannot come with me."

"Why not? I thought we were done with secrets."

"It's not that, Junya." She kept her thoughts hidden. "It may be possible later, but not now. I'm sorry. Go sightseeing."

"Are you going to the other side?"

"I cannot go there!" she snapped. "For once, just do as I ask!"

—

After a silent breakfast of white toast, a cold hard-boiled egg swimming on a saucer, and a small salad, all served by an old woman who looked half-asleep, we walked back to the house. But as we got close, I felt a presence nearby. I touched Okaasan's arm.

"Someone's up there," I mouthed to her, pointing directly above me. We both pulled back against the wall. I took a deep breath and felt a man's energy—he was here for us.

A loose roof tile creaked. A second later, a rock bounced up the alley behind me. We both looked.

"Damn it!" Okaasan looked down.

At our feet lay a small origami crane. She let her breath out and stooped to pick it up. When she saw my expression, she sighed.

"It's OK. It's just friends of my family playing a welcome-back joke." She smiled. "They like to be sneaky."

"Apparently."

Whoever it was, they were long gone.

CHAPTER
23

I GATHERED A DAY PACK and left the house at nine o'clock. I was mad at Okaasan, but I was looking forward to touring the grand shrine of Izumo-taisha—I almost felt as if it were calling to me. But as I walked up the street from Grandmother's house, a hill almost as steep as Arbutus Street, I felt myself growing nervous. I wondered how different it would look from my dreams. That was in the back of my mind as I replayed my conversation with Okaasan.

"What did you sense from the man on the roof?" she'd asked me when we got inside. "As much as from that airline clerk?"

"It's not the same," I said. "There was a sense of something, not exactly danger but …" I thought of that day on Market Street. "I can pick up on emotions, but they have to be close to me." I let out a nervous laugh.

Okaasan looked serious. "Go on."

"I think if I know them, or at least if I've met them, I can feel their presence from further away." I looked at her as it started to become clear. "That night when I helped Shoko, … I sensed the guys who attacked her, but now I'm sure I sensed Shoko, too, even though she was a block away—because I knew her."

Okaasan sat on the tatami. "I can sense emotions, but not at a distance, and I could never do what you did with the girl in the airport."

I gave her a look. "I thought you could read my mind."

She smiled. "I feel your emotions, usually guilt, and I make a calculated guess."

I rolled my eyes.

"Go to the Izumo shrine today, Junya. You must."

"You're still trying to get rid of me."

"Shoko was sent back after she awoke you," she said, "which means the Elders are interested in you. I want to know what they want and I want to keep you away until I know—for your own good."

"And you think you can find that out today?"

"I'm going to try."

"Great," I said. "Be sure to let me know."

She let out a deep sigh. "Junya, there was no need to tell you any of this, because none of this was supposed to happen." She crossed her arms. "You would have thought I was crazy and you know it."

I had to give her that.

She crawled across the floor to the corner of the room, lifted the tatami mat, and removed a section of floorboard. She reached under the floor and felt around. "They're still here," she whispered. When she sat back up, she held a short wooden bokuto the length of a wakizashi. She slid it across the floor to me. "It's small enough to fit into your backpack."

I gave the bokuto a twirl. It had a nice heft.

"So what's this for, in case I'm attacked by ninjas?"

Okaasan frowned. "If you're attacked by anyone, defend yourself with everything you've got and try to get back here."

—

I finally reached the parking lot, which was already filled with a row of tour buses and a few dozen small cars. I caught a glimpse of wooden buildings through the trees, but it wasn't until I passed the souvenir shops and entered through the west gates that I saw the main shrine rising above the wall that surrounded it. Only its massive X-shaped roof was visible, but that was enough to send shivers up my spine. It looked just like the shrine in my dream except that it sat firmly on the ground—no massive red pillars in sight.

The place was packed with tourists, mostly Japanese, carrying an arsenal of cameras and surging from one sight to the next, their energy as negative as the people on Market Street. Near the west gate, a long wooden roof ran along the wall, overhanging six rows of wooden stairs that rose like bleachers toward small rooms—like Grandpa's box seat at the stadium. The rooms faced the shrine, and there was an identical structure on the opposite side of the shrine.

I leaned back against a post and stared. It had been only a week since Shoko stole the journal—since she threw open the doors of my world and exposed me to what lay beyond. I suddenly felt so alone.

"This is where the gods stay when they come to visit."

I turned to see a gray-haired man, shorter than me, wearing the uniform of a taxi driver. He was pointing to the little rooms at the top of the wooden bleachers.

"The gods?"

He nodded. "According to the ancient Shinto myth, all the kami—the earth spirits—gather for a month of festivities here at Izumo-taisha." He smiled. "They hold meetings and decide what will happen to the earth in the next year. Perhaps it's also a holiday for them, a chance for fellowship." Then he pointed to the stack of sake barrels outside one of the buildings and grinned. "They drink, too."

I eyed the benches. "Are they here now?"

The man shook his head. "No, the time of Kamiarizuki is in the autumn. They arrive from the sea."

"You know a lot."

"And you speak Japanese well for an American." He chuckled. "It's helpful in my duties as a taxi driver."

"Do you think the shrine used to be higher off the ground, a long time ago?"

He pointed to a nondescript concrete building on the far side of the grounds. "Over there is a model and pictures of the huge posts they excavated here a few years ago. That leaves no doubt."

I stared at the replica of three huge red posts tied together with a black metal band.

The man cleared his throat. "I must be getting back to my taxi."

I turned and bowed low. "Thank you very much."

He returned the gesture. "I hope the rest of your day is pleasant."

I circled the shrine, but when I reached the back, far from the noise and negative energy of the tourists, I stopped. I felt something different here. It radiated from the shrine and crackled in the air like the hum of power lines. Entranced, I sat down cross-legged under a black pine and focused on the energy.

At first, it passed by me, like water washing over a stone, but ever so slowly my mind tuned in to its frequency. The energy brought serenity and peace, similar to the feeling Shoko gave me. But behind this energy was a force that rippled the air with its intensity. Like on that day outside Ghirardelli's, energy rose inside me, too fast, filling me until I felt as if I would burst.

The world around me started to spin and everything went black.

CHAPTER
24

I LAY IN A MEADOW, lush and green and speckled with wildflowers. A large buck with huge antlers grazed not far away, along with two spotted fawns. Behind them, familiar mountains were outlined against the sky.

I must have gone across.

I waited for the dizziness and the headache, but nothing happened. After a minute I sat up and let the sun warm my body and the peaceful energy fill my soul.

The two fawns moved closer. I glanced at the buck. Our eyes met, and then he went back to grazing. Obviously, the gods didn't eat venison.

I stood and took in a quick breath. In the distance, maybe four or five miles away, the Izumo shrine rose above the treetops, the same building from my dream. I couldn't see the staircase, but I knew it would be there.

I started toward the shrine, drawn by the energy that radiated from it. At the meadow's edge, I found a narrow trail meandering westward through a forest of pine trees. Raspberry and wild strawberry bushes lined the path, their branches heavy with fruit. I picked some and ate them as I walked. The sounds of birds' wings flapping and the breeze blowing through pine needles were the only disturbance. The only messages here, emanating from every leaf and blade of grass, spoke of peace and tranquility. I wondered when the Gatekeepers would come.

The trail wound closer to the forest's edge, and through the trees I saw a wide valley, lush and green, spread out below me. My brain told me it had to be the same river delta we'd traveled across on the train to Izumo, but here it was dotted with square fields of rice. Fruit trees and small vegetable gardens surrounded a scattering of huts with steep straw roofs. I saw people working and small children running in the fields. I sat down and stared at the valley, an overwhelming sense of awe growing with every moment. I was sure these people had problems—that was just the way things worked—but the energy that radiated from them was positive.

I caught a message, subtle but clear. Something was watching me—several somethings.

I heard a giggle and turned to see a group of children crouched in the forest, peeking at me from behind the trees. There were five or six of them, dirty little kids dressed in traditional clothing—they looked like extras in a samurai movie. One boy, about seven or eight, stepped forward. He had a small bow in his hand.

"Who are you?" he asked, his face serious.

"I'm Junya. What's your name?"

"Taro."

My eyes scanned the forest behind them. "Are you hunting?" There was no arrow notched on his bow.

He looked confused. "We are practicing shooting intruders."

I nodded and stood up. "Did you find any?"

"Perhaps. Where are you going?"

"To the shrine. Is it far?"

He pointed with his bow. "It is that way, not far." Then he looked me up and down. "You are not from here."

I nodded. "No, I'm not. Are you gonna shoot me?"

"No. If you are bad, you will be dead soon enough." With that, he turned and walked back into the trees, waving for his band to follow him.

About a half-hour later, I broke out of the forest and into another field of knee-high grass and wildflowers. I took about ten steps before my body went limp and I had to sit down. The shrine was just across the meadow, towering above the trees on thick red posts. Close by, a small house with a steep straw roof stood against the edge of the forested hills. It was the house I'd seen in my dream, with the girl watching from the doorway. I felt energy, something that made me turn and scan the forest.

The Gatekeepers were coming.

I stood up and waited. I wanted to see what Grandpa must have seen that first time.

There was a shimmering, like heat waves distorting the air and blurring the trees. Then figures began to materialize, three women down on one knee, their left palms pressed against the ground. They were beautiful, powerful, and their eyes shone with confidence. Their long black hair was tied in ponytails and topped with wide woven hats, peaked like low roofs. All were dressed in flowing green robes, the color of the underside of a leaf, the hems reaching just above the ground. Sleek muscular arms and legs showed through slits in the material. One woman looked older than Okaasan, but the other two were girls about the same age as Shoko. The older woman's robe was tied with a wide golden band, the girls' with plain braided belts. Each carried a katana.

At first they didn't move. They stood like statues, blending into the forest. Then as one they came toward me, their steps light and graceful. One of the girls notched an arrow onto her long bow. The older woman's hand went to the hilt of her katana.

I stood rooted to the earth, staring at her in amazement. I raised my hand. The older one was within a dozen feet. She faltered and fell to her knees, as if she'd hit an invisible wall. The other girls stopped, bewildered.

I studied the woman while she stared back at me. She was

beautiful, but her heart was heavy, a burden that dragged down her every thought.

"You must be Tomi."

She blinked twice and bowed, touching her head to the grass. The two girls dropped to the ground like stones and bowed as well, although I doubt they knew why.

Tomi looked up at me from the ground. "Are you ... a god?"

I laughed. "I am Junya, Edward's grandson."

Tomi's mouth dropped open and she stared wide-eyed as recognition dawned in her eyes.

"Yes ... you have his features ..." She collected herself. "How ... Is Edward well? Did he find what he sought?"

"He's rich and powerful."

A soft breeze swept across the meadow.

"Did he tell you about me?"

I nodded. "He did."

I didn't know what she was thinking, but I was trying to gather the courage to ask *the* question, and that was harder than facing a drawn sword. I took a deep breath.

"Do you remember my mother, Misako?"

Tomi studied me awhile before she answered. When she did, her voice was different. "I remember her."

"Is she a Gatekeeper?"

Tomi stood and brushed off her knees. "She left here before her final assignment. She can never be one of us."

"She's never been back?"

"It is forbidden ... though she was never one to follow the rules." Her lip curled. "I heard that she finished her assignment on the other side, where she was granted the ring."

"What was my mother's assignment?"

"Ask your mother why she *really* married your father."

Something shifted deep inside me and turned cold. I felt as if I saw into her more clearly than I'd ever seen anyone. "You couldn't go across to Edward if you wanted to. There's no purity left in you."

180

Her body jerked as if I'd struck her.

"If it's your duty to kill me, you'd better get on with it," I said. "You wouldn't want to screw up twice, would you?"

She lurched forward, but again she faltered—and not because of me. We all froze as a warm wind, its sound like air through a flute, drifted across the meadow toward us.

"Let him pass, Gatekeeper." The voice came from the wind itself. *"Would he be here if we did not permit it?"*

Tomi dropped flat onto the ground, her body pressed against the earth as if she were trying to avoid an inbound missile. I didn't know what to do, so I just waited, glued to the spot.

It took a few minutes before Tomi raised her head, looking amazed. The two young girls, as if by some prearranged plan, ran away across the meadow toward the buildings in the shrine compound. I was about to follow them when Shoko's energy reached me, stronger than ever before, and I turned to see her burst from the little house nearby. She ran toward us across the meadow in bare feet.

Shoko skidded to a stop beside Tomi, breathless. She pointed at me. "This is Junya."

Tomi kept her eyes on the ground. "We have met."

—

"I heard what happened." Shoko led me into the meadow, away from Tomi. "My mother did not know the gods brought you here."

I pointed toward the shrine. "I wanted to thank the gods for letting me see this. It's wonderful." But now all that peace was tainted.

Ask your mother why she really married your father.

Shoko laid her hand on my forearm. "Your energy is darting about like minnows in a pond," she said in a low voice. "What troubles you?"

"Tomi just told me ... She said my mom was ... is ..."

Her eyes narrowed. "She told you what?"

I took a step away from her and her hand dropped back to her side. That feeling of betrayal leaped back to the surface.

"She said Okaasan married my dad as part of her final assignment."

"Why?"

"How would I know?" I stopped to suck air into my lungs. "What am I supposed to do with that little gem of information?"

"What do you want to do with it?"

"I don't know. All this is so … premeditated." I spread my arms as if they could gather it all together into some coherent explanation. "Part of me wishes this was just another dream. You were there—"

"I was in your dream?"

I paused.

She flashed me a mischievous smile. "Perhaps this is my dream and you are in it." She wore a simple kimono, light and thin, tied with a single belt. She looked beautiful standing among the wildflowers.

While I stood there, awkward, she looked up at me. "Is your mother content?"

I shrugged. "I guess?"

"Does your father appear unhappy?"

"Not at all," I said, "but he will be when he hears about this."

She shook her head and sighed. "You say the stupidest things."

"What!?"

"What does this matter if they are both happy?"

"Are you kidding? It's another lie!"

"Answer the question."

I glared at her and then turned and started to walk away. "I'm going to the shrine," I said over my shoulder.

"Do not do that, Junya." There was an edge in her voice.

I didn't hear her move, but a second later I was on my back with her straddling me. The air whooshed out of my lungs, taking most of my anger with it.

She poked my chest. "Did your mother tell you where she and your father joined their bodies to create you?"

"Are you kidding?" I said, my voice about an octave higher than usual. I wasn't sure what she was getting at, and anyway it was hard to focus with her sitting on top of me like that.

Her face changed. "You must work harder keeping your mind closed." Then she looked at me in surprise.

My face flushed. "I'm sorry," I muttered, expecting to see Tomi running toward us with a raised sword any minute. "It kind of ... does that ... on its own."

She nodded. "I see." She moved farther up my hips. "May I ask another question?"

"Shoot," I said, my voice strained. "That means 'go ahead', by the way."

"Yes, I knew that one." She looked pleased with herself. "Up until the day we met, did you like your life?"

I had to give that some thought before I answered.

"Well, there are lots of things I'd like to change, but ... yeah, I did. I have great friends, plans for the future—lots of good things. Plus, no one was lying to me or trying to kill me." But I never had a girl straddle me.

She picked up a small flower and made a loop.

"But you were strolling aimlessly through a dream." She poked my chest again. "It seems to me that, like your parents' lovemaking, you do not need to know everything to be happy."

"Could you stop talking about sex?"

"I did not realize I was." She grinned. "With the awakening of your abilities, knowing this place exists and that you are a part of this, would you still choose the life you had over this life you believe is a bad dream?"

While I considered that, she added another flower to the chain she was weaving.

"I don't know. I—"

"To me, your old life and your dream life are almost the same," she said. "You still have your friends and your future—and now you have this." Her tone turned serious. "If you want to know everything, start by accepting what is right in front of you."

"But Okaasan—"

"Oh, gods!" She sighed and looked up at the shrine. "Could I not have a simple assignment? Perhaps kill an intruder or seal up a gateway?" Then she glared down at me. "Do you know why this is so hard for you?"

"Because you're not making it very easy?"

"No! It is because you *think* you have a choice!"

I stared up at the shrine, which glowed in the midday sun.

"You will help me?" I said.

She leaned forward and draped the flower chain around my neck. "What do you think I am doing?"

I took in a deep breath. She smelled good.

She smiled. "Thank you."

"Stop doing that."

She laughed. "You left your mind's door wide open again."

"How come I can't hear anyone's thoughts here?"

She shrugged. "Everyone keeps their minds closed. Can you imagine life if everyone could hear your thoughts?"

"I don't need to imagine it," I said. "I've lived it for sixteen years."

She stood and offered me her hand, which I took. She tugged hard and managed to get me off the ground.

I spun in a circle, my heart feeling lighter than it had in days— maybe ever.

Shoko smiled. "I believe your heart is now in a place suitable for praying to the gods."

—

The staircase, made of thick wooden planks, rose up before me. I suddenly felt so insignificant, like Earth compared with the entire Milky Way.

I started to climb, tentative at first. About halfway up, just as I had in my dream, I stopped and rested my hand on the wooden railing. The ocean, the distant green hills, the valley thick with crops and fruit trees, the straw-roofed houses clustered together—it was exactly as it had been in my dream. I looked toward the little house in the meadow. Shoko stood at the door, her hand shading her eyes. I waved and she waved back.

I resumed my ascent to the top of the stairs. The climb went on and on, the ground far below now. My heart began to pound, and every few steps I paused to fill my lungs. The closer I got to the top, the harder it was to breathe.

I stopped on the last step, the one below the platform where the shrine sat, and gazed at the building. The wood looked old, the pieces fitted together with skill, like nothing I'd seen before. The door was right in front of me.

It was faint at first, a sound so low I didn't perceive it as anything other than the breeze. Then, as it had in the meadow, the air became a beautiful rush of music, a symphony of peace and joy unlike anything I'd ever known. It swirled around me, increasing in force until I had to lean into it to stay upright.

It overwhelmed me.

—

The silence made me open my eyes. I was on the ground at the foot of the staircase, sprawled on the gravel. Not a leaf stirred. No child yelled and no dog barked. I pulled in a deep breath, sucking in the clean air until my lungs felt about to burst. As I let the air escape between my lips, sounds of life filled the air once again. I gazed up at the shrine.

Everything was the same—except me. I felt brand new.

Shoko was on her knees beside me, her hands together. When she saw me move, she clapped—two sharp cracks in the stillness.

"You have been gone a while, Junya."

"Gone where?"

She shrugged. "If you do not know where, then how can you expect me to?"

"I … was I up there?"

An eyebrow went up. "Do not be ridiculous. That is the house of Ōkuninushi."

"I'm pretty sure I was."

She stared up the staircase, a perplexed look on her face. Then her eyes widened and she dropped her face to the dirt in a low bow. A moment later, as if she'd been commanded to, she stood and strode toward a small building on the far side of the compound, about where the gift shops were on my side. As I stood to follow, I glanced toward the top of the shrine.

"Thank you, Ōkuninushi," I whispered.

―

Shoko emerged from the building with a light-colored bokuto as long as a katana. There were other people in the compound, but no one paid us any attention. When we met in the center of the compound, she swept her kimono between her legs and knelt before me. She handed the bokuto up to me with both hands.

"What's this?" I asked, in awe of both its beauty and her gesture. I took it from her as if she were handing me a newborn baby. The bokuto had good balance and it was heavy, more like steel than wood. But there was warmth and exceptional smoothness that felt surreal. And I was sure it vibrated—just a little shudder—when I touched it.

"It is *shirakashi*, the hardest Japanese white oak," Shoko said, "but this one is made from special trees, blessed by the gods." She smiled up at me. "It is for you."

I shook my head and tried to hand it back.

"I can't accept this. I'm not worthy."

"Our worth is decided by others," she said. "You would risk offending the gods—or me—by refusing their gift?"

I dropped to my knees and placed the bokuto on the ground in front of me. I bowed, first to thank the gods, then to the bokuto, and finally to Shoko.

"It is our pleasure."

"Did they tell you to do this?"

She stared at me in silence for a long moment. "The words of the gods can only be heard by the Elders." She stood up. "Now we will return you to your world—after I get changed."

—

"You are getting lighter," Shoko said as we appeared at the back of the shrine, the one on the ground in modern Izumo. "Are you doing anything different?"

I shrugged. "I was thinking about coming here as you said it—"

Darkness flooded over me, far worse than the last time I'd crossed back. Shoko gripped my hand and I clung to her as negative energy threatened to swallow me. I heard her voice from far above me.

"You do not need me, Junya. Come back."

I exhaled and the feeling lifted. I opened my eyes to the evening sky.

"How long were we over there?"

Shoko looked around. "A few hours. You have been gone longer here."

"There's a difference?"

She gave me an odd look. "Why do you think Tomi is so much younger than Edward now?"

CHAPTER
25

I WALKED INTO GRANDMOTHER'S HOUSE and slid the door closed behind me. I closed my eyes and breathed in the scents of Okaasan's cooking. It reminded me of when I was little, which made this all the more difficult.

I'd left Shoko outside in the alley, holding my bokuto. I needed to do this alone.

"I'm back," I called from the entryway.

"Welcome back." A moment later Okaasan came to the door to greet me. She looked innocent enough if you ignored the large white bandage on her arm.

"You were a Gatekeeper." It wasn't a question.

She held her breath for a few seconds. "I left all that behind. I'm your mother, nothing more." Her hands twisted her apron and I stared at the ring on her middle finger.

"If you were a Gatekeeper, what would that make me?"

She was silent for a long time. "A Gatekeeper's son, I suppose." She lifted her chin. "It isn't your place to be anything else."

"So why—"

"Are you going to make Shoko stand out there all night?"

—

Okaasan laid out dishes of food and we sat cross-legged at the low table to eat. Shoko sat beside me, across from Okaasan. Her only greeting to Okaasan had been a slight nod, and the tension in the room was unbelievable.

I studied Okaasan as if seeing her for the first time. The lines around her eyes and mouth seemed deeper, but she still looked younger than she should. It had nagged at me over the years, a slight tug on my cerebral coat sleeve, but never enough to question it. Now I couldn't ignore it: she was aging more slowly than the rest of us. Would Dad and I keep getting older while she and Shoko stayed young?

We began taking food with our chopsticks, but I noticed Shoko glance at the bandage on Okaasan's arm several times.

"What happened?" I said.

Okaasan repositioned her arm.

Shoko answered for her. "She called to me and said she wanted to fight me." She smiled as if she thought that was the cutest thing. "She was very angry, so I took her across."

"I thought she wasn't allowed."

"I did not want to kill her, but if need be, it was better to kill her there." She said it as casually as she might say melons were on sale at the grocers. "We fought, then someone called her name and she faltered. My blade cut her before I could stop."

Okaasan motioned for me to eat and poured herself a glass of sake.

"That's too modest. I couldn't beat you and I knew it."

Shoko nodded. "Tomi told me you were the best she had ever seen—until me."

Okaasan ignored the remark. "I believe we've resolved our differences. Would you agree, Shoko-chan?" I was surprised by her use of the familial suffix.

"Yes."

I looked at Shoko and then back at Okaasan. "What did the Elders tell you?"

"They said that because you are my blood and I trained you to fight, in their minds you are practically a Gatekeeper—except you're a boy and you live on this side."

"What if I was on that side?"

Shoko elbowed me. "Then you'd be an apprentice cook," she said through a mouthful of food. "But I am sure you wouldn't be half as good as her!"

Okaasan kept her eyes on me. "They're concerned. You may have the physical training of a Gatekeeper, but you lack the mental discipline."

I shrugged. "What does it matter?"

"It matters," Shoko said, "because without discipline, you may pose a threat to them."

I glanced at Okaasan. "How?"

Shoko put her chopsticks down. "Your energy is stronger than ours. What if you could travel, too?"

"The Elders don't believe that could ever happen," Okaasan said a bit too quickly.

I stared from one to the other.

"In any case, it was made clear to me that Shoko will continue to help you and ensure you continue on the right path." She couldn't hide the sadness in her voice. "That is her assignment now. I have no role to play in this. I need to let go."

"Speaking of assignments, … where'd you meet Dad?"

I don't think she expected that. She took a rather large sip of sake and dabbed her lips with a napkin. "It was a coincidence—not that I believe those—that your father came to Japan." She smiled, a happy-sad combination that confused me. "I didn't know who he was, but I'd seen him around Matsue. He was apprenticing with the Takahashi family, a family of woodworkers since feudal times. Your father lived with them, not far from our house."

I put my chopsticks down and leaned back to give my legs a stretch.

"My family asked me to keep an eye on him. I didn't mind. Your father was such a handsome boy and had a good heart. He still is, and still does." She gave me a quick smile.

Shoko looked puzzled. "Why did they want you to watch him?"

"My family ..." Okaasan glanced at me. "The ninja of Matsue have an allegiance with the Gatekeepers. They carry out the wishes of the Elders, for bags of silver."

I slapped the tabletop. "Your family *are* ninja! I knew it!"

Okaasan rolled her eyes. "Anyway, my ... adopted family was assigned to watch over Edward years ago. He'd been across, and one is never the same after that." She looked at me. "So, of course, they knew of your father. When he showed up here, it was reason enough to have him watched." She took another gulp of sake, reminding me of Lin. "It was a small assignment, fitting for my age and training, a way for me to contribute. You see, I wasn't a ninja and I was no longer a Gatekeeper's apprentice. I was just a girl with a very odd life."

"So you did your duty."

She nodded, unaware of my growing anger. "For a while, but there was a problem—well, a couple of problems."

"Like what?" Shoko asked, her chopsticks frozen in front of her mouth, the first time they'd stopped in a while.

Okaasan smiled. "First of all, he noticed me on the street one day and came right up to me—so bold, not like the local boys. I couldn't follow him around after that, could I?"

"What was the other problem?"

"Well, ... I fell in love with him the moment he spoke to me," she said, her cheeks turning pink. "Of course, when he asked me on a date, my family was pleased. To them, it made my job much easier ... but they didn't know. I hid my feelings from them as well as a teenage girl can." She gave me a quick smile. "If they'd known, they would have stopped it right away."

I glanced at Shoko. "Because love makes you weak?" I grabbed the bowl of fried chicken as she reached for another piece.

"Yes, it does." Okaasan took another gulp. When she noticed me eyeing the sake bottle, she poured a cup for both Shoko and me.

"You should be careful, Shoko-chan. I was curious about this world, too. Once I saw it, I couldn't go back."

Shoko nodded and grabbed a chicken leg from the bowl before I could react.

Okaasan looked down at her full plate and sighed. "You know, many people over there, including Tomi, called me weak and self-ish ... but it was the hardest decision I've ever made. I gave up everything I knew." She started to pick at her food.

Shoko had already finished hers and was going for seconds. I was too full of questions.

"Did you hear about Grandpa from Tomi?" I said.

"I was there when Edward came across."

"You were there?!" Shoko and I said at the same time.

She nodded. "I was only a child, but I remember everything. We were on a training exercise when the call came, an intrusion through one of the old gateways, and we were the closest."

I glanced at Shoko. She held her rice bowl close to her face, scooping out the last few grains, but her eyes were glued to Okaasan.

"I was sure Tomi would kill Edward. Her sword drew blood from his neck when she nudged him with it as he lay at her feet, half-dead from the desert heat." Okaasan got a far-off look in her eyes and laughed. "I remember how he looked at her, as if being killed by her would be wonderful. Tomi sent us students back to Izumo, and for the next three days she spent every waking minute with him. She fell so deeply in love—so obviously—it wasn't something any of us girls had seen before. It shocked us all." She paused. "I was there again when Tomi took Edward back across. And I must admit, I was surprised when she returned." She paused to take another sip of her sake. "She hated herself for letting him go. I didn't intend to repeat her mistake."

All of us were silent. Even Shoko had stopped eating. The emptiness in the small house became so crisp that to speak might break it like a frozen twig.

I cleared my throat. "Dad doesn't know any of this?"

"Good God no! When we met, I was just Misako Sota, the adopted daughter of highly respectable merchants." When I didn't respond, she continued. "We dated and got married a week after my twenty-first birthday. We had a simple Shinto wedding at the Izumo shrine. A few years later, you were born. We moved to America when you were five." She paused and wiped her mouth with a napkin. "I broke ties with both those worlds—completely severed—until today."

"How do I know that marrying Dad wasn't part of your assignment?"

Her eyes flared with anger. "I love your father."

"And?"

"And it's over and done! Let it go, Junya."

I pushed back from the table. "I deserve to know everything, and so does Dad."

Her face went white. "If he knew … I stand to lose everything."

"Tell me the truth!"

Shoko touched my arm. I shrugged it off.

"Fine." Her voice went flat. "My mother and the Kannushi came across one night when I was eighteen. You can imagine my surprise."

I couldn't, but apparently Shoko could. Her eyes went wide and she stopped chewing.

I made a face. "The Kannu-what?"

"The Kannushi," Shoko said. "One of the Elders. He who communicates the will of the gods."

Okaasan nodded. "The Kannushi told me I had to go back. Of course, I refused. I was in love."

Shoko looked astonished. "You disobeyed the Kannushi?" She lowered her eyes. "That is the greatest dishonor."

"Perhaps. But I still refused to return."

"You were willing to die?" Shoko asked, still not raising her eyes.

"Wait—what?" I asked.

"The punishment for disobedience is death," Shoko told me. "Ritual suicide preferred, of course."

"You're joking, right?"

"She's not," Okaasan said. "When it became clear that I wouldn't be returning alive *or* dead, the Kannushi allowed me to remain, on one condition."

My disappointment grew into a lump in my throat so big I couldn't speak.

"What was the condition?" Shoko asked.

Okaasan kept her eyes on the table. I couldn't sense anything from her. "I was to persuade your father to marry me."

I squeezed my eyes shut.

"Why?" Shoko asked.

Okaasan hesitated and I felt her eyes on me. "Edward had been *across*, and he had returned with the gold. There was something dark about the whole thing—and something dark within Edward himself at times. The Elders were concerned."

I put my face in my hands and tried to make sense of what I'd heard.

"Junya, ... I loved your father. I was crazy about him." I heard the plea in her voice. "Can you imagine how happy I was?"

"It sounds a little too convenient."

"*Convenient*? I was banished forever from the world you saw today, from my family, from everything I knew!" She took a deep breath. "I believe the Kannushi took a moderate approach with me—my family is quite powerful. But I took the assignment because I *wanted* to marry your father." Then she held up her hand and showed me the ring. "My mother came back and gave me this."

There was a moment of silence as we stared at each other.

I turned to Shoko. "I suppose you think this isn't a lie either?"

Okaasan slammed her cup down. "I don't give a damn what you think! I wouldn't change anything about my life, but I guess that's no longer up to me! So go ahead, Junya. You know the truth—now decide what you're going to do with it!"

CHAPTER
26

THE MORNING DAWNED SO QUIETLY I could hear the waves hitting the beach. I lay on my futon—Shoko and Okaasan were still asleep—and stared at the ceiling, this one made of wide planks stained dark by wood smoke and time. I had more information than I knew what to do with, but one thing seemed clear: all this had started the day my grandpa went into the desert. Shoko's crossing over, my awakening, the company's going under, Grandpa's naming me as his heir, those guys who'd tried to kill me—it couldn't be a coincidence that all this was happening now.

Over breakfast, I asked what I hoped were the last questions I needed to have answered.

"This Bartholomew guy that Grandpa's mixed up with," I said. "What's his deal?"

Okaasan and Shoko exchanged glances.

"Were it not for those like Bartholomew," Shoko said, "there would be little need for Gatekeepers."

Okaasan nodded. "There are those with great power in this world. Some are well-known, others dwell in the background, directing and influencing many things for their own ends. And they have people everywhere, people who have no idea what it is they truly serve."

I remembered Grandpa telling me about his *investment* group— the Committee—and that it had enough power to affect the economy.

"Bartholomew is one of those we call the *Evil Ones*," Shoko said as she stirred her egg into the rice in her bowl. "And they are not human."

My head jerked up. "Not *human*?"

"They are beasts—huge creatures with long claws and sharp teeth covered in deadly venom." She seemed to shudder. "And when they die, they bleed black blood—that, too, is poisonous."

"But they're businessmen. You just said Bartholomew—"

"They can assume human shape," Okaasan said, "though their inner character shines through."

An image of that old man in the bathroom flashed through my head. I licked my lips, which were suddenly dry. "I think I saw one. That night I had dinner with Lin. He was an old man, a really old man. He had a snake's tongue—"

"Oh, gods!" Okaasan's hand covered her mouth.

"Do you think that was Bartholomew?"

"I don't know," Okaasan said. "Did he say anything?"

"He said he could tell I was special and that we'd meet again. He noticed my gold watch." My brain was working overtime now, and I didn't like where it was going. "Grandpa and Bartholomew were business partners ... You don't think Grandpa is—"

"No!" Okaasan held up her hand. "Edward was under Bartholomew's influence, that's all. The Elders took notice. That's when my family received our assignment."

Something still didn't add up. "Grandpa said Bartholomew was trying to get his gold." I turned to Shoko. "Would the gold give Bartholomew access to your side?"

Shoko gave me an "Are you stupid?" look.

"Then why does Bartholomew want it so badly?" Come to think of it, why was Grandpa so determined to hang on to it?

Shoko shrugged. "That the Elders even bothered with Edward

amazes me—the Gatekeepers' only duty is to keep the evil out of the world of the gods."

I leaned forward onto the table. "So what are we going to do about Bartholomew?"

"Nothing," Shoko said, "unless he threatens our world."

I looked at Okaasan.

"The Evil Ones aren't my concern," she said.

"Bartholomew is threatening Grandpa. Doesn't that *concern* you?"

She looked away. "Evil exists everywhere in this world."

"So, we just let this ... this evil guy ... snake ... whatever ... attack Grandpa without doing anything?"

Shoko cleared her throat. "It is my understanding that Edward entered into the relationship with Bartholomew quite willingly. There is a price to be paid for everything."

I looked at Okaasan. "But ... you let me hang out with Grandpa for years. Didn't you think that this might become a problem?"

"Your grandfather has made a huge effort to change. He rejected Bartholomew and has tried hard to be there for you. I didn't consider him a problem."

—

Okaasan booked a flight back to San Francisco for early the next morning and reserved a room in a business hotel in Matsue for our last night in Japan. I'd spent almost the entire train ride back to Matsue Onsen Station deep in thought. I thought of Grandpa holding that MP5. What was so special about the gold? Maybe Shoko was right—maybe it was cursed.

Shoko sat beside me with her eyes closed and her legs stretched out, ankles crossed. I noticed a few men looking at her and was surprised at the jealousy that welled up inside me. I nudged her with my elbow and her eyes snapped open.

"If there was an Evil One on the train right now, could you tell?"

She shrugged. "Maybe if it showed us its tongue."

"Do you think *I* could tell?" I said as I studied the passengers in the half-full car.

She frowned. "Perhaps. Why?"

"Because one of them is after my family. Maybe if you did something to stop the evil on *this* side, you wouldn't need to guard your gates all the time."

She paused and then shook her head. "The gods do not want this world turned into a battleground."

"It's a little late for that."

—

Okaasan and I spent the afternoon walking and ended up by the north moat of Matsue Castle, in the old Samurai district. The estates stood in a row behind stone and wooden walls, facing the moat.

We walked in silence on the narrow street beside the moat under blooming cherry trees. This was the first time we'd been alone since she admitted the truth of her "assignment." Neither of us were ready to talk. Everything had changed, but into what I hadn't figured out.

Okaasan pointed to a narrow lane that twisted up the hill into a bamboo forest. A high concrete wall topped with security cameras ran parallel to the lane.

"What's that?" I said.

"That's where my family lives."

Three black BMW sedans turned up the lane and then into an opening in the wall. A high gate slid closed behind them.

"The respectable Sota merchant family, I presume."

She nodded and started walking again.

"Not very inconspicuous."

She pulled a twig bursting with pink blossoms off a low branch. "Everyone here knows not to ask questions."

I stopped. "Aren't you going to drop in and say hi?"

"I've already done that," she said, still walking.

"Well, I'd like to meet them."

She turned to look at me. "If you're lucky, you never will."

⌒

We got back to our hotel after dinner and were greeted by an anxious-looking desk clerk. He handed Okaasan a slip of paper. Her face grew pale as she read it, and then she turned to me with tears in her eyes.

"Your grandpa's had a massive heart attack. He's ... he's not expected to live."

CHAPTER
27

THE HOUSE WAS QUIET AND MESSY—dishes were piled in the sink and dust bunnies drifted along the floor. Tama wouldn't stop rubbing against our legs—I thought she'd missed us until I saw her empty food dish.

I threw my stuff onto my bed and headed back to the kitchen. Okaasan was already attacking the dishes.

"I'm going to the hospital."

"Go and call William from a pay phone," she said. "Ask him to send a car."

"Why a pay phone? And why William?"

"Because I'm sure they have our phones tapped, and because he has a car." She turned to look at me. "Make sure no one sees you. I don't want you getting into trouble again."

—

I got back about fifteen minutes later after bushwhacking through the neighbor's yard and climbing over the back fence. On the way back, I'd scouted out the neighborhood. A blue car was parked around the corner from our house, with one guy reclining inside. Two blocks away, south on Arbutus Street, two guys sat in a van, looking bored as hell. The blue car looked a lot like the car that had tailed me the day Shoko and I rode the cable cars. I figured they were either guarding us or spying on us. I couldn't tell which—their energy wasn't positive or negative, just the empty buzz of zoned-out minds.

"Twenty minutes," I called as I walked in the house.

Okaasan came out of her room. I stopped dead.

She'd changed into fresh clothes: high heels, a miniskirt, and a thin sweater that revealed more of her body than I cared to see. It sure wasn't hospital-visiting attire.

"How did William sound?" Okaasan said, smoothing her skirt.

"He sounded surprised we were already back," I called as I walked toward my bedroom. I figured I needed to change, too.

I emerged a few minutes later in clean jeans and a blue golf shirt. There was no sign of Okaasan.

A whisper of material sliding against something interrupted my thoughts. I spun but immediately tried to turn back around. Okaasan had her skirt pulled up and was strapping a knife to her inner thigh, hilt down.

She gave me a devilish smile. "*Kunoichi* sometimes use this. It's a good hiding place, don't you think?"

I wasn't sure about that. "What's a *kunoichi*?"

"Female ninja," she said. "I'll assume you know that men have nine openings in their body. Women have ten. One extra—*ichi*."

"OK," I said, doing a quick mental tally. "So what's with ... the, um ... outfit?"

"Kunoichi fight as well as the men, but they are most successful using other methods. Who suspects a pretty girl?"

As she adjusted her skirt, it struck me that all our lessons, even those Okaasan taught me when I was a kid, were about delivering death quickly. Shoko and Okaasan were trained killers, as were their families. Did that make me a trained killer, too? I stared at the ground.

"Is our life ever going back to normal?"

She was looking in the mirror, adjusting her sweater.

"You're the only one whose life has changed." She sounded less like my mother and more like Shoko.

We were two strangers in a familiar place. I'd lost so much. No—I wasn't losing things. I was throwing them away, and that wasn't what I wanted.

"I'm sorry about ... what I said about you and Dad."

She turned to look at me.

"I'm not going to say anything," I said.

She stood in front of me, arms crossed. "I won't let you pretend that everything's all peachy between us." Suddenly, there was anger in her eyes.

This wasn't going the way I'd hoped. "You've got to understand. The world I knew for sixteen years, the mother I thought I knew, disappeared"—I snapped my fingers—"pretty much overnight. The more answers I got, the more lost I felt. Please ... I'm doing my best here."

She stared at me silently, her stance unchanged.

"We've got to work this through," I said, "not just for Dad's sake but for ours." My voiced cracked. "You're still my mom, right?"

She buried her face against my chest and hugged me so hard I thought I'd break. We were both crying. When she finally pulled back, she wiped her nose and let out a giggle. "I think you'll need to change your shirt."

I looked down at my chest. "Yuck."

She sniffed. "What happened on the other side is a part of your life. It's not the end or the beginning, no more than any new day is. Shoko will help you, but I will make sure you always have a home, as long as I can." Then she smiled and patted the knife under her skirt. "And no matter what the Elders said, I'm uniquely qualified to support you."

—

On the ride to the hospital, the driver told us what he knew, but it wasn't much. Grandpa had had a heart attack while he was asleep, and the paramedics had to do CPR on the way to UCFS Medical Center—one of the best hospitals in the city, he said. If he'd meant to make me feel better, it didn't help. I didn't want my last memory of Grandpa to be that night in our backyard.

"Looks like we've picked up a tail," the driver muttered, his eyes on the rearview mirror. "I'll see what I can do."

"Don't worry about it," I said. "They know where we're going."

Dad met us outside the hospital entrance. Clearly tired and grumpy, he looked like hell. His hair was disheveled, his face a mass of brown stubble, and his clothes had that slept-in look. When he saw Okaasan, he looked as confused as I'd been when I first saw her outfit. She didn't smile at him. In the car, I'd felt her slip into a dark place. She was afraid—her secret was out. She looked guilty and distant.

All Dad saw was that his wife had changed. I felt the shifting of his thoughts: shock, suspicion, then sadness. I felt him start to deflate. She'd been away, back in her hometown, and had come back cold and distant—and dressed like a single woman.

"Misako?"

Okaasan must have felt it, too. Her head came up and she burst into tears, her hands reaching out for him.

"Robert," she whispered as she clung to him. "I love you so much."

They hugged for a long time. When they finally broke the embrace, Dad offered me a weak smile and he and Okaasan walked into the hospital holding hands.

—

Grandpa's people had taken over the area outside the cardiac-care unit, turning the place into a noisy mass of activity. An overweight nurse was yelling at a reporter to get out of the hallway. Two tough-looking men in suits stepped forward and assisted in the reporter's departure. Everyone looked a lot more serious than the last time we were here.

I felt a slight tingle in my neck as I looked around. I got a few dirty looks and saw one guy tap the sleeve of another man and point at me.

When Dad led us into the room, the only part of Grandpa I could see was his arm, pale and wrinkled. Machines surrounded him, and the heart monitor steadily ticked off the beats.

Lin was sitting near the bed, a tissue in her hand. I'd only ever seen her neat and impeccable, but now she looked exhausted, wrung out. She wore no makeup, her long hair was a mess, and she wore an oversize jacket—obviously one of Grandpa's—which she'd pulled tight around herself. She looked dazed, but when she saw us she stood up.

"Excuse me," she whispered as she walked toward the door.

My dad moved aside, but I grabbed her arm.

"You belong here, too, Lin."

She glanced at my parents, unsure what to do. Then she walked back and stood out of the way near the window.

I could see more of Grandpa now, and it wasn't encouraging. Wires and tubes stuck out everywhere, and the skin on his pale face sagged.

"Is he going to be OK?" I asked my dad.

"If anyone can survive, he can."

"Were you with him?" I asked Lin.

Dad shot me a look. "That's none of your business."

"Yes," she said in a low voice. "He was like this when I woke up." She looked out the window and wrapped her arms around herself. "His body felt so cold," she whispered. "I thought he was dead."

Dad cleared his throat. "He's got the best doctors looking after him."

"Can I touch him?" I asked the nurse who was changing his IV.

"For a minute." She was calm, professional, just going through a routine. "It's getting a little crowded in here. Make it quick."

My eyes met hers and she took a step back. I wedged myself between the machines and took Grandpa's hand. It was still far bigger than mine, but so cold and pale. I didn't feel anything from him—no energy, no warmth, nothing. How could a person so energetic and robust, with such a huge personality, end up like this?

I let my breath out. "Come back to us, Grandpa," I said as my eyes slid closed. "Get better and come back to us. We need you here."

There was an explosion of electronic beeps and alarms.

My eyes popped open. The monitors in the room were going crazy, computer screens flickering with horizontal static. A moment later, alarms in the hallway began to ring. I dropped his hand, terrified that he was dying right in front of me. My dad swore and Lin jumped toward the bed, her hand on her mouth.

Okaasan had her hands on her temples.

"What the hell?" the nurse yelled. A moment later, the alarms silenced as the machines began resetting themselves.

"You people need to get out of here!"

I backed away from the bed and faced her. "I want you to give him the best care you've ever given anyone in your career."

As I turned to go, the alarms went off again.

⁓

In the hallway, Okaasan came up beside me. She looked pale and depressed. I took her by the arm and led her to a corner.

"What's wrong?" I asked her in a whisper.

She stared at the floor. "My life was perfect. But the way you reacted ..." She looked up at me. "When he finds out ... he'll leave me."

I grabbed her shoulders. "Okaasan, you said you fell in love with him the moment you saw him. Who cares why you were there? It wasn't a lie—your intentions were pure." As I said it, I knew I believed it.

"Right," she whispered. I saw no hope in her eyes.

I glanced around to make sure no one was listening. "Look, you said there was no need to tell me anything, because none of this was supposed to happen, right?"

She nodded.

"Well, you're right." I gave her my best smile. "Dad's crazy about you. He's one of the happiest married men I know. It serves no purpose to tell him. Let him be happy."

When I walked away, I saw Dad watching us. I gave him a weak smile as I passed by. He reached out and touched my shoulder.

"Did something bad happen in Japan?" He cleared his throat. "I mean … worse than what happened here?"

"Going home … It wasn't what she expected," I said. "I think her family was really hard on her. You should give her another hug."

He stared at me. Then he ran his fingers through his hair. "You're getting to be a lot like your mother, you know that?"

It occurred to me, right then, that while Dad may have had no idea about his wife or her past, he wasn't walking around in a daze either. She was different—and he knew it.

I wandered around, not stopping until I noticed Mark Smith standing by the window at the end of the hall, a solitary silhouette.

"Mr. Smith?"

He turned from the window. "James." He put a hand on my shoulder. "I'm sorry about your grandfather." He turned back to the window and closed his eyes. "I'm sorry. This is way too soon after the last scare." He let out a long sigh. "I told him to take it easy, rest for a while."

I hesitated. I'd always liked Mark, and now I liked him even more.

"Is the company all right?"

He turned back to me. "For the most part, it runs itself," he said. "He worked his usual magic and several hundred million dollars appeared in our account the other day—and he canceled the layoffs, which was a stupid idea in the first place. If you cut staff, service suffers and you end up losing customers and revenue—it's a downward spiral."

I nodded and he gazed back outside for a long time, deep in thought. Finally, he cleared his throat.

"I hate to do this right now," he said, "but I'll need to meet with you and your father—the sooner the better."

I stared up at him. "Why?"

"Even though the Chairman's alive, he's unable to make decisions. That duty falls on his family—and his successor."

CHAPTER
28

Mark Smith sat across from us, looking uncomfortable behind a mountain of paperwork. Three lawyers in expensive suits sat off to the side, looking confident and relaxed.

"Your father's wishes are quite specific about this," Mark said, looking at my dad over his glasses. "If anything happened to him, he wanted you to be granted power of attorney over his personal financial affairs and, of course"—he spread his arms—"the Thompson Group."

My dad looked horrified. "Is this his idea of a sick joke?"

"Come on, Robert." Mark removed his glasses. "You're his son. Even if this makes you uncomfortable—"

"This is crazy!" My dad pushed back from the table and walked to the window. I felt sorry for him. We'd already been to the hospital that morning—no change. Grandpa looked as pale and fragile as he had the day before.

"What about you?" Dad turned back to Mark. "Can't you run things?"

"I am," Mark said, a hint of frustration in his voice. "I handle day-to-day operations, and the departments have their own management teams—they don't need anything from you. But your father ... his hands are in everything. You'll need to sign off on major expenditures—and there's his personal stock portfolio to consider."

Dad stared at the ground.

Mark sighed and plunged ahead. "And you need to go to Brussels right away."

"What?!"

"During that stock-market crash, he bought a controlling share of a minor European bank. There are papers to sign." Mark stood up. "I'll go with you, of course."

I lowered my eyes and wondered if Grandpa had caused the crash so he could buy it cheap.

"We *need* that financing, Robert," Mark said. "If the papers aren't signed this week, the Thompson Bayview Complex dies forever—"

"I don't give a damn about some office tower!"

"It could take the whole company down with it." Mark joined my dad at the window and laid a hand on his shoulder. "I'm sorry. This is a tough time for everyone, but your father spent ten years on the Bayview project. We can't let him down."

"Right." Dad didn't sound convinced, but he sat back down. One of the lawyers slid a stack of papers in front of him.

Mark sat down across from me as Dad started signing. "I'm sorry about all this, James," he said.

"So why am I here, Mr. Smith?"

"Call me Mark, OK?" He tapped the table with his pen. "The Chairman's legal papers reiterate what he announced on your birthday: you're the sole heir to the Thompson Group. And I know he expected you to help with the company, even if still underage—"

Dad slapped his pen down. "That's crazy!"

I glanced at Mark. He looked like he was about to say something but just shrugged.

After what I'd said to Grandpa, did he still want me to be here? I opened my mind and listened to the stream. I felt a gentle wash of reassurance.

"It's OK, Dad." I smiled. "Grandpa's been preparing me for this my whole life—and besides, Mark's still the boss."

"Actually ..." Mark cleared his throat. "That's a little unclear at the moment. Walter's been throwing his weight around."

My stomach sank.

Mark held his breath for a moment. "I work *with* Walter but not *for* him," he said, "so if Edward doesn't ... if he doesn't come back to work ... I'll resign. I can't stand by and watch Walter destroy everything your grandfather built."

I shook my head. "That's not going to happen—"

"Just work it out," Dad said. "I don't want to deal with this."

Just then, Walter Roacks walked in, his smile as thin as the pinstripes on his suit. "I know this is quite a burden your father dumped on you, Robert."

Dad nodded. "I've never wanted this—ever."

Walter smiled, but it looked like a grimace. "I understand that more than *some* do." He shot a sideways glance at Mark. "Fortunately, it doesn't have to be this way."

There it was—that tingling in the back of my neck. I sat up straight.

"Really?" my dad said, looking relieved. "I just don't have time to go to Brussels."

"Robert," Mark said, "what Walter's suggesting is practical, but it's contrary to your father's wishes."

Dad glared at Mark. "Maybe I'm a little tired of hearing about my father's wishes."

There was a brief, tense silence.

Walter nodded at one of the lawyers, who stood and handed my dad a single sheet of paper. Walter held out a pen. "All you need to do is sign right here."

As my dad's hand hovered over the page, I watched Walter. I remembered the night at the restaurant when Lin and I had seen Walter with Mr. Müller—who worked for Bartholomew.

All of a sudden I realized this was way bigger than Walter Roacks's wanting control of the company.

"Do it." Walter said it quietly. "Then you're free of this. You can go back to your woodworking, your wife."

"Do you even know what you're signing?" Mark said. "You should at least get legal counsel—"

"These men are company lawyers, Mr. Smith!" Walter said. "I think we can trust them."

I tapped the tabletop with my pen and cleared my throat. To my surprise, everyone turned.

"Actually," I said, "I haven't heard any advice from them at all. What does that paper do?" I directed my question at the lawyers. "Does it affect ownership?"

The oldest of the three straightened his tie. "It doesn't affect ownership *per se*, but it does move all financial control into Mr. Roacks's hands—"

"You're signing the goddamn company over to him!" Mark shouted.

Walter spun toward Mark. "Did you tell them you plan to resign if you aren't in control?"

Mark glared. "It's not like that."

Walter looked at my dad. "I need freedom to operate until Edward returns. There's no harm here. Edward's still the owner. Nothing can change that."

"Unless Edward doesn't come back." Mark stood up. "Who's in control then?"

Walter ignored him. "If your father dies—God forbid—do you want to run this company, Robert?"

"You can have it all, as far as I'm concerned."

Walter smiled. "Well, in that case—"

"No!" I stood so fast my chair toppled backward. I turned to my dad. "This company's not yours to give away!" Then I pointed at Walter. "And it's not yours to take!"

Dad stared at me and slowly put the pen down.

I turned to the lawyers. "My father will sign the original power-of-attorney papers, but that's all. And I want you to draw up a document giving me, under the supervision of my father, the authority to sign on his behalf."

The room was dead silent. Mark's eyes were wide, but Walter looked like he was about to choke on something.

"I thought you didn't want this," Dad said.

"I changed my mind."

He studied me for a long moment. "It always scared me how much like my father you were. If you really want this, ... just tell me what to sign and I'll do it."

I nodded and turned to Mark. "I need you here to run things, both now and in the future. I can't have you quitting on me now." I paused. "And you're both going to Brussels to get that money."

Both Mark and my dad looked surprised, but they nodded. I wished I could be sure they agreed of their own free will.

"You're fools!" Walter yelled. "I'm doing everything I can to keep this company afloat and you're signing its death warrant."

"Nothing has changed." I said, meeting his gaze. "It's exactly the same as if the Chairman were here, right?" Then I leaned toward him across the table and gave him my best stare—the one Okaasan reserved for when I was really in trouble. "And incidentally, I'm not impressed by how *afloat* you're keeping us."

"What?" Walter's eyes widened.

"I want you to understand this clearly. Mark is your boss, and from now on you don't do *anything* without his approval."

Looking as if he might implode, Walter stormed from the room and slammed the door behind him.

"How was that?" I asked Mark.

He managed a half-smile. "He still holds the purse strings."

"Then we'd better do something to change that." I turned to the three lawyers. "Fix this, and remember who you work for. As of now, this company is mine."

—

I left Dad in the conference room with Mark and the lawyers. I felt like I might throw up. I didn't want the goddamn company, but if Walter Roacks had something to do with Bartholomew, I couldn't just hand it over to him.

After I made two phone calls, I headed toward Grandpa's office, hoping to have a moment of peace, maybe sit in his big chair and absorb some of his energy—and some clue to what the hell I should do next.

Lin was at her desk outside the Chairman's office.

"Hi, Lin."

She wiped her nose with a tissue and tossed it onto the pile in her wastebasket.

"Hello, Junya." She was back in her usual high heels and business suit, but her makeup couldn't hide the state she was in.

I pointed toward the office. "I'm going in here for a bit. Will you come, please?"

She looked down as if examining her French manicure. "If that's what you want."

I didn't sit in his chair. Instead, I sank onto the leather sofa. Lin sat in the stiff-backed leather chair across from me, her knees clamped tight together, her hands folded on her lap. It felt odd being here with her like this, like some crazy role-reversal had occurred.

"I'm sorry about what you've had to go through ..." My words dropped away, meaningless, because I had no idea what she'd gone through.

She gave me a strained smile. "I'm sorry, too. I know how much you care for him."

There—why hadn't I said something like that?

"Was there any more trouble after I left for Japan?"

She looked up. "Like what?"

"Where do I start? The company's going broke, Grandpa's bodyguards tried to kill me, and let's not forget about Walter and Mr. Müller."

It took a while for her to answer. "The Chairman's been worried about Walter, but ... he's changed." She stared at the floor. "He doesn't trust anyone. I think that's why he got so upset with me that night."

"What did you do?"

The eyes that met mine were less friendly than they'd been a minute ago. "It's what *you* did. You opened his safe, betrayed his trust, then you destroyed him with your words." She glared. "It's like the fire inside him went out that night."

I closed my eyes, but I'd rather have closed my ears. Her words felt like a kick in the gut and my anger rose, faster than before—always coming faster now. For a moment, I wanted to hurt her, but the wave of anguish I felt from her ended that.

"He was under so much stress that night, more than usual," she said, her tone no longer accusing. "Something about missing accounting files—dozens of boxes had vanished. When he refused to talk to me, I went outside to get some air." She sucked in a breath. "A while later, he came to find me." She was struggling to speak. "He found me in Sugimoto-san's workshop ... We were only talking, but maybe we looked suspicious. Edward looked so—so betrayed."

"Why were you with Mr. Sugimoto?"

She shrugged. "Sometimes it's nice to talk with someone familiar, you know? Someone who understands how lonely it can be when you've left everything you know far away."

"I know what you mean," I said, but there was something bothering me, some thought trying to surface in my mind. I looked back up to find her staring at me.

"You're different since you got back," she said. "The way you look, talk, even the way you move."

I gave her a half-smile. "It was quite the trip." Then I stood and walked over to her. "May I see your hands?"

She looked up at me, confused, but she held them out. I took them in mine and turned them over, examining them. They were slender and beautiful, manicured and pampered, not worn by hard physical training like Okaasan's.

Lin giggled, but it had a nervous edge. "Are you a palm-reader now?"

I didn't answer, because I couldn't—there was so much energy flowing between us I could barely stay upright. She looked up and our eyes met. I dropped her hands.

"I don't know your last name," I said.

"Sota."

Her dark eyes followed me as I backed away. She was about to say something when her phone rang, startling us both. She ran to her desk and pounced on the phone. Her eyes came to rest on me as she listened to the caller. A moment later she hung up.

"That was Mr. Barrymore. He's assembled all the security teams, as you requested." She cocked her head and frowned, her right index finger tapping the desktop. "What're you up to?"

I grinned. "I'm going to kick some ass."

She gave me a little smile, amused, maybe even impressed, but I couldn't go yet. I stood in front of her desk and stared at her, feeling her energy.

"What?" she said.

"Are you in love with Edward?"

Her eyes narrowed. "That's none of your damn business!"

I walked to the elevator and punched the "down" button. I winked at her as the doors slid open.

Her eyes went wide.

I stepped backward into the elevator, twirling a pen I'd stolen from her desk.

"I'm sorry, Lin, but I've gotta know—" I flicked the pen toward her, low and hard, like a throwing star.

She snatched it out of the air as it sailed past while her other hand reached up and pulled a long thin pin from her hair.

"Nice catch, kunoichi." I took in a deep breath. "Sorry. That was mean." My voice was somber now. "I'm really happy Grandpa has someone that loves him, especially now." I managed a smile. "Please, go to the hospital. Protect him."

Her face and energy betrayed everything she was feeling. "But—"

"Go to Edward. That's an order."

The doors slid closed.

CHAPTER
29

THE SECURITY BRIEFING ROOM, nicknamed the Bunker, was in the basement of the Thompson Building. When I walked in, about five dozen tough-looking men and women faced me, some sitting, others leaning against the walls.

I stood at the front of the room and scanned the faces. The most common expression was boredom, but I also spotted dislike and a dash of hatred.

The room grew quiet. I let the silence take over while I took in a deep breath and tuned in to the stream.

Mr. Barrymore sat on the edge of a table, his suit jacket pulled open, his face a professional mask of disinterested alertness.

"This isn't everyone," I said.

"These are the bodyguard and surveillance teams," he said, pointing a pen at each cluster of people. "The regular uniformed security guards aren't part of this unit."

I scanned the crowd again. "Which one of you is Johnny?" I asked, raising my voice so that it would reach the back.

A man with graying hair stepped away from the wall. "That'd be me," he said, his arms folded.

I tried to feel his energy, but I couldn't get a fix on him, not with so many people in the room.

"It's good to put a face to a voice," I said. "That was a big Doberman, huh?"

He looked startled for a millisecond. "It … I got bit by my neighbor's dog."

I hopped up to sit on the table, not far from Mr. Barrymore. Unlike his, my feet didn't reach the floor. I glanced at him and wondered what kind of support I could expect.

"Let's talk about last Wednesday evening."

There was an outbreak of murmurs, but Mr. Barrymore shut them down with a look. When it was quiet again, I turned to him.

"Tell me what you've found out."

He ran a hand over his buzz cut. "Two of my guys—who were off duty—got into an altercation with a bunch of drunks outside a bar. Both ended up in the hospital, along with three of the drunks." Then he looked out at his officers. "And contrary to the rumors, I didn't fire them. Steve and Mike resigned."

"They weren't on duty?"

"No." Mr. Barrymore didn't look pleased at all. "None of the injured men were on duty."

"And how many got hurt?"

Mr. Barrymore thought for a moment. "Ten, counting Johnny's dog bite. One guy's still missing. We presume he took off."

I nodded and tried to remain expressionless. Did he mean the man Shoko had killed?

I realized I was staring, and the longer I did, the more uncomfortable everyone began to look.

"Does anyone know why those men were out there?" Mr. Barrymore said.

Silence. Then someone at the back stood up—Anthony Roacks. "I called them out."

"Aren't you from *accounting*?" Mr. Barrymore practically choked on the word.

Anthony scowled. "That was temporary. My uncle's put me in charge of his personal security."

Mr. Barrymore laughed. "And what does Uncle Walter's office boy know about security?"

Anthony hesitated. A few of the guys around him made faces. "Walter asked me to bring in extra men that night."

"Why?" Mr. Barrymore asked.

Anthony shrugged. "Mr. Roacks doesn't need to explain anything to you. What matters is that when my men heard Steve and Mike were getting beat on, they moved in to help—and he"—Anthony pointed at me—"nearly killed them."

"So Steve and Mike were working for you?" I said.

Anthony hesitated again. "They work for the company."

"And what about the rest of the guys who chased me?"

"Why don't you tell us?" Anthony raised his voice. "You all know what he did to your buddies!"

A woman near the front spoke up. "I heard he had a sword."

There was muttering in the room.

"That's right," Anthony said, sounding more confident. "He attacked them, just like he did with Steve and Mike!"

Beside me, Mr. Barrymore cleared his throat. "I'm confused," he said. "How did these men of yours know where James was?"

No one answered.

"Who else was part of Walter Roacks's personal security team that night?"

A group at the back, all those near Anthony, put up their hands, although they looked reluctant. They were all new guys, the ex-soldiers. I did the math, but Mr. Barrymore beat me.

"So counting the men who ended up in the hospital, you had *sixteen men* out there? We don't even put sixteen men on the Chairman!"

"What I use *my* people for is none of your damn business!"

"It *is* my business!" Mr. Barrymore bellowed, which caused everyone to jump. "You used my men to attack James!"

Anthony took a deep breath. "Prove it."

The crowd began to break into two groups. I noticed that Johnny stayed on our side.

"Your little stint as security chief just ended," I said to Anthony, my fists clenched at my sides. "Now get off my property!"

—

I interviewed every member of the security service, even the office staff. Those who were loyal to Grandpa—based on the energy they emitted—stayed. I fired those who weren't. By the time I was done, Mr. Barrymore had lost over a third of his staff, including Johnny.

Afterward, we headed up to his plush twenty-first floor office.

"So what's your system for testing loyalty?" he said, not looking happy. "You flip a coin?"

I sat in his office chair—not my choice, actually. He'd chosen to sit on the sofa across the room, in front of a window. I had to squint to see his expression. I wondered if he'd done that on purpose.

"I'm weeding out the cancer, Mr. Barrymore." I leaned back and stared at him. "Do you have a problem with any of the decisions I made?"

He shook his head. I felt his anger, but there was sadness there, too, and guilt. It was his responsibility to protect the Chairman, but he couldn't. That was up to the doctors and the gods now.

"How'd you allow this to happen?" I said.

His head snapped up, eyes flaring. "Oh, so it's my turn now, is it?" He stood up. "Fine. I was delinquent in my duties, and as I told the Chairman, I take full responsibility for this matter." He shook his head. "This place has gone to hell anyhow."

I sighed. "Relax, OK? Please, sit down."

And he did. We remained quiet for a while, each of us lost in thought.

"To tell you the truth," he said after a while, "I've had my suspicions ever since those new guys arrived—little things, stuff I couldn't put my finger on, you know? But Johnny recruited them, and I always thought he was solid. But like I told the Chairman, I just don't have time to supervise all of them." He stretched his arms wide. "Besides the close protection teams, surveillance teams, and the building security force, I'm also overseeing a goddamn intelligence service here. I may be the chief, but the new influx of employees—it was too much. I work sixty hours a week as it is."

"Why does Grandpa need an intelligence service?"

Mr. Barrymore sighed and put his arm on the back of the sofa.

"It's for business," he said after a minute. "We've got wiretaps, surveillance, paid sources inside companies all around the world. It's quite sophisticated."

I frowned. "Isn't that illegal?"

"Only if you get caught." He flashed a grin. "The Chairman likes to know what his competitors are up to. He learned that when he first started the business. He'd hire taxi drivers, waiters, bell hops, anyone who had access to information."

"What information does a taxi driver have?"

"See?" He wagged a finger at me. "That's what everybody thinks. We talk in front of these people like they're not there—the invisible service providers, overlooked and ignored. It was an amazing idea—still is."

I tried to think about what Lin and I had talked about on our taxi ride. "And all the bodyguards?"

"That's a different matter," Mr. Barrymore said, his voice guarded now. "No one's ever attacked him, never threatened him either, other than the usual hate mail and a few wacky protesters. He does need security, but three or four guys would be enough. Right now we're kitted out like an army."

I leaned forward. "But why?"

"My guess, he's scared of something—and I think it's Bartholomew." Mr. Barrymore shook his head. "Who, by the way, my intelligence people can't prove exists. And I don't know what he keeps inside that safe." He raised an eyebrow. "Maybe I should ask you?"

I put my feet up on his desk. He glared at me until I dropped them back to the floor. "You ever see Bartholomew?" I asked as I brushed the marks off the desktop.

He nodded. "Once or twice, back in the old days. He was still part of the Committee then, came for the meetings. And his body-guards ..." He paused and stared at the wall behind me. "Those guys were something else." I felt a chill. If what Shoko and Okaasan had told me was true, they were something else all right—something far from human.

"What'd you think about Anthony?" I said.

He rolled his eyes. "Anthony Roacks is a spoiled jerk. He's full of bluster, but he's got nothing to back it up except his uncle. I guess him using our guys as thugs shouldn't surprise me."

His eyes met mine. There was that guilt again.

I nodded. "At first I thought it was a kidnapping, or at least a forced ride home, but then they got so violent ... I heard them say they had orders from the *old man*." A short silence ensued. "Why haven't there been any arrests?"

"The police found empty shells, lots of blood, but there's no wit-nesses—or victims. They figure it's the start of a gang war."

I sat for a moment staring into space, trying to put things together. "I know Walter wasn't happy about me being named as Grandpa's successor ... but do you really think he tried to have me killed?"

"I don't think he's that stupid," Mr. Barrymore said. "But the Chairman did order me to follow Walter and tap his phones. He thought Walter was acting odd, a little too defensive about the money situation. Why would you fire your accounting staff in the middle of a financial crisis? And then there was that alleged meeting with Mr. Müller you told him about."

He stood and rolled his shoulders. "Of course, we weren't mak-ing much progress with the investigation. Probably because most of the people I'd assigned to the task were the ones you fired today. I suspect they weren't working too hard."

I suddenly felt exhausted. "So what should we do?" I asked.

"We need to start a forensic audit of all the accounts. That's out of my league, but I know a couple of experts here in San Francisco—old colleagues. I'll keep going with the Walter investigation, but I'll add Anthony, too." He frowned at me. "And we need to make sure you're safe."

"I'll handle my own security."

He studied me. "Yes, she's quite the bodyguard. Who is she anyway?"

I hesitated. "I can't tell you."

He nodded slowly. "Did she kill that man in Lower Pacific Heights?"

Hesitating, I couldn't meet his eyes. "I thought you said one of your men ran away."

"There was no connection to us, so no one knew anything … except me. I'm inclined to leave it that way." He ran a hand over his buzz cut. "I wish the Chairman were here. This is gonna blow up, and soon."

"We have to do it without him for now."

"Won't be easy. Mark Smith isn't interested in security stuff, and Mr. Roacks has a lot of power here."

I was instantly angry. "Mr. Roacks was demoted an hour ago, and I made damn sure he knew that Mark's the president!"

His mouth puckered. "Walter isn't going to like that."

"I'll worry about that. You just find out what's going on. Oh, and send two guys to Brussels with my dad and Mark Smith."

Mr. Barrymore didn't move.

"What are you waiting for?"

His eyebrows rose. "You're a lot like your grandfather, right down to the yelling." He chuckled. "Yes, sir, I'll get right on it."

"Very good, Mr. Barrymore," I said, lowering my voice to a growl, imitating Grandpa. "That's more like it."

CHAPTER
30

MR. BARRYMORE GAVE ME A RIDE home in his company car, a gray four-door sedan with an array of antennae on the roof and trunk—when I first saw it I thought it was an unmarked police car. But the inside was something else: leather seats, plush carpet, power everything, and a kick-ass aftermarket sound system. Not such a bad deal, working for Edward Thompson.

It was getting dark, with gray clouds hanging low over the city and a light rain falling as we emerged from the underground garage. A river of black umbrellas flowed down the sidewalks, away from the financial district. I stared out the window and sighed. My eyelids grew heavy and eventually slid closed.

I knew I'd done the right thing today—I'd kept the company out of Walter's hands. But I was worried. Today hadn't been a spur-of-the-moment power grab—the lawyers were there, the paperwork already drawn up. Walter must have been planning this for a while.

I opened my eyes to see the last rays of daylight shining through the clouds. I pulled the visor down to block it out, but when I caught my reflection in the vanity mirror, I froze.

"What's wrong?" Mr. Barrymore asked.

Dark eyes stared right through me. I looked away, but I forced myself to turn back. The face—my face—was still there. Those eyes had gazed toward the top of the Izumo shrine and into the eyes of Shoko. They looked different ... powerful.

"Nothing."

I glanced in the mirror again. They were my new eyes and I liked them.

—

We saw nothing suspicious, no surveillance vans or occupied cars, when Mr. Barrymore dropped me off at home. Still, I felt something dark and menacing, like the storm clouds above us. I couldn't pin it down.

The house was dark when I walked in, no smells of dinner cooking. Tama ambled down the hall toward me, looking bleary-eyed and disheveled. She meowed and rubbed against my leg and sauntered into the kitchen toward her food dish. I followed her, heading toward my own food dish—the cookie jar—and found a note on the counter.

Okaasan had gone to see Dad off at the airport and wouldn't be home until later. I grabbed a handful of cookies and headed to my bedroom.

While I waited for my laptop to power up, I thought about Walter. He'd shown his true colors today, and he obviously didn't think Grandpa was coming back.

I was fuming when Tama strolled into my room. She looked at me with her bored cat expression and headed straight for my legs. I reached down, lifted her onto my lap, and stroked her back for a minute before I started to laugh, realizing I looked like some crazy movie villain. I rubbed her fuzzy chin. Her purrs vibrated through my body and my anger began to subside.

My thoughts wandered—from Grandpa's announcement on my birthday to the way Walter had looked at me, then to Lin and how she'd smelled when she kissed me. My thoughts lingered on Lin for a while, and then I thought of the day Shoko had stolen the journal.

I opened my eyes and sat up straight, knocking Tama to the floor. She let out a meow of indignation. Something about Grandpa's office ... specifically his desk.

Passwords! I still remembered the passwords on that yellow sticky note.

It felt good to touch a keyboard again, something I understood. A minute later, I was inside his account on the Thompson Group's network. I wasn't sure what I'd find, but I needed more information—about the company, about everything.

I spotted a dull-looking paper-and-pencil icon and clicked. It opened what looked like accounts, showing financial transactions, with more numbers and commas than I'd ever seen together. I rested my elbows on the desk and stared at the screen, scrolling at full speed until the numbers started to melt together. The evidence of what Walter was up to—what he'd *been* up to—was probably right in front of me, but I knew as much about accounting as a turnip did.

I stood up and paced, treading a path from my doorway to my bed, trying to get my thoughts together.

I needed to find out what Walter was plotting. If I could get into his e-mail, I was sure I'd find what I needed. But cracking into the corporate computers would be a nightmare—way beyond my skill level—and Grandpa's security department would track me down in minutes.

Besides, I doubted Walter would keep any records at the office, and from what Lin had said, he'd packed all the paper records into that van and made them disappear while Mack and I enjoyed the baseball game. But Walter was bound to have a computer at home, and getting into that wouldn't be a challenge at all.

But getting *to* his computer was another matter. Walter lived in a penthouse apartment. To get in there, I'd need to be some kind of ...

Ninja.

I logged out of Grandpa's account and shut off the screen. Outside, the rain had stopped. I'd just finished calling Shoko, asking her to help me later, when I felt someone coming—Okaasan.

When I strolled into the kitchen, she was struggling to close the door with her foot, her arms loaded with grocery bags. I took two bags from her and peered inside.

"I didn't know you were home," she said, sounding annoyed. "You're getting good at hiding your energy."

"Yeah? I felt you coming a block away."

Her eyes narrowed. "Then why didn't you get off your lazy butt and come help me?"

—

While Okaasan unloaded the groceries, I told her what had happened at the office. Her mood grew darker the more I talked.

I frowned. "What's wrong?"

She turned to me, holding a cabbage in her hand like a basketball. "Your father already told me what happened." She didn't look impressed. "You're trying to fill very big shoes and you made a powerful enemy today."

"Walter was already the enemy. I'm not worried about him."

"A log can block a creek but not a river. You don't know what's coming. Don't get overconfident."

"Walter's trying to take the company. I can't sit back and do nothing."

She gave me a look as she pulled some strange root out of the bag. "Are you sure that's what he's doing?"

"It's obvious." I shook my head. "And Dad almost gave it to him. If it wasn't for me ..." I stopped as a cloud of disappointment moved across her face.

"Please tell me you didn't use your energy on him. He never would have gone to Brussels otherwise."

My gaze dropped to the floor. "I didn't force him to do anything." Had I?

She sat down and stared at the table, not saying anything. I glanced around the kitchen, at the groceries still on the counter, then back at Okaasan.

"Your father's spent his whole life trying to stay away." Her voice was so quiet I had to strain to hear her. "You understand that?"

"You're talking about Grandpa and maybe Bartholomew, though," I said. "Not the business itself ... right?"

She stood up. "They're one and the same." Her voice was strained. "Damn it, Junya, you just put him right into the middle of it!"

I let out a deep sigh. "He just needs to sign a few papers in Brussels, then every once in a while when he's back. He doesn't have to even go the office."

"Junya—"

"No, Mom! It's not just about the business and it's not just about Dad. If we save the company, we stop Bartholomew. Grandpa will finally be free of him." I pointed at her. "I'm going to find out what Walter's up to—tonight—and Mr. Barrymore's looking into the accounting. We got this buttoned down."

"How can you possibly have this *buttoned down*?" She was angry now. "You don't even know who tried to kill you."

"It was Walter."

"Can you prove it?" When I didn't reply, she crossed her arms. "You pulled your father into this, but no one knows what *this is*!"

I heaved a huge sigh. "I need to focus on what I understand, and that's getting into Walter's computer."

—

Okasan threw a meal together in about ten minutes, some meat-and-vegetable thing over rice, and I gulped it down, eager to get started on my clandestine operation. I was clearing the dishes off the table when I felt a disturbance in the earth's energy. A long moment later, Okaasan jumped to her feet.

"Took you long enough," I said.

She gave me a look. "You've been oblivious for the last sixteen years and now you're an expert?" She pointed at the stack of dishes. "I'll go meet Shoko. Wash the pots!"

I was up to my elbows in soap bubbles, grumbling under my breath and wondering if there was some way to travel the pots somewhere, when Shoko strolled into the kitchen.

"This house is amazing!" She pointed at the skylights. "I can see the sky!" She was dressed in skinny black jeans and a tight-fitting T-shirt. Her only accessories were her silver ring and a black hair band, holding her hair in a high ponytail. A black jacket completed the look.

"Wow!" I tried not to stare. "You look great!"

"Thank you," she said and her cheeks reddened. "I had a friend help me buy them." She moved closer. "I did not expect you to be useful around the house."

I flicked a wad of soap bubbles at her before rinsing the last pot.

"Okaasan works me like a horse." I tried to sound grumpy, but I was happy to see her. "Thanks for coming."

She tilted her head to the side and looked at me. An uncomfortable silence settled over us. There were things we needed to talk about, but I didn't have a clue how to start. From the look on her face, I figured she felt it, too, but she wasn't ready to say anything either. Our thoughts—and our feelings—would remain unspoken, at least for now.

She broke the silence. "I felt no distress when you called."

"Do I need a reason to call you?"

"You always have before."

I sighed. "We're going to break into someone's house. We can be sneaky like ninja."

She brightened. "That sounds fun … in a silly sort of way."

"You're not going anywhere until I make sure those pots are clean," Okaasan said as she strode in from the hallway.

"They're clean," I grumbled and turned back to Shoko. "We're going to Walter's apartment. I need to get inside his computer."

"Really? Then why do I need to rewash them half the time?" Okaasan said, hands on hips.

"Why don't you do them yourself and save all the trouble?"

Shoko poked my arm. "What is a computer? Will we both fit inside it?"

Okaasan and I stared at her. Then Okaasan started to laugh.

"We'll be OK," I said.

Shoko didn't look impressed with our laughter, but my thoughts were back on my plan, on what software I needed and how we'd get to the tenth floor of Walter's apartment building.

"Do you have any climbing gear?" I asked Okaasan.

"I have a few things … from long ago."

"Can you get Shoko set up? I need to load my memory stick."

"Do not bother yourself, Misako-san." Shoko glared across the kitchen at me. "If you want to climb, go ahead. I will meet you at the top."

—

It was late when Shoko and I left the house and walked to the dojo. The air had a heavy, close feeling, and the damp seeped through my jacket, chilling my body. The rain was holding off, but the low clouds looked heavy.

Shoko carried her school bag slung over the shoulder of her new jacket. I hadn't brought much, only a small pack with a few computer tools and a memory stick. I'd done all I could think of to prepare. Walter's apartment was near Nobb Hill—Snob Hill I liked to call it—about a thirty-minute bus ride away. I'd studied a map online, checked the street-view images, and found a small park across from his building that looked promising—a patch of grass with enough shrubs and trees to give us a place to hide.

As we knelt side by side on the tatami mats, our eyes met. The soft glow of the house lights illuminated Shoko's face. My chest clenched and I felt a flush come over me. I had to look away.

Her hand touched mine. "You are troubled?"

"No." I kept my gaze on the mats. "It's just that …" *I really like you and I'd love to take you out after we finish up tonight. I know this great pizza place near the library that's open late, a real Italian place, and the owner uses a real brick oven. Would you like to go with me?* "I'm a bit nervous, that's all."

She nodded and moved her hand away. "Then let's begin." She was all business now. "I need you to view our destination and feel if it is safe."

"I can't do that."

"You must. Focus, Junya, see it in your mind."

I closed my eyes, focused on my breathing, and tried to push thoughts of Shoko out of my head. I pictured the park and let my mind clear. I saw the street-view picture in my head, but—

"Use less energy," Shoko said in a strained voice. "Let the Mother Earth do the work. Go there, feel the energy. Try to *see* what is there."

I tried again, but there was nothing, only the usual noise in my brain. I sighed.

"This is important, Junya," she said, sounding a bit annoyed. "We cannot appear like a gopher from his hole."

I was about to give up when I felt the energy of Mother Earth seep up through the tatami and into my body. A distorted image began to form in my mind. A moment later, I was in the park—at least a part of me was. The air swirled around me like mist. Through it I saw a thermal image of shapes and energy—warm red and orange shapes and the cool greens and blues of the earth. Above me, a bird rested in a nest, three warm eggs beneath it. Near the fence, a cat stalked through the bushes behind a smaller orange shape that moved ahead of it, unaware.

Two people, a mix of glowing orange and red, passed by on the sidewalk. I could have reached out and touched them. Would they have felt me, or I them? I waited until they were gone to open my eyes. "That's amazing!"

"If you believe it, you can do it. Nothing is impossible." She was smiling. "It is safe there?"

"I think so." I suddenly felt drained and emotional. "It's quiet."

Shoko's eyebrows came together. "What is it?"

"I just feel so strange." I paused, trying to find the right words. "Since I got back, I've been so caught up in all this business crap. I feel so far away from Izumo ... from the gods."

Shoko looked confused. "The energy of the gods is always with us. It is not an afterthought—it is *the* thought."

I took her hand. "Let's go."

CHAPTER
31

WHEN WE APPEARED IN THE PARK, it was nothing like what I'd seen with my energy. The light from street lamps flooded across the dew-covered grass, sparkling in the light. It might have been a beautiful sight at any other time, but now we were in the open, exposed.

We both dived into the shadows but in different directions.

I glanced over at Shoko. She was behind a small bush, peering out at the street. Unlike me, she looked calm, but I caught the glint of light on steel—she'd drawn her wakizashi. She ran across the grass, bent low, and dropped down next to me.

"Next time," she whispered, "pick a hiding spot *before* you travel."

"You didn't tell me that," I whispered back.

"It is common sense."

I turned to her, ready to argue, but she was smiling.

"Being with you is always interesting," she said. "Every moment is an adventure."

I looked across the street, suppressing a smile. Walter's apartment building wasn't new but it looked well-kept and tidy, luxury evident even from the outside. The doorman, dressed in a long red jacket and black cap, stood outside the glass lobby doors, watching and waiting. A dozen expensive cars lined the curb in front of him. Through the glass, I saw two men in dark suits sitting on a sofa in the lobby. They looked familiar and I closed my eyes, reaching out, trying to sense something from them, but I felt nothing.

I pulled binoculars from my pack, a pair of decent Nikons I'd grabbed from Dad's camping gear. I studied the men and felt a knot tighten in my stomach: they were two of the men I'd fired this morning.

"They found a new job pretty quick," I muttered.

I got a yawn in reply and I turned to Shoko. She sat cross-legged on the grass, looking bored.

"Are we going to sit here all night?" she said. "My new pants are getting wet."

"There're guards in the lobby," I whispered. "We'll have to be careful."

"Those men are nothing."

I sighed. Everything had been so clear back at home but out here, I was losing confidence fast and she wasn't helping. "Can we travel straight up to his suite?"

"Do you even know what awaits us inside? You want to be stealthy, but if I have to cut someone down—"

"I don't want you to kill anyone!"

"Then do what you did in the dojo and see what's up there. Do I need to explain everything?"

"Look, I'm not very good at this."

"I know nothing about the limits you have placed on yourself."

I sighed and closed my eyes. I thought of Walter's apartment, thought of him, thought of where I wanted to land, but nothing came to me. I opened my eyes and glanced around. With the park, I'd had an image to get me started, the aerial and street views, but with the apartment, I had nothing.

"I'm not getting anything. What should we do?"

She shook her head. "Perhaps you can tell me what we are doing, besides going inside some computer thing."

I squatted on the grass beside her and she listened while I

explained what I knew about Walter and what I intended to do. She nodded and occasionally grunted, all the while staring at me with those big dark eyes of hers. And then a smile spread across her face.

"What?"

She started to giggle. "You sound like my brother, Toro, planning an adventure in the forest. It is so cute!" She fell backward and lay there laughing.

"Shhh."

She nodded and covered her mouth. "OK, we are going to go in there, sneaky like ninja. You are going to enter a computer and do … something." She paused. "And I will kill anyone I see." She started to laugh again.

"Shoko, be serious." I already felt like abandoning this crazy mission and going for pizza. I shook my head and tried to regain my focus. "Let's travel to the balcony first. I'll try to feel for Walter from there."

"Yes, sir." She giggled.

I glared at her.

"OK, OK." She put her wakizashi away.

I took one more look at the top-floor balcony, imagining us there. She grasped my hand and I squeezed it, glad this was a necessary part of traveling. A moment later, we were on his balcony.

I was peering into the dark suite when I noticed the change: the warmth and energy of the earth was gone. I glanced up at Shoko to see if she'd noticed, but she was cupping her hands against the glass, trying to see inside.

"Um, Shoko … how far above the ground does the earth's energy reach?"

She turned to look at me and shrugged. "Its energy reaches through anything that is still a part of her. Why?"

I touched the cold reinforced concrete, saw the steel and glass railing, the metal patio furniture. "Because I don't feel her anymore."

She frowned. "That's interesting," she said and turned to look into the suite again.

I peered through the railing, ten stories to the street below. "So we can't travel in or back down?"

"Perhaps we will find something inside that still has some of her energy left in it."

"I didn't plan to break in," I said as I dug into my backpack. There was nothing useful in there, only a small set of computer tools. What I needed was a hammer.

Shoko grabbed the handle and slid the glass door open.

Great. Next time I needed a hammer, I could just use my head—it wasn't much good for anything else.

A faint sound—three electronic beeps—registered in my brain.

"Shoko, stop!" I froze, waiting for the wail of the alarm.

"What is that?" she asked, her tone higher than usual now, sounding more than just curious. She was pointing at a red light on the wall.

"Motion detector," I whispered, feeling another shot of adrenaline. It was glowing red, sensing our movements and body temperature. I pulled myself together and ran to the front door. The alarm panel had to be there—and it was—but the lights were green.

Shoko came up beside me and I pointed to the green LEDs.

"It's not turned on," I said. Walter had only the door chime turned on.

"What is it?"

"It's an alarm system. It detects intruders and rings a loud bell."

"There is a magic eye, too."

"Magic eye?" I peered over her shoulder. A small monitor displayed an alternating view of the elevator doors, the hallway outside and the lobby downstairs. The guards down there looked bored—one was lying on the sofa. Obviously no silent alarms were ringing.

"Do you think he has other ... things to see inside here, like in Edward's study?"

"I doubt it."

I looked around. I'd somehow imagined outdated furniture and yellowing wallpaper, maybe even a velvet painting of dogs playing poker. Now I wondered if I'd broken into the wrong apartment.

The glow of the city lights illuminated the room enough to see his ultra-modern suite, minimalist with strange steel and leather furniture and chrome lighting. Several large paintings, abstracts with geometric shapes and bright colors—the kind that looked like a kid had painted them—hung in the hall and the living room. And the kitchen was right out of a magazine, sleek and commercial, with stainless steel counters and glossy red cabinets.

Shoko rubbed her shoe on the floor and took a tentative step toward the windows. "It is like walking on a pond," she whispered as she tiptoed across the smooth, polished concrete.

—

We found an office down the hallway, past the kitchen—a spacious corner room with large windows and the same polished concrete floors. The desk was a thick slab of glass, nearly invisible in front of the windows, held up by steel legs. The two large flat-screen monitors and the keyboard, the only things on the desk, appeared to float above the floor. The walls were stark white and blank except for two things: a large flat-screen TV on one wall and a framed illustration on the opposite wall. The TV didn't interest me, but the illustration did. I moved closer. It was a caricature, a cartoon portrait of a laughing man with an enlarged head, standing on top of a huge pile of money shaped like the hills of San Francisco. There was no mistaking the subject. It was Walter.

I decided two things right then: I was definitely in the right apartment, and I knew nothing about Walter Roacks.

Shoko stood watching me, looking curious, but when I sat on Walter's weird clear plastic chair and slipped on a pair of latex gloves, she wandered away. I took a deep breath and tapped a key. Both screens flashed to life, flooding the room with light. One monitor opened to a stock-market page. Real-time quotes from the European and Asian markets glided across the screen, a steady flow of letters and numbers. The other screen opened to a Web browser, with the search screen waiting. And the Internet was connected.

I got to work.

Shoko came back a few minutes later. I'd sensed her so I wasn't startled when she came up behind me.

"This place is huge," she whispered. "And so high up. It is like the shrine at Izumo, a house fit for a god. Only one man lives here?"

"Yup, the whole top floor of the building." I was concentrating on the boot sequence. He didn't have any security software or virus scanners. I could have sent him an infected e-mail and saved us all this trouble.

I began uploading a new version of his browser from my memory stick, a special altered copy I'd bought on the Internet from a guy in China.

"You are good with this ... this computer?"

"Yeah," I turned to look at her. "Sometimes I feel like it's the only thing I'm good at."

"You are better than you realize." She bent to look at the screen and her cheek came close to mine. I breathed in her scent and had to close my eyes for a moment as butterflies began to spin in my stomach. When I turned toward her, my face brushed lightly against hers. She pulled away and stared at me, her eyebrows knitted together. The lighting wasn't good, but I swear she was blushing. I realized I was, too.

"Uh ... did you see anything interesting out there?" I said.

She hesitated a moment. "He has a huge bed and a whole room for his clothes. There are dark suits, white shirts and black shoes, all in rows along one wall. The other side has very fancy clothes, colorful and shiny like spring kimonos."

I looked up at her. "Shiny clothes?"

She didn't answer. She was staring at the screen again, squinting at the data cascading down the screen. She shook her head and looked outside at the panorama of twinkling lights of the city below us and far across the dark water to the lights of Sausalito. "I have no knowledge of what you are doing or why. I understand too little about this place, this city."

"Can you start looking for a way to travel out of here?"

As I waited for the computer to reboot, allowing for the final installation of my software, I flipped the keyboard over and looked underneath it. Unlike Grandpa's, there were no sticky notes with log-in passwords, but I figured he'd have them written down somewhere. Old people always wrote things down. I closed my eyes and concentrated.

A moment later, a string of letters and digits flooded my mind, too many to process, but I felt their source. I reached into the top drawer of the cabinet next to his desk. Inside was a red leather-bound book, and when I opened the page at the ribbon bookmark, I found six pages of user names and passwords, written neatly in blue ink.

"Gotcha." I pulled out my phone and snapped a photo of each page. Then, with the book open on the desk, I opened the browser and went to his favorites. He had dozens of them, neatly organized, including a few porn sites. I considered opening one to see what his tastes were but clicked on "banking" instead.

I logged into his account and let out a low whistle. The jerk had one and a half million dollars in savings! Well, maybe that was about right for the workaholic CFO of a large corporation with no wife or kids. I scrolled through his other bookmarks, boring stuff like tax and finance sites. His browsing history wasn't any better. I was about to shut the browser down when I noticed a link that said "Turks and Caicos." He'd visited that one a dozen times in the past month. The site opened to a plain white page interrupted only by two gray rectangular input boxes—ID and password required.

I sat back and looked at the page. I knew Grandpa had a few accounts in the Turks and Caicos. His and thousands of other foreign companies had tax-exempt status there—after all, only poor people pay taxes.

I entered the log-in info, and while I waited I flipped a few pages of his book and laughed aloud. Almost all his passwords were the same.

I stopped laughing when his account opened. There was over fifty million dollars in there. I recounted the zeroes to make sure I wasn't wrong—nope. And the bastard had deposited thirty million since Grandpa's first heart attack. There was no way this was Walter's money. I had to assume he'd been stealing from the company for years.

"Junya."

I spun around.

"There is nothing natural here." Shoko looked worried. "He does not even have a plant."

"Then I guess we'll have to kick some ass downstairs," I said.

I opened his e-mail account. I'd only scanned a few lines when I saw a familiar name: Müller.

"Junya." Shoko was by the doorway again. "I hear something, a rumbling sound."

The elevator? "Damn," I said, forgetting to whisper. "I'm not done yet."

I scanned the latest e-mail from Mr. Müller. It was obviously a continuation of an ongoing conversation. His employer was getting impatient ... Edward was old ... maybe dead soon ...

There—an e-mail from Mr. Muller asking Walter to locate Edward's map.

"Someone is coming!"

"Stand guard while I finish." As she moved away from the door, I called after her, "But don't kill anyone."

I started to clear the history. The hum of the hard drive was loud in the quiet room, but the sound of keys going into a lock was unmistakable. For the first time in a while, I started to panic. The front door squeaked opened, the alarm chimed three times, and I felt him.

Walter was home, and he wasn't alone.

"Come on, come on, come on," I whispered, my eyes glued to the screen.

"You don't need to walk me in." Walter's voice shattered the stillness. "I'm not a child."

"We have to make sure everything's OK, Mr. Roacks," a man said, his voice and energy slightly familiar. "That's our job, sir."

"I've been coming home alone for forty years," Walter yelled. "Get the hell out of here!"

The door slammed, rattling the pictures on the walls.

"Idiots," Walter grumbled and keys clattered onto something metal.

I turned off the monitors. That wasn't how I'd found them, but they couldn't be on when he came in here. Shoko appeared beside me, quiet as a spirit, and yanked me out of the office and into the room across the hall. We were sliding behind the half-open door when Walter came down the hall.

My heart thumped loud and fast. I was afraid Walter would discover my software before it had a chance to do its thing.

I stopped thinking about computers when I realized that Shoko's body was pressed tight against me—there wasn't much room behind the door. I peered past her, trying to distract myself. This looked like a guest bedroom, with contemporary furnishings and a queen-sized bed. Even in here the floor was polished concrete, with only a small rug near the bed. There wasn't a piece of natural material in the room that I could see. Even the door looked synthetic.

I tried to squirm past Shoko to give her some room, but somehow we ended up face-to-face, so close that my nose was inches from that cute freckle under her right eye. She turned her face away and pulled back, as much as she could in the small space. I swallowed hard, suddenly uncomfortable—I'd started to sweat. I noticed she was biting her bottom lip, and when her eyes turned back to me, she blushed again.

A noise came from Walter's office that brought reality crashing back.

"We've got to get out of here," I mouthed.

I peeked around the door. The only sounds were the occasional squeak of Walter's office chair and the sound of Walter typing, oblivious to the fact that my software was transferring the contents of his hard drive a trickle at a time.

We tiptoed down the hall toward the living room. Shoko walked backward, watching his door. We'd made it to the kitchen when Walter's chair rolled back with a sudden squawk. I pushed Shoko toward the front door and dived behind the sofa. I landed as softly as I could on the concrete floor.

From under the sofa, I watched Walter's sock feet shuffle down the hall and turn in to the kitchen. The sound of ice hitting glass came next, then liquid pouring. He let out a loud fart, and I put a hand to my mouth to stop a laugh. I shot a glance at Shoko. She squatted near the front door, her back pressed up against the wall, a strand of hair falling across her expressionless face.

I didn't want him to find me lying there like some scared dog, but I had nowhere to go. He took a slurp of his drink, the ice cubes tinkling. I looked at Shoko again. She hadn't moved. I made up my mind. If he found me, I'd confront him. If he walked away, we'd slip out—somehow.

I closed my eyes, relaxed, and extended my energy.

I saw Walter leave the kitchen, his body glowing bright orange against the cool blue walls. The shape moved back toward the office and I looked at Shoko again. She was looking at me. I opened my eyes and the colors vanished. As I started to get up, the telephone rang, a jangling electronic bell that sent me back to the floor.

Walter stopped, swore, and came back to the kitchen and picked up the handset.

"What?" A short pause. "Anthony? Where the hell have you been?" A longer pause. His left foot tapped the concrete. "Don't worry about that. Nothing's changed." There was another pause. "Tell the sergeant to stand down for now but to stay ready. I might need them to take care of any *problems*."

I assumed that meant me.

"No! Do it now, you idiot. Save your celebrating for after this is done!" The phone slammed down and Walter shuffled back to his office, the ice tinkling in his glass.

Shoko stood up and looked toward me. "Junya, get over here," she said inside my head, startling me. Her hand was on the front door. "I think it is wood. Come see."

I started toward her, moving through the open space like a ghost, invisible and silent—until I struck a lamp with my shoulder and it made a metallic clang as it rocked back into the wall. I caught it, but a loud "Damn it!" escaped me.

Walter's chair groaned. "Who's there?" he called out.

I felt a subtle suggestion of wood grain followed by the wonderful feeling of the earth's energy surging through me.

"Anthony, is that you?" He was in the hallway now.

Shoko and I put our hands on the door at the same time.

"Take us back to the park outside," Shoko whispered. She squeezed my hand and the apartment began to disappear, lost in the swirl of color.

The last thing I saw was Walter coming around the corner, his eyes wide. I have no idea what he saw.

CHAPTER
32

OKAASAN AND SHOKO SAT AT THE kitchen table across from me, drinking tea. They were looking at a fashion magazine, pointing at the pictures, sometimes laughing. For the first time in days, Okaasan looked relaxed.

They'd become a bit too close as far as I was concerned.

I'd given Okaasan a brief rundown of what I'd found at Walter's. She was as surprised as I'd been. You never know people like you think you do.

As I worked on my laptop, Okaasan looked up from the magazine. "What if he notices you're on his computer?"

"I'm not on his computer. I'm using a copy of his hard drive that I moved to a server I have in ..." I looked up at her. I'd been about to say "Panama," where I rented two servers, a cheap and easy thing to do anonymously. But somehow, I was reluctant to tell her that. She was still my mother, after all.

"Panama?" she asked.

I glared at her.

"You leave a sentence like that hanging *and* leave your mind open, I'm going to look." She lifted her teacup and traced her finger around the ring it had left on the table. "Tell me what you've found."

"More bank accounts in the Turks and Caicos." I paused to take a bite of a cookie. "They've been open for about twenty years, but they're definitely not company accounts, and there's no way all this is Walter's money." I spun the screen toward them. "Look at these routine deposits, all in amounts of three to five thousand dollars." I pointed to a deposit in Walter's account and then tabbed back to the general account for the Thompson Hotel Group. "There's a withdrawal for the same amount on the same day. And there's been a withdrawal once a month for years, starting with two thousand dollars and gradually increasing to five thousand dollars. The hotel managers must think it's some kind of regular bill or something, and they'll do whatever Walter says, right? He's the chief financial officer. And by the looks of these other deposits, he's doing the same thing with a bunch of Grandpa's companies, over a dozen." I did a quick tally in my head. "He's transferring over seventy grand a month."

"That would add up fast." Okaasan started to do the math on her fingers.

"Look at this!" I spun the computer around again to show her another account I'd found.

Shoko looked, too, but her face was blank, like a cat staring at a wall.

"This is an actual Thompson Group account but linked to Walter's. He opened this account about two months before the Bayview project started having trouble."

"And?"

"Look at the balance!" I said, louder than I intended.

"I don't know what I'm looking at!" Okaasan yelled back.

I pointed at the bottom line. "There's over eight hundred million in there!"

"Holy crap!" Okaasan yelled and slapped her hand over her mouth. I started laughing before she did.

Shoko looked curious. "Is that a lot of money?"

"Yes, Shoko, that's a lot of money." Okaasan turned to her. "You could buy ... a nice meal for every person in Japan."

Shoko frowned. "Why would I do that?"

I leaned back. "Mark Smith and Grandpa can't understand why they're in financial trouble when all the divisions are doing well. Walter's telling them it's the Bayview project that's sinking the company, but he's the one emptying the Bayview accounts." I shook my head in disbelief. "Maybe Walter knew this would stress Grandpa out ... Maybe he hoped he'd have a heart attack." My eyes widened. "Bartholomew can't cause heart attacks, can he?"

Okaasan shook her head. "He has nothing but the power of persuasion. He uses sex, money, and power to influence people."

"Well, it's working. From what I've read in the e-mails, they want the Thompson Group to go under, and Walter gets to ransack the company in the process."

"And with Edward in the hospital ..." Okaasan said, understanding dawning on her face.

My head began to spin. "And if I'm not in the picture—"

Okaasan looked at me in alarm. "Then there's no one to stop him! Oh, Junya, be careful!"

I felt that now-familiar anger begin to rise inside me. "I'm not dead yet. And neither is Grandpa."

"Junya, ... please." It was Shoko. Her hands were on her temples.

I let out my breath slowly, trying to control the release. After a moment, she nodded and gave me a little smile.

—

Grandpa had once told me about the banks in the Turks and Caicos. I found it an especially boring lecture at the time. He said the laws there allowed total anonymity for the account owners. They only needed a resident of the Islands, usually a lawyer, to represent them, so whoever had the access codes controlled the account, no identification required.

I changed the password on Walter's account to a long and complicated one. I did the same to the Thompson Group accounts. Then, more for fun than anything else, I transferred the balance of his three investment accounts and his checking account into my bank account. I doubted the transfer would go through, not without someone confirming it, but I wanted him to know I was on to him. And unless he had another account I didn't know about, he wouldn't be able to buy a cup of coffee.

Walter had lost access to almost a billion dollars. I leaned back in the chair, linked my fingers behind my head, and let out a sigh of satisfaction.

"What are you looking so smug about?" Okaasan asked.

"I'm savoring the feeling of victory."

She snorted. "One skirmish doesn't decide a war."

"It's one heck of a first strike."

She pushed the magazine aside and frowned. "You're thinking only of the money and the power that comes with it. That worries me."

I gave her a look. "You and Shoko *kill* people, but I'm a bad person for thinking about *money*?"

"Purity is determined by one's intentions, not their actions."

"So, you can massacre a crowd of people as long as your intentions are pure?"

Okaasan crossed her arms. "Shoko killed for you, but she had no malice toward those men. Her intention was to do her duty and save you. She has no other agenda." She gazed into my eyes. "What's your agenda?"

"I'm fighting for my family."

"Do you think your father wants this fight?"

"I doubt it, but I need to take back what's mine."

Her eyebrows lifted. "Isn't it still your grandfather's?"

I didn't answer.

"You need to maintain balance," Shoko said. "Your heart is leaning too far one way. The Elders will be concerned."

"So if I get *unbalanced*, what will the Elders do?"

"They told me you may be useful to them," Okaasan said. "But Shoko also said you could be a liability." Now she looked worried. "I have no idea what they'll do."

—

It was after eleven when Okaasan finally went off for her bath, leaving Shoko and me alone.

"Let's go for a walk," I said. "I need some fresh air."

"A walk?" She shrugged. "OK."

It was cooler now and the clouds had drifted east without dropping their payload, leaving the sky clear. The moon was rising over the city.

Shoko had her hands stuffed into the pockets of her jacket, staring straight ahead. It felt odd being with her now, with no distractions. We hadn't ever talked about anything personal—we'd never had a chance.

"You are quiet," Shoko said. "What are you thinking about?"

"Just how much my life has changed." I let out a sigh. "I did things today I could've never done a week ago, and yet"—I turned my face away, pretending I was looking at the passing car—"I'm still the same old Junya in a lot of ways." Like being afraid to talk to a girl.

A slight smile turned the corners of her mouth. "I have felt like a different person lately, too." She stopped at the red fire box, the same one we'd stopped at days before. "It feels like a long time ago that we last stood here."

It felt like another lifetime.

"I said I wanted to get to know you better, and yet … I understand you less now than I did then."

I tried to swallow the sudden lump in my throat. I pointed to the east. "Have you ever eaten pizza?"

She tilted her head and frowned. "I have never even heard of pizza."

"It's Italian food, round, flat dough with tomato sauce, cheese, sliced meat and stuff on top, baked in an oven. It's delicious." I looked away. "Would … would you like to have some with me?"

"Well, I am hungry." She smiled. "Yes, I would like to try this pizza—with you."

I gave her a big smile back.

CHAPTER
33

THE STREETS WERE EMPTY OF PEDESTRIANS as we walked along Sacramento Street toward the pizza shop. Shoko walked close beside me and when her hand brushed against mine a few times, I felt my heart speed up. I glanced sideways at her the third time it happened—she was biting her lower lip.

"Excuse me," she whispered.

I took a deep breath and grasped her hand, interlocking my fingers in hers—we'd never held hands like that before.

She gave me a smile, a kind I'd never seen on a girl before, and she added a little bounce to her stride. Happiness erupted inside me.

"Were you OK inside Walter's place?" I said. "I was worried about you."

She shrugged. "I do not like being without my senses, but I had my weapons ... and *your* senses. You had no need to worry about my feelings, although ..." A smile moved onto her face. "It is nice that you were." She looked away. Her grip on my hand tightened, as if she were afraid she'd fall.

"Are you all right?"

"I am confused. I feel torn inside by mixed emotions."

"Like what?"

"I still do not understand what you did with that computer thing. I feel stupid."

I laughed. "Don't, it's complicated. The important thing is, I found a lot of information about how Walter is stealing Grandpa's money—and now we know he's working with Bartholomew."

She nodded.

"I keep thinking about what Grandpa said about Bartholomew wanting his gold," I said. "But Mr. Müller asked Walter for the *map*, not the gold. Why would Bartholomew need that?"

She thought for a moment. "Perhaps he wants to know where Edward found the gold."

I stopped walking. "So then ... maybe the gold isn't the treasure after all. Maybe the gateway is."

She didn't answer at first but I felt her energy change. She turned to me. "If that is so, then we must go back. There is no reason to delay this."

"Delay what?"

"Killing him."

My mouth dropped open.

"This Walter stole your grandfather's money, acting on Bartholomew's wishes, and his men tried to kill you. What if he does find the map? He needs to die."

"No, he doesn't! I wiped Walter out tonight! I got all of Grandpa's money back, and without money he can't pay his men. They're going to desert him. Plus we know where the map is, and there's no way Walter can access it."

"You cannot be sure. We must cut him down and end this."

I scowled at her. "That's murder."

She shook her head. "Your way is so complicated ... and weak."

I let go of her hand. "Has it ever occurred to you that there are other options besides your sword?" I took a deep breath. "You told me to embrace change. Maybe you should give it a try."

She looked down at her hands. "You laugh at my obedience," she said, almost too quiet to hear, "but rules are all I know." She moved farther away from me. "The more I know you, the less I understand my life, and I do not like that." Her voice faltered, and when she looked up at me I saw the glimmer of a tear on her cheek. "My duty is to the gods, but ... I feel free here." She looked away. "Perhaps that is the poison my mother is always warning me about."

"Are you talking about this world or me?"

She stopped under the green awning of a flower shop, in front of a window bursting with flowers. "We are being foolish. I must remember my duty."

"What? To kill me if the Elders tell you to?"

Her eyes narrowed. "You are wavering." She tilted her head to the side. "On one side, you have overwhelming power. You find it exciting, yes?"

I nodded. I couldn't deny that.

"Well, that power is not from the gods," she said. "On the other side are the gods, the Gatekeepers, your mother—a life of duty, and purity." She stood up straight. "You have both inside you, and I do not understand how."

I ran my hands through my hair, pushing it back. "Doesn't everybody?"

"I do not."

I let out a sigh. "Sometimes I wish I had a rulebook to follow. It might make life easier. I react the way I do because it's all that I know. Maybe all of this is my path or whatever, but I have my own dreams, too."

She snorted. "Dreams are a waste of time."

"Are you serious?" I stared. "Every goal ever reached started out as a dream. They're what keep us going."

"The path of our life is already laid out for us. Our duty is to follow that path, not dream of a different way."

"So when you sneaked away to ride trains and eat ice cream, that was part of your destiny?"

"Who says I cannot ride trains and eat ice cream?"

I gave up. "Let's just go have pizza and stop talking about this."

"No!" She sank onto a bus bench and turned away.

I sat beside her, an arm's length away, unsure what to do. Why did we have to have all these complications? Couldn't I just be a teenage boy with a crush on a cute girl?

"We must stop this now," she said. "I am a Gatekeeper. I have dedicated my life to the gods, and I will never forsake them."

"I don't think I could ever be like you Gatekeepers."

"And I can never be like you." She slid off the bench and onto her knees. "I am sorry. I think … I think I should go home." Then she slapped her hand against the ground and faded away as if she'd never existed.

—

A half-hour later I was on the bench in our Zen garden, my head in my hands. It was colder now and the air curled around me, giving me goose bumps.

It was motion more than any feelings that made me look toward the house, brightly lighted and warm. Okaasan was silhouetted in the doorway.

"What happened?" she said.

"I just wanted to go for pizza."

She let out a sigh. "That girl likes you."

I rolled my eyes. "Don't be surprised if she kills me one day."

Okaasan chuckled. "That's how I know she likes you."

She stepped down into the garden and sat on the bench, crossing her arms against the damp night air. "You two are very different, and both young. You're both struggling, but she has a code she can never violate. She's a warrior, Junya."

I was shivering now.

"We were trained like soldiers—obedient, no need to think—but we had good reason for our discipline," she said, her voice soft in the night. "How many times did I see my mother come home, her clothing splattered with human blood or the black blood of Evil Ones? Whether you like it or not, you will never change her."

"But I don't *want* to change her." Did I?

She sniffed and rubbed her arms. "I can feel evil, close by, closing in, and I feel the darkness inside you, growing more and more each day."

I looked at the sky. "That's what Shoko said."

"Anger strengthens you. I've seen it."

"That happens to everyone when they get mad—it's just adrenaline."

"But you are not just anyone. I heard you were able to stop Tomi with a burst of energy that hit her like a wall. If you had done that in anger, what would have happened?"

"I don't know."

"Neither do I." She put her arm around me and held me. We stayed that way for a while, and then she pulled back and looked at me. "Have I ever told you how proud I am of you?"

I made a face. "Never," I said, only half-joking.

"Well, I am. And no matter what you think, I love you and I love your father, more than anything in the world."

I squeezed her back. "I know."

"And I believe you'll do the right thing." With that, she walked back inside, leaving me alone in the quiet of the Zen garden.

CHAPTER
34

I LEFT MY HOUSE A LITTLE AFTER EIGHT the next morning.
I'd awoken with an urgent need to see Grandpa—he wasn't doing
any better, but I needed some reassurance that I was doing the right
things. I hoped I could get that much from him.

As I started up the hill, I scanned the area with my eyes and my
mind but didn't sense anything—the stream ran clear and quiet. In
fact, there were no messages at all.

That changed the minute I reached the bus stop. Negative
thoughts and energy bombarded me. I dropped to the bench, holding my head in my hands. A dark sensation descended, growing
stronger every moment—but it wasn't coming from these people.

"Are you all right?" It was a woman, the only source of positive
energy here.

"Yeah, just tired," I said, keeping my head down.

"He's obviously on drugs," an old woman said.

"Not every kid's on drugs, you know."

I looked up and saw a man across the street dressed in a long black
coat. His face was expressionless, ageless, his eyes like black holes in
his head. Then the bus arrived, slicing between us, and the woman
called to me again.

"Come on."

I looked up. A young black woman, the one who'd asked me if I was all right, beckoned me towards the bus.

"I'll catch the next one," I said. "Thank you for your kindness."

She looked surprised but disappeared into the bus without looking back. When the bus pulled away, the man in black was gone, but the dark sensation lingered. I was just turning to search for him when a black car almost as long as the bus stopped in front of me. The rear window slid down.

"I suppose I'd be wasting my time if I asked you to step inside," a deep male voice said.

When I offered no response, the elderly driver, wearing an old-fashioned uniform, hurried around and opened the rear door. A tall man stepped out, wearing a blue suit so crisp it could have cut glass. He straightened his tie, not that he needed to, and inspected me, his face expressionless. Then he smiled, revealing a perfect set of white teeth.

"Good morning, James." He had an accent, slight and indefinable.

"What do you want?"

He took a business card from his suit pocket and passed it to me. It was cold, and when I flicked the edge, it sprang back. It was metal that was thin as paper, embossed with the name Mr. Müller and a telephone number with an area code I didn't recognize.

"Do you have a first name, since you know mine?" I said.

"I have many given names, European aristocrats being what they are. I wouldn't want to burden you with all of them."

"I see." I felt a slight tingle in my neck and looked up. The man in black was back, and another guy just like him now stood farther up the block.

"They're with me," Mr. Müller said. "One can't be too careful, especially in this country. Who knows when violence may erupt?"

"Yes, who knows?"

He studied the bench and then sat beside me, placing as little of his pants on it as possible.

"My employer noticed your banking transactions last night."

That caught me off guard. "Bartholomew knows about all my transactions?"

Mr. Müller raised his brows. "We always notice when someone moves several hundred million dollars. But we have a special interest in Edward Thompson and his family."

"Because you're helping Walter Roacks destroy his company?"

"The other way around, actually." Mr. Müller scowled. "Personally, such treachery disgusts me. Mr. Roacks seems to think that he is somehow entitled to the company."

"I noticed that when he tried to have me killed."

He smiled again. "Mr. Roacks has focused too much on his own goals and has failed to deliver what he promised. My employer does not take such things lightly."

"Meaning?"

He shrugged. "He is no longer of use to us."

"Because of me."

He smiled. "Did you enjoy taking it all away from him? There's nothing like beating an enemy at their own game."

It had felt good at the time, but I wasn't so sure now.

"I was told to inform you that you may keep the money."

I laughed. "I intend to—since it's mine."

He frowned, and for the first time his steely façade cracked, but only for a moment.

"Edward chose to alienate us, but with one phone call"—he snapped his fingers—"my employer destroyed his dream. With another call he could bring it all back."

"I have enough money to save my grandfather. *We* don't need you."

"I disagree. What will happen when my employer contacts the bank in the Turks and Caicos? And with Mr. Roacks in such a panic, no one can foresee Edward's future … or yours. Whatever happens next is up to destiny, I'm afraid."

"I make my own destiny, Mr. Müller."

He gave that some thought. "Perhaps we can make a deal."

"Like what?"

A smile spread across his face. "You possess something my employer has sought for a very long time."

I let out a snort. "The gold?"

Mr. Müller waved his hand in dismissal. "Gold is a transitional metal, nothing more."

"So he doesn't care how my grandfather went *across* to get it?"

Mr. Müller's lips tightened. "He is far more interested that *you've* been across."

I sucked in a breath.

"He wants to meet you."

I nodded slowly, trying to think fast enough to keep up.

"If I do … he'll leave my grandfather alone?"

"Edward is already lost, but perhaps you can save his company."

My fists clenched. "Then tell Bartholomew he can go to hell."

An unpleasant smile came to his face. "He will be amused to hear that." He turned and strode toward his car. "We'll be in touch," he called out as the car door slammed.

As it sped away, I saw the longhaired man across the street. My anger rose up instantly. I breathed out and sent my energy hurtling toward him.

He jerked as if I'd hit him and then turned and strode away, pushing through the pedestrians like a battering ram. Most people moved out of his way. Others swore at him, but he kept walking, unfazed.

I stood up and ran after him, even as he disappeared among the cars and shops. I followed his energy, a dark magnet that pulled me to him. He was moving faster now, but I was closing in. Everything else faded away—pedestrians, cars, blaring horns, screeching tires. We were the only ones moving and breathing.

The man turned to face me. I felt his energy, negative and powerful, but mine was more intense than I'd ever felt. The man jerked backward into a store's brick wall, dazed. After a long moment, he swung his long hair like a stallion, his eyes wide and fierce. Then he hissed, a horrible, high-pitched sound, and bared his teeth. From between long incisors, his forked tongue flicked out, tasting the air, smelling me.

I took a step back. The man—if that was what he was—let out another hiss and turned and ran down the side street, his black coat billowing behind him. As I watched him go, my heart thumped like a drum.

CHAPTER
35

THE ONLY BODYGUARD OUTSIDE Grandpa's hospital room when I got there was John, and he looked exhausted. I forced a smile as I approached him. He didn't return it.

"Hey," I said. "Everything OK?"

He crossed his thick arms and glowered at me. "You can fire me, but I'm not leaving."

I blinked. "Why would I fire you?"

"Save it," he said, loud enough that the nurses at the central station looked up. He stood up, and I backed up a few steps. "You want it all so bad you just leave him unprotected—fire everyone—with those special-ops guys running wild?"

"John!" the head nurse called. "Keep it down please!"

He actually looked sheepish, but my anger exploded. "You honestly think I want him dead? I didn't fire anyone today—especially not you—so back off!"

He looked confused and a bit taken aback. "Well someone did. I got let go this morning."

I let out my breath, releasing some of my anger. "Where's Barrymore? I need to straighten this out."

John shrugged. "I don't know. He got fired, too."

I put my hands to my face. "Damn it!" When I opened my eyes, John was looking at me.

"You really had nothing to do with this, did you?"

"Indirectly maybe." Walter was moving fast, eliminating all the obstacles. It was an act of desperation, as Mr. Müller had warned me—which made it scarier.

"Look, John, consider yourself unfired. You'll get all your pay plus overtime, even if I have to take it from my piggy bank. Please stay—and don't let Walter Roacks near him."

His expression softened. "I already told you, I'm not going anywhere ... but if you plan to pay me, you'd better make it quick. I have a mortgage payment due and the wife's already pissed."

—

The door to Grandpa's room was only half-open when Lin attacked me. Seeing a hand come at my face, I ducked—right as a knife came up at me. I jerked sideways, grabbed her wrist, and twisted it around so that the blade of the knife brushed her throat. Our eyes were inches apart.

"Junya," Lin whispered, "I didn't know it was you."

I let go. "A little paranoid, aren't you?"

"I'm scared."

I walked toward the bed. Grandpa was pale, his eyes sunk deep into the sockets.

"They say he's stable, but ... I feel him slipping away."

I turned to find tears running down Lin's cheeks and I fought a wave of shame. Ms. Lin had been my personal porn star since I hit puberty. Now I knew her as a friend, and I began to understand all the things she'd given up, or had had taken from her.

"Lin ..."

She grabbed me and buried her face in my neck. Her sobbing made her whole body shake, and for the first time in days I let my own emotions go. My tears began to drop onto her hair. The only sounds were our sobbing, the hum of the machines, and Grandpa's breath going in and out.

Lin finally let me go and I wiped my face with my sleeve.

"I'll go get us some tea," she said.

I waited until the door closed behind her and sat on the edge of the bed. I felt exhausted, overwhelmed as I took his cold hand in mine. I couldn't feel anything from him, no energy at all. I closed my eyes and tried to focus, but I grew colder and felt myself begin to drift.

—

I found myself in a meadow, warm and full of life and color. A small hut, its walls glowing bright in the sun, sat at the far edge against a backdrop of lush vegetation. A warm breeze touched my face and dried my cheeks.

"This is where it all began," Grandpa said in a low voice, standing at the doorway of the hut. He turned to look at me. "I'm sorry, James, ... but I can't stay."

My eyes snapped open. Grandpa lay on the bed beside me. I squeezed his hand.

"Don't—you can't leave me!"

"Edward!" Lin ran toward me, two steaming cups of tea nearly falling from her hands. "No, no, no—"

I grabbed the cups, my hands over hers to steady them.

"He's alive." I kept my voice steady, hoping it would calm me as much as her. "Nothing's changed."

"Then why ..."

I gently pushed her backward to a chair, took one of the cups, and knelt in front of her. "I'm sorry I scared you," I whispered. "I don't know what happened. I'm sorry."

She nodded, but the shock was still evident on her face and in her shaking hands. I moved into the chair beside her and we sat in silence, lost in thought.

After a while I turned to her. "You're pretty good with a knife. Lucky it wasn't the nurse."

She sniffed and wiped her face with her sleeve. "I knew your mom when I was a little girl, did you know that?"

I shook my head.

"She helped inspire me to follow my own path, in a way." She took a sip of tea. "But no one told me what she was until later."

"So you know she's a Gatekeeper?"

She nodded.

"Does Grandpa know?"

"I don't think so."

I studied her face. "I guess being on Grandpa's flight that day was no accident."

She nodded. "I was sent to assist another who grows older." Then she laughed. "And we all knew he'd fall for my *bait*."

I laughed. "Who doesn't?" Then my mouth dropped open. "Wait! Are you telling me Mr. Sugimoto is a ninja, too?"

"Gardeners have been the disguise for ninja bodyguards since the Edo period."

I tried to absorb that. "Why'd they send a kunoichi this time?"

She frowned. "I consider kunoichi to be a rather insulting term."

I cringed. "Sorry."

She took a sip of tea. "They wanted someone close to him, to his business." She shrugged. "They didn't ask me to seduce him—becoming his executive assistant was enough … but he was so lonely and it did make things easier."

I smiled. "You know you're not fooling me, right?"

She managed a weak smile. "I do love him." She looked down at her lap, and neither of us spoke for a while. I was about to stand up when she cleared her throat.

"Junya?" She was staring intently at the floor when I turned to her. "Do you … do you think he'd marry me? If I suggested it?"

"Marry you?"

Her cheeks turned pink. "Never mind … I could never be a wife. I'm sure I couldn't stand it."

"Lin." I put my hand on her arm. "He'd be a fool to say no."

There was an awkward pause.

"You know what happened today?" I finally said.

She nodded. "Walter threatened to fire me, too, if I don't go back to the office, but the bodyguards are gone. Sugimoto-san is guarding the house, so I stayed here. I don't know what else to do."

"Walter shouldn't be a problem much longer. I started to fight back last night. He's reacting, but he's not thinking straight. We're going to win."

"How do you figure that?" She sounded skeptical.

I told her about the money missing from the company accounts and about the Turks and Caicos accounts.

"When his men find out he's broke, they won't stick around."

"Damn," she said. "I never liked him."

"And I had a visit from Mr. Müller this morning."

Her hand rose to cover her mouth. "What?"

"Bartholomew's supporting Walter, or at least he was. Now he's offered to return everything to normal, except he'd prefer that Grandpa isn't around." I decided not to mention the map just yet.

She looked horrified.

"I don't know what to do about Bartholomew right now, but I know I can save the company from Walter. Will you help me?"

She sat up straighter. "What do you want me to do?"

I pulled her out of the chair and headed for the door, but before we could get there, there was a tap and Mr. Barrymore peered in. He looked embarrassed when he saw us.

"I'm sorry to interrupt. I thought I'd check in on him before I left."

"There's no change," Lin said.

He nodded.

"Let's go talk in the meeting room down the hall," I said to him.

Mr. Barrymore didn't move. "If the Chairman's still unconscious, then there's nothing to talk about."

"Please come," I said as I pushed past him.

⎯

I took the seat at the head of the table and waited. Lin strode in a moment later, her heels clicking, and sat down and opened a notebook in front of her.

"He'll come," she said.

Mr. Barrymore walked in a few minutes later. He stood against the wall opposite me with his arms crossed.

I leaned back in the chair. "I'm not going to let this happen."

"It already has. No one's going to stick around, not even John," Mr. Barrymore said.

"Not even you?"

"Damn it, James, I've been fired! I know when to give up."

Lin clicked her pen. "I never thought of you as a man who'd give up so easily, Maurice." She turned back to me. "Where do we start?"

"First of all, Barrymore, you're rehired, and 'no' isn't an option. Second, rehire everyone."

"But—"

"Lin," I said, "I know this isn't your area, but can you do payroll?"

She smiled. "Of course. We need to get paychecks out ... but where's the money coming from if Walter cleaned us out?"

I slid her a piece of paper with an account number on it.

She pulled a laptop out of her bag and flipped it open. "I'll get started."

"Good." I looked up at Mr. Barrymore. "Did you start that audit we talked about?"

He nodded. "It was the first thing I did this morning, before I got fired—ex-IRS auditors." He adjusted his jacket and stood up straighter. "Started their own business a few years back. They're working from their office, nothing official, as you wanted." He paused. "I forgot to tell them I was fired."

"They'll never even notice."

He looked thoughtful. "I wasn't able to take Walter's computer access away, though. The IT department won't do it without an order from the Chairman—"

"Screw them!" I shouted. "Take him offline now!"

"I can do it," Lin said, her fingers tapping the keyboard. "I have Edward's codes. No one can override them."

I leveled my gaze at Mr. Barrymore, who was studying me with interest. "I want a full team here in an hour," I said. "Then you go and escort Walter out of the office."

He glanced at Lin. "You can pay my guys?"

She tapped a few keys and looked up. "Auto deposits just went out." She looked at me. "And Walter's account is locked. What's next?"

"You call and speak to the people in charge of every department of our company—top people, the ones who report directly to Grandpa. Tell them that any orders they've received from Walter since my birthday are canceled." I paused, trying to remember how far back that was. "Any layoffs, any accounting changes, anything Walter told them to do is to be reversed." I looked her in the eye. "Will they listen to you?"

She raised her eyebrows. "Oh, they'll listen."

I nodded. "Transfer cash from that account to any of them that need it to stay afloat."

"What about the Bayview Project? We're in default."

I sighed. "I don't know what to do about that." I ran a hand over my face. "When are Mark and my dad due back?"

"Not until tomorrow at the earliest. The papers aren't even signed yet."

"Well, after what Mr. Müller said, I don't think we should bother with the Bayview right now."

Mr. Barrymore hadn't moved yet. He was standing there, watching us.

"Are you with me, Mr. Barrymore?"

275

He nodded.

"Well, then what are you waiting for? Get on it!"

CHAPTER
36

I MET MACK LATER THAT AFTERNOON at a coffee house not
far from his place, a funky little joint with an eclectic mix of mis-
matched tables and chairs and old sofas. They had wraps and salads,
the usual espresso, and a few treats under the glass. Their pumpkin
pie was the best I'd ever tasted.

I showed up fifteen minutes late—I wanted to make sure I wasn't
followed. Mack was sitting alone at a table near the washrooms,
his backpack at his feet and his back to the door. I ordered a vanilla
steamed milk and a piece of pumpkin pie and sat across from him,
grinning like a goof. I gave him a quick once-over but saw only a few
light bruises near one eye. "Man, is it good to see you!"

"Been a long time." He frowned at me before he took a bite of his
chicken-Caesar wrap.

I cringed. "I know … I'm sorry. I didn't even check to see if you
were OK."

"I was freaking out when I didn't hear anything." He looked serious, not a normal thing for Mack. "And I was pretty pissed when you
took off without a word."

"I'm really sorry. Everything was so crazy."

"Yeah, I called your house. Your dad told me you went to Japan."
He put his wrap down. "I don't blame you for having other things

on your mind. I saw the news the next day. The guys that jumped us—you really did that?"

I dropped my eyes to the table. "They were trying to kill me. I thought my grandpa sent them—accused him of it … Turns out he didn't."

Then I told him—at least the parts I could. I told him about my grandpa's heart attack and that Walter was trying to take over the company. I left out the part about Izumo and the ninja and the map. I did tell him a bit about Shoko, though.

Mack mulled it over and leaned back in his chair. "This is nuts," he said.

I was about to reply when I felt a disruption in the energy outside, like a leaf dropping into a stream. Men were gathering outside, and they were here for me.

I swore. "Mack, you need to get out of here."

He looked confused.

"Pretend you don't know me and get the hell out of here, now!"

He looked like he was about to say something, but he stood and walked away, making it to the counter with his empty plates as the first man came in, slamming the door open so hard it hit the wall and rattled the windows. Another guy leaned against the wall outside, watching the street. As Mack walked out, he brushed past Anthony Roacks, who was on his way in.

"Uh, what's going on, guys?" the barista asked, almost cowering behind the espresso machine.

"Relax," one of the men said. "Everything's cool." He stepped up to the bar and set what looked like a stack of bills on the counter. "We want to have a private gathering here. Close up shop and take a break. We won't be long."

The barista's eyes lighted up. "Sorry, folks," he called, "we have to close. See you again tomorrow." The customers glanced up from their laptops and phones, grumbling.

"Move!" the man said.

They shuffled toward the door, glancing over their shoulders as they hurried out. The barista disappeared into the back room, and a moment later a door closed.

Anthony straddled a chair at my table and sat down. He looked tired and red-eyed. Two men sat at a table behind him, and a big guy circled around behind me.

"These guys are dangerous," Anthony said. "It's all we can do to keep them from killing you, after what you did to their pals."

"This office boy is keeping you guys on a leash?" I shook my head. "That must be tough." The expression on the men's faces told me that their opinion of Anthony wasn't far from mine. "I guess I should buy you boys a coffee—I don't think Anthony's bank card works anymore."

"Yeah, and that there is a major problem," a scar-faced man behind Anthony said. "I'm getting pissed, and that's not good for either of you."

Anthony glared at the man. "I told you, Jackson, I'll get everything back."

"Walter's finished," I said. "We're auditing everything."

The man named Jackson laughed. "Auditors aren't going to find much. Not with those holes in their heads."

I felt sick. "You think the police won't figure this out?"

"I'll be killing a lot more people if I don't get paid."

Anthony gave Jackson a nervous smile. "I told you, it's not a problem."

"Then get on with it, *Tony.*"

Anthony slapped my cup off the table, spreading foam across the floor. "Tell me the new passwords, now!" he shouted.

I smiled. "I'd rather stick a fork in my eye."

"I'll do it for you!" He snatched Mack's used fork off the table and came at me.

I moved without thinking, and a second later, I had the fork. I slammed it into Anthony's hand, deep enough to hit the tabletop. His eyes bulged and he let out a scream. He lunged across the table toward me. I don't remember moving but Anthony crashed into the wall beside me and crumpled to the floor, the fork still protruding from his hand.

"Nice," someone said.

No one stirred as Anthony struggled into a seated position against the wall, whimpering, while blood dripped from his hand.

"Mr. Müller paid me a visit today," I said.

His eyes went wide. "You know Müller?"

"He said I can keep the money because *his employer* is very unhappy with Walter." I shook my head and smirked. "You're *so* screwed."

"Who's this Müller guy?" Jackson asked. "We may have to pay him a visit, too."

"Good luck with that."

The man behind me started to move, but Jackson stopped him. "Easy, Bubba." Then he slid a business card across the table. There were two sets of numbers written in blue ink, one obviously a phone number. "We just want our payment," he said. "Transfer two million into that account and we go away."

"Two million?" Anthony cried. "Your fee is one!"

The man's eyes never left mine. "Or we start collecting collateral."

I thought fast. If I paid these guys, there'd be no one to protect Walter and no one to threaten me. But they represented something so wrong. "I don't think so."

Jackson sighed. "Then we're going to take a ride. I've got something that should change your mind."

That got my attention. "What?"

"It's not a *what*, it's a *who*." He smiled, but there was no humor in it. "Your mommy."

My fury surged and Bubba chose that moment to drop his hand onto my shoulder.

I grabbed two fingers, spun out of the chair, and felt his fingers and wrist snap. Then I ran toward the bathrooms.

The women's-room door was open, and I darted inside and slammed the door. My heart dropped: there was no window. My heart was about to burst from my chest as I looked around for an escape. Heavy fists began pounding on the door as I climbed onto the toilet, and a moment later the door burst open with a loud crack.

"He's not in here!" Bubba yelled.

Another crash came from across the hall. "The window's open."

"Get outside!" That was Jackson. I heard their retreating footsteps and the slam of the front door.

My arms and legs were shaking, but I didn't dare let go yet. I was wedged between two walls of the narrow bathroom, hands against one, feet against the other, right above the door. I held on while my muscles screamed. I managed a deep breath and waited until I sensed they were gone. I dropped to the floor.

"Shoko, I need you," I whispered.

CHAPTER
37

I SPRINTED HOME, ALL SIX BLOCKS, not once looking back. I cut through the neighbor's yard, cleared our back fence, and crashed to the ground near the dojo. A sensation of darkness lingered in the air, and then it was gone, like the shadow of a plane passing overhead.

The house was quiet. I listened for Okaasan and searched for her presence but felt nothing. Scared but angry, I was walking toward the house when I felt a dark wave of energy, followed by the crunch of feet on gravel behind me.

I spun, ready to fight.

"Shoko!" Relief flooded into me.

She ran toward me. "I heard you call."

I started to tell her what had happened, but she stopped me with a finger to my lips. It felt like a kiss.

"Don't worry. I'm here, I came back."

"I'm glad." I glanced at the back of the house. "Okaasan—"

"She's safe inside."

"But I don't feel—"

"Trust me, Junya." She flashed those long lashes of hers and her eyes crinkled that cute freckle under her left eye. "Who knows more about this, you or me?" Then she kissed me. The warmth of her lips spread through my body and filled me with more desire than I'd ever felt before. Mind you, I'd never been kissed like that before.

"Why ..." I said as our lips parted.

"Isn't this what you wanted?"

I nodded, but something didn't feel right. There was no warmth to her touch, none of her usual positive energy.

She pulled me toward the back of the dojo, out of view of the house, and started kissing me again. When she took my hands and put them under her blouse on the bare skin of her stomach, I decided I must be dreaming.

But the stream was screaming at me. Something was wrong here.

"Shoko, ... I'm not ready for this."

"Are you sure?" I felt her hips press against mine, and suddenly I wasn't sure. She kissed me again and then pulled back, grabbed my hand, and dragged me toward the dojo.

I hesitated. "Shoko, ... maybe this isn't ... the best time."

"I thought you wanted this." She looked sad. "Junya, I came back here for *you*."

Inside the dojo, she kicked off her shoes and started pulling my T-shirt off. I fumbled with the tiny buttons on her blouse. I was nervous and excited, but everything about this was so wrong.

She pushed my hands away and then stood back and gave me a sexy smile as her blouse fell open. I took a deep breath, so excited I could barely think, but I still felt that something was wrong—and this time I couldn't ignore it.

She frowned. "Don't you like me?"

"No—I mean yes, yes, but ... I'm getting the weirdest feeling." Something was very wrong here.

She knocked me down to the mats and straddled me like she had that day in the meadow. I looked up at her. There was an odd smell, sort of like ... cars? Gas stations?

Gasoline.

I shoved her away and she toppled backward off me. For the first time, I took a good look around the dojo, squinting in the dim light.

Sparring gear lay scattered on the floor, the sword rack tipped over. There was a dark stain on the tatami.

I crawled past her. "Its blood," I whispered. Near the stains were footprints, the crisp outline of a boot tread. I spun in a quick circle. Jackson's men *had* been here, but Shoko had said—

I turned slowly and looked at Shoko.

She was upright on her knees now, her face expressionless, eyes like ice. One hand buttoned her blouse. The other hand held Okaasan's best katana, its tip stabbed into the tatami like an exclamation mark.

"She fought back," Shoko said, "but once they shot her, she was easy to take."

I choked on my breath. "How do you know?"

"Because I watched."

I sucked in a breath. "Why are you doing this?"

"The Kannushi has decided you must die," she said in a conversational tone. "You can't be trusted. He believes you'll be corrupted by the Evil Ones and bring them across. It cannot be risked."

My mouth gaped open. "Shoko, please." I wasn't having much luck choking back my tears. "Don't do this."

"You're dealing with a war that's been raging for a thousand years. You're nothing but a grain of sand in the river of time. Your death—and your mother's—will have no more significance."

A lighter sparked, and an instant later a wall of flame circled me, following a track of fuel on the tatami. The heat and the smoke were instantaneous—I couldn't see anything. My throat and nose burned, and I retched as the smoke seared my lungs.

"Good-bye, Junya."

The flames spread at an unbelievable pace, feeding on the tatami and the paper shoji panels before attacking the dry straw of the roof. Burning embers hit my jeans and ignited them, hungry for more fuel.

I threw my arms across my face and dived through the flames toward the nearest wall, hoping I'd break through.

—

The dojo was engulfed. Flames shot toward the sky, and billowing black smoke filled the air as I staggered toward the house, shielding my face from the heat. Somehow I made it to my bedroom. I grabbed my bokuto and energy surged into me as soon as I gripped the handle. I sucked in a deep breath, then another. My energy began to expand inside me. By the time I'd taken the third breath, I felt ready to explode.

I focused all my energy. Shoko was gone and so was Okaasan. As I stood up, bokuto in hand, I swore through gritted teeth that I'd make Shoko and the rest of the Gatekeepers pay for this.

The air was thick with smoke when I walked out my bedroom door. I heard sirens now. The dojo was gone, reduced to a pile of flaming logs, still roaring like a summer campfire.

On my way to the side door, I pulled a wakizashi out of the broom closet—another of Okaasan's stashes—and fed it through my belt. Then I went over the fence, squatted in the bushes in my neighbor's yard, and studied the street.

A huge ladder truck jerked to a stop with a hiss of air brakes. A pumper truck came down Arbutus Street, dragging hoses from the fire hydrant. What interested me most, though, was the black SUV parked up the block.

I started toward it, sneaking through the neighbor's yards. When I was behind the SUV, I stepped into the open and strode toward it in the driver's blind spot. There were two men inside, both from the café. Bubba was in the passenger side with his right arm in a sling. The driver's arm dangled out the open window.

I swung the bokuto full force through the open window and felt it shudder as it connected, followed by a sickening crack. Then I yanked the back door open and climbed in. The driver was slumped over the blood-covered steering wheel, and Bubba was swearing and reaching for his gun, but his bandaged arm didn't respond.

"Where's my mother?!"

He stared at me, and in his eyes I saw disbelief quickly turning to panic.

I shoved my energy at him. "Answer the question!"

He blinked twice and his body jerked. "I don't know." His voice was flat, almost mechanical. "A different group hit here before we went to the café."

"Where do you *think* they'd take her?"

"Probably to the warehouse by Crissy Field, on the Presidio grounds."

"Why there?" It was an old concrete building, once part of the military base. Grandpa had bought it years ago. It wasn't more than a mile and a half from here. I'd jogged to Crissy Field tons of times— the road was practically behind our fence.

"That's where we're staging out of."

I pushed the back door open with my foot. "That's enough. Now, you have a nice nap for a few minutes, and when you wake up you won't remember me being here. Do you understand?"

He stared straight ahead. "Yes."

"But you'll feel guilty. You can't live with all this on your conscience." I pointed down the hill. "When you wake up, go to that police officer and tell her everything. Do you understand?"

"Yes."

I swung out of the SUV and looked at the cloud of gray smoke that hung over the neighborhood like fog. Then I ran north.

CHAPTER
38

As I RAN UP THE CURVING ROAD through the Presidio, I tried to push all thoughts of Shoko from my mind. I couldn't believe she would be so heartless, so cold. And there had been something else different about her, something physical…

I jogged down the hill behind the old military barracks, a three-story Spanish-style building dwarfed by the elevated highway to the Golden Gate Bridge above it. Its windows were dark, but the parking lot glowed under amber streetlights. I stumbled down the grassy slope and went to my knees on the damp grass beside a palm tree.

I blinked the sweat from my eyes. Crissy Field was empty, the grass uncut, the dew sparkling as the breeze off the bay swept over it. Beyond the field lay a narrow beach, a bright strip of sand against black water. The Golden Gate Bridge stood to my left, its lights blurred by a haze of fog.

As I concentrated my energy, I began to pick up messages. I jogged toward the warehouses, and the energy grew stronger with each step, a deluge of emotions and energy, all of it negative, all of it speaking my name. As if I'd summoned it, dark energy swept across the field, bending the grass like ripples on a pond. It surged and circled around me, spinning, menacing. This time it didn't overcome me—I felt energized.

The closest warehouse—not Grandpa's—was a featureless white concrete structure with two loading doors at the end. I considered my options. I could walk up the road beside the building, but if anyone looked, I'd stick out like a bug in a bathtub.

I looked up at the roof. There was a downspout, the old-fashioned sturdy, steel kind. I tucked the bokuto into my belt and checked my wakizashi and started climbing. I ran the length of the building's flat roof and then went to my knees and peered over the edge.

Dim lights over the loading door of Grandpa's warehouse illuminated a shiny black SUV. Two men, each toting a small submachine gun, stood beside it. One of them was smoking. Both looked bored. Both had their backs to me.

"Sergeant Jackson's taking this personally," one said.

The other man nodded.

"You think he'll kill her?"

"Who cares?"

Anger surged inside me, too much for me to contain, and blasted from me like steam. A moment later I was on the ground, the bokuto already in motion. Both men crumpled to the ground, blood flowing from their ears and smashed faces.

When I touched the door frame of the old warehouse, the wood spoke to me. It had stood proud for six hundred years before men cut it and brought its pieces here. I closed my eyes and focused my energy. After a moment, I sent my mind into the warehouse, just like I'd done when I scouted the park outside Walter's penthouse.

A huge floor space lay in front of me, a cool blue that stretched the length of the warehouse. Besides several huge wooden crates stacked to one side, the only other objects here were three SUVs at the far end, their engines bright red and white, hot from their race to get here. Several warm-colored shapes milled around them.

Okaasan was here … and someone else.

A moment later, I was back in my body. I glanced around. The two men still lay unconscious. I crouched and opened the door.

At the far end, near the SUVs, Okaasan lay on the concrete, her blouse red with blotches of blood. Her pant leg was soaked in it. Jackson had a laptop open on the hood of the SUV. Its screen glared at me, critical and unforgiving. He spoke—I didn't hear what he said—and a man hauled something out from the backseat of an SUV, something heavy that hit the concrete with a dull thump. Jackson strode over to the shape and kicked it. The bundle reacted with a moan.

"Your friend didn't deposit the money," Jackson yelled. Then he turned the lump over with his foot and I gasped.

It was Mack.

—

Jackson noticed me first. I must have looked small and insignificant walking across the floor with a wooden stick in my hand, but he cocked his weapon and pointed at me.

"No, Junya!" Okaasan yelled in Japanese. "Get away from here!" The man beside her rewarded her with a kick in the stomach.

Seven men stepped forward to face me, weapons up and ready. Their anger was palpable and I was an easy target. But I felt as if I was watching everything in slow motion, every detail vivid, every motion accounted for.

"Don't shoot him! We need the money!" Anthony rushed toward Jackson and grabbed for his gun. Jackson responded with a swing of his rifle butt and smashed Anthony in the jaw. He crumpled like a stack of wooden blocks.

"Get him!" Jackson yelled.

Three guys spread out. I slowed down, sucked in a deep breath, and let my anger rise.

The shortest of the three leaped forward and I sent him sprawling onto the concrete. The other two moved forward, but now they really were moving in slow motion.

I exploded into action. Limbs flailed and bones snapped. As the last man fell to the concrete, I turned to Jackson. The remaining men moved to flank me, their weapons up. Anger seethed out of me—I couldn't stop it—and I thought of Shoko, remembered her saying this energy wasn't from the gods, but I didn't care.

I took another breath and started forward, my body expanding with rage I could no longer control.

Jackson squinted at me. "What the hell?" He swung his submachine gun up and leveled it at me.

My neck tingled in warning, and a long moment later a muzzle flash expanded in front of the gun, widening into a plume of fire. Okaasan screamed, or at least it looked like a scream. Her mouth dropped opened, but the sound that came out was deep and low, like a slowed-down recording. I let go of the bokuto. Part of my mind registered how long it took to fall, but the rest of me was focused on those bullets.

I squeezed my eyes shut and threw all my energy outward. Somewhere far in the distance I thought I heard someone laugh. Then silence.

When I opened my eyes, they were all motionless. I stepped to the side and watched the line of the bullets drift past at walking speed. I drew my wakizashi and walked toward Okassan. She was a mess. Her face was bruised, swollen and bloody, but that was nothing compared with how her thigh looked. The bullet wound lay open, a bloody gash caked in dry blood. By the look of her blood-soaked pants, she'd lost a lot.

I turned toward Jackson. There was humor in his eyes. He liked what he did, I could tell. He liked the money, too. He had an offshore bank account, and his mind whispered the account number and password into mine.

I smashed my elbow into his throat. He tipped backward and crashed onto the concrete then I knelt beside Okaasan and slipped the hilt of the wakizashi into her right hand. I noticed she wore a smile that hadn't been there before.

"You know what's going on, don't you?"

I was tiring fast. Using my energy to keep them all frozen in place was like sprinting while holding up a barbell.

My energy slipped as my rage lessened. Men started to stir, and my neck screamed out a warning. From outside, I sensed boots on asphalt, SWAT teams in black armor, police cars easing to a stop.

Suddenly everyone was moving. Okaasan rose to her knees and in a single motion buried the blade deep into the man who'd kicked her. I dived and pushed Okaasan to the floor as gunfire erupted, so many shots I couldn't keep track. I lay on top of her, my rage dissolving into terror.

Then it was over. Police in black tactical clothing stood over us, their guns pointed at me.

CHAPTER
39

BUBBA HAD SPILLED HIS GUTS to the police, so as far as they were concerned, it was a clear case of kidnapping. The sword, found near the body of one of the men, they took as evidence that these were the men responsible for the carnage that had occurred that night in the alley.

I rode with Okaasan in an ambulance. Mack, still unconscious, went in another. Most of the other men were dead. I hadn't seen what happened to Anthony or Jackson, but I hoped they were dead, too.

"Thank God this is over," Okaasan said later that night from her hospital bed. We were alone, the nurses having finally left and Lin having gone back to Grandpa's bedside.

"You know it's not."

She stared at me a long time. Then she squeezed my hand. "Junya, that energy you used …" She suddenly looked scared. "Don't ever use it again! If you accept this power, Bartholomew will have you, stronger than he ever had Edward."

"But I feel it inside me. And it saved you, so how can it be bad?"

She shook her head. "I'd rather die than watch you carry this inside you."

"All you ever talk about is death!" I yelled, suddenly angry. "It doesn't solve everything!"

She looked stunned. "Go to the Elders, Junya. They will help you—"

"The Elders already made up their mind." I told her what Shoko had done.

She emitted a low cry, like the sound of an injured animal.

I stood up. "So you tell me who the evil ones are, because I don't know anymore."

"Don't say that!"

"I'm going to return the gold and burn the map. Then I'm going to find Bartholomew."

"No, Junya," she whispered, reaching for my hand. "You'll die!"

I walked away without looking back.

Grandpa's driver was waiting outside the hospital. I got into the car. "Take me to the Mojave Desert."

—

A little over six hours later, the exhausted man dropped me off beside Highway 62, several miles east of Twentynine Palms. With the nearest town miles away, I was alone under a dome of a billion stars, something I had time to appreciate now, perhaps for the first time in my life. And like the sky, things were clearer now.

The eastern sky grew pink, silhouetting distant jagged mountains. I'd always wanted to see a sunrise in the desert. As the light grew, it revealed strange-looking trees with long prickly branches, low bushes, and piles of huge smooth stones. At first glance, the desert seemed empty, but I could feel life, hear the scurrying of small creatures.

A large diamondback rattlesnake lay coiled nearby on a smooth slab of granite. We sat side by side, lulled into awe by the wonder of the dawn. The birds kept up a constant chatter. For them, the night was almost over. But the darkness in my heart was deep, and even the light of day couldn't touch it.

I glanced at the snake. Its tongue flicked out every so often, unconcerned by my presence. Its energy was in sync with mine. We'd been drawn to each other for a reason yet unknown, so together we watched a thin slice of sun peek over the distant mountains, casting long shadows, bringing light but not yet warmth to the cold ground. I'd worn my leather jacket over a T-shirt but it wasn't enough to keep me warm. Oh, well—in less than three hours, this rocky land would become an inferno.

I looked at the snake. "I bet you've seen this a thousand times."

The snake flicked its tongue and stood its rattle up a little higher, perhaps a little more proudly. As the sun cleared the mountains, the snake slithered off toward the rocks. I called after it. "You'll help me find it?"

The snake looked back at me, flicked its tongue, and disappeared among the rocks. I lifted the heavy canvas bag, checked my katana and bokuto, and followed the snake.

I heard the rattle and, not long after, found the snake coiled in the shade. When it saw me, it stopped rattling and tested the air with its tongue. In the pile of rocks behind the snake I found a narrow vertical opening, just big enough to fit through if I crouched. Without help, I'd never have found the entrance—the opening was invisible from a yard away. The cave itself was roomy, large enough for three or four men, and surprisingly bright, with daylight streaming through the gaps between the boulders overhead. The ceiling was black from ancient fires. I sensed nothing, good or bad—it was a cave, nothing more. I unloaded the gold and stacked it near the back wall. My watch went on the top of the pile.

"That's all of it," I said as I stood up.

The earth gave a small rumble. I reached for the wall, nervous, but only a gust of wind passed over the rocks. It blew sand through the cracks.

I crawled out of the cave. The heat struck me and I stumbled. Another gust of wind roared toward me, spinning and twisting, becoming a dust devil as it boiled across the dirt road. I ducked back inside the cave to escape it.

Inside, I stopped dead. There was a layer of dust on the pile of gold now, and the watch was gone. The earth gave another shudder, more violent this time. The ground moaned and rattled, sending dust and small rocks down onto me.

After what seemed like hours, the earth became silent and I crawled back out of the cave. I braced for the heat, but instead a cool breeze touched me. The mountains were the same but the desert was gone. Now banana trees and date palms swayed in the warm breeze, the rocks replaced by deep green vegetation.

Somehow, I was on the other side.

A thin trail led away from the cave and I followed it, wary but enjoying the squawk of parrots and the feel of the breeze on my face. I pulled a mango off a low branch, peeled the thick skin with my teeth, and ate it as I walked, juice dripping off my chin. But even here I felt the darkness inside me. My bokuto and katana were heavy, but I'd need them soon enough. Shoko had tried to kill me. I knew she, or others, would try again.

After a few minutes I came to a wide clearing with a stream trickling through the center. Off to the side, under a stand of date palms, stood a pueblo-style hut, a mud block structure with a straw roof—the same one I'd seen when I was daydreaming on Grandpa's hospital bed. I walked through the soft grass and peered through the doorway.

"Come in, James."

The inside was humble but comfortable, with colorful woven rugs on the dirt floor, a simple wooden bed, and a low table. Square-cut timbers crossed above me, supporting the straw roof. Grandpa sat on a straw mat, looking healthy and strong.

He smiled. "Come inside. I promise this won't hurt a bit." He motioned with his hand and I sat on the rug across from him. He looked more relaxed than I'd ever seen him, and happier, too. Before I could assemble a reply, two young girls, with almond skin and dark shiny hair, maybe ten or eleven years old, entered the hut. They wore white robes and beaded turquoise jewelry, and they carried earthen bowls overflowing with fruit, nuts and dates. After they placed the bowls on the mat, they knelt nearby, their faces impassive but their eyes curious.

"I put the gold back," I said.

He nodded.

"So what are we doing here?"

He chuckled. "I thought maybe you could tell me. I assume I'm dead."

"You're not dead." I was quite sure of that.

"Too bad. I would happily stay here forever."

I motioned around us. "What is this place?"

"This is where I woke up after the old Indian found me in the desert." His face was radiant, lost in his memories, before a cloud moved across his features. Maybe, like me, he was waiting for the Gatekeepers to come again—but the only movement outside was the swaying of the grass and the rustle of palm leaves.

"I wish I could change things," he whispered.

"The gold wasn't the treasure. You know that, right?"

He sighed. "The gold was real. I could feel its weight, feel its power." He shook his head. "To me it was the road to the happiness I craved."

"But you live like a prisoner."

He shrugged. "We make our own hell. I made my deal with Bartholomew, and off I went to conquer the world." He thought for a while. "But later, wealth and power began to lose their luster." He spread his arms to take in everything around us. "I understand now. This place was the treasure. The gold became my obsession."

"When I saw you with that machine gun, ... you were like a stranger to me."

His eyes met mine. "Deep down I always knew Bartholomew wanted the map but it was mine to keep ... and protect. It was my ticket back here." He shrugged. "The only thing that kept me going was the thought of this place." He stared down at his hands, turning them over. "Where did my dreams go?" He looked up at me. "This wasn't supposed to be my destiny."

I stared at him, feeling sad. It was as if he never knew that his life was his to make. When he looked back at me, his eyes were hollow and expressionless.

"They watched me all my life, afraid of what Bartholomew might do or what I might become."

"You know all that?"

"I know it now."

I became annoyed at him. "You have choices—you've always had choices. Maybe not with Tomi, but you had a chance to get out, to give the gold back—to live a different life. Look at what I've inherited from you."

"Well, I'm not going back." He reached for a plump date. "There's nothing left for me but a world of lies—theirs and mine. Maybe in death I can find peace."

I stood and walked out into the sunlight. A few minutes later, he followed me.

"You go back, Grandpa, and make things right. Don't leave us. Don't leave Lin."

His gaze dropped to the ground.

"You can become a new man if you want."

He shook his head. "It's too late."

"Bartholomew will leave you alone. I'm going to make sure of that."

His eyes widened. "How? What can—"

"He wants to meet me."

He stared at me a long moment. "There's no such thing as a fair deal."

"We'll see. Now go back."

He shook his head. "Go back to what?"

I glared at him. "If you really can't see what's waiting for you, don't bother." I turned away. "You're such an idiot."

"Guess it runs in the family."

CHAPTER
40

I RETURNED TO THE CAVE AND PASSED back through the gateway, back to the wicked heat of the Mojave. When I emerged, the diamondback was coiled not far from the cave entrance, its rattle shaking like a maraca. I stopped about five feet away, not liking the energy it was giving off.

"What's wrong?"

It shot out at me, its mouth open wide, its fangs bared. My katana sliced through the air. The snake's headless body swung away and thumped against the rocks, but its head, still very much alive, sank its fangs deep into my left forearm.

I screamed and dropped the katana, but the bodiless head held on, jaws locked, fangs buried deep into the muscle. I slammed my arm into a boulder again and again until the head finally came off. It bounced once and came to rest on the sand.

I fell to my knees, clutching my arm. It felt like someone had hit it with a red-hot sledgehammer. I stared at the snake's head. Its eyes still showed life, its tongue still moved.

Then I understood. I was alone in the Mojave, without water, with a poisonous snake bite—a death sentence.

Bartholomew was waiting for me.

My energy drained away like water wrung from a sponge and the desert sand sucked it up, leaving no trace of it, taking me with it.

I fumbled with my leather jacket and left it on the ground. I did a slow spin, assessing each direction, wondering where I should go—not that it mattered. A gust of wind surged past me and sent a dried-up sage bush tumbling toward the shimmering haze to the east. I followed it.

The pain radiated from the four small holes and was getting worse. I managed to walk for about half an hour, weaving between the boulders and small bushes, trying to pick the straightest route between them. The sun was high and hot, well over a hundred degrees. I stopped and looked around. There was nothing to see, just sand and boulders, all the way to the distant mountains.

I was tired, more tired than I would have imagined I could be. The pain was horrible and I couldn't move my left arm. The forearm was twice its normal size, swollen like a red water balloon. I sat on a flat rock and mopped my face with the bottom of my shirt to get the grit and sweat off. I looked at the shirt—it was dry. I wasn't even sweating. Well, that was good; it must not have been as hot as I'd thought. Screw Bartholomew. I'd make it to the highway, to help, after all.

A nice cold drink would have been great, and the thought of it got me up, but as I stood I got a head rush far worse than any brain freeze. My head throbbed and I staggered, holding my head. I looked around through half-open eyes. I needed to figure out which way to go, but I wondered why I even cared. I was sleepy and the heat was nice, so unlike the cold and fog of San Francisco, and it wasn't that hot after all.

I looked down at my feet, confused. They weren't cooperating. I was kicking stones, shuffling through the sand like a toddler. Little cacti, balls the size of brussels sprouts, stuck to my socks. Brussels sprouts—I hated them! Okaasan said they tasted like candy, but she must have eaten some horrible candy in her time. Maybe while she was washing clothes in the creek.

That was so funny that my eyes must have filled with tears. Why else would everything be blurry?

Three steps later I dropped to my knees. I was so tired, so very tired.

It surprised me when my face hit the sand.

—

I hit the ground so hard it knocked the breath out of me. I lay gasping on the cool grass. Grass? The smell of the earth filled my nose while the sun warmed my back. It wasn't the heat of the desert—this was just regular old sunshine. The songs of birds and the buzzing of insects filled the air, but my mind was quiet. No feelings came to me, no sensations of evil or good—there was nothing. I felt like my old self, before Shoko had awakened me.

I still had my bokuto and katana. When I could manage it, I opened my eyes and looked around. Surprised, I rose onto one elbow to get a better look. I lay on the bottom of a wide canyon, a lush green place, watered by a wide shallow river that left the air cool and pleasant. Trees grew near the river but thinned out as the canyon sides sloped up into red and gray granite walls that climbed hundreds of feet above me.

A distant memory nagged at me. I'd been here before, I was sure of that, but long ago, in a different lifetime. I worked myself up onto my knees and stared around me. Yes, I'd come here with Dad and Okaasan one spring, long ago. There was no lodge, no roads or tour buses, but this had to be Zion Canyon in Utah.

Across the river, two men sat on a boulder, both dressed in black suits, a style from another age, with long black hair that hung past their shoulders. I don't know if they'd noticed me, but they looked as if they were waiting for something, so I started across the river, hopping on rocks and logs.

"Hello," one of the men said as I approached. They weren't armed but didn't seem concerned about my weapons.

"Hi."

"Going for a hike?" the other man said. His tone was pleasant enough. Behind them, a narrow dirt trail curved up the hill toward the towering cliffs above.

"We've been waiting for you," the first one said.

"You must really want to see him," the other man said in the same voice as the first.

The first one gave me a once-over. He looked skeptical. "Think he'll make it?"

The other one shrugged. "Don't know. How's the arm?"

I glanced down. My arm looked normal. "It's good."

"All right. Ready to go?"

"I guess so."

"It's not far and the view is pleasant," the first man said as we turned to go.

So we started up the trail, one man in the lead and the other behind me. They were silent, marching up the trail at a steady pace. The path was steep but nothing compared with Arbutus Street, and it felt good to work my muscles. I moved easily as my strength and energy returned.

As we climbed away from the canyon floor, it became hotter, the soil drier, each step raising dust that covered my shoes. The bushes that had looked so green from the canyon floor were parched and brown up close—only the newest growth on the branch tips was green. Every so often, one of us kicked a stone over the edge and it bounced down the slope, tumbling toward a stream far below. The man in front would look back occasionally, perhaps to see if I was lagging behind. I wasn't.

We climbed until we came to a wide plateau of solid rock, the surface smooth and flat like a balcony, the view unbelievable. A small stream flowed across the rock and spread out before disappearing over the edge. I moved closer and then jerked back. We were hundreds of feet above the canyon floor.

The men sat on the rock, cross-legged, facing the towering

red-gray cliffs on the other side of the canyon. One of them pointed upstream.

"Bartholomew's up there."

—

After a few minutes' hike beside the shallow stream, I came to a series of huge red boulders, some bigger than a truck, that forced the stream to weave around them and pool in places. A man in a Hawaiian shirt sat beside one of the rocks, his bare feet dangling in the clear water, canvas boat shoes beside him. He looked like an aging surfer, with a tangle of curly brown hair under a yellow baseball hat. He looked more like Jimmy Buffet than the old man I'd seen in the restaurant bathroom, but I knew it was Bartholomew.

"So, you chose to come through death's door," he said, concentrating on the ripples his feet made in the water. "There are easier ways."

I squatted near him. His hat said "*Relax*" on the front. "You're not what I expected," I said.

He laughed. "I get that a lot." He looked over at me. "Hey, do you board?"

"I've done some surfing, and I've got a skateboard."

"There you go." He nodded at me. "Skateboarders are bad, right? Graffiti-painting vandals, a menace on the streets. Surfers are worse—lazy bums, probably on drugs—at least until you get to know one." He paused while he readjusted his hat to block the sun. "Hell, it wasn't that long ago that being Japanese would get you locked up in America. Now Americans think Japanese stuff is better than their own." He looked back at the water. "Evil's just a word, like *tasty* or *beautiful*."

I considered that. "Surfers don't have snakes' tongues."

"It happens to be a lizard tongue." He sounded hurt.

I sat down, leaned back on my elbows and basked in the sun, enjoying its warmth and the sound of the water trickling over a small waterfall upstream. "Where are we?"

"In another dimension of your world." He wriggled his feet in the water. "Over on your side, the Mormons named this place Zion. Ironic, wouldn't you say?"

So I was in the place Shoko had called evil. The place you couldn't go with a pure heart.

He turned and faced me, sitting cross-legged, and inspected me with eyes that didn't stop at my skin. Then he nodded his approval. "I heard about Walter," he said. "But you surprised me." He chuckled. "And now you have almost a billion dollars."

"I took back what was mine, ... Grandpa's."

"You wanna have a Ferrari?"

I hesitated. "Yeah, I'd like one someday."

"Why wait? You can buy ten right now."

"It's not my money."

His eyebrows rose. "Edward lost it, you found it. Without you, he'd be broke."

I didn't say anything.

Bartholomew stretched his arms over his head. "Ever wonder why they *really* wanted a Gatekeeper to marry your father?"

Something froze inside me. I sat up.

"They say you have to balance the good and evil, right? Yin and Yang, all of that crap." He crinkled his nose and gazed skyward. "So, when you take the son of Edward—apparently tainted by my *evil* influence—and you combine that with a Gatekeeper's blood, what do you get?"

"You get me."

He clapped. "That's right, and look at what you've become."

I looked away. "I don't know what I am."

"Don't you get it? The gods made you. They wanted this. You don't really think that Shoko girl crossed over by accident, do you?" He waved his hand. "They sent a cute girl to watch you, and if you crossed the line and became a threat, she was supposed to kill you. Isn't that right?"

Anger simmered deep inside me. "She said the Elders were afraid I'd give you that map."

He looked interested by that. "And will you?"

I hesitated, choosing my words carefully. "I want you to make Grandpa better and leave him alone. That's all I care about anymore." I dropped my head into my hands. I thought of Shoko's kiss, the feel of her body against mine. "She didn't even ... It was like she never cared about me."

"I hope it *was* all a lie," he said, "because if she really cared about you but came back to kill you anyway, I think that's far worse."

While I fumed, Bartholomew pulled on his shoes and started to tie them. "Maybe you should ask her."

I looked at him, confused.

"She followed you, came through the desert gateway I opened up for you." He gestured downstream with his chin. "She came to finish the assignment."

CHAPTER
41

WE WALKED BACK DOWNSTREAM, Bartholomew in the lead, my hand tight on the hilt of the katana. As we broke into the open, there was Shoko—sprawled on the rock face, teetering on the cliff's edge. A chain was looped around her neck, the other end welded to a steel bar drilled into the rock. Another chain, unused, lay beside it. She was leashed like a dog with no hope of escape. On three sides, she could move only about ten feet. If she moved toward the fourth side, she'd drop over the cliff and hang herself.

She looked like hell. Her lips were cracked and swollen, and dried blood blotted her face and matted her hair. Her uniform was ripped and dirty, and one shoe was missing. A mass of cuts and bruises covered her arms and legs. She'd had the crap beaten out of her, but she straightened up as soon as she saw me.

"What have you done?" Her voice was hoarse.

Bartholomew smiled and pulled his Hawaiian shirt away from his chest, as if he were sweating a lot. "I'm willing to make a deal with you, kid."

I turned to Bartholomew. "What kind of deal?"

Shoko struggled against the chain. "No, Junya!"

He laughed at her. "You tried to burn him alive. I don't think he's in the mood to hear what you have to say."

She looked confused as she staggered to her feet. I saw disappointment in her eyes. Whether she was disappointed because she'd failed to kill me or because she thought I'd cut a deal with Bartholomew, I couldn't tell. I couldn't sense anything from her.

"Kill her," Bartholomew said. "Then we can discuss what to do about Edward." I felt his eyes bore into me. "I can heal Edward," he said. "Her life for his."

Shoko jerked against the chain, fury in her eyes. "You are far stupider than I thought!"

She was in front of me now, just out of arm's reach. She was crying, and her tears began to wash the blood from under her eyes. I could see her freckle now, the one I'd thought was cute. I faltered. There was something wrong ...

Bartholomew sighed. "What are you waiting for?"

I turned to him. "What did you do?"

He snapped his fingers, and the two men who'd brought me here appeared from behind the brush.

"If you don't kill her," he said, "they will."

I took a step back as they approached her. Bartholomew looked at me and shook his head slowly. "You're sure we can't come to an agreement?"

I shot one more look at Shoko's face. Then I swung my katana and cut the first man's head off. The second man leaped at me, and I sent his arm spiraling over the edge. A thrust into his stomach and a twist and his body landed next to the first. Black blood oozed across the rocks.

"That was awesome!" Bartholomew yelled. "Seriously, I loved it! You're a killer after all." He laughed a dry, horrible laugh. "That's all I needed to know."

I held up my finger and thumb, almost touching, as my fury surged. "You were *this* close to convincing me!"

"What changed your mind?"

I jerked a thumb back at Shoko. "She wasn't the girl at the dojo! You sent a fake!"

He pushed his hat up to scratch his scalp. "So?" He looked puzzled. "That doesn't change anything—the lies she told you, the lies your mother told you. And what about *Grandpa*?"

I looked at Shoko and then back at Bartholomew. "We're done here."

He snapped his fingers again and at least half a dozen men, all dressed in black, burst from the bush. I stared in horror as they began to transform, clothes rippling away, skin turning to scales, their bodies stretching and growing. They dropped to all fours, their tails as long as their bodies, all easily over two hundred pounds. They looked like Komodo dragons, with long claws and huge jaws full of inch-long serrated teeth.

I attacked the lizards, the sword alive in my grip, striking from every angle, driving them back and away from Shoko. But they were fast, heavy, and vicious, the black blood flowing from their wounds driving them into a frenzy. They alternated their attacks, claws and teeth snapping inches from my skin.

One got me, its claw cutting my lower leg to the bone. I went down and crawled away, dragging my leg. Two more came at me. I tried to run, but my leg wouldn't cooperate. I stumbled and heard Bartholomew laugh as more lizards came swarming across the rock toward me. I staggered back, teetered, and gasped. I was right on the edge of a cliff, the canyon floor hundreds of feet below. Stones shifted underfoot and my feet went out from under me. The katana fell from my hand and disappeared into the abyss as I grasped at rocks, roots, anything that might stop me. I clutched a small bush that clung to the rock face, but it pulled loose and I fell. I heard myself scream, but it died as a bright flash exploded behind my eyes. Somewhere in the darkness, Bartholomew laughed.

Junya, get up!

I forced my eyes open. Dark forms loomed above me. The lizards peered over the edge, barely six feet away, their tongues flicking, their disease-laden saliva splashing on the rocks around me. One lunged at me. I twisted sideways and it tumbled over the edge. The others hissed but didn't come after me.

I climbed to my knees and felt for my bokuto. Somehow, it was still in my belt, not that it was much use. I touched my throbbing head, still watching the beasts above me. My hand came back sticky with blood. The lizards liked that and stretched their massive jaws toward me.

A second later, Shoko screamed, a sound of rage and fear. I looked up again—the lizards were gone. I whispered a prayer, gritted my teeth against the pain, and started to climb.

Two were closing in on Shoko when I pulled myself over the edge and started toward her. I was weak and wavering on my feet, as frail as a blade of grass as I moved in-between the beasts and Shoko. I clenched my fists and tried to find my energy, but nothing happened.

I glanced over my shoulder at Shoko, terrified. When our eyes met, I watched the faint light of hope go out—I was in no shape to help her and she knew it.

"Save yourself," she whispered.

I collapsed to my knees, touched Mother Earth, and asked her for help.

She answered with a burst of energy that flung me onto my feet. I yanked the bokuto from my belt.

I stole a look at Bartholomew. He wasn't laughing now.

And then they were on me, charging like bulls. I swung the bokuto as if I were the last batter up with the bases loaded. I connected with the first one—a solid hit. It hurtled past me, its head cracked and gushing black tar. My mind was empty as I moved through the kata I'd practiced a thousand times, my body dancing among the dragons. The whistle of wood through still air, the thump of impact on flesh, the groans and screeches of the dying—these were the drumbeat, the cadence of my dance, and one after another the beasts died until only two were left.

One came at me while the other circled and raced toward Shoko. I dived and smashed its head, but momentum sent the dying lizard skidding across the rock toward her. She yelled, kicked, and deflected it toward the cliff, but her balance was off—she toppled over the cliff after it.

The chain played out until it jerked to a stop.

I watched that in slow motion as I slid across the slime-covered rock after her, propelled by my own dive. My fingers grabbed at the second chain as I slid over the edge, and I jerked to a stop beside her.

She clawed at the chain around her neck, but her face was already blue. I swung my legs around her, clamped her body, and tried to lift her and give her enough slack to breathe. The chain tore into my hands—I couldn't hold us both. Desperate, I grabbed inside her noose and hauled up on the chain. She gasped and sucked a breath in.

"Shoko, I can't hold on!"

I looked down but shouldn't have, because we were swinging over nothing.

A hiss came from above and the chain ripped against my hand as I was yanked upward, bringing Shoko with me. Pain exploded in my shoulder and arm as the lizard's teeth sank in and dragged me onto the flat rock. Shoko gasped and thrashed, rattling her chain as she struggled with the noose. The lizard hovered over me, its putrid breath in my face, its teeth inches away.

My arm was already going numb. Shoko's legs, entwined in mine, weren't moving anymore, and I struggled out from under her. I dug my fingers under the chain and worked it away from her neck, trying to untangle it. Finally, the chain fell off.

Relief surged through me when she sucked in a breath of air.

Then I turned. The big lizard, the one that had bit me, hissed once more before transforming into a man in a Hawaiian shirt. Bartholomew staggered to his feet, panting but smiling. "That was great!"

I sank back to the ground, staring at him, bewildered.

He pointed at me. "It looks like a shark bite! That'll impress the hell out of the babes." He scowled. "I wish I had one." He glanced at the other lizard pacing nearby.

I gasped when I saw the semicircle of teeth marks on my left biceps and shoulder, my red blood mixing with black, both dripping off my elbow onto the dirt. "You're insane." No better words came to mind.

"And you're not dead yet." His tone betrayed a touch of pride. "And that's interesting."

"What ... what've you done to me?"

He laughed. "You've got a little Bartholomew flowing in your veins now."

"This ... this will kill me."

He waved a hand, dismissing me. "If it doesn't, consider it a permanent reminder of how stupid you're acting right now." Then he looked at Shoko and rolled his eyes. "All right, be her hero and take her back."

I swallowed, trying to force my tongue to cooperate against the growing numbness. "How can I?"

"Travel her out. You've got my power inside you now."

No! My eyes locked on his. "I don't want it!"

"Would you rather be dead?"

I fell back onto the rock. "I burned the map."

He kicked the bokuto toward me. "I don't need the map anymore."

"Then why ..."

"I've got you to bring me across."

It took a moment for the weight of his statement to reach my brain. "I'll never do that ... ever."

"Forever is a long time, kid." He turned to the last lizard. "Let's go."

⁓

Shoko and I were alone under the noonday sun, whose intensity had doubled. I tried to move but couldn't. After three agonizing attempts, I persuaded my left hand to move and it touched bare rock.

I felt the Mother Earth, the rush of the stream of life surging into my body—but it wasn't enough to let us travel, not from here.

I'd use Bartholomew's power. Just this once.

CHAPTER
42

I TOOK HER TO IZUMO. We needed to cleanse ourselves of evil—both the blood and their energy. We slammed down hard on arrival, but my body had become so numb I barely felt the impact. When I managed to open my eyes, we were on the fourth step of the grand staircase. Shoko was lying on top of me. As I stirred, she rolled off and sat on the step below me, her back against me, head in her hands. She tried to call out, but her voice was hoarse. The shrine grounds were dark and empty. Everyone was home with their families, eating dinner or having their evening bath in deep wooden tubs.

The black poison spread through my body like lava, far worse than the snakebite. I groaned. Shoko turned and put her hands on my chest. We stared at each other and she began to cry.

"I felt the energy from the other side, ... so much evil. I traveled to your house, but then I saw you, ... saw you with that girl."

I felt her disappointment and hurt and had to look away. I was embarrassed, but more than that I felt ashamed.

She sniffed. "You ... you really thought it was me?"

I took a breath. "I knew something was wrong, but ..." I couldn't meet her eyes. "I thought maybe you changed your mind and ... came back to me. That maybe you felt ..." I gritted my teeth against the pain as my shoulder flared again, a good excuse not to answer her.

"They used our emotions against us," she whispered. "There were only three Evil Ones, yet they seized me outside the burning dojo. I was upset. I hesitated."

I didn't answer, couldn't answer. After a while, she laid her head on my chest.

"I screwed everything up." I didn't know if she'd heard me whisper it in the dark. And I didn't know if it was the darkness in my heart or the darkness of the night closing in.

—

Shoko was asleep or unconscious, her head on my chest, when the first girl arrived. She was young, still a child, but wore the green robes of an apprentice Gatekeeper. When she saw us her face went white and she screamed. A moment later, another Gatekeeper—a few years older than Shoko—appeared out of the darkness beside her.

"Summon the Kannushi!"

I felt familiar energy as more Gatekeepers appeared, their green garments glowing in the twilight. I stared, transfixed by their raw physical power, their radiance and beauty.

Not long after, a man dressed in a long black robe and a tall hat hurried over. He stopped dead when he saw us and his face went white. He leaned on his long staff to steady himself.

"What is this?"

Shoko stirred and tried to bow, but all she managed was a slight nod of her head. "Kannushi."

"Shoko!" Tomi burst through the line of stoic Gatekeepers, dressed in a simple kimono—obviously evening wear—but holding a katana. And she looked scared.

"Is that ... the blood of an Evil One?"

"Be still, Gatekeeper." The Kannushi moved to stand beside Tomi.

"The blood itself is not poison. If she was bitten, she would already be dead."

Shoko turned toward me. "Junya was bitten!"

Tomi and the Kannushi seemed to notice me for the first time, although I was still flat on my back behind Shoko, not hard to miss. Tomi leaned closer to get a better look. She looked astonished. "She is right," she whispered. "Oh, gods."

I looked past them at the young Gatekeepers gathering.

"They look like angels," I said.

The Kannushi didn't turn. "A snake would look like an angel to you."

"Kannushi," Tomi said. "How is he still alive?"

He silenced Tomi with a wave of his hand and stared down at Shoko. "Open your mind, young one," he said in a severe tone. "Tell me what happened." A moment later, he looked at her in astonishment. "The Evil Ones seized you and took you *there?*" He glanced at me. "And you came back ... alive?"

She pointed at me. "He killed a dozen lizards." Her voice grew in volume. "He saved my life!"

His eyes met mine. "No human can travel from there."

At that moment, two miko hurried across the grounds toward us, carrying black lacquer boxes. They wore long silk jackets with wide drooping sleeves, their long hair tied back with red and white ribbons. They bowed to the Kannushi and then knelt and began to wash Shoko, carefully removing the black blood first and then her own blood. They worked on her one section at a time, keeping her body covered, but from what I could see, there were large, ugly bruises, already purple and black, all over her body. The older one clicked her tongue when she saw the red welt that circled Shoko's neck.

"Is she infected?" the Kannushi asked.

"She was not bitten," the older miko said.

Before they bandaged Shoko, they poured a clear liquid onto her open wounds. To my amazement, the cuts closed and shriveled, like morning glory in the evening, leaving behind scabs that looked a day old. When the miko moved toward me, the Kannushi shook his head.

"He was bitten and will die," the Kannushi said. "It is only his dark energy that is slowing it."

The older miko looked angry, but her voice was calm. "It is our duty to treat all."

The Kannushi hesitated. "Bandage it to contain his rancid blood, but do not waste medicine on him."

They pulled my jeans up and took my T-shirt off, exposing the wounds. I kept my eyes squeezed shut and tried to make the pain stop. My energy rose until only a dull throbbing remained in my left shoulder and leg. They worked quickly, in silence, and their touch was gentle.

When they were done, I whispered a word of thanks and stood up. Everyone gasped, but my eyes were on the Kannushi. "Was I really an experiment?"

"What kind of an experiment?" he barked.

"Why did you really ask Misako to marry my father?"

He made a face. "Your mother is not the first to cross over and mate with a man from the other side." He hesitated and looked over his shoulder at the gathered Gatekeepers. "Of course, her assignment was important to us … But it was only when the young one told us about your awakening that we became interested."

"Because I might be … useful?"

He shrugged. "It is a rare opportunity, not to be taken lightly. And the gods favored you."

"And now?" My voice grew louder. "What do they think now?"

He glared at me. "The will of the gods is now unclear. With this event, it is my belief that the gods will not want this to continue." He moved up onto the bottom step. "Let me pass!"

"I'll save you the climb. You're not the only one they speak to." I turned to look up at the shrine, far above us. "Do I still find favor with you?"

The Kannushi's face burst with fury. "Blasphemy! Insolent devil!" He thumped the ground with his staff. "I sentence you to death!"

Tomi drew her katana and came at me, but Shoko pushed herself between us.

"He is a Gatekeeper's son," Shoko said. "He saved my life and brought me back when no one else could."

Tomi faltered, but five other Gatekeepers came at me as one, an organized chaos of swords and bodies converging on a single point. I shoved Shoko away, and without willing it, my hand came up.

Like a ball meeting the bat, they stopped for a split-second and then flew backward in a jumble of arms and legs. The Kannushi's hat flew off and his robes billowed as he staggered backward, trying to stay upright. I lowered my hand, amazed and reassured.

It wasn't Bartholomew's power that had done that.

The Kannushi stared up at me. When he made it to his feet, he pointed his staff at me. "You are in their favor … for now," he said, his voice hoarse. "When they decide otherwise—and they will—we will hunt you wherever you go, in this world or in yours."

I stared at him. "If I see or feel *anyone* on my side … I'll deal with them and then I'll come for you."

Shoko stood up. "Junya," she whispered, her face pained, her eyes wide, "thank you for saving my life. I … I have always believed in you."

Something caught in my throat and I had to look away. Beyond the small group at the bottom of the stairs, a multitude of Gatekeepers had gathered among the trees behind, barely visible in the fading light—far too many for me to fight.

I tried to keep my face expressionless as I knelt on the steps and looked at Shoko again.

"I won't let the evil win," I said. "I promise."

CHAPTER
43

I STAGGERED THROUGH THE FRONT DOOR of my house and came face to face with my dad. He was in work clothes, walking through the living room carrying a glass of water. I hadn't expected him. I'd come straight from Izumo and the pain was growing. I needed Okaasan, but I was relieved to see a familiar face.

"Hey, Dad."

He came toward me, frowning. "What happened to you? You're covered in black stuff."

I glanced down at my ripped, dirty jeans, glad he couldn't see the wide white bandages that circled my calf and shoulder.

"It's a long story," I said through gritted teeth. "Where's Mom?"

"She's downtown with Lin." He was still frowning, but now he looked more angry than worried. "I can't believe you took off to Japan for six weeks!" Yep, definitely angry. "Your mom was in the hospital when I got home from Brussels, and you were gone—not to mention the damn fire!" He pointed to the garden.

"I've been gone six weeks?"

Our eyes met and the fury in his made me take a step back.

"Damn it, Junya, I don't know what the hell you've been up to—"

I looked him in the eye. "Do you *really* want to know, Dad?"

He stared at me. His energy changed. He looked away.

I felt Okaasan. Her energy was loud, her fear palpable, but she was still far away. My body was slowly becoming numb—from the poison, I guessed. It was a wonderful feeling, and it became a bit easier to stay upright.

Through the new glass windows, a building was taking shape beyond the Zen garden. A small crane lowered a beam while half a dozen Japanese workers waited, ready to secure it. This building looked different from the original dojo, smaller and older. I felt the wood call to me and I longed to touch it, to hear its story.

I nodded toward the backyard. "What's with that?"

He followed my gaze. "We shipped an old teahouse over from Japan a few years ago. Had it stored in crates in your grandfather's warehouse ... where those men died." He paused. When he spoke again, his anger had faded. "It's over two hundred years old, a victim of a new rail line."

"It's small." I slurred the words.

"That's what your mom wanted—just a teahouse."

The pain flooded back and I couldn't say any more—if I opened my mouth I'd be screaming. I tried to raise some of my energy, but I had nothing left. The venom had me. I started to slouch. From the corner of my eye, I saw Okaasan standing in the kitchen doorway, her hand over her mouth. I sent my scream to the inside of her head.

"Go back outside, Robert," she said. "Now."

He took off like a nervous child, and the second he was out the door, Okaasan limped toward me. "Is that ...?" She pointed to the black stuff.

When I nodded, she let out a small cry, and with a grunt she picked me up as if I weighed nothing and carried me into the shower, clothes and all. Her clothes and hair got drenched as she washed me from head to toe three or four times. Besides a few whispered curses, she didn't show much reaction, even when she began to remove the bandage from my leg.

I nearly passed out. The gash was over six inches long and straight, as if cut with a knife. She sat me on a stool while my head spun.

"Is it bad?" I croaked.

"I'd take you to the hospital if I could," she said after a moment's hesitation. "It needs stitches." But she didn't pull out a needle and thread, much to my relief. Instead, she applied a dozen little Band-aid like strips that pulled the edges of the cut together. Okaasan had an impressive first-aid kit—a necessity because of our training.

"That doesn't look like a sword wound."

"Lizard's claw."

She sucked in a breath and held her hands out toward me, a calming gesture that seemed to be more for her than for me.

"That's OK ... People survive claws."

"You haven't seen my shoulder yet."

She started to undo the bandage on my shoulder. When she got the last piece off, her face went white. "Oh, gods!" she whispered, her hands frozen above the wound. "It bit you?!"

I looked at the tiles, my eyes unfocused. "I'm going to die, aren't I?" I whispered.

She grabbed my chin. "Junya," she said, her voice shaking as much as her hands, "you're different from the rest of us. You shouldn't be alive right now, so I'm going to assume—I'm going to pray to every god in Izumo—you'll stay that way."

After taking a deep breath, she leaned closer and inspected the wound.

"There are eight teeth marks on the front, as far down as your pectoral." She paused as she looked at my back. "And nine on the back." She hesitated. "There's venom in there, ... in you."

I bent my head to look and she had to push me back onto the stool before I fell over. The teeth marks were deep ugly holes and the skin around them was swollen and blotched red and black like decaying meat.

Her hands were shaking as she worked, dabbing at the wound with a cloth soaked in antiseptic. It hurt like hell and my body jerked every time she touched me. "Use your energy, Junya. Don't worry about hurting me. Let it build slowly. I'll be OK. I'll use my energy, too."

Even though I saw her cringe when I started, I concentrated on my breathing, and within a minute warmth began to build in my abdomen. This energy felt different—it wasn't built from anger. I let it flow and the pain began to recede.

When she'd cleaned the wound as best as she could, she wrapped my arm and shoulder as if she were preparing a mummy. Then she sat back and looked at me.

"I've never seen a lizard bite. There's never anything left of the body to see."

Okaasan made me a huge bowl of udon noodles and sat across the table from me. As I slowly ate, I told her everything.

"Junya …"

I felt the thought she was trying so hard to suppress. "I know it was Bartholomew's power that let me travel Shoko from Zion to Izumo," I said. "It was the only way I could save Shoko, and myself. But that's not what I used on the Kannushi and the Gatekeepers—I swear."

She took her time replying. "I just worry … I'm scared to death actually, that you'll be tempted to use Bartholomew's power again. It's far beyond the power of any Gatekeeper, and many of the gods."

I looked at my empty bowl. "I don't want to. I can't let Bartholomew get control of me."

She reached across the table and put her hand on mine. "I believe in you, Junya. You aren't alone in this."

The two of us were quiet for a while, content just to sit there together. Then she gave me a little smile. "How are we going to hide *this* from your father?"

I smiled, but I felt sad. "He'll never ask."

She nodded. She knew that, too.

"How's your leg?" I said.

She straightened it and put her foot back on the floor. "It's good, only muscle injuries. I'm almost back to normal."

"And Mack?"

"There was no permanent damage, just a lot of bruises. I've only talked to him once since that night."

Her mind was elsewhere, and I picked up on a stray thought. "Where's Lin going?"

Okaasan shrugged. "The South Pacific, maybe Fiji."

I guessed she had lots of time for a vacation now.

Okaasan put her cup down with a thud. "Aren't you going to ask about your grandfather?"

"I already talked to him, over … somewhere." I met her gaze. "I know he's dead."

She smacked my hand. "He's not dead! And it's bad luck to say such things." She tried to look mad but couldn't. "He woke up a few days after you disappeared."

My mouth must have dropped open, because Okaasan began to laugh.

"The doctors can't believe it, but he's up and about and getting stronger. He's like a new man. And he's decided to start using his yacht for something other than a floating office."

"He's taking a vacation?" I asked, unable to hide my surprise.

She smiled. "He's taking it out for a South Pacific cruise."

"He should change the name. Tomi's a bitch." Then I sighed. "So Lin's going with him?"

"Of course. Why?"

"She's my friend and she deserves a better life—someone who will love her back."

"For your information, Lin's wearing a very large diamond ring, and it's obvious it means a lot to both of them. They're acting like newlyweds already."

I blinked a few times and I had to ask. "Did she ask him?"

Okaasan smiled. "As I recall, they pretty much said it at the same time."

I looked around, trying to see as much of the house as I could from my chair. The kitchen was familiar, the smells the same, but I couldn't find comfort there. My worlds were so far apart. I saw no way for the chasm to close.

"I'm starting to feel like you did when we came back from Japan," Okaasan said. She put her hands together on the table and forced a smile. "I wonder if *my* life will ever go back to normal."

"I don't even know what normal is anymore."

She let out a deep sigh. "We must keep moving forward. I recall you saying something like that to me not so long ago."

She helped me to the living room, where I stood and watched the workers assembling the old teahouse. How long had it sat in that box, wondering if it would ever get to be itself again? Did it ever imagine it would end up halfway around the world, in our backyard? I started to feel sorry for it, but I stopped because I had a lot in common with that teahouse.

I felt myself starting to glaze over, and a moment later Okaasan was beside me, steering me to the sofa. I was so weak, so tired I couldn't stand anymore.

"Watch from here," she said. "This will take a while."

CHAPTER
44

A SHORT BUS RIDE FROM MY HOUSE, close to Golden Gate Park, is the best burger place in San Francisco. It's on a side street, sandwiched between a laundromat and a produce store, the kind that displays fruit and vegetables on the sidewalk in front. It's easy to miss.

Inside, there are six small tables and three booths in the back that are never available—I'd never once sat there. Most of the time, people are lined up on the sidewalk waiting, but when I got there, Mack was already inside sitting in a booth, looking as if he'd won the lottery.

September is San Francisco's warmest month, and today was pushing seventy-two degrees, definitely T-shirt weather. It was good to feel the sun. I'd got off the bus in Golden Gate Park and walked the rest of the way, feeling proud that after two months of recuperating, I could finally move around more or less like normal. The scars would never go away, though. I guess I'd take Bartholomew's advice and tell my future girlfriends it was a shark bite. I could never tell anyone the truth. Would that make me a liar?

Our conversation started casually, like a conversation between any two friends who hadn't seen one another in a while, but the small talk felt wrong. Mack was an alien to me now, a part of that other world so far removed from my reality. I could barely concentrate on his words. He noticed and the conversation faltered. Pretending to search the menu was a brief distraction, but we both knew what we wanted—we always ordered the same thing. Once the waitress had taken our order, Mack tried to carry the conversation by himself, but he eventually ran out of things to say.

I realized I was nervous. I cleared my throat. "I'm sorry about all this, Mack."

He looked as if he had a response all prepared, but just then our burgers arrived. We both began to eat, but after the first bite, I put mine down. Mack was looking down at the table. He noticed me staring at him.

"Look, I don't blame you, OK?" he said in a low voice. "I didn't go home like you said to. That's my fault. One of those goons remembered me and grabbed me. Things got kind of fuzzy after that."

I nodded, uncertain. "Do you ... do you remember anything from the warehouse?"

"Not much."

I let out a sigh of relief. "It's a good thing those cops rescued us when they did—"

"Don't," he said, louder than he meant to. He stopped and glanced around. There was fury in his eyes as he lowered his voice. "Don't treat me like I'm stupid. I saw what you did, I *saw* how you moved!"

"You had a head injury—"

He hit the table, shaking the cutlery and drawing stares. "Don't lie to me!" He paused for a moment as he struggled to control himself. "I don't know what's happened to you, but don't insult me by thinking I'm still the same old clueless Mack, all right?"

I hesitated. "It's just ... a lot's changed."

He glared. "I got kidnapped and had the crap beaten out of me. And people were dropping all around me in that warehouse—bleeding and dying, gunshots, heads cut off. You think *I'm* ever going to be the same?"

I looked down at the table, but he wasn't finished.

"I know your mom lied to you and that sucks, but you hated it, so don't do the same thing to me. I've been your friend for ten years. I'm still your friend, if you'll let me be."

For the first time I realized I wasn't the only one who'd grown up too fast over the summer.

"I could really use a friend." Then I grinned. "And you have no idea how bad I've wanted to tell you all this!"

He cocked his head, and a slow smile spread on his face. "First I've got two demands."

"Demands?"

"One: you never lie to me again. Two: don't get me beat up anymore, OK?"

I laughed. "I can only promise you the first one."

We both dug into our burgers. Small talk resumed, with a promise of real answers later in a more private setting. It wasn't until I'd finished my second burger and sat sucking the last remnants of my root beer float that I felt the energy of the earth shudder. I put my glass down.

"I have to go." I tossed some money onto the table, more than enough—I'd kept both Walter's and Jackson's money in my new offshore account.

Mack looked surprised, but he followed me outside. "What's wrong?"

It was our first test. "You won't understand until I give you the whole story, but I have to deal with something and you said you were tired of getting beat up."

"Sounds interesting."

"Maybe. I'll see you later, Mack."

CHAPTER
45

I WAS PASSING THE BOTANICAL GARDENS, about to turn toward the Japanese gardens, when I finally saw them. Two young girls, maybe twelve or thirteen, wearing matching school uniforms with racket cases strapped to their backpacks. They stood in the shade of the smaller gate of the Japanese gardens with their attention focused on me. They were apprentices—no silver rings adorned their right middle fingers.

I walked past them toward the main gates of the gardens, where the all-too-familiar energy resonated.

Shoko sat on the steps in front of the gates, bathed in sunlight against a backdrop of manicured black pine and maple trees. She looked stronger, her confidence and power more obvious. She didn't wear a uniform, and she'd cut her hair into a ragged style that ended at the collar of a well-worn black leather jacket.

She noticed me as soon as I stepped into view.

"Hello, Junya." She gave a small bow and then shook her hair and gave me a smile—noncommittal, uncertain. Her fingers went to the hem of her jean skirt. "What do you think of my new look?"

"I like it."

"I have never been here before," she said, nodding toward the gates. "This garden is beautiful, a fine replica of those in Kyoto. You almost cannot tell the difference."

"You can if you look close enough."

She turned back to me, her eyes burning with intensity.

"I saw the apprentices back there. They're kind of young for this, aren't they?"

She stepped down off the stairs. "They are the best in their class." A slight smile crossed her face. "And they are petrified. You have become quite a legend."

I didn't respond. Instead I stood watching her, saw the breeze move her hair, the sunlight on her face. Had the gods changed their minds? Keeping the darkness at bay was a daily struggle, but I hadn't faltered.

"Why are you here, Shoko?"

A sad smile turned the corners of her lips. "My duty is my life, Junya. The only life I have ever known"—she paused and her eyes met mine—"until I met you. But the gods need warriors, and thanks to you, I have experience that no other warrior has ever had. I will pass that experience on to others."

"I'm sorry for what you went through."

She laughed softly. "But I will not grow bitter like my mother, wasting my days wondering what could have been. I will perform my duties, but I will make my own destiny and trust my heart. I have made that clear to the Kannushi. Neither he nor *you* will stop me from doing as I please—including traveling here." Then she moved closer, within an arm's length, and crossed her arms. "Tell me, Junya, what mistake did Bartholomew make that saved my life?"

I reached out and touched the freckle under her right eye. "I don't know why, but *she* had the freckle under her left eye," I said. "It made me look harder, deep into your eyes, and when I did, the darkness vanished from my heart."

She touched her face where my hand had been. "The balance of life and death in a freckle." She fell silent for a moment. "You have so many reasons to be angry at us. I understand how you feel."

"You can't understand, because I never had the guts to tell you anything."

Our eyes met again. "You still have not told me anything, Junya."

I reached out and took her hand. She looked down. I felt the warmth of her energy flow through me, pure and sweet, like a kiss from the gods.

"Would you like to ride the cable cars with me and drink hot chocolate?" I said. "I want to get to know you better."

Shoko smiled. "Maybe I will not kill you after all."

NOTE FROM THE AUTHOR:

Thank you for reading *The Gatekeeper's Son*!

Whether you loved it—or didn't—your opinion is important to me, and I'd appreciate hearing from you! Please consider taking five minutes right now and writing a review on Goodreads, Kobo, Amazon, Barnes & Noble or wherever you browse and shop for books. You can also tell your friends on Facebook or your blog.

Of course, you can also email me directly and tell me what you think: chris@crfladmark.com

I really enjoyed bringing Junya's and Shoko's world to life and I hope you will help me introduce them to many more people.

Chris

COMING SOON

The sequel to *The Gatekeeper's Son* will take off where this novel ends, because Junya's journey is far from over.

My neck tingled. Somewhere in the darkness, evil moved closer.

My bokuto felt good in my hand.

I moved a few paces in their direction, probing, sending my energy out. Behind me, a young gatekeeper notched an arrow. Shoko moved off to my right, squinting against my energy.

"There."

Between the trees, about twenty yards away, stood two men dressed in black, their long black hair shining in the moonlight. A shudder traveled up my spine.

What would I do if they came? What if they transformed into lizards?

One of the men moved and I took a step forward. From behind me, I heard the whisper of a katana sliding from its sheath.

Shoko moved up beside me. "If they come, we will cut them down ... together."

For the latest news on its release, visit my website, www.crfladmark.com, join my mailing list, or follow me on Facebook.

ABOUT THE AUTHOR

C. R. Fladmark lives in a small, historic town in British Columbia and travels often to Japan, where he researches his novels among the ancient sites in Shimane Prefecture. To learn more, visit www. crfladmark.com or find him on Facebook at www.facebook.com/ CRFladmark.

CPSIA information can be obtained
at www.ICGtesting.com
Printed in the USA
LVOW03s1923140917
548743LV00001B/180/P